GW00584864

NEITHER HOPE NOR FEAR

BOOK THREE OF

'Jack Tucker of Exmoor'
A Family Saga 1815-1875

Paddy King-Fretts

ryelands

First published in Great Britain in 2009

Copyright © Paddy King-Fretts 2009

British Library Cataloguing-in-Publication Data
A CIP record for this title is available from the British Library

ISBN 978 1 906551 10 0

RYELANDS
Halsgrove House,
Ryelands Industrial Estate,
Bagley Road, Wellington, Somerset TA21 9PZ
Tel: 01823 653777   Fax: 01823 216796
email: sales@halsgrove.com

Part of the Halsgrove group of companies
Information on all Halsgrove titles is available at: www.halsgrove.com

Printed and bound by Short Run Press Ltd, Exeter

Cover illustration: *St Mary's, Molland and The London Inn,* by Jack Hoar
Tel: 01769 572131 e-mail: jackhoar@hotmail.com

The Tuckers

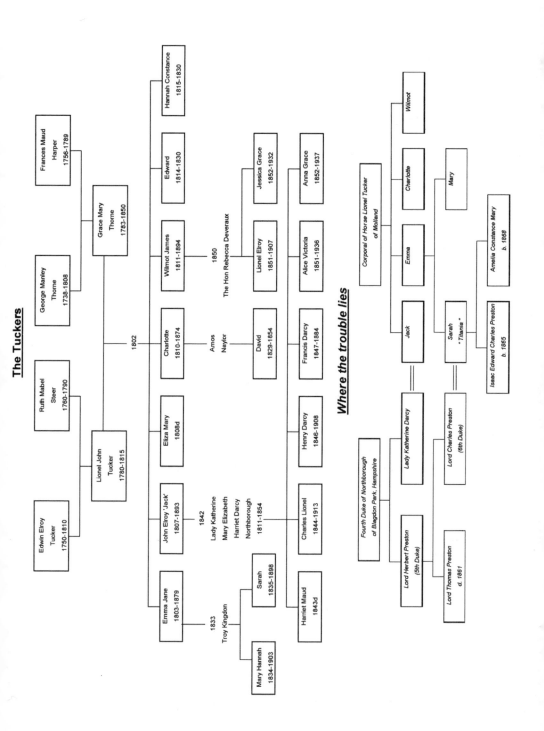

Where the trouble lies

Principal Characters

(apart from the family tree)

Baillie, Dr Edgar. Dulverton doctor and junior partner to Dr Collyns.

Barclay, Captain Marcus, Life Guards. Sarah Preston's lover.

Barclay, Mrs Lucinda-Katherine. Captain Barclay's wife.

Brodie, Mr Milton. Another of Sarah Preston's lovers.

Chichester, Mr and Mrs John and Caroline. Owners of Arlington Court and friends of the Knights.

Cockram, Mr. The old butler at Whitechapel Manor.

Collyns, Dr Charles Palk. A well known doctor and benefactor from Dulverton.

Davey, Jed. Shepherd to the Orchard family at Hartland Abbey.

Disraeli, Benjamin. British Prime Minister 1868 and 1874-1880.

Frobisher, Lord and Lady. Landowner and M.P. from Filleigh near South Molton.

Gladstone, William Ewart. British Prime Minister 1868-1874,1880-1885, 1886 and 1892-1894.

Harper, Mervyn. Freebooter and assassin. Nephew of Jasper Harper, the highwayman.

Heard, Bamber. Farmer from Withypool and husband of Charlotte 'Lottie' Tucker.

Kingdon, Mr and Mrs Troy and Emma. Parents of Sarah and Mary. Emma is Jack Tucker's sister.

Knight, Elizabeth-Jane. Mother of Frederic Knight.

Knight, Colonel The Hon Sir Frederic Knight, KCB, M.P. Owner of Exmoor Forest.

Knight, Florence and Sebright. Wife and son (only child) of Sir Frederic Knight.

Locke, Mr Malcolm. Duke of Northborough's butler at Whitechapel Manor.

Maynard, Mr. Frederic Knight's butler at Portland Place, London.

Morgan, Sir Durnford. City banker.

Morton, Miss Eileen. Irish governess to Isaac and Amelia – Sarah's children.

Newton, Tam. Harbour Master at Ilfracombe.

Northborough, Duke of. Family seat at Blagdon, Hampshire and owner of Whitechapel Manor.

Orchard, Mr and Mrs Desmond and Jocelyn. Owners of Hartland Abbey, North Devon.

Orchard, Cardew, Jemima, Edwin and Jocasta, the Orchard children.

Palmerston, The Viscount. British Prime Minister 1855-1858 and1859-1865.

Preston, The Lord Thomas. Heir to the Duke of Northborough.

Preston, The Lord Sharland. Second son.

Price, Miss Daisy. Lady's maid to Sarah, Lady Preston.

Quartly, Mr and Mrs Joseph and Mabel. Farmers at Great Champson Farm, Molland.

Quartly, Edwin. Son and husband of Victoria Tucker (Jack's daughter).

Rawle, Kitty. Widow of Gillan who becomes Jack Tucker's second wife.

Richards, 'Black'. Small time villain in Exeter.

Steer, Mr Jacob. Sir Wilmot Tucker's butler at Court Hall, North Molton.

Tarr, Mr Able. Resident butler to the Knight family at Simonsbath Manor.

Tennyson, Alfred. Poet Laureate and long time friend of Sir Wilmot Tucker.

Thornton, The Reverend William. First vicar of St Luke's Church, Simonsbath, Parish of Exmoor.

Tissini, Madam. Soothsayer at the Hartland Abbey Christmas Fair.

Westcott, Billy. Survivor of Balaclava, now manager of livery stables in Exford.

PART ONE
Sarah
November 1856

Chapter One

The visitor glanced down at the rough-coated head nuzzling her hip. The eyes looking up were soft and they were smiling. Elizabeth-Jane Knight smiled back, fondling the silken ear, before glancing up and acknowledging the parlour maid as she curtsied and backed away.

Moments earlier, the young wolfhound had pulled himself up and shook clumsily. His mother, darker and heavier, lay still with her chin resting flat on the rush matting. As she watched her son crossing the flagstones so her tail thumped rhythmically. Behind her, a log fell between the ornate fire-dogs sending a cloud of sparks racing up the chimney. Then she, too, rose and stretched before following him into the deep bay of the window. In spite of the warmth of the fire, Elizabeth-Jane shivered and left her blue-grey coat well buttoned. But her narrow dark blue velvet hat, the one with the black plumes she knew her son would remember, she unpinned and placed on the table. Then she took a deep breath and sighed contentedly.

It had been a long time, a very long time, since she had been mistress of Simonsbath Manor yet here she was again. Once more she took in the view she knew so well. The tall beeches lining the track down to the bridge over the River Barle had grown and she watched as the gaunt branches dipped to the sharp breeze coming up the valley. Even now she remembered the afternoon almost thirty years ago when her husband, John, planted the saplings. It was the year they moved in: March, she thought to herself, and it had been a stormy day. John had rushed about like a mad thing directing operations, his mane of hair tangled and wild. Elizabeth-Jane smiled again.

An eddy of leaves whirled into the air. The gardens running down to the road had been extended and she could see that the rhododendrons now filled the corner by the gate to the stables.

*

The two dogs heard the footfalls first and turned towards the door. Beowulf, the younger, cocked his head to one side, took a pace forward then stopped again before lowering his head and listening intently. As the door opened both dogs moved to greet the new arrival. Elizabeth-Jane turned.

"*Mother.*" Frederic Knight stopped then raised his arms wide. "Mother," he whispered. "You're back...back at last." He moved swiftly, gathering her up in his arms to hug her closely. "Wonderful," he cried laughing out loud. "How wonderful...*wonderful.*"

"Yes," she gasped, her feet now back on the ground. "Yes, dear...back at last but now I'm a little old lady with nothing to do and nowhere to go.

"But you're here, here with us all and that's what matters." Frederic stood back, wrestling with the fastening of his fur-trimmed cloak. Without looking, he threw it across the oak table causing a pewter jug to topple over. Then he swept back his dark hair. It had been a little over four years since he had last seen his mother at the villa in the Tivoli hills, half a day's drive from Rome. He had begged her to come home then but she refused, preferring instead to stay where his father had died. But time had moved her. Gradually, year by year, her letters told them how much she missed Exmoor, how she pined for the wild open spaces she loved and how much she missed her family.

Then suddenly, less than a year ago, she had changed her mind and her return had been arranged. He thought she had been worried about growing old but neither he nor the others knew that someone else had been urging her to come home. Tomorrow they would visit the house he had bought for her. Not too big she had demanded and not too isolated either, but somewhere close to the moors. Bremridge Manor, just outside South Molton was ideal.

✳

It was not until after lunch that their conversation made much progress. It was their own fault for they kept going back over some topic or other, both determined to take their time and to savour everything. "And who else?" she queried lightly, hoping her voice would not give her away. "Who on earth is there left who has not been enquiring about my well being? You've mentioned everyone." Frederic stretched his legs then bent to scratch at some mud on his breeches. He had been expecting her to ask him directly, even so the suddenness of her question startled him. Had he guessed right, he wondered? Had the one uppermost in his mind been pleading with her to return as well?

If so, then whoever it was had won a hard fought battle. Little more than a year after his father had died, Rome society began to pay court to the elegant widow. There had been the Barcinnis of Palazzo di Giustazia and Jean-Alfonso d'Avosa, the count's younger brother; not to mention the obnoxious little Marquis Sambrerro, the diminutive and cunning French Ambassador. They and Heaven knows who else had followed one another out to Villa Orsini, each set on ingratiating himself with his mother, no doubt set on gaining her favours if not her hand.

He remembered how, on the final night he was there, she had laughed as she ticked them off her fingers at dinner. Later, when she had played for him, he had seen through her gaiety. It was false: the piano told him so. She was lonely and vulnerable to the attention of the Latin wolves who prowled tirelessly and he left determined that she should come home. "Well…" Frederic caught her eye.

"Durnford?" she half whispered, her eyes wide and bright. "Yes?" she asked again seeing immediately the answer in his look. "Aaah…dear Durnford," she mused. "He's…he's been wonderfully faithful."

"Was it him mother?"

"Him, dear?"

"Was it he who brought you home? Did Durnford finally persuade you?" He put his hand on hers, surprised at her sudden hesitancy before she lowered her head. She was so young to be his mother. Often she had seemed little more than an elder sister yet suddenly, now, she looked her sixty-two years. Her hair, once that great auburn-red cascade, was shorter and flecked with grey. The fine bone structure of her face had not changed but the lines around her mouth had deepened. He rose and placed both hands on her shoulders, sensing her unease at being asked to reveal something so intimate. "I hope it was." He felt her stiffen. "He's always been such a good friend and you'll be needing company, mother. Exmoor hasn't changed you know…at least as far as society goes. It's still the same wonderful empty wilderness."

"I have to say his letters did help me make up my mind." Elizabeth-Jane looked away then up at her son. She turned her hand and caught his fingers in hers. "You're not cross, are you, dear? I mean, I've always cherished his friendship and you always seemed to get on so well…all of you. What does Florence think?" She hardly knew her son's wife, yet Durnford Morgan had intimated in his letters that she had little time for the solitude at Simonsbath preferring instead their Worcestershire home or Portland Place. Her maternal instinct told her that her son, too, was lonely. Perhaps she should be careful for if she began to fill her life with company then Frederic would be reminded of his own solitude. Her attention would be drawn away from him and a gulf might appear between them where there had always been such a close bond.

"She enjoys his company, we all do." The answer came too quickly. He could not stop himself and watched her eyes searching his. "Florrie's away quite a lot but I find Durnford's fellowship most welcome. I must say he's an easy companion and a great help…whenever I ask."

Sir Durnford Morgan, now head of Esdaile's banking in the South West had often ridden out from Exeter to stay at Simonsbath where he could escape from the claustrophobic, competitive tensions of the banking world. He never offered his advice yet Frederic knew it would be there and, from time to time, he sought it. The two had indeed become close, each able to offer something to the other. "No, mother; Durnford is welcome here at any time and if his presence pleases you then I shall be more than happy."

"Come now." He released her hand and patted her shoulder gently. "I'll tell Tarr to bring Maudie in for you. She's Florrie's girl but I've told them I want her to see to you while you're here. You'll like her…she's a Lynton girl. Her mother comes from one of those fisherman's cottages behind the market." He eased himself round the mahogany fold-over table and stretched for the bell rope. "I'll go and get out of these things and when you're down we can start *all* over again. There's so much to tell."

Elizabeth-Jane rose and smoothed her coat, watching fondly as he rang then held out her arms as he moved to embrace her once more.

2

"'Bain't easy, y'know." Charlotte reset her mob cap and folded her arms. "'Er's not easy at all and the young're not taking to her like they ought. Well, not all of them anyways."

Bamber Heard glanced up at his wife. It never was going to be easy at Sherdon and he nodded thoughtfully. He knew only too well what life was like for a farmer on his own and thanked his good fortune that Charlotte had accepted his hand. She was not the slip of a girl he would once have sought, he had to admit, but she had done wonders for him and he could never understand how he had managed without her before she came into his life. He could imagine how Jack must have struggled to keep the house going after Katherine's death almost two years ago. Sherdon was out in the wilds and difficult enough on its own, but Jack had the five children as well.

Kitty Rawle had done what she could but her own husband, Gillan, was ailing and, as he got weaker, so she became more and more tied to his bedside leaving those at the farm to fend for themselves. Charlotte had taken it upon herself to ride out every day from Withypool to Sherdon and cook for her brother's family. The two had managed between them but Sherdon needed more: it needed a woman to run the home. Three months after Gillan had gone Jack asked the young widow to join him. She was given the large attic room above the main landing, once home to the young farm boys.

"Tod's fine with 'er," Charlotte continued. "Get's on real well they do." Charles, at twelve the eldest and known as 'Tod' by the family ever since they could remember, had always liked Kitty. After his mother's death, it was she who had nursed the tall, fair-haired boy through his long illness. He remained frail and Jack had agonised when Wilmot, the children's uncle, had paid for him to attend Blundell's School in Tiverton. Kitty had been shocked at the idea of the quiet, thoughtful boy leaving home. "Almost like mother an' son they are," Charlotte mused. "But, it's she an' Harry that don't get on…always summat between 'em. Can't be half a day afore they're off again."

"Lively lad." Bamber pulled thoughtfully on his pipe, exhaled and wiped vaguely at the worst of the smoke. "'E's the one in trouble at school, eh?" He looked at his wife inquiringly. "Jack said 'e were one for finding the trouble. If trouble were about then Harry'd find it. Or more'n likely trouble would come looking for 'im, an' all." He chuckled, stroking his mutton chops as he did so.

"Proper mazed so 'e can be...fightin' an' scrappin' all the time." Charlotte wiped her hands on her apron. "Anyways, whatever it is, Harry an' Kitty don't get on. Not always the lad's fault mind...Kitty jumps in right quick sometime. Bites off his head afore 'e's started an' you can't blame the lad fer gettin' back. T'other day Jack almost had to pull 'em apart...summat daft about wet clothes an' that."

"Shame reely." Bamber leant forward in the high-backed kitchen chair and examined his toes. The fire, now little more than embers, for it was late, had done its job. They were warm and he wriggled them contentedly. "'Er does what 'er can for all of 'em...cookin' an' cleanin' an' that."

"But her should never have moved in so quick. I told Jack...an' I told 'er an all." Charlotte stepped over her husband's legs and turned her back to the fire. "'Twas all too quick. The littl'uns weren't ready for such a change...missed their mother they did, poor little mites. 'Twas Katherine they was pining for and didn't want nobody else."

"Don't be goin' too hard, dear. Jack had to 'ave somebody up there. 'Ad to...he could never manage by 'iself." Bamber eased himself in the chair. "'Tis all very well folk sayin' this an' that about what should 'ave bin done. Point was, they chillen needed a mother up there, an' Jack needed help. Can't 'spect no man to go runnin' a farm out there without someone lookin' after 'im an'his children...can't be done."

The two were silent, each remembering the gossip and comments there had been when Kitty joined the family at Sherdon. Jack had been unable to go on, so he told his sister but she, Charlotte, could give him no more time than she had been doing. No man could run a farm as well as looking after five youngsters and three farm hands. Even so there had been those who thought it wasn't right for a young woman who had just lost her own husband to move like she had. Most had been sympathetic but others less than charitable.

"Well, whether t'was right or wrong 'tis bin difficult and some of they littl'uns can't make 'er out...can't take to 'er like I s'pect they should." Charlotte shook her head. "Frank's all right an' Victoria but little Anna misses her mum dreadful, poor little dear. Still barely five her is...*cuh*."

"An' that's just it." Bamber struggled to his feet. "When you've got little tackers like that there's got to be a mother about...just like sheep. Can't 'spect 'em to look after theyselves...no ways. Anyhows, Jack says she's doin' a wunnerful job, an' says that fer you, too, m'dear. Says that it wouldn't be possible without the pair o'yer." She watched as the slow smile creased up his eyes and turned his cheeks into rosy apples. "Aye, 'tis difficult, that's fer sure an' will be difficult fer some time yet but us've got to be patient. Can't go expecting the chillen to un'erstand. Again, they're like lambs...some takes to the new ewe more quickly'n others."

"I know, I know." Charlotte felt the heat of the hearth through her skirt and shuffled further away, folding her arms and rubbing the warmth into them. "Still, 'tis a worry though. I can't help worryin' about that little Anna. She comes runnin' to me every time. Throws 'er little arms around me legs an' won't let go. 'Tis awkward reely seein' Kitty standing there an' the little maid all clinging to me. Don't feel right."

"She'll come round, don't 'e worry. 'Tisn't though Kitty's not 'urting her nor nuthin...'tis just 'cos she knows you so well. 'Er can tell, y'know. Take's time." He sucked on his pipe, packing down into the bowl what little tobacco was left. "If there be a worry wiv any o'them then 'tis young Harry. There's word about that 'ees getting' in with they Denholms...right wild lot they are and we don't want to see any o' that. An' Jack don't either, that's fer sure." Bamber settled the two larger pots in the embers and packed the still-hot ash round to keep the water warm through the night. He had indeed heard that young Harry Tucker was something of a tearaway but that might just have been more talk. The trouble was that country folk had to talk about something. It didn't seem to matter whether they had been told the facts or not, gossip was gossip and he had heard more than enough about life at Sherdon.

Bamber Heard could well remember what it was like to farm on one's own. It had been difficult enough for him and both Walter and Edgar, his two sons, were almost grown men when Jessie died. Nobody could blame Jack, nor Kitty for that matter. It had been well over a year now since Katherine had died and the struggle had brought the man to his knees. All the chit-chat should have stopped long ago. Charlotte, bless her, was doing what she could out there and, between them all, the farm was moving on. It would be all right in the end.

3

"The girl has done well." Delia, Dowager Lady Frobisher looked at Emma. "My goodness me, she has. You must be very proud."

"Yes, ma'am." Emma nodded and took back the report. "It's a wonderful chance for her to get on...to make her way in life." Sarah, Emma and Troy Kingdon's younger girl, had left Edgehill School in Bideford before Christmas. Wilmot Tucker, the girl's uncle, had once again stepped in to help his family, this time ensuring that Sarah and her elder sister, Mary, had received the best education available. Mary, it seemed, had squandered her opportunity and was supposed to be somewhere in Plymouth but, Sarah, so her final report had said, was a gifted young lady.

'She is blessed with many natural gifts,' the headmistress had written. *'Academically she has done very well. Sarah, however, is a headstrong and ambitious girl who, on occasions, needs to pause for thought while selecting the most suitable direction. She must appreciate also that there are those who might not possess such an abundance of talent:*

tolerance and caution do not come easily to her. That said she can look back on a most successful time at Edgehill and regard the future with optimism. I wish her all good fortune.'

"And we all know Sarah." Lady Frobisher laughed as Emma finished re-reading the report. "There's a very strong character there…ever since she was a little girl." Emma smiled and raised her eyebrows in agreement.

"And what now? Mrs Patterson's would you suppose?" Lady Frobisher, bent with arthritis and her hair now snow white yet still the same neat and elegant figure, rested her hand on the arm of the mahogany and gilt morning room sofa. She enjoyed Emma's company, if possible fonder of her now than ever she had been. She remembered when the tall young parlour maid arrived from Lynton, recommended to her by Elizabeth-Jane Knight. Emma, Jack Tucker's elder sister, had come to Filleigh initially to marry Troy Kingdon, the second butler, but it had not been long before she had taken her on as her personal maid. Now Emma had retired. Living in South Molton, in their little home tucked away up the narrow, cobbled Church Street, she and her husband were running their own haberdashery business and very successful it was too. Once a month Emma would drive herself out to Filleigh in their little dog cart when they would take tea together. Lady Frobisher smiled fondly.

"Oh, I think so, ma'am. That's if you still think it's for her." Two weeks earlier, Lady Frobisher had come into her shop, supposedly to look at some material but, inevitably, she had stopped to chat and the subject of Sarah's future had come up. It was then that she had suggested the select School for Young Ladies in Barnstaple.

"Abso-*lutely*…and *quite* right. It will develop the girl…bring her out. She's a beautiful creature and as bright as a button but…well…there's a deal to be learned yet. Mrs Patterson has a marvellous reputation and a very special way with the young. I've seen it myself. *Uh.*" Her face was a picture of horror as she lifted her hand in mock surprise. "Oh dear me, the girls arrive thinking they know everything about life but they're as raw as raw – until Mrs Patterson sets about them. What she does to them is quite remarkable, and if Sarah survives…*if* she can take the routine and the discipline, which I'm *sure* she can, then she'll benefit for the rest of her life."

"It'd be wonderful, ma'am, as I said it's such a chance for her." The two women looked at each other both trying to imagine the scene. "She says she'd be ever so grateful for the opportunity. And I know she'd do her best." Emma remembered how her daughter had clapped her hands and twirled in delight more like a child of half her years. "And her uncle has offered to help us with her wardrobe."

"And that's important." A finger wagged knowingly. "So we shall go through it together. Perhaps you'll be able to recommend some materials." Lady Frobisher reached for her Malacca cane and started to lever herself up, nodding automatically as Emma put down her cup and saucer and hurried to steady her. She gasped as she stood and stretched before reaching for the small of her back. "There won't be a great deal, not initially anyway. But the school lasts for almost a year, y'know, what with the tour to Europe in the middle, so we'll have to make sure she's got what's required."

Emma helped the old lady to the drawing room door where she was dismissed just as she always had been. It was the same little ritual that had been repeated countless times in the past and if Lady Frobisher thought anything should be different now she gave no indication. But perhaps it was just one of her ways that had become habit and Emma loved her for it.

✻

"And it has come to my notice that my advice has been forgotten…worse still, forsaken." Mrs Patterson was a tall woman, aged somewhere between forty and fifty, so it was believed, but nobody had ever asked her. Her black hair, pinned back severely in a tight bun and part hidden under her lace bonnet with a pleated edge, accentuated her pale features. The eyes, although sunken and perpetually redrimmed as though they were sore, missed nothing. She dressed well as Sarah and the others had to admit, and today she had chosen a midnight-blue dress with a braided trim which she wore over a crinoline frame and petticoats. The image was one of a certain forbidding grandeur. If there was supposed to be humour or bonhomie at this early hour, there was none today.

" I do not suppose it ever occurred to you that I would arrange for reports on your behaviour over these last ten days. Easter, you should well know, is when all the world is out and about and your conduct and your demeanour have been commented upon." As she talked so she walked slowly up and down the eight young women seated against the wall. A small coal fire kept most of the spring chill off the middle of the room which had been cleared except for a three-pillar rosewood dining table at one end. The rest of the room was empty, as though prepared for dancing classes. "I have to tell you that what I have heard has not been favourable. Very little of, how shall I say, 'couleur de rose'…rather quite the opposite; a situation I find positively disquieting.

"And pray bear yourself up – you, Matilda Webber…and you, Catherine James. Sit properly. Now I shall speak plainly," Mrs Patterson stopped where she could be seen by them all. "Kindly look me in the eye." Sarah glanced quickly at the two who had been reprimanded then did as she had been asked. She disliked the woman intensely as did the others, but where so many had wilted under the sharp tongue and critical eye, Sarah Kingdon had made it her business to gain from the experience. Such early morning tirades no longer upset her. It was typical of Mrs Patterson that after a short break she should claim without justification that they, her precious charges and symbols of her good name, should have disgraced themselves in public.

At first the other girls had laughed at those who had been selected for criticism but their turn came, each one identified and humiliated by the acerbic tongue. Some cried with shame, two girls left altogether but others, Sarah included, bore it doggedly. They had no idea how to sit properly, they were told this morning, not even how to stand while waiting to be seated. And they had forgotten how to hold themselves up as young ladies should. They did not know how to laugh gracefully, their tutor complained, or how to cough or carry their parasols. And when it came to young men, why they simply conducted themselves howsoever they desired. Everything but everything that had been learned to date, they had elected to ignore.

But Sarah was determined. She would learn the subtleties and the delicate touches of what to do and what not to do, of what to say and how it should be said. As the term progressed so she became ever more angry, not with herself or her tormentor, but with her own humble background and with those who had not corrected her clumsy ways earlier. The depth of the gulf between her own family and those with whom she was determined to associate she viewed as a challenge to be overcome. She was angry but she was resolved.

Hour after hour she would walk alone, talking to herself and refining her accent that had been so cruelly exposed. Since she was a child she had heard how others spoke but had thought nothing of it. Now she knew that it mattered a great deal. Mrs Patterson had impressed upon them how opening the mouth was like drawing back the curtains: it revealed everything. Not so much *what* was said but *how* it was said. Later, when the day was done she would come down to the dining room, take the books from the shelf and see how the various dinner tables should be set, where the mass of cutlery and accoutrements should go and learn by heart what should be called what, what a lady was supposed to touch and what was to be left well alone.

Little by little she mastered the traditions and the propriety, the etiquette and the demeanour of the *beau monde*, those gifts that had been granted by God to some through birthright. Great wealth, she appreciated, although a poor second to the blood line, was power nonetheless and there were those who had bought their way into society; their vulgarity tolerated solely on account of the fortunes that came with them. Why was it, she asked herself, that she had not been born into such a privileged elite and why was it that she and her family had been seen as fit merely to serve? It hurt and it grated.

Such bitterness served only to fuel her determination. The others noticed the change and kept their distance but Sarah remained unmoved. She had her looks, even Alfred Lord Tennyson had told her that when she had met him with Wilmot. 'Titania' he had christened her: Titania the beautiful fairy queen. Her uncle had dressed her well; she had her contacts and, with whatever Mrs Patterson had to offer, she would face the world. For all she cared the devil himself could take those she would be leaving behind, as well as any who might try to stand in her way.

*

"That's right, Sarah Kingdon...beautifully done. Thank you...fine....very neat." Mrs Patterson clapped her hands. "Gather round everyone and watch. See how the bustle and hoops are arranged to one side when the chair is proffered. Again, Sarah, please. First show how you must turn should it be the footman who is holding your chair, and, now, how it should be done if your escort at the table proffers his hand. Watch...that's right...and thank you." Sarah sat, her eyes moving automatically to the array of glass and cutlery in front of her. "And now lean back just a shade, a touch more, so the napkin may be taken from your plate and placed in your lap. Then turn ready for the iced water or the first wine...from your right. Do not look up at the waiter...such familiarity is unacceptable...good, that's prettily done."

Well, let the others be jealous. Let them leave her to take her meals on her own, to read by herself in the evenings while they prattled away together. It mattered not, for her determination to take what she could from Mrs Patterson would pay handsome dividends. Just a week ago she had heard that Lady Frobisher had suggested to her mother that she should apply for the post of second governess at Hartland Abbey and that she would be pleased to recommend her if she so wished. She had replied by return of post saying that she would indeed be more than happy to be considered for such an appointment. Lady Frobisher, so she was told, wished to see her this coming weekend.

*

"You've changed, Sarah...and changed a great deal." Their eyes met, Sarah looking back unflinchingly before looking away as she had been taught. She had it in mind to stare back at Lady Frobisher, to see if her nerve would hold, unlike so many who were petrified at the very thought of such a confrontation. But no, she considered it wiser to demur; there would be challenges enough ahead. "Mrs Jocelyn Orchard will see you herself at Hartland. You must realise there will be competition, and you should take nothing for granted...that will show and serve only to cause concern. Be yourself, girl. Remember all that Mrs Patterson has taught you and you will come to no harm. My letter of recommendation will not go unnoticed."

"Thank you, ma'am. Permit me to say how much I appreciate all the trouble you have taken on my behalf. Mother has told me that you have done much, a great deal, and I am indeed most grateful." This time she held the other's gaze.

Lady Frobisher inclined her head. "I'm very fond of your mother...she has looked after me for more years than either of us dare count and this, if it is anything at all, is but a mere token of my gratitude. She deserves more. But thank you." Sarah knew instinctively that the interview was over.

"Thank you ma'am. If it pleases you I'll take my leave." She smiled at the nod then backed away before turning and leaving the room.

4

Frederic pursed his lips and looked down to study his finger nails. The moment had come and he knew there was precious little he could do about it.

Florence was as lonely as a lost soul. At twenty-three, the dark-haired petite was barely half his age and he, himself, was younger than most of his friends. From the start he knew it would be difficult and had been anxious about his young wife. All the signs were there. The other night, after dinner together, there had been tears and it had been the same last night. There was no one for her, she complained, no one at all and the bleak solitude was forbidding.

He rose and went to sit on the arm of her chair. "Never mind," he murmured, his fingers playing lightly through the velvet ribbons that tied her long ringlets. "We'll give it a bit of time and see how you feel."

For a moment she was silent, staring ahead; her eyes wide, reflecting the light from the fire. Then she sighed. "Oh, I don't know, Freddie. I feel awful. It's as though I'm letting you down so, complaining like this. Half of me wants to stay…to be here with you. It really does." She leant back and looked up at him. "I mean, I'm your wife, after all, and I should be *here…here* with you at your side. There's so much to be done and I hate the thought of you being on your own."

"*Poof*, that side of it's nothing at all." He raised a hand and let it fall. "It's just that…well I had hoped you might love it up here. There's a magic about the place, y'know. Either you feel it and are in…."

"I know, I know and I've tried so hard. Believe me I have. Perhaps it might have been different if we'd had a few of our friends around…the Dempseys, for instance or the Packenhams." She twisted herself further round and put a hand on his knee. "Just a few like them. It would have been so different for me, so much more fun…then the riding and the picnics would have been a delight."

Frederic looked along the line of stags' heads above the fire then on to the tapestry hanging above the long, black Elizabethan table but he was not taking it in. His mind had gone back to Sherdon six or seven years ago. He remembered sitting alone with Katherine: dear, lovely, sad Katherine Darcy when she had confessed her loneliness to him. Her plight had hurt him grieviously and he had been drawn to her. He had seen then how a woman nurtured on a full and busy life could be brought to the edge of despair. His heart had gone out to her but she was Jack's and although he knew then that he loved her dearly, it had been too late. There was nothing he could do and when he met the shy, teenage Florence Gibbs in London he had asked for her hand.

Now here it was again: this time it was his frail and timid wife who had bravely born him his firstborn – a son - in this very house, born while the larks were singing in the spring sunshine outside. It had been as though nature was serenading the tiny newcomer, welcoming him to what one day would be his. But his expectations had not lasted. The young Frederic Sebright Winn had not been born with his father's vigorous, rude health nor his zest for life. More like his mother, the child had not taken kindly to the fresh moorland air. Before he was a year old Florence had taken him off to Worcestershire complaining that the damp and the cold were doing him no good. They had been away for three months and it was the same the following year and the year after.

And now he feared it might be for good. "I'll be coming up, my dear. Perhaps it *might* be better for you to be at Wolverley…I'll need somebody there to keep the constituency happy. And old Sir Thane Grantham, dear old Mister Gout himself, will love having you there. Checking up on the lifestyle and family of the Member for West Worcestershire will give him every excuse to call on you, and frequently at that. And the Bathursts too." He pulled her towards him. "It could be a blessing y'know."

"You're just being brave, aren't you." Florence rested her head against him. "Dear Freddie, you'll be here all on your own and yet you say it might be for the better. I do love you, you know, really I do." She sat up, turned and faced him squarely. "I do, you know." He bent down and brushed her forehead with his lips.

"I know," he whispered then cleared his throat. "But it's not only here that takes my time. There's London, don't forget, and parliament. Since Derby made me Secretary I've spent more and more time trying to keep that lot together. It's like collecting up spilt mercury…every member of the board runs around in different directions. It's a nightmare and I'll be glad to be shot of it."

"D'you have to do it all, dear? You're driving yourself so hard. There must be others."

"Not really. Sometimes I fight against it but it's a fascinating time to be there…and at the centre of things. The old order is breaking up. More and more on both sides are seeing the need for change. People are following their conscience. Like me," he laughed. "A whole host of Tories watched me like hawks when I spoke for reform…Evelyn Denholm from Tonbridge, for instance, Arthur Peake and William Gladstone to name but a few. There's a mood of change afoot, y'know. Fresh life is being breathed and it's exhilarating. You'll feel it when you're next in town. Number fifty-two Portland Place has become quite a centre of intrigue and you'll love it."

Tarr opened the doors through to the hall then turned and led the way to the dining room where he nodded to the footmen. Knight chuckled to himself. "But come on let's eat and hear no more about you feeling guilty. In any case I'll be needing you more and more in London. And, here's a thought…a little absence now and then never hurt. If the boy's better off elsewhere then all well and good." Husband and wife rose together.

Chapter Two

Jack Tucker spat on his hand, took up the billhook and toyed with it until he found the right balance. Leaning forward, he stretched out and bent the beech sapling away from him, then cut deeply a few inches above the base. The blade bit just hard enough for the young wood to split. *"Jest enough so's you can bend 'er down an' lay 'er flat."* Years ago Harry Fisher from Ferny Ball had showed him how. *"That way a new shoot comes up from the stump and life begins all over again."*

He remembered watching as the old farmer laid the first beech hedge. Once the sapling branches had been pegged flat along the hedge top, earth and sods were packed in between making the high bank taller still and almost impenetrable. The banks at Sherdon had never needed repair before but the sheep, seeking shade in the summer and shelter from the winter winds, had started to break them down. The young saplings, some almost thirty feet high, first had to be thinned before those left could be laid. It was cruel work and, standing on top of the hedgerow in the March wind, it was cold as well.

*

Jack paused, wiped his brow on his sleeve and studied the sky like farmers do. The clouds were high and broken, little more than thin lines of smoke trails tinged pink by the setting sun. They would clear and that meant another cold night yet it was high time for some warmth to get into the ground. That would come only when the wind backed to the west and stayed there bringing with it the much needed rain. Of that there was little sign. It had been another hard winter, and difficult in more ways than one. January had been bitter with two falls of snow that covered the roots. The snow had frozen and, no matter how hard they tried, the sheep had been unable to break through the icy crust. Jack had no option other than to dig into his reserves of hay. The three small ricks below the house had gone first followed by the two behind the shearing barn. The trouble now was that the pastures were still bare with not a blade of grass in sight. March in the high hills was a hungry month.

Below him the dogs stirred and stood, then the younger one growled softly. Jack shielded his eyes, calling to them quietly then raised his arm in salute. Slowly, and taking care not to trip over the latticework of branches, he made his way to the ground. A few years ago he would have jumped, his legs easily taking the shock but no longer: he would soon be fifty-one and sometimes felt like it. In any case today had been long enough.

"Ooh, just passin' through, like. Thought to drop by." Jack watched as Bamber slid easily from the pony's back and went to secure the head collar. As he turned so his visitor took off his battered felt hat, scratched vigorously at his bald pate, then replaced it a shade further back than before.

17

"Cold enough, Bamber?" Jack bent down and picked up the two jute sacks he had brought out with him. One he threw around his shoulders before moving into the lee of the hedge, the other he offered to his visitor. Bamber always came with news from the village and he watched attentively as the older man went through the ritual of bringing life to his pipe.

"Aye," Bamber agreed. "'Tis sharp all over an' I don't spec 'tis over yet. Next month can be hard, too, mind." Jack eased his shirt around his leather belt, pulled his sack tighter and listened as talk turned to sheep. His own views, usually kept to himself, were based on his years at Sherdon.

"I can't be certain these hornies are right for this high ground." Jack nodded towards the young Exmoor horn ewes picking at the remnants of the hay. "'Tis all right further down the hill…that's where they come from but up here, and 'specially where we're still breakin' the land, they're not doing so well." Bamber followed his gaze. "They're all right on the roots but not for long. Trouble is, they cut up the wet ground terrible an' there's nowhere dry for them to lie. The fleeces're all heavy with mud an' they're none too happy 'bout that…not in February anyway."

"Aye." Bamber considered the problem. "Several've bin lost back in that cold spell."

"And up here, too. Dozens out at Emmets and more at Wintershead. And its bin hard out at Simonsbath as well. We had Master Frederic over t'other day an' he was saying that the Scottish shepherd, the one out to Black Pits, 'e reckons that Devon sheep are best left down on the lower ground. Reckons that Scottish sheep'd be better up top. Scottish sheep an' they from up north." The two men were silent. "The fact is, Bamber, we're losing as many as what us must sell to buy in next winter's keep. Losing more than we're making…all of us are. Year on year it's the same. No man can farm when 'es losing money like that."

"'Ave heard they new tenants up at Driver 'ave had enough. The ones that lost that littl'un before Christmas. A young lad, wer'n it? Up sticks an' left so they did. Dead stock all over the place an' the farm's still empty. 'Tis bitter out there, mind."

"Well no local man's going to come this far out…except me, that is." Jack laughed at his own words. The chill wind had begun to feel through the sweat on his clothes so he pulled the sack tighter around his shoulders. "More sense and there's the problem. Told Master Frederic many a time. The local man knows what 'tis like up here come the winter and what's to be done, an' won't come near the place. So then the lan'lord has to go lookin' elsewhere and brings in those who've got no idea…no idea at all, they haven't."

"You'm all right, boy?"

"Aye, Bamber, we're strugglin' on. I don't know what we'd do without Wilmot, though." Jack paused. "I hate going to him but he insists on it. Says it's his farm and it's up to him to keep the place running. Can't imagine what it must be like without someone such as him behind you." Jack, once angry and shamed that his younger brother had bought Sherdon from Frederic Knight, had long since come to terms with the situation. Wilmot, as he now knew, had enough money to see all his farms through the worst of the weather, and time and again if necessary. What was more he enjoyed coming out to Sherdon and the brothers spent hours together walking the land or inspecting the stock.

"An' the family?" Bamber turned from the wind and struggled with the tobacco and flint. "I hear from Lottie that things are goin' along." Jack sighed. He knew his sister would have passed on all she had heard and seen at the farm and that some of it, embellished no doubt to suit her case, would cause eyebrows to be raised. But Bamber had said nothing to anyone, even when Katherine had confided in him. He had kept her secrets to himself, allowing her to take them to the grave.

"Phhhew." Jack leant against the hedge. "Half an' half, Bamber." He shook his head trying to find the right words. "Sometimes its peace…and laughter an' that but other times 'tis difficult…and then there're times when I dunno where to turn next." Bamber leant back beside him. "Kitty an' Lottie are wonderful, really they are but they're two very different sorts an' no matter how hard they try – an' they do try, sometimes they get scratchin' at one another. Then the young get started and then 'tis all madness…an' then suddenly it'll stop." He let his hand fall and smiled weakly. "That's the honest truth, Bamber…an' I dunno where to go from here."

"Aye." The old man spoke slowly. "Aye I've heard 'tis more or less like that. Lottie comes back worried sore sometimes…other times 'ers larkin' an'jokin' an as happy as can be."

"What d'yer reckon, Bamber? What can a man do about it? There's mouths to be fed and clothes to be washed an' that…an' the children to see. It's not easy."

Bamber looked down, prodding at a stone with his boot. He glanced at the sky and then down again. "You'm fond of the maid? Kitty, that is?"

"Aye. Dearly so."

"An' she you?" Jack shrugged and Bamber took his arm, suddenly embarrassed at what he had asked. "'Ere, Jack, should never have asked yer that, lad. The maid's 'ansome for yer, we can all see that." Again the two were lost in thought. "Well," Bamber pushed back his hat. "Since you'm asking…my advice, an' 'tis only mine, mind. My advice is that if yer feel right on the maid then take 'er to yer proper."

"Get married, you mean?"

"Aye, that's what I reckon. You'm not getting' no younger, neither of yer. An' yer have to say that Katherine's bin gone now…an' I know how yer feel, lad, 'cos I lost

Jessie likewise, mind. Katherine's gone on and Gillan's bin gone also and there's the two of yer. Trouble is, see, the littl'uns don't know what's what. Kitty's up there with you an' yet she's not there proper like. You'm sort of half way but neither one thing nor t'other. P'raps if yer both feel so sure about the way of things then, p'raps the time might be right."

"It's still soon enough, Bamber. Every time I'm in the house I can feel her, Katherine that is. I sense she's there…see her almost. She's there somewhere, you know." Jack looked down and shook his head. "'Tis hard, my God it's hard. I loved that girl more than any man could have loved anyone. I know what folks 'ave been saying…about Kitty an' me. I'm truly fond of her but there was nothing in it, nothing at all. You know that, don't you. The only one for me was Katherine and when she died like she did…well." His voice trailed off and he turned away suddenly.

"Aye," Bamber muttered softly. "Aye, we all knows that. But then," he paused again. "But life goes on, lad. None of us can do nort about the past. An' there's the girl, y'know, Kitty that is. You must spare a thought for her, fer all she's done. An' for the children, mind. They needs to know what's what…then they'll settle better. Take things easy, mind, an' don't go rushin', but if you an' Kitty feel 'tis right then my advice'd be to see the vicar. He'll tell yer when's right. The reverend up to Simonsbath, that Mr Thornton. He'll tell yer, but that's the way I'd be thinkin' if I were you."

"'Y'ere." Bamber struggled to his feet. "Us can't be stoppin' 'ere like this…getting' all maudlin' like. Best be better gettin' on. 'Tis goin' to be sharp tonight what with that sky. Not a cloud, look." Jack straightened also, glanced upwards then stamped his feet and eased his shoulders where they had stiffened. Bamber was right. The dogs had to be fed and the young bullocks in the shippon as well. And he had planned to get a load of roots out of the clamp.

He ought really to have stepped out but he walked slowly, pondering what the old farmer had advised. He was right, he knew he was. It made sense as did most things he said, but it was not going to be easy.

✳

Kitty hitched her skirt then bent forward and lifted the lid. The stew was simmering nicely so she added some salt and stood back from the hearth. Squinting past the lamp hanging from the beam she checked the clock on the delf-case. Jack was late but it had given her time to put the girls down. She turned the potatoes in the bread oven and wiped her hands on the folds of her grey apron before pausing to pick at something under one of her nails. Then slowly, her mind deep in thought, she walked to collect the washing basket.

Upstairs, little Anna, barely six, had rejected her bedtime embrace, turning her back instead and saying nothing. However Alice Victoria had been pleased to see her and had thrown her arms around her neck to hug her tight.

"Don't be silly, Anna." Victoria, lying next to her sister, had tried to pull her round. "Come on, say good night."

"Leave me a-*lone*," Anna had cried, waving her away. "I don't *want* to…not to her anyways."

The elder girl had hugged Kitty again. "Don't worry, Kitty. She doesn't mean it…not really."

"Yes I *do*…I don't like her. Go away and leave me alone." Kitty had hesitated, holding the dimmed lamp high in order to see better but the child's back remained turned.

"Night, night, dear." Kitty brushed Victoria's hair from her face. The child was lying staring up at her, with her eyes wide and her small piece of cloth pressed to her cheek. "Night, Kitty." As she backed towards the door they smiled at one another but from Anna there was no sound.

For a moment she stood in the darkness. Why, she asked herself. How could it be? Did Anna feel that she, Kitty, was trying to push her way in place of her mother? Or did the child see her as some sort of imposter who was forcing herself between her and her father, taking his love and attention? And why had she turned to Charlotte? What had *she* done to deserve the little girl's affection? But there was nothing she could do about it, nothing at all. She had tried, tried to give love to the girl just as she had tried to ease the bitterness she saw in Harry. But it was hard.

And then there was Jack himself. Why this indifference from him? Why had he not taken her to him? She longed to hold him in her arms, to cradle his head on her breast and comfort the grief she saw was still there. She longed for the time when he came in at the end of a busy day, tired and worn out, when she could help him ease his pain and listen patiently to his woes.

She knew he cared for her, cared deeply sometimes but sensed his struggle within. He had been so good to her when Katherine was alive and he had comforted her tenderly when Gillan was dying. He had never done anything more than hold her close yet she could remember the warmth and the desire in the man…and that was while Katherine lived. Why, therefore this change? His wife had gone and been gone for two years yet still he hung back from her. Was it the children? Was it the other woman's ghost that kept coming back to him or was it that she, Kitty, was not the woman he was seeking, and would never be so? Would he ever pledge his love or would he continue to offer simple affection for ever and a day until their relationship grew stale? Sometimes he would hold her tight in his arms and press her to him yet that was all: a sudden moment of love which was soon gone. It was as if he was afraid, shy like a child of doing something he might later regret. She needed his love, dear God she did. Without it her life was empty and becoming ever more so.

21

Sometimes, like now when she shut the door behind her, she wanted to run head-long into the night escaping forever his cool brooding and all the pain it brought. Have faith in me, she begged him. Take me for who I am and what I am. Have trust in the love I have for you. Please let me into your world for I have nowhere else to go. There are no other arms out there waiting to sweep me up. What you see is all I have. Everything I have to give I have given and all I seek in return is a share of your love.

Slowly, and with the lamp held in front of her, she walked away from the children's door. Downstairs she picked the wet clothes from the basket one at a time. They had been left screwed tight after Frank had helped her squeeze out the water. It had been fun and the two had laughed together as they twisted the clothes, each trying to outdo the other. He was a lovely, gentle lad but it was unnerving to see how closely the tall eleven year-old resembled his father. The eyebrows were darker but the straightness of the nose and the high forehead were Jack all over. And all he wanted to do was to follow his father on to the farm. She warmed at the thought of him and, for a moment, her spirits were lifted yet her heart remained heavy.

But it was Anna. As she shook the clothes open and placed them along the cord line so her mind returned to the child. Small and neat with her uncle's dark features, she had always hung back from her advances. Somewhere there was a barrier. No matter what she did or how she tried, the little girl always ran to her father, or to Lottie. She was a dear little soul and she longed to pick her up and ruffle her curls but she would have none of it. And it had been the same tonight.

Just as she was pulling the creases from the last of the clothes, she heard Jack's call as the door opened. "Seen Harry's arm, have you?" She watched as Jack steadied himself against the door frame before bending slowly to unlace his boots. "Slipped when he was on the rocks above Whitewater. Up there with Ernie lookin' for young ravens. Swears blind there's a second nest up there somewhere but he wouldn't hear that birds like that wouldn't nest so close…not ravens."

She had heard the boy had fallen but thought no more of it. "Not so bad as it looks though," Jack continued. "'E an' Frank are up there in the room with they elder two. All four of 'em together talkin' an' chatterin' away. I said they could stay 'til supper." She remembered how, when she arrived, Ernie Snell and Stan Bawden, the two farm lads, had moved out into the barn loft, a snug place once occupied by Declan, the Irishman. She had taken their room in the attic and, at first, felt guilty about it until they told her they would rather be outside. Eventually she believed them for their new room had become a meeting place where the young tended to congregate.

She hoped the boy might have come to her but he, too, fought shy of her company and once more she sensed failure. "Come on, dear." Jack took her gently by the hand and pulled her towards him. "Tired, eh? Never stop, you don't"

"An' who's doin' the talking then?" Kitty smiled bravely. "Aye," she sighed. "I'll have to say there's always summat or other, but I don't mind. No different to outside." She smiled again and brushed a lock of grey-brown hair back from over his eyes. "An' you've had a day, an' all. I can see that."

"Aye, long enough." He sat heavily and watched as she bustled about. Once, as she was setting the places around him, he took her hand again and rubbed it gently with his thumb.

*

The meal had gone well and for once, so it seemed, there had been nothing to argue about. Jack listened as Harry and Ernie Snell described the climb up to the ravens' nest and how the young birds had flattened themselves, lying low and still in the hope they would be missed. "About a week," Harry had announced. "I'll have a pair o' them and ought t'get two pence for each down at The Royal Oak."

Jack chided him gently, remarking that he wanted no more talk of selling birds at tavern doors. "Stay away from they places," he warned, his knife emphasising the point. "Time enough fer hawkin' things about later. And any more o' that messin' around down at the inn an' yer away to Blundell's with Tod." It was an idle threat for Harry was no academic, a point noted by Wilmot. Harry, the adventurer, was bound for the outdoor life rather than books. He grinned at his father then scowled darkly at the very idea of school.

*

Jack sat in the high-backed chair, turning the day's events over in his mind. Kitty, her day done at last, sat in the rocking chair beyond the fire. It was one of the few pieces of furniture she owned. Given to her by Gillan's mother, it remained her favourite and the family recognised it as her chair. He could see her now, out of the corner of his eye, dipping into the endless pile of clothes that needed mending or patching.

It all depended on which way you looked at it, he thought to himself. There were problems and more problems at Sherdon if you went looking for them yet he still loved the life and was blessed with five wonderful children. Wilmot had all the trappings of life and, from what he had heard, there were plenty more on the way. But he, too, loved it here and was always telling his brother that he had the better life. Huh. Then there was Emma, his sister; she seemed as content as ever. And Lottie; now happy at last with Bamber. And Bamber himself…what he had said earlier kept returning and he glanced at Kitty.

The chair was still. Her hands were in her lap and her head had fallen forward. The shirt she was darning had slipped to the floor. He rose silently and crept towards her. He thought he had reached her but she started just as he knelt by her side. "Come on, love, you're dead beat. Come on, come over with me a minute." Both hands steadied her as she stood and he drew her over to his chair, sitting first then helping her onto his lap. She settled like a kitten, her knees tucked up and her head resting high on his chest.

23

"Quiet this evening, so you were." He stroked her hair then nuzzled his face down breathing her fragrance. It was still the same dark auburn hair he remembered. She snuggled closer. "Bin thinking again, 'ave you?"

"Always thinking," she mumbled.

"Go on."

"Mmm?"

"What's up? Summat's there, that's fer sure." Kitty remained still. "It's us you're thinking on, isn't it?" He continued and she nodded. "Eh? Wonderin' what's to come of us, I'll be bound." She nodded again. What indeed. Bamber's advice came to him again and Jack let his head loll back against the high wooden chair. It was clear enough and, he suspected, most men would have jumped at the chance there and then. Kitty was more than any man in his position could ask for, and yet, and yet. Even as he closed his eyes, Katherine's face returned out of the darkness. Her radiant smile with the children crawling all over her; her tears of anguish at the sight of the dead sheep after the storm and that terrible look of pain on her face when she found him with Kitty. But there had been nothing, yet the sight of the other woman in his arms as he was comforting her had broken his wife. It had been his fault and he had not been able to forgive himself. It was no good. He was not ready to give his love to anyone else: it was all too soon. The memory of her fall into the stairwell was still fresh and his anguish still deep.

He moved his head sideways and tried to look at the face on his chest but it was hidden by the mass of hair. Her breathing had slowed and she was asleep. Suddenly he was torn. He would never be able to love another as he had loved his wife yet here was a woman whose loyalty and devotion was saving him. Day after day she was slaving away yet asked for nothing in return. She had heard the talk and the gossip and had seen the backs turning at the market yet she never complained. Lottie had been sharp with her, Harry had shouted and little Anna had forsaken her yet she remained at his side. And here she was now, exhausted and helpless in his arms. He had never thought of her, only for himself and his grief. She had given him everything.

He rose slowly, lifted her into his arms and started to carry her up to her bed. Half way up the stairs she woke and clung to him. When he lay her down she pulled his face down to hers and he felt the warmth of her kiss. Even so he backed away. "Not yet, my little one," he whispered to himself. "I can't, not just yet."

2

Sarah rose on her toes, turned sideways and looked at herself in her mother's full-length mirror. She turned further, straining to see how the loose, three-quarter length amber coat fell away over her skirts. More of a cloak than a long jacket and trimmed lightly with fur, the coat was fastened at the throat and hung open over her apple-green bodice and her dress which was darker and edged with pleats.

"Lovely, that is." Mary, her elder sister, had returned from Plymouth three days ago. Sarah had met her off the stage outside The George and immediately noticed the changes. She was no longer the elegant, sophisticated sister she had once admired. There was too much rouge on the cheeks and her unwashed hair had been cut badly. Worse still there was the bitter smell of gin and her clothes, now frayed and stained in places, reeked of tobacco. She could see, also, that the skin on her face had become puffy and slack, typical of those who have been drinking too much.

Their parents had been shocked at the state of her and her coarse manners had reduced their mother to tears. Yesterday the two sisters had rowed and even today, Sarah's last day at home, an atmosphere prevailed. "You can do it, you know." Sarah looked at her sister. "Honestly, you can if you really want."

"Oh, it's easy for you to say that." Mary bit her lip and watched as Sarah selected the jade bracelet from her black, oval-shaped jewel case. "You wait…you haven't taken a knock yet. Life's not all that easy out there."

"Well I don't intend to sit around waiting for these knocks." Sarah tossed her head defiantly and turned towards the smaller of the two mirrors where she toyed with her hair, now curled into ringlets by Mrs Simpkins in her South Street salon. "If you think I'm going to wait for life to have it's wicked ways with me then you're mistaken. It's what you make it, not what it does to you."

"Hey, *steady*. You can't go saying that. Sometimes things just…well, just happen an' there's no way of knowin'."

"Most surely. But what d'you expect when you go consorting with the sort of people who do *this* to you." She waved a hand at her sister now sitting on the bed. "Just look at yourself, Mary…go on, look in the mirror. You were given *every* chance by Uncle Wilmot; all that education, the new clothes and then the allowance. And what have you done with it all?"

"Oh get over. 'Taint right goin' on like that. 'Tis unfair…cruel, sayin' that sort of thing."

"And stop speaking like that…in that dreadful, common accent. You've got to make an effort with yourself, you know."

"Well, that's how mother an' father taught us. That's how us were brought up. 'Baint my fault."

"Oh, come on. You had every chance at Edgehill…and you know it. You just didn't bother and mixed with all those roughnecks as soon as you were home."

"Weren't nobody else, were there? Not round where us were at Filleigh. And

NEITHER HOPE NOR FEAR

anyway, us grew up with mother 'n father's friends and that were it."

"Exactly. So if you want to stay like that...like them, then that's up to you, my dear."

"'Ere come on, Sarah. Don'e dare go speakin' of mother all hoity-toity like that. Don'e ever say nuthin like that." Mary rose, her face flushed. " That's right dreadful of yer."

"Poof, and so say you. Maybe that's the way things were once but I've seen a different world and so've you. If you want it like this...slaving and scraping away in all that muck for the rest of your life then that's fine. But don't come and tell me *I'm* the lucky one or how *lovely* my clothes are. I started down there, too, you know. I didn't like it and I'm getting out of it."

"Well *go*, then." Mary came closer, her voice raised. "An' if you're so ashamed of our Mum and Dad and our home, then the devil take you, Sarah Kingdon. They've done *everything* for us so they have, *everything*, bless 'em, and they don't need that from anyone...not least you."

"Oh, stop shouting like that." Sarah went to push past her then changed her mind and sat at her mother's dressing table. "Look, I'm going and don't you worry about me." She paused and looked disdainfully into the mirror at the figure behind her. "I've had enough of this draggle-tailed world of ours where we're expected to go round bobbing and curtseying like lackeys...keeping our place and minding our peace."

"Cuh, right proper uppity, so you are. A right madam. They'll see you comin', all right, Sarah. They'll be watchin' you pushin' yer way in an' creepin' around. An' d'you know what'll be sayin'? *Eh? A right little gold digger, 'er is, they'll be sayin'. They'll see you comin'...you mark my words."

 Sarah rose and faced her sister. "Good," she said acidly. "Well, let them. And let me tell you something, shall I? Let me tell you this, Mary." She looked her up and down. "You *smell*. It's horrid but I don't suppose you even notice it. You stink of the taverns and the alleyways of the docks where you've come from and if that's what you like then get back there. You go your way and I'll go mine."

"Ohh...yooouu." Mary clenched her fists but her sister swept past.

3

Wilmot stepped down from the brougham. He eased his legs then bent down to rub the old mine injury which always ached after such a rattling around. The journey home to Court Hall from South Molton had taken little more than half an hour and he now had time enough before Sir Durnford Morgan would be here. He had asked the banker to meet him on behalf of The Bristol Steamship Company, on whose board he was now a member.

"Ah, Steer…a pleasant day, I see. Anything from Mrs Tucker?" Jacob Steer, the butler, had come from Arlington Court three years earlier. Short, plump and jolly, his enormous mutton chops compensated more than adequately for the lack of hair on his head. Another of his quirks was that he always tried to look taller than he was, the result being that he tended to strut about with his back ramrod straight and his arms well away from his body.

"She promised to write her itinerary for next week," Wilmot continued. Rebecca could not wait to escape from Clifton where the fine house they had taken meant little to either of them. She, like her husband, adored Exmoor and would be bringing the children with her. Lionel, as black as a coal scuttle according to his father and now seven, would be hunting this season but Jessica was not so sure. The three year-old had decided that horses, and that included Pepper, her matronly Exmoor pony, should be treated with caution.

"A letter yesterday, sir. No, two would you believe. They're on the hall table along with the despatches from Bristol." Steer beckoned to Grainger, the new coachman, to follow them with the luggage but only as far as the hall. Wilmot shrugged his beige taglioni into a more comfortable position and flicked at whatever it was on his tartan-check trousers before following them inside. The butler turned with the mail on the salver.

"Well, how's everything here?" Wilmot glanced at the handwriting and looked up. "Mmm?"

"Very well, sir, thank you." The butler felt his master's dark eyes searching him for the answer. "I've another footman coming tomorrow…remember we got rid of that Bannister fellow…a right grubby little man 'e was." Steer rose on his toes. "And Mrs Lock gets in tomorrow as well, sir. I know she's lookin' forward to seeing you all again." Wilmot nodded. The housekeeper from Dunster was a success; for once a friendly soul to run the house rather than one of those frigid creatures carved out of ice. "And Bulled will be up directly, sir. Wants to talk about the release pens…says the pheasants won't take to a couple of 'em. Well, summat like that." Steer had little time for country pursuits.

"Good…good. Look, I'll take my tea in the study. I want to wade through this lot before the house fills." He held up the mail. "Anyone else expected tonight? No? Then peace and thank goodness for that. Just Sir Durnford." He smiled with relief.

✳

Wilmot re-read the minutes of last week's board meeting. The subject of expanding the company, always difficult, had been hotly debated. There were those who wanted to break into the shipping lines that held the monopolies further north. Port Talbot and Tenby on the Welsh coast had been mentioned. These ports would not have been too bad but then two of directors, Alfred Swithen and the loquacious Blake James, had wanted to go much further – they had identified Ellesmere, in Cheshire, and the Red Funnel line at Bootle as possible targets.

He had contested such ideas vehemently arguing that to do so would shift the whole balance of the company to the north and they would have to start importing and exporting different commodities, which meant new ships. And the new markets they had acquired recently, well used to the previous administration, would be suspicious. Far better he reasoned, to remain in the South West. The smaller ports such as Watchet in Somerset, Bideford and the new seaport at Countess Weir, just south of Exeter, were the best bets in Devon and there were several in Cornwall. The future of all of them would depend on the arrival of the railways. Some would be bypassed while others would flourish.

If they decided now and struck before the rest of the world woke up, the company could hardly lose. He had swung the meeting, but before the vote was taken a caveat was added that the banks would have to agree to underwrite any such venture. And so it would be tonight, at dinner, that Sir Durnford Morgan would be appraised of their plans. It was difficult to see how the banker could be anything but sympathetic to their requirements

Wilmot wiped the tiredness from his eyes before resting his chin in his hands and gazing thoughtfully across the valley towards Barcombe Down. Beyond that the land rose further still and it was there, way over the skyline, that Sherdon lay. And that meant Jack. Wilmot rubbed his eyes again and yawned expansively. He had been worrying for some time, ever since Charlotte had alerted him to his brother's plight. Jack was almost five years older than him and life, rather than easing, seemed to be getting ever harder. Eighteen fifty-nine already, he thought, wondering how life might look for them all ten years hence. The thought of the poor man struggling, as their sister claimed he was, unsettled him and he was determined to get out there.

Tod, his nephew, would soon be home from school and he had brought some more books for the boy. The youngster devoured them, just as his mother used to and never ceased questioning him in that slow voice of his. Kitty, he knew, fussed over him, something that tended to upset the others. But they had not been ill like Tod and he could remember the grave look on Dr Collyns' face when he told them about the boy's pneumonia. So it was fair, he decided, that the one who was away for most of the time should have that little bit of extra attention when home.

*

Sir Durnford Morgan was punctual as he invariably was. Stating a time, the banker affirmed, was like quoting a price: you should stick to your word, for those who heard you would then depend on it.

Wilmot, now changed and ready, had barely time to study the news. Lord Derby, so 'The Times' reported, had been defeated over Disraeli's Reform Bill and Palmerston was back. Hmm, the man had only been gone for a year or so and they were now due for another dose of his Liberalism as they liked to call it. The company would be none too pleased: all these changes promised by the new government would make it difficult to plan ahead which was exactly what they were intending to do.

But Frederic Knight would be happier. He had done well in the House, making his name when Derby appointed him as Secretary to The Poor Law board. But that had been several years ago since when he had started to speak out as a radical. Palmerston, so Freddy told him, was a man with vision and, if ever he got back, would form a coalition of Whigs and Radicals, even Peelites. Well, here he was, back in office once more and it would be interesting to see how many of these changes there would be. But Freddy, 'Young Knight' as he was known, as opposed to the other member of that name – a grizzled old Scot from Renfrewshire – remained a Tory, but only just it appeared. He had made his views known by keeping on about the plight of the workers, upsetting those around him while drawing murmurs of approval from across the floor. And here on Exmoor he had been as good as his word. He had done much and, without him, there would be nobody living up there.

✳

"Beg pardon, sir." Steer walked round to where Wilmot could see him without having to turn. "One of Sir Durnford Morgan's outriders has just pulled up." Steer was bobbing on his toes. "Says the coach will be just a minute or two, sir. No more'n that."

"Splendid. Alert the stables if you will." Wilmot rose, wincing at the sharp stab of pain in his foot. "We won't dine for a bit…we'll take drinks in here as soon as he's settled."

"Very good, sir." It was going to be an interesting evening and as he stood waiting to greet his visitor, Wilmot took a deep breath.

Chapter Three

In spite of the hour, the day was still burning hot. Frederic walked across the first floor drawing room and looked down on the junction of Portland Place and Devonshire Street. Maynard, the butler, had thrown open the windows to catch whatever breeze there might be but not even the leaves at the very tip of the limes along the middle of the broad avenue were moving. Number fifty-two faced the evening sun and as he waited for his visitor so he wondered if his hunch might be right. Florence was still out with Sebright. Their son was home and they had gone into Hyde Park, promising not to disturb what might be a delicate meeting.

✳

"Mr Gladstone, sir." Maynard waited until the visitor, dressed in his customary black frock coat, had entered the room. The butler then bowed and retreated, closing both doors as he did so.

"Freddy, dear boy. It's so good of you to see me…and at such short notice." William Gladstone, beaming warmly, clasped his host's hand in both his. There were but three years between them yet the wily parliamentarian had made his maiden speech in the House almost thirty years before. Later, and soon after Frederic entered the Commons, Peel had appointed him to be his President of the Board of Trade. In spite of his meteoric rise to power, the young Gladstone had sought company of his own age in order to see him through the rare moments he allowed himself between his furious political demands. 'Young Knight' had caught his eye and they had become good friends, often dining together.

But there was something else. As his authority increased, so Gladstone had become ever more disenchanted at the lack of sympathy shown by so many members on both sides towards reform. Seven years ago he had declined to join Derby's Tories, instead declaring openly his liberal philosophies. Eyebrows had been raised and it was then he discovered that the Tory member for West Worcestershire shared similar views. He had watched with growing admiration how Frederic, time and again, stood alone on his side of the House demanding change; how he had argued passionately on behalf of the poor and how sometimes he had thrown down his papers in disgust.

"Well, I had it in mind that sooner or later you would have had enough. Am I not right?" Frederic waved his visitor to a seat, noticing how the hooked nose and hollow eyes enhanced the look of studied melancholy. "You see, word's out that you're anxious to move on. The Reform has sharp ears y'know."

"Indeed, indeed." Gladstone nodded sagely and lifted his chin to stroke where the whiskers met underneath. "I'm certain there has been much talk outside the House, just as there has been within. I suppose it would be stretching a point to say that

30

I'm not exactly the most popular member there right now…and that goes for The Carlton, too." He smiled ruefully and waited while Maynard served drinks, his sad eyes following the butler to the door. "So, yes…I'm of the opinion that the time is right."

"And you'd like me to test the water for you?" Frederic, sitting opposite, crossed his legs.

"I'll need somebody to let me know how such a move would be received and what the Prime Minister might have in store for me. I've no intention of jumping too soon and then being commited to a life on the back benches, humiliated and ridiculed." Gladstone nodded slowly to himself. "It would hardly be wise to stumble on blindly like this and I need to be sure that it will be worth my while. Who knows what may lie ahead."

"But you must have heard word. Has no one said anything?" Frederic wrinkled his nose.

"Word yes, but what's word in politics. Rumours by the score, most telling me what I'm about to do and even more warning of the dire consequences."

"For certain it will not go unannounced," Frederic mused. "Its not every day that a senior minister…how shall we say…switches allegiance like this. But why me, William? Surely to goodness you have many wiser heads out there who'd be more than willing to help." For a moment the other was silent.

"Trust, my friend." The words came slowly as Gladstone studied his glass. "You see, Freddy, I know you as a friend. Also, I know your political mind and, let's face it, you also hold dear certain liberal ideals. I have my friends, of course, and I have many good political colleagues, some of whom, like you, have made their views well known. But…and *this* is the point, it was imperative to find somebody who meets all three such prerequisites. And who else is there…mm? Who else?"

Frederic rose and walked to the window once more, pausing to lift the edge of a curtain from the small table where a sudden and welcome gust had wafted it. He could feel the other waiting for his answer. He had a fair idea that such a request would be coming, but was flattered nonetheless. And after all, he, too, needed allies if ever he was going to make headway. Here he had one of the most astute politi- cal minds in the House requesting a favour. Gladstone was a brilliant debater who had untold scalps attached to his belt, Benjamin Disraeli's included. More than that, his friend had come to him, perhaps not with cap in hand, but in his hour of need. Right - he would see to it.

"Yes…yes, it makes all sorts of sense and perhaps it will help get us out of this dreadful impasse." He turned. "I'll do it, William. I'll see the Whips and find out. It should not take long for there're others who will have been watching and waiting. Of that I have no doubt."

Gladstone rose. "My thanks, Freddie. My thanks indeed. I would not have asked anyone else. It's been rolling around in me for months now, like some dreadful storm cloud getting blacker and angrier all the while." Frederic held up his hand then waved him back to his seat and summoned Maynard.

*

It took less than a week. As Frederic surmised there were others, including Viscount Palmerston himself, who had been anticipating Gladstone making his move.

June the eighth began wet yet, by mid-morning, it had cleared and the sun made valiant though unsuccessful attempts to disperse the low cloud. The result was an oppressive grey-brown haze brought on by the smoke from the multitude of coal fires still burning in Mayfair, battling its way heavenwards with little success. As he passed through St James's Square and waited for a gap in the tangle of traffic moving down Pall Mall, the back of Frederic's mouth burned and his eyes began to water.

There was nothing to identify number one hundred and four Pall Mall, simply the typical, nondescript main door at the top of a short flight of steps. Frederic ran up briskly, passed the porter's lobby and then took in a second, shorter flight before reaching the main hall. Truberry, the head porter of The Reform Club and, as vigilant as ever, greeted him warmly. He knew him, of course, from his many previous visits and today he had been asked to look out for him.

"Good day to you, sir." The head porter inclined his head and smiled, then summoned a steward to take the visitor's gloves and grey beaver top hat. "Sir Henry's this way, sir. Allow me." Truberry, tall, angular and fashionably bewhiskered, moved towards the main reception area where small groups, including several he recognised, had gathered before lunch.

Frederic paused. The two main floors around and above him were open to the ornate, skylit ceiling. The effect on all those who stood where he was now standing, was inspirational: height, breadth and space, exactly as Barry had intended when he brought the image of Sangallo's Palazzo Farnese to central London. Each floor was supported by two dozen massive columns of ochre, Italianate marble which stood one upon the other, Corinthian and Doric. He stood for a moment gazing up into the cathedral-like space. As he moved to meet his hosts so his boots rang out on the mosaic floor. The architect, he surmised, had set out to create an aura of timeless splendour, and had succeeded.

*

Lunch, in the far corner of the Coffee Room where the windows looked over the club gardens, was a somewhat tense affair rather than the usual, more cordial occasion.

Sir Henry Brand, the Chief Whip and a shrewd, ferrety little man, remained suspicious of the member for West Worcestershire's political leanings, and considerably more so of the request he had brought with him a week earlier. "Doubtless the Prime Minister will wish to consider the matter further." Brand nodded to the portly James Caird for support but the Agricultural Minister, wary of displaying any such allegiance, focussed his attention on the contents of the ornate vegetable toureen in front of him.

"But you've just told me that the Prime Minister's going to offer him the post of Chancellor." Frederic felt the hot hand of exasperation beginning to stifle him and had no wish to play the go-between for a moment longer than necessary. The government had one of the richest prizes of all in its grasp yet it was prevaricating. "We all agree that he'll feel bound to accept it. I mean, he could not have been offered more."

Brand chewed laboriously on his veal, occasionally sipping from his glass in a miserly fashion, no doubt intent on keeping his head clear and his mind sharp. "We may *think* he will accept but we cannot be sure."

"Then I will ascertain it from the man himself without delay and I will confirm it." Frederic caught the Chief Whip's sharp look. "It will be his final word I assure you and, knowing William Gladstone better than most, I'm confident he will wish to proceed."

"Then the Prime Minister must meet with him beforehand to discuss the matter."

Frederic nodded. "And have you any idea where he might wish to conduct such a meeting? It is an occasion that must be kept well clear of the public gaze...what is more the newspapers, by now, will surely have their eyes wide open." He dabbed his mouth. "If you consider it might be of any assistance I would be glad to offer the facilities of Portland Place...it's a little further out and away from prying eyes.

"Nn, nn." Sir Henry Brand waved his hand and swallowed quickly. "My pardon...no, we will do it here."

"*Here.*" Frederic sat back and looked around. "But here? Then surely all the world will know something's afoot. I mean...if a senior Tory is seen dining with the Prime Minister *here*...we could hardly advertise our intentions more brazenly."

"Show him." Brand smiled smugly at Thomas Potter, a short, undernourished merchant whose appearance did no justice to the coffee and cocoa fortune he had amassed recently.

Potter looked round, initially to see who might overhear what he had to say then concerned himself with the survival of his untidily pinned cravat. "Behind you, Knight." He nodded and Frederic turned. "Behind that small William and Mary davenport. Can you see anything?" Frederic shook his head. "Look at the line of wall paper carefully. No? Well, go on look, take a closer look…look at the faint line, barely more than a hairline, about a foot away from the corner."

Frederic rose from his seat and stepped closer. "Aha. Why, yes indeed." He turned back to the table. "Go on, pray satisfy my curiosity."

"It's a door," Brand interjected quietly, leaning forward. "A narrow door that leads right through the wall and into a room, more a chamber in fact, albeit there's a window that looks onto the garden. Those who know of it refer to it as The Cabinet Room, and with good reason. *That* is where the Prime Minister will meet his man. He, together with whoever he wishes to accompany him, will meet Mr Gladstone there…in comfort, I hasten to add, for they will dine together. But it will be undertaken in complete secrecy. And *you*," Brand pointed to Frederic. "You, Knight, will see that your friend makes good his rendezvous at the appointed hour…then, and only then, will we be able to satisfy ourselves about what is in the offing. Is that clear?"

Frederic nodded.

✳

There was nothing particularly unusual about the thirteenth of June. It was a Sunday and it was raining heavily which meant that there were less people about than usual: a matter of some satisfaction for those about to take a short walk.

The handsome cab trotted smartly down the deserted Haymarket and turned into Cockspur Street. Here, even this evening, the cabbie had no option but to slow as he forced his way between the carts and cabs negotiating the filthy, narrow confines of Spring Street. But, at last, they were in The Mall. Frederic leant forward and tapped him on his shoulder. "About three hundred yards down on the right. Go past Waterloo Place and pull in under the trees a bit further on…by Marlborough House."

"Aye, sir. 'Tis wet mind. Wet on the grass."

"No matter." In fact the heavy shower was a blessing and there was hardly a soul to be seen. And as for the wet, his father had always advised the wearing of high leather boots in London, maintaining that the streets of the capital were dirtier than the average Devon farmyard. He adjusted his cloak, stepped down and paid the man his dues. Stopping briefly at the bottom of the steps to Carlton Gardens he pressed two pennies into the old flower seller's hand, waving aside her show of gratitude. He then moved quickly, trusting the rain to continue, and rapped the heavy brass knocker on the door of the first house.

The valet, or whoever it was, must have been waiting for the door opened almost immediately. "Mr Knight, sir?"

"The same…and is everything in hand?" Frederic waited in the outer hall. Barely time to satisfy himself as to how a wealthy, senior parliamentarian might choose to furnish his home, when there were footsteps. William Gladstone appeared first followed by another who, he learned later, was his secretary. Frederic smiled then laughed out loud. Gladstone had prepared himself for the worst of weather and stood half hidden under the high, turned up collar of his cloak. His hair, usually brushed flat now stood proud from under his black top hat. The picture was one of a large and mournful hound that was feeling sorry for itself.

"A comedy for you, perhaps, Young Knight." Gladstone allowed himself a wry smile. "You'll be spending the rest of your political life trying to convince me that these fun and games were necessary."

"Well, maybe, but so far everything has worked well, has it not?" Frederic was still laughing, but to himself. "Look, it's not long now and as far as everyone can tell, the word's not out. Seriously, my friend, we've all been at great pains to keep it thus…that is the purpose behind all this clandestine activity." He chuckled again, gesticulating at the figure in front of him. "Oh, William, look. Once tonight has passed then all the world can know…and no more of this theatre."

The door shut behind them and the three walked smartly towards Waterloo Place where they turned to follow the railings bordering The Reform Club gardens. Half way along they went through the narrow wrought iron gate which had been left unlocked, crossed the lawn and descended the steps at the back of the building. "Servants' entrance." Frederic announced, holding the door for his guest. "The first and last time you'll be coming in this way, I'll be bound."

"And *that's* the truth." Gladstone's face was impassive. Frederic lead the way past the kitchens until the corridor ended at the bottom of a flight of carpeted stairs. At the top they turned and stopped, confronted by a heavy door. He knocked then, as soon as the door was opened, blinked at the gas light that shone from within.

"Ha, Gladstone, at last, at last." Henry John Temple, Viscount Palmerston, rose to greet the newcomer. "A very warm welcome, I do assure you and my most humble apologies for this miserable charade. Tonight we might have got away with it for the weather was with us, but my house is rarely free from prying eyes. Come in, my dear good fellow. Come in, come in."

Palmerston, as elegant as ever, helped Gladstone with his cloak. Tall, slim and finely dressed, the Prime Minister appeared younger than he was and bore himself well. Frederic noticed the lidded eyes and the sensuously cruel mouth. He was a fine looking man indeed, the high, intelligent forehead and straight nose giving a sense of calm authority to the formidable intellect that lay behind. He looked every inch a leader and this time, so he had made it plain to his newly formed cabinet, he was here to stay.

"My thanks Freddy. The last fence, yes?" Gladstone took his hand with one of his own, the other fell on his shoulder. "It's all been something of a challenge, what? My thanks again."

"Indeed, Knight, and on behalf of us all." Palmerston's grasp was firm.

"My pleasure, sir." Frederic inclined his head.

2

The stars were bright enough but it was the moon, lying low on its back in the southern sky that bathed the house in such ghostly light. The old manor at Whitechapel had been built in the style of the age, a stamp of authenticity favoured by the Elizabethan craftsmen. Herbert Preston, the fifth and current Duke of Northborough stood alone on the terrace looking over the parkland towards the distant oak woods through which the mile long driveway wound. Comfortably replete and well pleased with himself, he drew deeply on his cigar and exhaled slowly.

He had bought the house almost six years ago, three years after his father died, and only now was he minded to spend more time here. The manor, set low in the wooded hills beneath Exmoor and just three miles from South Molton, had been crying out to be brought back to life. Used previously as a mere hunting lodge it was to be the base for his new found business enterprise. It was only after he accepted a ridiculously high price for two of his larger cotton mills in Urmston, a grimy suburb to the south west of Manchester, that he felt ready to proceed.

Now in his mid-fifties, the effects of his sybaritic existence were plain, even by the light of the late-August moon. Throughout his life he had fed well, a fact borne out by his ample girth. He had drunk better still and whatever energies he cared to expend were confined mainly to the salons and morning rooms of the great houses belonging to his various friends and, whenever the situation presented itself, to the bedrooms above. His hair, scented, grey-white and tightly curled was cut carefully to lie on his collar. Two large eyes, round and owl-like, together with a petulant mouth, gave a look of piqued and permanent surprise. But he was a shrewd man, or so he liked to think, and prided himself on missing little. And just occasionally, when the dark red blood stirred his loins, he missed nothing at all.

The documents setting out the final details for the sale of Ilfracombe harbour had been signed two days ago. It had long since been his intention to secure a port of his own and now, if the American cotton belt had begun to export its own finished products, he would be glad to assist. His port and his ships would see to that. There were plenty of other such establishments dispersed along the south west coastline yet none, so his agents assured him, had hit upon a similar idea. The cheap cotton clothes would be brought one way and as many thousands of the wretched working class emigrants as he could cram aboard his ships would be sent the other.

He, Northborough, would retain the controlling share of the company and

Thomas, his elder and commercially minded son would run the business. It made sound sense and it was simple, as were all the best plans. The idea was his and would be seen as such. As he turned back to the house, the Duke patted his hair gently then drew once more on his cigar.

✳

"Come, father. What's this about Deborah Farleigh…and *Mrs* Farleigh, no less?" Lord Thomas Preston let his legs fall from the chaise longue and rolled to his feet. The elder of the two boys, so it was claimed, was a physical reincarnation of his father when a younger man, yet one blessed with a sunnier disposition. Jocular and languid, a slow smile never far from his face, Thomas rode easily through his father's rapidly changing emotions, his good nature able to turn the blackest of moods. The boy, his mother used to say, could play his father like a salmon, always bringing him deftly to the bank.

"What's mine's mine, yer young pup…you take care of yer own affairs." The Duke walked purposefully towards the mahogany lowboy on which the butler had left the night tray. "Have you no regard for your elders and the manner by which they're entitled to conduct themselves, eh?"

"Ah well, it's just that the word's come down from Blagdon."

"And whose word's that, might I ask? Whose been minding my business up there…and dipping their words in spice? Mmm? No more'n a pack of lies."

Lord Charles Preston known as Sharland, held the decanter for his father. "The trouble is, father, your hand is too well read. Wherever and however you choose to play, it's the same old cards time and again. They're all wise to your game."

"And don't you start preaching to me either, my lad…*you* of all people. You're a menace, Sharland Preston…there's hardly a maiden in the county that's safe when you're about. Least that's what their fathers're telling me…braying away like a load of old mules." The Duke lifted his glass, wrinkled his nose and drank deeply. Sharland, quiet and cynical, the thinker, had left his mark more than once so it was said. His father had warned him, indeed he had had him stand in front of him while he shouted and waved his arms yet he was fond of the boy and envied him his lotharian conquests. Sometimes he wished they could all play together but he was too old for that. The fire in him, once so bright, had cooled. If the embers were to glow then a fan was required and she had to be good.

"Now look, enough of that saucy impertinence. Hear this, the pair of yer, and mark it well." The Duke rounded on his sons, the mischief in his eyes mocking any attempt at severity. "We're away shooting in a day or two. The partridges're are lining themselves up so Desmond tells me and I don't want the party spoiled. D'yer hear? So keep yer eyes an' yer hands where they're supposed to be."

37

"Oh, come, father. Why so…why all these threats? Jocelyn Orchard knows us well enough."

"*Mrs* Jocelyn Orchard to you, my boy. And yes, I know she does and that's exactly what I mean, so hold your fire. There'll be others there too, you know, so don't go letting me down…I command it. It's an order."

"And you, too, father."

"Away with you, the pair of you. I've had enough…but listen. We ride for Ilfracombe in the morning and…" the Duke forced himself round in his deep armchair to squint at the diminutive bracket clock. "It's late enough now," he wheezed. "Horses at half-seven, and we'll ride on the hour."

3

"I simply don't know how he does it." Sir Durnford Morgan trapped her hand between his elbow and body. He delighted at the light touch of her fingers on his arm and the feel of her silk and cotton day dress as it brushed against his plaid tweed trousers.

Elizabeth-Jane moved her parasol to shade her eyes and glanced up from under her lavender silk bonnet. "It's his father all over again," she replied. "They're just the same…unless they've a dozen things to do at once and all of them in different directions, they'd never be happy, neither one." She felt a deep contentment. Only when his last letter arrived announcing that he would be staying at The George and that he would be delighted to ride out to Bremridge to see her if she so wished; only then did she realise how much she looked forward to his visits. "He's simply exhausting sometimes…just to observe, let alone keep pace with. He's loaded himself down with responsibilities and I have it in mind to suggest he pauses to takes stock. London is demanding more and more of his time…and now he's off with the Yeomanry again, fighting their cause as doggedly as ever. At least, so I hear." Sir Durnford noticed how her hand remained on his arm in spite of the fact that they had reached level ground. The gravel path through the glade of beech trees led towards a small wooden and wrought iron seat overlooking the lake. As they made their way slowly towards it so a waterfowl flapped wetly through the rushes. In the distance a moorhen croaked.

Elizabeth-Jane sighed. The sheer pace of Frederic's life had begun to take its toll and she rarely saw her son. Furthermore the absence of Florence and Sebright was worrying. She let go of his hand to adjust her skirts before sitting carefully then moved politely, the gesture no less than a subtle invitation for him to sit beside her. He took off his calfskin gloves and tucked them under one arm before removing his grey top hat. When he had done so he smoothed his hair which, she noticed, had greyed further and started to thin. Then he sat. Their hips were touching but she did not move. "Perhaps *you* should, Durnford…say something, I mean. I'm worried about the girl. All this absence and rushing about is not good for them…not good for the marriage. They need to see more of each other."

The two watched in silence as a pair of swans, the Bremridge residents, floated into sight. Their four cygnets, now drab youngsters rather than the balls of fluff they once had been, glided behind. In a month they would be flying. "I'll see what I can do," he replied. "We're due to meet in Exeter next week to discuss the farm projects. He's been concerned that the sheep're doing none too well and is considering changing the breed. That's yet more expense…and now there's talk of a pony stud as well." Sir Durnford paused. "But the mines are quiet…for the moment anyway, thank goodness."

Elizabeth-Jane adjusted her mantlet. "Yes, thank goodness for that. Oh, poor Freddie. He was so convinced that there was something out there just waiting to be unearthed." Again they were silent. His hand, when it rested lightly on the back of hers, felt for her fingers and she turned her palm upwards, allowing hers to intertwine with his.

"And what about you?" His question came quietly yet she felt her heart quicken. Throughout his last two visits she had been waiting expectantly for him to enquire about her plans or perhaps *their* plans. When, at the end of his last visit, he failed to do so she found herself dejected and, if she was honest with herself, a touch alarmed but it did not last and she had laughed at her silliness. She was behaving like a youngster at a ball, she told herself, when the young man she hoped might have asked her to dance again had failed to do so. It *was* rather childish, she had to admit, but the doubts kept returning to taunt her and as his visit today grew ever closer, she had grown increasingly anxious.

"Me? Ohh," she shrugged. "There's a host of matters to be addressed just now. Bremridge needs an expert eye to tell me what has to be done and where I should make a start. Then, next month, I'm away to Worcestershire…I've been asked to stay for the Kidderminster festival. I try to get up there every year. It's become something of a tradition, more of an annual pilgrimage." She found herself talking too quickly.

"No, no. It's you I mean, Elizabeth-Jane. You, yourself." Morgan's fingers tightened and he shook her hand gently. "You've been back now for over a year and, well, I have to say that I often wonder how you might be preparing to face the future."

"*Often*, Durnford? My goodness, you flatter me."

"Oh, come. You know exactly what I mean…how I feel. What I have just said is no idle flattery….it's the truth. Look…" He turned towards her now taking her hand in both his. "Surely you must see it. I'm thinking of the two of us…together." He raised her hand to his lips. "Can it be that you have been preparing to face the long lonely walk ahead on your own. And you *will* be on your own. You no longer have your responsibilities towards a powerful man…the family are grown and have gone." He paused. "And the moors here have cast their spell over you as never before: you're never going to leave again. I can see all that clearly but surely you cannot imagine such a future by your*self*...surely not?"

"I don't know." She looked away, shaking her head, afraid yet excited by his persistence. She could feel the colour rising in her face and suddenly felt ashamed that she, a woman of such mature years, could still feel so bewildered and awkward on such an occasion. Thinking about it only made it worse. She should have prepared herself for this then played with his emotions and parried his questions. "Oh, I don't know, Durnford. I mean...."

"Then allow me to put it to you that we might face whatever lies ahead together. Will you...permit me to make such a suggestion...such a proposal? Come," he reached across and pulled her towards him. He took her chin in his hand and gently lifted her face. "Answer me, Elizabeth-Jane. Please answer me."

She moved her face away and his hand fell. "I must think, Durnford, think carefully. I am no longer a young woman." He watched as she studied her hands in her lap. "And to do as you are suggesting at my stage in life is, well, it's not something to be taken lightly. Mind you," she added hurriedly. "Such a proposition is never, ever to be taken lightly but now, at this period in our lives, there is so much more to think about."

"No, *less*. When we were young there was the whole of life ahead to consider...our homes and professions, our children...parents, neighbours, friends but all that has now gone. It's too late for any of that. All we have now is ourselves...just the two us." He took her hand again. "But you will consider what I ask, will you not?" For a moment she was still. Then, after looking across the lake and up at the canopy of leaves above them, she caught his eye. He had not moved, rather he had sat motionless watching her face, his own one of anxious expectation. Suddenly she smiled and lifted one hand to touch his cheek.

"Yes," she murmured, her eyes now searching his. "I'll consider it...I'll consider it carefully, of course I will. And thank you for paying me such a compliment," she whispered, looking up at him. He smiled, took her hand in his and raised it to his lips once more.

Chapter Four

Neither Harry nor Frank Tucker took to books. The younger boy, by now thirteen, wanted nothing more than to stay at Sherdon and work on the farm. He remained the tall, quiet lad he had always been, gentle and loving towards his younger sisters and devoted to his father between whom a close bond had formed. It was Charlotte who remarked to Bamber that she swore Jack could feel the mother in his son. "Frank's got Katherine all over 'im. There's summat about the way he stands and looks out the window sometimes…when 'es just starin' an' thinking, like. It's his eyes and his nose…an' the way he turns to look at yer. An' then the way he smiles. Cuh, 'tis the very mark of his mother. Gives me a proper turn sometimes, it does."

If Frank resembled his mother then he had taken Harry's share of her. Kitty and Jack worried for the older boy. He grew more quickly than any of them, tearing or wearing through the clothes passed down. Not the height of his brothers, Harry's body broadened. His shoulders became rounder and he stood more like a young fighter than a boy at peace with himself. No matter how she tried, Kitty was never able to get close to the youngster, his affections remaining firmly with Charlotte. And that is where the likeness lay: whenever Kitty saw them together, she noticed it. It was not so much that they joked together but the very way they laughed with their mouths open and their eyes wide: even the way they walked together to do the hens or bring in logs from the shed.

❋

"Can't get the lad interested." Jack dug the fork into the ground, straightened slowly and eased his back. Kitty, a row of pea seedlings away and bent almost double in order to stake the tiny plants, now stood also. "All he wants to do is to ride like the very devil after the hounds an' fish the waters…or do summat out there in the wild. Can't get him near the farm."

"Well, what *about* Billy Westcott then?" Kitty eased her back, glancing proudly at the neat rows of spring vegetables. The long lines of delicate leaves ran the length of the piece of high ground behind the house they had been working on since the last of the primroses had gone from the bank. The rabbits, she knew, would have their share but would leave enough to see them well into summer. She would come back later and give them their first good soak. "Harry took to him real well when us were down in Exford. Said then you were minded to ask if 'e'd find a place for 'im. Be like his father wouldn't it…startin' out a stable lad. Didn't do *you* no harm."

Jack began to wind in the string he had pegged out earlier to mark the lines for the seedlings. If anyone could handle the boy it would be Billy Westcott. It seemed only a year or so since he and Charlotte's Davey had left to join the army. And it was as if though they had hardly been gone when the trooper from Barnstaple had ridden out to the farm with the news that Davey had been lost in the great charge. Then Billy brought the full story home. Wilmot had been there at the time with Tennyson, the poet, who sat writing about it after listening to what Billy had told them. But all that was six long years ago, now, and Billy, out of the army as a sergeant, had taken the livery stables behind The White Horse in Exford.

Jack arranged it. He was proud in a way but worried nonetheless. The lad was big enough and strong but there was a wild streak and a cussedness about him that needed to be watched.

*

"Aye, an' doin' me well." Billy Westcott smiled in delight and watched his friend slip from the little mare's back. Jack had been checking his cattle summering out on Bradimoor above Chibbet Ford and had decided to call by to see his son. Billy took his hand. "He's up at the forge just now but he'll be back directly if you'd mind to wait. Time for a brew?"

Jack grinned at the soldier in the man. The stables, he knew, would be run like military horse lines, just as old Sergeant Fanshawe had taught them at Ebberley Lawn Barracks when he, Hector and Leonard Grant together with Master Frederic had joined the Royal North Devons. "Aye, dare say, Billy. So the lad's not makin' you tear yer hair out then?"

"Nooo." Billy Westcott paused while Jack tied the pony. "Wild enough tho'…an' a scrapper if ever there's a spot of bother around. Where did 'e get that from then? Father or what, eh?" Jack smiled at the banter and followed him into the harness room. "No, I'll have to say the lad's doin' me proper…and a firm seat if ever I saw one. Now that's more like his dad."

"Watch the boy, Billy." Jack leant against the saddle rack, his eyes taking in the neat rows of gleaming and well-oiled saddlery. The room smelled of leather and horse. "He's as wild as a hawk when 'e has a mind to be an' us don't want the lad to go down that way."

Billy paused and glanced through the window at the sound of hooves in the yard. He had noticed the wild streak and had seen the company young Harry was heading towards. There were these two brothers and a cousin of theirs who were up to no good and he was watching them. "Lewis Denholm," he said quietly. "Lewis and Eric Denholm and 'Black' Richards, so he's called. Know 'em, Jack? Out to Newlands…one of they cottages there."

"Aye. I've heard tell. Their old man, old Reg Denholm. Always up to summat…poachin' usually."

"That's them. And a few sheep, an' all. Rough lot they are." Billy nodded. "I've a mind young Harry fancies a run out with them. I've warned him mind but when you're a lad a warnin' only adds to the excitement, don' it." Billy took the blackened pan from the embers of the small coal fire and checked the water. The tea leaves came from a tin on the workbench. "I'll keep an eye open there, Jack. Wouldn't want fer the lad to get in with they lot."

Jack nodded. It would be Harry, all right, he thought to himself. Just what the lad was looking for.

*

"Stay on this bank. Right." Harry nodded. Lewis Denholm, no taller but now a man past his teens, crouched down and pulled the boy down after him so they could see the skyline better. The last of the drizzle had gone but the low cloud blotted out whatever light there might have been.

They had left the two ponies in the small thicket above Landacre Bridge and walked the last few hundreds of yards downstream. For almost a week the river had been in spate but today the level had dropped. Even so there was good water coming down and the salmon were on the move. They had hoped for a moon but there was none tonight and they would have to use a lantern. Only then would they be able to see the outline of the great fish as they lay in the deeper pools waiting to begin their run upstream. But a light was risky.

"We'll be behind you, a coupla hundred yards or so." The hoarse whisper blew into his ear. "Keep stoppin' every now an' then to listen. Right? They bailiffs stick together on nights like this. Likely as not you'll hear 'em chatterin' an' coughin' an' that, if they're there. Hear anythin' then get back an tell us…no shoutin' out nor nuthin mind. Keep yer voice down." Denholm gave the boy a shove.

Harry was thrilled. A week ago Lewis Denholm had come to him and offered him a job. A shilling it would be if the run was successful, but it was not the lure of the money that tempted him. He knew the Denholm brothers from the stories he had heard. For months, ever since he arrived at the yard, Harry Tucker had watched the way they swaggered and bragged their way about the village, how there was always a girl with a story to tell and how Jade Westcott and the other village women muttered darkly. He envied the reputation for it gave them an aura of power and daring. If he could join them then a tag like that would get him known and he, too, would be talked about.

A week ago he had slipped out of his bunk and gone to the store behind the bar where Black Richards looked him over and quizzed him. They had tested his strength by arm wrestling in the shed where the kegs were kept. Black had beaten him but he had held his own against Lewis and had driven Eric down. It was Lewis who pulled him off his brother after Harry had wrestled him to the floor. The lad was not fifteen but they liked what they saw and, the next day, they talked to him.

Harry moved slowly. The rushes and sedge along the riverbank kept tripping him.

43

Sometimes he had to feel his way, but it was easier to judge his pace when he saw the dim yellow glow of the lantern behind him. He had taken off his boots. Time and again his feet sunk into the mud where a spring, now bubbling after the recent rains, made the surface soft and spongy. He was doing well and the others were following him, but then came the first hedgerow running down to the water's edge. He should have gone round by going into the river and feeling his way along the bank but he chose to climb through instead.

He missed the first call for he was struggling in the branches. But he heard the shout that followed and saw the lantern when they lifted the shade. He never saw the dog until it was in the hedge alongside him. It was a big one; he could tell that easily enough by the way it was forcing its way towards him. He couldn't run without his boots and, anyway, the dog's throaty snarl made him freeze. He looked around for the others but their light had gone.

"Here's one…'ere, look." The fresh voice was behind him and the heavy breathing told him that they were upon him. "Right there, Jed. Up in the bank look." The hand that gripped Harry's leg above the ankle was rough. *"Got 'im, Mal…*jest the one, I reckon.

"Come 'ere, you." It was the same voice, now directly below him, and it belonged to the hand. "Come on, yer bloody villain." Another hand grabbed him and the two men pulled him back. His body was twisted and he yelped at the sudden pain. "The lantern, Jed…let's 'ave a look. See what us 'ave gaffed tonight."

He was down in the water and mud of the ditch and the knee on the side of his head was forcing his face down. Another hand twisted his arm up behind his back. He tried to shout but, as soon as he opened his mouth, it filled with the cold, gritty water of the ditch. He spat and coughed then tried to catch his breath but the water filled his mouth again. He felt himself being dragged backwards through the rushes. Rough hands turned him over and the light of the lantern made him blink. He looked up but could see nothing behind the flame.

" Tis but a lad."   "He'll do…us'll make 'e sing."   "Tie 'im?"   *"Naah,* 'es goin' nowhere…got no boots nor nuthin." "Reckon 'e'll talk?"   "Bloody right, he will."

As he lay helpless on his back, he could feel the ditch water soaking through the rest of his clothes. They turned him again, twisting his arm further than before. Two knees were pressing into the small of his back. He lifted his head to try and breathe more easily and never saw the fist that smashed into his cheekbone.

"I'll ask yer one more time…who were they others? Eh? Answer…or you'll go under again." The two either side of him had his arms pinned. He was on his feet in the river, that he knew, and felt the water washing against his thighs. "Answer me, lad." A hand grabbed his hair and jerked his head backwards. "Answer me." He shook his head weakly. "Right…in again."

The water was ice cold. He tried to struggle but it was no use for they were holding him too tightly. His lungs were straining, desperate for air and he could feel the water pressing up his nose. Suddenly he could hold no longer and his mouth opened. The water was everywhere, eyes, nose, mouth and he was swallowing trying to get past it to reach air. He swallowed again and a third time, never feeling the arms that were pulling him up. The choking, suffocating water had filled his throat; much had gone down to his lungs. They threw him onto the bank then turned him round to lower his head into the ditch. He choked, then choked again and retched before gasping for air. It was then that the beating began.

✳

When Billy Westcott came in from the yard, Jack was sitting alone. He was leaning forward in front of the fire with his head in his hands as if in prayer. Jade was upstairs with the boy. Billy put a hand on his shoulder. "He'll be fine, Jack…fine. Don't'e go worryin' now. Us've squared Hawkins, the bailiff. 'Tis agreed the hiding he took were punishment enough. Jade'll see to the lad…he'll soon be back on his feet." He patted the back. "'E're come on, man…'tis nort."

Billy admitted later that he was shocked by the face that looked up. It was drained, mournful almost as though the man had lost his son. Jack barely knew where he was. "The devil, Billy," he whispered then cleared his throat. "What's to be done? Eh? We thought better of the lad, y'know. 'Tis not the beatin' 'e took…done him good, dare say. 'Tis *what* he did…thievin' like that. Plain thievin' it was an' when it's yer own boy it's hard to take."

Billy knelt by the chair. For an hour they talked, one trying to persuade the other that it was no more than what every young man tried. Poaching and smuggling on Exmoor was rife and always had been: it was part of life and the two of them had tried it themselves. The lad had come to no harm and the cuts would heal. But Jack was hurt: his name had been tarnished and nothing could alter the fact.

Billy saw it all. It was the same proud Jack Tucker who had fought and killed for the family name, the same man who, on one dreadful winter's night, had carried his master's flock to safety one at a time. Billy knew his man and he knew his moods. What had happened would weigh heavily and his heart went out to him. He had always looked up to him, worshipped him and when, eventually, he went on his way, Billy knew that what he had said would have little effect.

2

Sometimes, when they broke into an easy trot, the hooves were in step. Hounds had killed above North Molton and the two brothers were making their way home. Their father was hosting a dinner party at Whitechapel and, already, the first of the evening chill had begun to cool the air. The autumn gales had brought down most of the leaves and, as they made their way down the track through the woods, they could hear cock pheasants noisily claiming their roosting places for the night.

"He seems dead certain on you running it all for him. D'you think you can manage?" Sharland Preston, half a length in front, kept his eye on the track.

"Don't see why not. We've got the shipping agents at Barnstaple *and* the local port authorities working for us. And, let's face it, it's hardly beyond the wit of man. We've only got the three schooners to begin with and they'll be at sea most of the time…should give us plenty of time to organise the turnaround." Lord Thomas Preston was confident that the Ilfracombe harbour project was in hand. "Father's given me a good team."

"What about the other end? Charleston, isn't it?"

"Yes, there and much further round…place called Baton Rouge, up the Mississippi from New Orleans. The agent there's French, like most of them, and he's ready right now. We had a letter last week telling us the warehouses are full to the rafters." The two were silent, each one contemplating the new venture.

"Why d'you think he suddenly embarked on this great idea, and down here of all places?" Sharland reined back and looked at his brother. "It's fine by me but I thought he wasn't keen on this part of the world. Mother always used to say he'd try to keep clear of the place…something about the Knights. About the duel, wasn't it, when Kenton Knight was killed?"

"They were good friends." Thomas Preston tilted his top hat and wiped his mouth with the back of his glove. Earlier in the day he had come off when putting his horse at a fallen tree in the woods behind Molland. His left shoulder ached and he rubbed his coat where the bruise had formed. "I've never really heard the full story but apparently it took place up beyond Simonsbath. They'd never get away with it now but then… phhh, fifteen years ago or something. It was still more or less legal then… frowned upon mind but the chap got away with it. Father's never forgiven him. And it was him, the fella that killed Kenton… who married our aunt… Katherine, the one they never wanted to talk about." Thomas eased his shoulder and rolled his arm.

"Painful?"

"Could be worse." He grimaced then stood and stretched his back. "I'll live."

"What sort of person was he…the man who killed him?"

"Some yokel." Thomas shrugged. "A farmer of sorts…just an ordinary peasant straight off the hill. Grandpapa went mad apparently and that's why Aunt Katherine left home." For a moment he was quiet. "And then she was killed at the farm…fell in the house or something. Father saw her husband soon after but that was that. Strange, really…rather sad, too."

"For sure." Sharland shook his head. "But that all makes it even more difficult to see why papa wants to get involved down *here*. I wouldn't want to come near the place if I was him."

"But you're not him, Sharland." Thomas gathered up the reins. His voice sounded more positive. "You're not papa. He's got this idea into his head that what he's doing simply cannot fail and that down here is the best place. But then he's got any number of good friends in this part of the world…the Orchards down at Hartland, for instance. Then he's got the Bracknells and that strange crowd near Barnstaple…the Smythes, I think they're called. No, father's got it worked out all right. And, anyway, he loves Whitechapel."

"So what about these farmers…the fellow Aunt Katherine married? Are they around still?"

"Up in the hills, apparently. They've still got the farm where Kenton had the row that began it all."

"Isn't father worried about it…that they bump into each other or something? Old wounds and all that?"

"I don't think he could care less. Honestly. The man's stuck away out in the wilds and father never goes up on the moor. He hardly ever rides these days, let alone hunts. Just shoots…a shooting man through and through…says he leaves the falling off to me." The brothers laughed.

"But there must be a family? They breed like mad down here and they can't all be hidden away out of sight…I mean they've got to emerge now and then."

"Heaven knows, but he'll take that as and when it comes and you can be sure that he's hardly going to go looking for the man…or any of them for that matter."

"Mmm…not so sure about that." Sharland took out his red kerchief and blew then rose in his stirrups to tuck it back into his breeches. "Wouldn't like to see him taken by surprise…he's not as quick as he used to be, y'know."

"Don't you bet on it." Thomas turned his horse into the Whitechapel driveway. "There's plenty of fire there yet. I wouldn't like to cross him, even now. But, there again, he's pretty shrewd and it's hardly likely to come about. Not now anyhow."

3

The weather seemed to have made up its mind at last. Earlier it had been bright as the breeze from the north west kept the high, broken clouds moving along. Later, though, the wind dropped and backed to the west, bringing with it the grey, wet, enveloping mist that rolled in from the coast and up over the shoulders of Exmoor. By noon it had 'clagged in' as old Fisher would have said, and everything was sodden. Even for a late autumn afternoon it was dull. It was wet and it was miserable.

Jack's face and hair were soaking, his hands slippery with mud and dark green sheep's dung. He took a deep breath, half lifted the ewe and turned her, sitting her on end with her back resting against him. Next he bent forward, blew the water drip from the end of his nose and picked up one of her hind legs. Prising apart the two toes of her hoof he inspected the flesh in between and saw the tenderness that had caused her to hobble so painfully. It was the soft autumn mud that had caused it. Bending further forward he took a pinch of sulphur-blue crystal from his tin and rubbed it into the sore.

The other feet were healthy but the horn of the toes had become overgrown. Holding the foot with one hand, he cut carefully, the sharp blade of his clasp knife paring away the surplus horn. Once he had checked the other feet, he let her go, pushing her away with his knee. Then he stood and eased his back before picking his way to the drier ground under the bank.

Ralph and Stan Bawden should have been helping but the cattle on the lower cleeve had broken out and he had sent them to round up the beasts and repair the damage. Frederic Knight was due to call later, yet there were still twenty ewes to be done. Wilmot had told him about Knight's plans for the stud at Simonsbath and warned that Frederic wanted to seek his advice. It would never work and he sighed heavily. The little Exmoor ponies wanted every drop of their own thick blood to survive up here. Any cross breeding would only water it down and dilute the very strength that made them the hardy creatures they were.

As he worked on so he wondered how he might dissuade his old master. His new sheep had done well, he had to admit, and now Wilmot was following him. His brother's Cheviots from the north and the Scottish Blackface would be here in a week or two, time enough for the rams to go on. The ones he was working on today, the last of the Exmoor Horns, would then go down to Withypool.

He had done more than a hundred since dawn and the last few were harder to catch and certainly heavier to turn. His back was getting no easier and his feet, long since wet through, were numb. A day like this now made him more tired than he cared to think about.

✳

The welcome had been as warm as could be. Jack had called the children forward one at a time and Kitty brought griddle cakes and tea, fussing about the visitor and taking his cloak before seeing to his men. There was barely time to see outside but Frederic insisted: there were too many memories to miss and he wanted to see how Jack had covered the root clamps.

The two of them, friends since early childhood, stood together by the lantern hanging from the shippon beam. Behind, and already chained up, the cattle stood patiently chewing their cud waiting to be milked. A cat, the dark tabby that had lost a front paw in a trap, rubbed against their leggings.

"Since you've asked me, Master Frederic, I'd bide more time if I was you, sir. The sheep're doing nicely…very well, in fact, and us'll see more of that at lambing time for certain. If I'm not wrong they'll be easier to lamb than the hornies. They'm bigger and more used to our weather." Frederic watched him as he spoke. The lines across the forehead and those running down beside his nose were deeper. The grey-blue eyes seemed to have sunk a bit and the hairline had receded. It had indeed been more than two years since they last met, but he could see how the remorseless grind and the elements had begun to tell. The loss of Katherine had all but brought the man to his knees, but he was back again and from what he had seen earlier and had heard there was someone in his life again.

"I'm not going to go mad at it, Jack, but if I can get a few, say half a dozen or ten even, of the bigger Exmoor mares to go with a part-Arab then I'll be looking for the best of both worlds. Think of the blood there'd be in a cross like that. There's nothing around for an older child or a young woman to ride…either it's a clodhopper from the Fells or else something too big an' too strong. There has to be a market for what I've in mind."

"Aye, up country maybe but hardly here, sir. They'd never winter out, and *you* find me the farmer on Exmoor who's got shelter to spare for horses such as that. Cuh…every drop o'cover we've got's filled to the rafters with keep. Bain't no room for nothin' like that."

"But my market's not here, Jack. I *am* looking up country for that's where they'll sell. There's many a place where a little horse with the sure feet and the staying power of an Exmoor would win the day. I'm certain of it, people have been asking me. Near London, too, for Heaven's sake."

"P'raps up there, sir, but all I'm sayin' is for you to take yer time and don't let no one go pressing you into anythin' like this too quickly…not out here." Frederic knew he was right and that he had to take one thing at a time. Every visit to Simonsbath he found himself surrounded by those who wanted to push ahead on some madcap venture or to experiment with something or other. Always their ideas but always his money. But, here at last, was a man whose word he could trust and who said what he believed without anything to gain.

It was dark and he would have to take the long way back to Simonsbath but, tonight there was no rush, and in any case he had accepted the invitation to stay on and share their supper. They had offered it at first, then pleaded with him and he could think of nothing better.

✳

"Well, your brother's a wise man." Frederic sat with his feet outstretched. The meal with the youngsters had been a happy and noisy affair. At first they were shy for he was almost a stranger and he could see them casting glances at his clothes, the chain of his fob and his brown-topped high boots. Twice little Victoria had blushed when he caught her looking at the ruby in the eye of his fox head on his gold cravat pin. But it must have been the way he and their father talked that let them know instinctively that he was a friend, and a good one, rather than some forbidding stranger. At first the laughter had been nervous, then louder, and after that came the cheerful banter and tomfoolery until Jack banged the table. They had gone now, the stew and bread pudding cleared away: just he and Jack alone together.

"Done well, Wilmot, so he has." Jack leant forward and crackled his knuckles. "Never knew where he got his mind from but it's done him well."

"Amen to that…and good luck to him." Frederic moved to make room for the little terrier bitch that was telling him she wanted to join him on the chair. "*Cuuum on,*" he groaned, bending down for her. He helped her settle beside him then fondled her ear to let her know how welcome she was. She knew she had found a friend and rolled onto her side staring up at him out of the corner of one eye. "He's doing well at Bristol…goodness me, he is. The shipping line's going from strength to strength and now he's thinking of banking as well."

"*Banking*? Cuh, our Wil a banker…how come then, sir?"

"Durnford Morgan let it on the other day. Perhaps I shouldn't have said as much but I'm sure Wilmot'll let you know just as soon as it's settled but it looks as though the bank wants him."

"Why's that? For 'is ships or what?"

"No, his brains. Your brother's blessed with enough grey matter for us all to have a share. He really has, y'know, and when the banks see something like that walking past they want it for themselves." For a moment the two were silent. Frederic glanced at his friend, head down and lost in thought. He half turned and filled his tankard. "Talking of Durnford, Jack, there's something perhaps you should know. Have you heard anything? " Their eyes met. "About mother? About how she and Durnford Morgan are seeing rather more of each other now?"

"Courtin', sir?"

"Well." He laughed, but politely at the innocence of the remark. "What you've said just about sums it up. Yes, I believe that's it exactly."

"An you're pleased enough, Master Frederic?" Jack struggled to sit up. "Happy with that are yer?" For a moment he was silent his mind going back many years. Once there was a time when they had all seen rather too much of the suave young Durnford Morgan, the debonair man about town who found himself at Simonsbath just a mite too often and more likely when John Knight was away. But nothing had come of it, or that's what was said. And, in any case, it was all many years ago. Life had moved on and Mrs Knight, the fine lady she was, was on her own.

"Oh yes...yes indeed, I am. All of us are. We're delighted. Couldn't bear the thought of her being out here without company. They're very fond of each other and...who knows, I daresay they'll make an announcement in time." He saw the other nod and watched while he, too, filled his tankard of watery beer from the earthenware jug. Suddenly the silence sharpened, each man reading the other's thoughts. "And what about you, Jack. It's been a while now...a while since...."

"Katherine, sir?" Frederic noticed him looking down at his hands. Perhaps he should never have mentioned it. He had heard from Wilmot how difficult Jack found it to move on from the past. "Aye, well, us struggle on sort of. Plenty up 'ere to keep us going." The smile was wry yet unconvincing. "Not sure I'm ready for any o' that just yet." Frederic waited. Jack pulled at his trouser leg then eased the stiffness in his knee. "Hasn't bin easy y'know, Master Frederic."

"You've found yourself good company...Kitty, I mean. She adores you, even I can see that. And you her, or so it looks." He watched the other nod slowly. "Don't leave it too long, my friend. Can't have you alone out here and grieving for what can never be changed."

"Aye, sir, an' that's what they all say." The voice was barely a whisper. "Aye, you're right but she's still too close, Katherine, that is."

Kitty had left them and stayed away until Frederic had gone when she crept back to set the water pots around the fire for the night. She said nothing but, as Jack watched her, he could tell she knew they had been talking about her. Suddenly she looked small and frail again, vulnerable and alone. He wanted to pick her up in his arms there and then, smothering her in the love and affection she craved. But he hesitated, afraid to make such a move, and when she left him with a kiss on his brow, he knew how her heart would be aching and it was him that had made it so.

4

Sarah sat at her mother's dressing table and looked across the cobbled alleyway to the neat, half-timbered cottage opposite. Mrs Orchard had given her the two days off. She had not been home for three months and tomorrow she would be away again, away back to Hartland.

Her new life had begun well, so she told herself. At first she thought Mrs Jocelyn Orchard was a rather haughty woman and a little unnerving. Conversation at the interview had been difficult, with her mistress seemingly incapable of little more than a tremulous "Uh," or an "Oh" in reply to whatever she said. But it was shyness, Sarah concluded. She was shy and she was lonely, her husband, Desmond, remaining distant and aloof to them all, but most of all to his wife.

She was an attractive woman, of that there was no doubt, with a fine looking rather than beautiful face, dominated by a longish, Roman nose and a firmly set mouth. She wore her fair hair in neat ringlets and was always, so it seemed, beautifully dressed and attired; her jewellery and clothes the very model of fashion, though perhaps a little more London than Hartland. But it was when she smiled that she came to life. Her face would light up, displaying the most beautiful set of teeth Sarah had ever seen.

But for her, Jocelyn Orchard, her children were everything. Mercifully, Sarah had taken to them and they, also, to her. It was this, she suspected, that drew her and her mistress to one other and already they had begun to enjoy each another's company. Often, when there were no guests to entertain, they would walk together or sit side by side sewing in the drawing room after the children had gone to bed and when her husband had buried himself in the library.

The new nanny, a heavy, rather common woman with thick arms and unkempt hair, had taken over her room next to the nursery. Next week, she, Sarah, would be moving into the altogether superior accommodation high in the north wing over-looking the park. There were deer and white charolais cattle there and, to the left and at the edge of the wood beyond, a little trout stream wended its way down to the beach a mile further on. Above the trees she could see the tower of St Nectan's where the family had worshipped for hundreds of years and beyond that again, perched high on the cliff top from where they could see Lundy, a folly had been built. It was little more than a single stone arch over a seat but she loved it there, relishing the solitude with only the cry of the sea birds and the distant rumble of breakers for company.

Better still, she would be taking her meals with the family and had already been asked to be present on all family occasions. Her duties were, of course, bound entirely with the two elder children, Cardew, the thin, flaxen-haired boy of eleven and Jemima, his sister, less than two years younger. Jemima had taken a particular liking to her and now followed her everywhere, badgering her constantly about clothes and jewellery. But for Sarah, nothing could have been better and she was delighted: the doors of the dining room, the day room and the principal salons were now open to her. She could come and go as she pleased and would be able to see exactly what went on and between whom. She was lucky. She knew it and longed to get back.

Mary had gone, as had whatever affection remained between them. She had become impossible and Sarah tossed her head angrily at the memory. Dirty, heavy-fleshed and little more than a gin soak, her sister had thrown her life away: she cared neither where she had gone nor with whom she was now emptying the bottles of cheap gin.

✳

Little had escaped Sarah during her first six months at Hartland. She had listened carefully and watched closely, in particular the Orchard women. She listened to what each said to the others and how they said it, then compared it with what was said behind each other's backs, noting the malice and the spite, the double-talk and the constant intrigue. She studied their mannerisms and their little ways, how they stalked about and preened themselves and how they treated their men folk: the posturing, the posing and the cunning. She noticed their dresses, how they carried themselves and how they were made up by their lady's maids. And she was determined that she, too, would look like them. Her time at Mrs Patterson's had, indeed, been well spent but there remained much to learn.

Leaning forward to see herself better in the mirror, she checked the line of her eyebrows, remembering well that the higher the arch meant the greater the dignity. For a moment she plucked at whatever might spoil the curve then picked up her pot of kohl. Deftly and with the stick the apothecary had provided, she applied the black paste taking care to darken only those hairs that highlighted the arrogant sweep. The eyelashes were next and here she used the tiny horsehair manicurist's brush. Just the tips and not too much and, for certain, nothing more. She sat back, blinked, then checked her handiwork by turning this way and that. The eyes, she had heard one of the gentleman guests affirm, were the windows of the soul. Everything, he assured those listening, began or finished there.

The faces were white; she didn't know why but that was the way it was. Her pot of marble rice and alabaster from Bourjois of Paris had been given to her by her uncle Wilmot as had the auchonsa and the rosette brun rouge. She smiled at the memory of his warning. Just a delicate touch, he had cautioned as he came up to her with his Malacca cane and his limp, and his lock of lank, dark hair hanging down. The less the better, he ordained: seduction rather than violation. A face must attract and beguile but never offend. And just one tiny black taffeta beauty spot close to the mouth, for that is where the eye falls. Rebecca, his wife, had then shown her how.

Sarah pulled a face at herself in the mirror then pouted and wrinkled her nose, screwed up her mouth and pursed her lips. She turned her face, lifted her chin, even stuck out her tongue. Then she stood, checking herself before moving back and checking yet again. Satisfied at last, she reached for the dress and ran her hand lovingly over the soft material but, before that, there was the corset. Plain white and with whalebone stays it was dull and cumbersome. As she laced herself so she pulled herself in, her high, full breasts trapped and flattened.

Her figure, she knew, had attracted the eye of one of the footmen in particular. He was shortish but a handsome man and she had caught him studying her. She should have remained imperiously indifferent to such familiarity but had been unable to. Instead, and much to her annoyance, thrills of excitement had coursed through her each time they passed one another and it was she who averted her eyes rather than him.

The dress, green silk over the crinoline, the grey paletot trimmed with claret velvet, was cut low at the front but flattened to lie over the corset as was the fashion. She demurred, bent forward and eased her breasts until a mere impression of her cleavage was exposed. Then she turned and bowed to check. Perhaps not the height of fashion, she mused but such a hint of daring would, nonetheless, catch the eye. She was ready and opened the door.

Emma's hands went to her mouth. "Oh, it's a fine dress, dear. It's beautiful…really handsome, just look at the flounces and those pretty ribbons where 'tis held back…and the ruches." She moved forward to touch the material. "And your face, dear. That's just how 'tis done…oh, my goodness you look the part. They'll never know…."

"Know *what*, mother?" Sarah turned to look at her eyebrows raised suspiciously. "What d'you think they might know about me?"

"That you're from here, my love. That you're one of us…just, well. That you're just a normal country girl, like."

"But I'm not normal…not now. I've seen my way ahead, mother. Seen where I want to go. There's another life out there and I like what I see. No more of this." Her hands rose dismissively. It's as simple as that."

"Shush, never forget your roots, dear." Emma adjusted the neckline of the dress to cover the bodice. Her eyes flicked to her daughter's face but then returned to what her hands were doing. "Look, dear. Here" She picked at the material. "Or you'll be falling out of that. 'Tisn't right to have anything showing…I'll tuck it in a bit. There look…that's better."

"Leave it alone, mother." Sarah drew back and pushed her mother's hand away. "I like it like that and it's the way I want it to be." She eased her chest, smoothing down the material.

"'Tain't right though, dear. Here, let me…."

"*Leave it,* mother." Emma stepped back, surprised at her daughter's sudden tone. "I said I want it like that…stop fussing so."

"Listen, dear. I only want you to look right. There's ways to do things, properly like, an' ways not do them. I'm only trying to help."

"Mother, listen." Sarah's hands dropped in a show of exasperation. "Just leave me, will you. I've seen what's what and I know what I'm doing. Just stop fussing me about."

Emma was silent. Hurt by her daughter's manner, she was worried. Worried that under all the paint and the silks and the finery there remained the little local girl. It was so plain to see. And they would find her out; not the gentlemen perhaps, for their eyes would be elsewhere; but the ladies would. For sure it was always the ladies who were the most discerning. It was a game of theirs and a cruel one at that.

Chapter Five

For a moment Elizabeth-Jane stood with her head bowed. Not only was the Bremridge midday sun highlighting the yellow and greens of her silk ruching, but the pattern of shadows from the tiny Elizabethan window panes criss-crossed the front of her dress. Although he was standing behind her, she knew he was watching closely. As she looked up to glance out of the window she caught her breath then blinked and pursed her lips.

He had made no mention of it for two months, since that evening in March when they dined with Frederic at Simonsbath while the blizzard raged. But now this. As she turned, she tried to compose herself and when she replied she was surprised at how calm she sounded. "Yes," she said, nodding and then smiling delightedly at the expression on his face. Afterwards they laughed about it, when she teased him mercilessly about his nerve failing.

"Oh, Durnford...my dear, dear man." She placed her hands on his lapels and it was only then that he reached out for her. "Yes, I will," she whispered, standing on her toes to reach up to him. "Most certainly I will, kind sir."

"Well, my goodness, what can I say?" He cleared his throat and laughed. "I'm sure there should be some traditional response...I should be on bended knee or making some noble gesture such as one reads about. What I asked seemed no more than a matter of course...and then came your reply. But, thank you, my dear Elizabeth-Jane...the future Lady Durnford to be exact. He gathered her in his arms and pulled her close.

"Y-yes," she gasped, easing back from him. "But not yet. There's all manner of things we have to consider. First, though, and very much first we must tell the family. We must see to that before anything."

"Of course. Now look, before that even." Durnford reached into his pocket. "I...I fear this should be conducted with far more aplomb and finesse, but...here." He opened the tiny maroon velvet box with his thumb. "I thought emeralds would suit you best. Emeralds...and the odd diamond or two. Emeralds are your stone, you know. Allow me." She let him fit the ring then held her fingers out straight in front of her.

"Perfect," she whispered. "Perfect." Her lips brushed his cheek. "Ooh dear," Elizabeth-Jane touched her chest. "It's made me feel quite weak." She held on to his hand. "Dear Durnford, this *is* a lovely surprise...really, it's wonderful. But, what to do now? Where do we start?"

"Well, at the beginning, I suppose. But, first, allow me to make a confession. Here. Come and sit." He drew her towards the window seat. "Now then, you must not be cross. Promise me that."

"That depends," she cautioned. "Suppose I find this confession of yours too outrageous for words. Nothing has yet been sealed or signed, you understand. You have but my word and I shall consider myself at liberty to withdraw it just exactly as I please until...well, until our betrothal has been legitimised by man and by God."

"Exactly." He took her hands in his. "But I have not allowed matters to rest. D'you remember when we were riding together at Simonsbath and I asked you then? The day of the snow, when you were proving to be even more elusive than usual, and quite deliberately so? Yes? *I have a number of matters still to consider,*" he mimicked. "Just as some ledger clerk might protest when a hand reaches out to check his books. Yes? Well, I took such a response to be positive if not actual acceptance itself. And I have been making, shall we say, enquiries..."

"What *do* you mean? Enquiring about *what*?" She sat back and looked at him. "Not me I hope...you've not been searching behind the cushions around the salons of North Devon for tittle-tattle about me, have you? I most sincerely hope you've not been doing that, Sir Durnford." It was said mostly in jest but he could see she was anxious to hear more.

"Most *certainly* not." It was his turn to feign pique yet with a touch of genuine indignation that told her he considered she had called his integrity into question. "Nothing like that at all, I promise you." He squeezed her hands. "All I did was to suppose, to take the extreme liberty of concluding that I was at last breaking down your truly obstinate resistance and that, one day perhaps, you would consent to be mine. As such I took it upon myself to visit the Archdeacon in Barnstaple, he is the surrogate to the Bishop of Exeter, and ascertain how we might proceed...that is if ever you would submit to such an idea...which you now have."

"And? Go on...I'm intrigued by this impertinence. *Alarmed* might describe my emotions more accurately." Elizabeth-Jane smiled coyly. "So what are we supposed to do?"

"Well, as it so happens, it's surprisingly simple. First of all, we are bound by law to obtain a licence...that, of course, will make our situation legally binding but then, and if we so desire, we can apply to have our union blessed in church...thus we shall be bound in Holy matrimony. I daresay you might find such an occasion to your liking?"

"Indeed...I could not imagine it any other way." Elizabeth-Jane nodded thoughtfully. "Yes, most certainly...it must be done like that." She hesitated further. "And *where*, d'you suggest?"

"Well." He chose his words carefully. "I must tell you that we are bound here also." He paused. "It has to be the parish in which you were residing when we first met...but I suspect you will have no objection." Morgan caught her eye. "Lynton," he said quietly. "And for me, that is where it all began. Years ago...far, far too many years ago but the memories are still fresh. Perhaps at the little church of St Mary's above Castle Heights."

"Yes." For a moment she was pensive. "Oh yes, I would like that, too. Yes…it has to be there."

*

The marriage was in June that year. It was a quiet family affair but they asked Jack and Wilmot to be present. Wilmot and Rebecca stayed at The Castle Hotel with Frederic and Florence. Jack stayed with Hector and Nancy.

For hours, the two brothers walked together where Jack had roamed alone as a child more than forty years before. Old Corwen, the blacksmith had gone, and so had the forge. Jack found a pile of old shoes half hidden in the nettles. Somebody had bought the stables at Castle Heights and built a fine house just where he had met the toddler called Frederic Knight. The gardens where Leonard and Hector worked had gone also and more houses had been built along the cliffs where they ferreted for rabbits and lay looking over the edge with the wind buffeting their faces. The next day they walked to the spot where the path once dipped into the woods before winding its way, ever more steeply, to the beach below. Now a road had been built and they watched as carriages and ox carts struggled up from the harbour. The passengers walked while extra animals strained to help with the cargoes of lime and barrels of fish.

And it was here, somewhere just behind the stables, that he had first set eyes on Katherine, then no more than a playful girl in her bright summer frock. Later, he returned alone and sat trying to remember the exact spot where she had stood and asked him about riding the next day, before skipping away to join the others. But he couldn't; it had gone, as had so much else.

For Jack it was difficult, not so much for what they were doing or that he remembered how things once were but because of the news from home. A week earlier Edgar Heard, Bamber's elder son, had ridden to Sherdon with the news about his father. There had been pains and then a fall. His father had risen but fallen again and Jack had called to see him the day before he left for Lynton.

2

Nobody knew exactly when it was that he died.

Lottie and Edgar's wife, Nessie, had left him sitting up in the bed they had placed between the pine dresser and the kitchen window after his first fall. They had cleared away the window ledge in front of him and tied the curtain back so he could see out and into the yard. That particular morning it was raining but he had insisted on leaving the window ajar. It helped the smoke from the hearth to find its way up the chimney so he claimed: in fact it made it worse but they left it open just the same.

Edgar and Walter saw him when they came in to change after checking the sheep. He had been dozing but woke cheerily. Later he claimed to be a mite pinnicky, as he put it, grumbling about the fog-bred pestilence that had laid him low. But it was not his cough, the pipe smoke had given him that years before. Rather it was his heart and, sometime between Edgar calling out as he shut the door and Lottie returning from the village, it decided to stop. When they found him he was lying just as if he was asleep but when Edgar went to sit him up his head rolled to one side. He still had his empty pipe in one hand and the crow's feather he used to clean it in the other.

＊

"Lottie's taken it bad, that's for sure." Jack glanced at his brother. Wilmot, slimmer now and limping quite badly, looked smaller than he remembered. "Wally said her was poorly when we were at church and I went down to Brightworthy to see. 'Er's not good, Wil...in a bit of a state, really. Gin an' all sorts, so it is...gets it up from Withypool somehow." Jack had asked his brother to come out and see the freshly broken ground on Sixty Acres, the high ground behind the farm. They had limed the soil well and already the first signs of the roots they had sown were showing.

"Damned drink. Like the very devil itself. It'll get to you all right if you give it half a chance." Wilmot cursed and backed his horse into the wind. "You'd have thought that she of all people would have been terrified of the stuff after what she's been through."

"Aye, that man of hers...Naylor or summat." Jack steadied his horse. "Mind you, I'm not saying she's real bad just yet but 'tis something we need to watch...or she'll go right down."

"So...what's to be done? We can't leave her at the farm like that. One of the brothers there's married and there's hardly room for another woman...not one in Lottie's state. They've got enough to do and we can't expect them to cope with her. She's nothing to do with them really."

"Aye, she's ours, Wil, that's fer sure. But she's got nowhere else. She's right by herself...an' she's our sister."

"What d'you suggest?" Wilmot's head was on one side. "She can't come in with you. I mean there's Kitty...she's made Sherdon your home and Lottie in there...in the state she's in." He laughed sardonically. Jack said nothing, merely raised his eyebrows in resignation but his brother knew it had been considered already. "No, there's no way we could do that. But what about the cottage down by the bridge...where Kitty and Gillan used to be?" He paused. "Now there's a thought. Empty isn't it?"

"Aye, Wally Sexton's from Barkham, it belongs to him."

"Then if it's empty we'll take it...buy it if we have to." Jack saw his brother's face harden. Suddenly it was drawn tight, mean almost, and he watched as he flicked back a lock of black hair. It was that stubborn, determined streak that had always been there. "She can go in there and I'll help her a bit but she'll be close enough to you, Jack...yet not too close, I hope."

"No, I'll see to her, Wil...we'll make a home for her down there." He shrugged at the look on his brother's face. "We could never just leave her...we owe it to her." They rode back one behind the other, forced into single file by the high bracken. As they rode, the younger man watched his tall, angular brother in front, sitting easily, his body moving naturally with his mount. The drab shirt barely disguised the lean frame. His hair, still long and tied back, had greyed. The shoulders appeared to have rounded and the back had become a little more hunched.

His own life seemed so easy in comparison, what with the servants and the carriages, the power and authority yet for the one in front it remained hard. His brother had never had the good fortune that had come his way and now he was the patriarch of the family. Nothing could change that, whatever their differing circumstances. His elder brother saw it as his job to look after them all and bore his responsibilities heavily. As he watched him leading the way, Wilmot wondered if their own father had been like that.

※

The noise of the pans in the sink meant only one thing and Kitty's heart sank. She went into the girls' room and began to tidy hoping the woman would go away but the noise continued and when she heard the tuneless singing she had no option but to go down.

"Hullo, Lottie." The figure half turned. She barely lifted her head in acknowledgment then turned back to the sink." Kitty paused in the doorway. Her hands clenched and she took a deep breath. "Now what's this? What are you doing here? I thought we'd settled all this."

"Settled what? The pans are dirty and you can't go leaving 'em in this state."

"Lottie, listen. They'll be done directly...that's my job." Charlotte ignored her. "Lottie, will you *please* listen. That's my job. I live here and I know what's to be done. And in any case, I can manage thank you."

"Don't look like it...the state of these 'yere pans're nort but a disgrace."

"Well, they've still to be done fer goodness sake, and it's my kitchen, I'll have you know."

"*Your* kitchen?" Charlotte swung round, water dripping from her hands. "*Your* kitchen?" Her face was puffed and her voice slurred. Kitty's heart sank. "Who're you to tell me about this kitchen? Eh? The devil on yer, Kitty Rawle. This is my brother's house and I'm 'ere to help…it's his an' the chillern's. Nort to do with you so don't you go givin' me none o'that. Anyways," she stepped closer. "What're you doin' up 'ere at Sherdon Farm? What business 'ave you got 'ere?"

"What do you mean, *business*? It's because Jack, your brother, asked me to come here, that's why. He asked me to move in upstairs and to help with the house an' the little ones. I live here now and yer know it."

"Well, that's my job to do them dishes. Always has bin an' always will. Bin like that ever since Katherine were 'ere."

"Well it's different now. Things 'ave changed. Jack's on his own and the children need someone to look after 'em. He's asked *me* to help an' that's that." She walked to the sink. "So please leave all this an' leave the house to me." She picked up the dishcloth but Charlotte went to wrestle it from her hand.

"*Leeeave* it, Lottie." Kitty tried to twist it away but the other woman was too strong for her."

"Get out of 'ere, you slut." Charlotte's face was contorted. "*Gid on,* bugger off, you Kitty Rawle or whatever yer name is. *Gid out of my sight.*" She went to grapple with her but Kitty was too quick. "Get out, d'you hear…afores I bloody *throw* you out."

"Don't you *dare* speak to me or anyone like that, Charlotte Heard. As far as the master of this house is concerned, my place is *here* and I'll be pleased for you to take yourself away."

"Oh, away with yer, child. I'll not be pushed around by no slattern like you. I'll soon see Jack about what's what…'e'll know what's right fer his own."

Kitty was trembling. She felt weak and she staggered to the table where she sat even before Charlotte had left the room. She heard another curse and the scullery door slam. She saw that her hands were shaking and felt her face twitching. Inside, her heart was thumping and a deep surge of anger and fear churned through her. Jack had asked her to come and live with them to help and she had, but now, suddenly, it was different. Bamber had gone and Charlotte was on her own. The woman saw Sherdon as her refuge and was going to fight for it. She was, as she said, a Tucker through and through while she, Kitty, had no call on the place. It was only Jack's word but now he was going to be torn between the two of them and there was only room for one. Gradually, and as the day wore on, the anger subsided but the fear remained.

✳

Jack sat at the table with his hands clasped in front of him. He knew it had to come. Earlier he had settled Charlotte back in the cottage having heard her tale. He left her for a while and when he returned she had been drinking again. It was, as Wilmot said, the very devil himself once it got to you. And now he had heard Kitty out.

His head dropped. Solomon himself would have been hard pressed. His heart ached for his sister and her wretched state but she had a home and Wilmot's allowance. It was not much but if he were to ask Kitty to leave she would have nothing. And besides, she had come to him in his hour of need. She had asked for nothing save the chance to help and he could never turn her out. But there was something else: she brought with her the warmth and affection he craved and which he, like any other man, needed. For him Sherdon was once more a happy place, and he was determined that it should remain that way.

He took a deep breath. Kitty, having said her piece, had left the room and gone into the parlour. Jack rose and followed. The room, not used for weeks, was cold and damp. He saw her standing by the window and knew she had been weeping. His heart ached for her yet, even as he reached out to console her, he agonised for his sister who had lost so much and who he would now be turning away. He paused with his hand still raised, once more doubting his judgement. She must have heard him for she turned and it was the look on her face that gave him the answer he sought.

✳

Kitty knocked and waited with her head inclined, listening for signs of life. A week had passed since the dreadful confrontation. Charlotte had said little since Jack had called them together and made clear the situation. She had seen how he was torn by the decision yet had seen it as his duty. He had hated doing it. He had looked tired and strained, his voice weaker and more hesitant than she could remember and he was having to force himself to confront them both. Later they had talked about it and twice Kitty had been down to the cottage. The first time was difficult enough but yesterday, when she went for the second time, there had been the scourge of drink about the place. Charlotte had been incoherent.

She stood back, noticing once more how the door had warped and what was left of the paint had flaked. Then she knocked again. Hearing nothing, she pushed gently. The top hinge creaked just like it always did but inside it was gloomy and unwelcoming.

As she came in from the kitchen, Charlotte stumbled. She was trying to smile but it was more of a leer. "Ha, Kitty Rawle." When she reached the back of the chair, she put out her hand to steady herself but it slipped and she stumbled again. Kitty saw it at once.

"I've brought you these, Lottie." She lowered the can of milk to the floor then put the basket on the bare table before removing the patterned cloth she had covered it with. The eggs were half wrapped but the carrots and potatoes surrounded the leeks and other greens in neat circles. "Not much, I'm afraid but we'll get a nice bit o' lamb down directly."

"Whassat for?" Charlotte wiped her mouth and stepped back to steady herself. "Don't need none of that. Don't need nuthin' from you, Kitty Rawle. Still Kitty Rawle, ain't it? Eh? Not Jack's then?" For a moment Kitty hesitated. She would have to choose her words. There was a brooding menace lurking in the woman just waiting to erupt and she could sense the bitterness about what had happened. Arguing would be no good, neither would sympathy for she would see it as a patronising insult and rise accordingly.

"Just thought you'd like a bit of something to eat, Lottie…help you along a bit." Charlotte swayed as she stood but the eyes remained fixed on her visitor, giving her an uncomfortable feeling that she was being studied closely. "Here, come and sit, Lottie. Looks like yer a bit tired. Bin working, I dare say." The older woman pushed away her hand. She was smiling again with that stupid, superior smile drunks give when trying to look sober. Then she sat and waved her hand dismissively. Kitty perched warily on the edge of the chair opposite and watched as Charlotte tried to concentrate.

"They're Jack's…not yours." She waved her hand at the basket. "Tell yer to come, did 'e? Go an' see Lottie. Eh? See if her's all right now we've thrown her out." Her eyes narrowed as she tried to focus. "You'm Kitty Rawle, bain't yer. Eh? Kitty Rawle what's bin smarmin' up to my Jack." She frowned, searching hazily for words. "Well, you leave 'im be an' cum back 'ere…where you belong. Right? 'Tis my place up at the farm…the chillern need me up there, not no Kitty Rawle. Can't abide yer they can't…all this smarmin' up ter their dad. You'm not their mum, y'know."

"It's not like that, Lottie. You know yer brother asked me to go an' help an' there's none o' this smarmin' as yer say. Us lives our own lives up there an' that's that."

"Oh aye. Well, I've seen yer." Charlotte's voice was raised. "Seen yer canoodlin' about in front of the chillern. All cuddlin' up just in case 'e chucks yer out. Eh?" She threw her head back and cackled.

"Bain't nort wrong wi' that. Jack's a lonely man an' I love 'im dear. Tis his house an'…."

"An' I loves 'im an' all. D'yer hear that…you Kitty Rawle?" Suddenly, and quicker than Kitty knew how, the face had changed. The woman in front of her crouched low. "Us all loves Jack, all of us an' it don't take for you to come pokin' yer way in." Charlotte rose heavily. Kitty stood also and stepped back. "You gid out of it up there, d'yer hear." For one so drunk, she moved quickly. "Just you gid on." Her finger stubbed harshly into Kitty's chest, the half-blow that followed caused her to stagger. "An' gid on out of 'ere as well."

"That's for Jack to decide, Lottie." Kitty stepped back again then stood her ground.

"And he's said his piece…it's nothin' to do with you or me. Anyways, I'll be leavin' yer now."

"An' keep out, d'yer hear." She tried to push her again but Kitty moved first. She had left her basket and turned to get it but the door crashed in her face. As she climbed the path behind the cottage she could hear the cackling laughter. The sobs came later but, by then, Kitty had long gone.

Her walk back to the farm was slow and she barely felt the evening wind that tugged at her hair and the hem of her dress. Charlotte was there to stay, of that there was no doubt. What she might try to tell her brother, Kitty had no idea but she, herself, would say nothing. There was no point. Jack, poor man, had made his decision and needed help not more worries. Harry had left Exford. He had slipped away in the night without taking his leave, so Billy Westcott told them when he rode out to see them. For days, Jack had worried about his son and only now was he coming to terms with his loss. Ernie, the young farm boy had left also, leaving just Stan Bawden and Ralph to help, but it was Jack who had taken on the extra work and she had seen how he tired more quickly than before.

Charlotte, she knew, would only worry him further. She would not be kept away and would keep causing trouble. There would be shouting and falling about. She, Kitty, would have to see to the woman: somehow she would have to be kept away from the house. But then, in spite of everything, she was still Jack's sister, his own flesh and blood. As she approached the farm at the end of the lane, she saw the light of the lamps in the windows, and suddenly she was afraid again: afraid for herself and for what might come to pass.

3

Harry had always been in awe of Black Richards. His hair, his thick eyebrows and his chin really were black. The man rarely smiled and his red kerchief stood out from his dirty clothes but there was something smart about him. It was his way with words: he always knew what was what and how things should be done. But he was an evil one as well, and as cunning as could be. So when Richards asked him to go to Exeter with him, Harry didn't hesitate. The journey took three days. It should have been longer but Richards stole a pony and its bridle from a shed by the bridge in Dulverton. Two days later Harry watched as he sold the animal to some gypsies at Rewe. They walked the last few miles together.

The money for the pony, Richards explained, would see them through the week and the next one as well. After that Harry would be on his own and would have to work for his keep. The two others in the third floor of the unoccupied terraced house in Friars Gate showed him how it was to be done. 'Snakey' Masters, older and fatter than Black Richards and with most of his red face, except for his pock-marked nose, covered with wiry, dark hair, warned Harry to watch him and to watch carefully.

'The Three Birds' and 'The Bell', both in narrow cobbled alleyways behind the market, together with the tangled mess of houses either side of Cow Lane where the harlots lurked, was their pitch. Twice Snakey and Tom Hall, a squat, strongly built man with a lazy eye, had to clear away those who wanted to run their affairs there as well. Tom was violent and used to beat the flower sellers and pie boys as well as the whores who strayed on to the pitch. Harry saw it had to be done that way or else there would be loud arguments about it and people would gather to watch the fun.

Only the gents what's drunk an' them what's going with a woman were to be taken, Snakey decreed. *They might make a bit of noise but they'd never cause no trouble, not when they're with a woman and not when they were down Cow Lane. Wouldn't want to be seen down there, would they? Eh? Only gents, right, for they're the ones with the money. Only the ones with money.*

✳

Harry learned fast. At first they wanted him to dress as a woman but he was too big and his voice had gone so they found a younger lad for that. Harry would watch over the boy as he made his approach and it would be his job to snatch the purse or the bag and the watch together with anything else he could find. Snakey and Tom would be there to watch his back while Harry and the little fella made off into the night. It seemed so easy.

Harry knew the back streets from Burnthouse Lane to The Custom's House quay and from Shilhay Street up to Thomas Carnall's Coffee House. He was quick on his feet, far quicker than the constables in their heavy boots, and he was strong for a lad of sixteen. He had his friends and his safe houses where his knock in the night would open the door only for it to be quickly bolted again behind him. He could climb like a cat and run along high beams. He could jump across gaps in the dark and twice he had to swim the river.

But then he began to swagger and brag. They ate well, up in the loft at Friar's Gate and Harry watched and listened as Snakey and Tom brought women home. He bought himself new boots, a fancy jacket and a pair of buckskin breeches. He won and lost in the cockpit behind Northernhay. Only twice were they nearly caught, once by friends who came to the aid of the gent they were robbing and once when Harry ran into the Night Watch. They caught him, but he twisted and turned out of his jacket and ran off. They learned as they went along and the better they became, the bolder they got.

✳

"Shops is easier," Snakey advised as they sat around the brazier of coals they had built on tiles in the loft. "Wiv gents an' that you never know." Snakey's finger waved in front of them. "Some come quietly but others begin to holler. Some are easy, come all quiet, like, but others make a showing of it. An' look," he shrugged his shoulders expansively. "All this fightin' an' scrabblin' about when they're on the ground and the hussy's screamin' an' yellin'...'tis dodgy and takes time. Takes *too* long." The others listened in silence, their faces long and serious by the light of the oil lamp. "Now shops are different. We know *what's* in there 'cos we've looked...an' we know *who's* in there 'cos we use our bread."

"Until us get caught that is." Tom Hall sniffed and wiped his nose. "You know what they do to those they catch, Snakey? Eh? Up in front of the gaol...gets their necks cracked. That's what." Harry inched forward to hear more, blowing on his hands, his eyes moving from one to the other.

"Don't fancy it, Snakey...don't fancy none of that." It was the lad and the three of them looked at him. "Don't fancy swinging not for that...not for nothin' like that." Harry could never remember who moved first but Snakey had the boy on his back and by his throat. His hat had fallen off and his mane of untidy hair had fallen forward as he knelt on the struggling figure.

"See here, boy, and see well. You got no choice." Snakey's thumbs pressed hard and he shook the neck in his hands. His body was bent over the boy like a big dog would tower over a pup that had angered him. "You're here with us an' you're stayin'. See? And you'll do what's what. I know where you's from, Jason, my lad, and if yer thinkin' of tryin' ort I'll be coming for yer...like we did fer that Jack Fry."

Harry saw the glint of the blade in front of the boy's face. "You're here, an' yer'll do what's to be done, see." Snakey clenched the knife then pressed the blade forward against the boy's throat. Harry watched as the sharp tip pressed into the white flesh. "You hear me, lad, an' you hear me well." He rolled off the boy and got to his feet. When he spoke next his voice was soft. "I need yer, my boy...need yer bad and you wouldn't be letting me down. Not me and not Tom...you wouldn't do nuthin' like that."

Harry shrank behind the twisted beam. It was one of the several that supported the roof and they hung their clothes from nails they had driven into it. He looked from Snakey to Tom and then back at the boy. There was no going back. Snakey Masters knew too much and would come for him if he tried to run and, anyway, he had no money. Tom held it all. So, shops it would have to be. But he was excited; the thought of it sent a thrill surging through him. There were risks, to be sure, just as there had been with picking pockets but this was bigger and better. And it would work; Snakey and Tom would see to that.

For a time it did. It worked very well and Harry thought no more about going back to mucking out horses and cleaning leather. When they had done the jeweller's shop behind the Cathedral Close they went to Plymouth for a while and it was when they returned that the uncle of the lad asked Harry to join him. They cut a deal and it was just a matter of moving when the timing was right.

4

Rebecca Tucker watched the two men in the garden. Sir Durnford Morgan, in spite of stooping as he walked, towered over her husband. They were both dressed in identical frock coats, a sight which always reminded her of rooks looking for food in the fields behind the church. She had taken an immediate liking to the tall banker with the crinkly grey hair and the worried look, and smiled to herself as he put a hand on Wilmot's shoulder. It was as if he was emphasizing the point he had been making. They had stopped by the sundial in front of the wall and turned to face each other, her husband leaning on his Malacca cane to ease the pain in his leg. She was too far away to hear but had a fair idea of what held their attention.

"I'm sure it'll work, dear boy. Sure of it." Morgan patted the shoulder.

"Well, you've certainly covered yourself well with that rate of interest you've wrung from us." As he spoke, Wilmot glanced idly at the head of the other's cravat pin. It was a golden claw grasping a single pearl and, for some reason or other, it caught his eye. He pushed back a lock of his still black hair. "It's a devil of a hard bargain you've driven but I have to say the docks and harbour are in very good order. Our team from Bristol know what they're looking for and they're satisfied well enough. We got their report a week ago." He wrinkled his nose at the thought going through his mind. "However, I'd have to say there seems to be an element of doubt...over-caution, built into the rate you're demanding...rather as though you've seen something you need to safeguard against. Have you no faith in our judgement, Sir Durnford?" Now their eyes met.

"It's not that, not at all." Morgan stood back then followed the other to a semi-circular granite seat set under an arch of the palest of yellow roses. He lifted his tails and sat. "No...we have absolute faith in both your judgement and in the company itself. To this extent we're planning to lower the rates after two years and propose to halve them after that...if the loan hasn't been cleared by then. It's just that we're living in uncertain times right now. Nobody can say what effect the rail network is going to have on maritime traffic...or with any new industrial venture, for that matter."

"But we're hardly dependant upon *that*." Wilmot prodded at the gravel with his cane. "Anyway the railway's due to come through to Bideford...we've checked that out with the London South West in Exeter. I mean, they're in Barnstaple already and we've seen plans for the line that's to be pushed through."

"I know, I know." Morgan held up his hand. "It all looks splendid but there's an awful lot of jockeying for position yet...ownership rights, track gauges...standard or broad and goodness knows what else. Most banks are getting very wary...you'd never get a better offer, y'know. We've done you well, Wilmot."

"Hmmph. That's the standard speech all bankers make once they've got you in the bag." He jabbed at the gravel and eased his leg. "A thank you and good bye until we meet again."

Morgan ignored the taunt and, for a moment, the two were silent. "You've heard word of Ilfracombe, I suppose?" He leant forward to catch the other's eye. "Likely to be a spot of competition up there from what we hear."

"Ilfracombe…*Ilfracombe*? Pit props and lime…and a bit of coal, perhaps." The cane jabbed harder at the gravel. "Not much else out there. It's a very poorly angled harbour and precious little deep water. We had it surveyed way back. Little more than a haven for fisherman and coastal traffic…and that's about it." Wilmot lifted his chin and rubbed thoughtfully. "So what's this news you're telling me I should know about?"

"A fella called Preston. Lord Herbert Preston, the Duke of Northborough, apparently. Took completion a couple of months ago and he wants to develop the place. Frederic Knight knows about him. Florence said so when I called at Simonsbath and I want to get up to see him about it." Others on Exmoor, so Florence Knight had told him, knew the man as well, but he could not draw her. He had been keen to know more but had gained nothing from her other than having his instinct sharpened.

Wilmot sat without moving, both hands now on his cane and his chin resting on his hands. "Yes," he half whispered. "Yes, we know the man all right. He's my brother's brother-in-law. Didn't they tell you that?" In spite of the question he looked straight ahead but Morgan could see his face had hardened. Something had struck home. He sensed that whatever humour had lain within this dry intense man had gone, evaporated.

"Well?"

"Phwww." Wilmot blew and raised his eyebrows then looked down at his feet. "Say nothing of this to by brother, Jack, mind." The words came more as a command. "Oh, it'll be out sooner or later no doubt about that…when a man like Northborough comes around and starts buying harbours the place is going to fairly buzz. Frederic'll know for sure and word will get about but the man's…well, how should we say, he's hardly a friend of the family."

"A rival?"

"Commercially no. There's no rivalry there and I'll see it stays that way. It's just that…oh, Heaven's, Durnford, it was a long time ago and we've all moved on. Well, perhaps it would have been better had he not come down this way. It's a pity really but it can't be helped." He was silent for a while and, when he spoke again, all his vital energy had returned as though his mind had been focussed elsewhere. "But, have no fear, my friend." Wilmot leant forward and slapped the banker on the thigh. "The Bristol Steamship Company at Bideford will be able to look after itself; of that I can assure you. On that particular score there'll be no trouble at all. Come, Rebecca and the others await us." He rose and stretched his injured leg. "But thank you none the less for such information. I'll be watching Ilfracombe with great interest."

5

As she stood in the library doorway, Sarah lifted a finger to dismiss the footman offering her a glass from the tray. It looked as though she was the last to appear. Nobody from the large group of twenty or so who had assembled for dinner turned and it was Mrs Jocelyn Orchard, her mistress and the first lady of Hartland Abbey, who came across to greet her.

Earlier, and as soon as her daily routine was done, Sarah had handed the children to the nanny and tidied the schoolroom next to the nursery. Mrs Orchard had asked to see her concerning Cardew's final preparation before he went away to boarding school in May. It was agreed that as soon as he had gone the two youngest, Edwin aged seven and the diminutive Jocasta, now six, would become her responsibility. There would be the three of them but, by then, she would be the only governess.

After that she had taken a bath. It was her turn and the two watermen brought hot water from the kitchen to the copper tub set up in the old day nursery next to her room. After soaping herself she lay back luxuriating until the water had cooled. It was a wonderful new experience and her body felt alive and invigorated. Nothing was to be hurried so she took time to prepare her face; a little more white kaolin, this time, and a touch less rosette brun.

Olive, the new lady's maid, a silent, dark skinned girl from Guadeloupe, set her hair. Later, when she could be spared from seeing to her mistress, the girl padded back in her bare feet to help with the back buttons and puffed sleeves of her dress. The silk and cotton material was cut more to the figure, allowing the rose and lily patterned folds to be swept back, so she chose the smaller of her two crinolines. Instead of a bustle, which she and most of the others at Mrs Patterson's hated, the seamstress had given the dress a frilled back panel of Lincoln green edged with lace.

Even as she stood there, twisting and turning in front of her mirror, she could detect the fragrance of the eau de jasmin her uncle had brought back from Lille. Olive had sprinkled it lightly onto the single, pink rose that nestled in her cleavage and whose exact position continued to exercise her. She was ready but ignored the assembly bell, preferring to enter quietly, by herself when she could gauge the mood rather than being part of it. Then, and when she was ready, she would move quietly to the edge of the melee around the marble and oak panelled fireplace.

*

It was Sharland who noticed her first. He had been talking to Henslowe Debroan, Jocelyn Orchard's nephew, and only happened to glance up when he heard his father's laugh. He, too, had come down later than the others and must have just missed her on the stairs. The Debroans, the final members of the shooting party had arrived late from Wiltshire. He and Henslowe had not seen each other for over a year and had sat talking in the morning room until the butler reminded them of the time.

He watched, intrigued by the way the newcomer stood and surveyed the room, and waited until her eyes met his. There was a boldness about her steady gaze and when she gave a hint of acknowledging his attention, it was he who looked away. Stung by this audacity and curious about the hint of a smile, he moved to see more but his hostess had blocked his view. He never heard what Henslowe was saying to the others and turned back to them only when his sleeve was tugged. He caught her eye once more when she was standing by the bay window listening to Elsie Summerfield. The short, plump and over-made-up cousin of Hector Galbraith laughed uproariously at the sound of her own voice but the newcomer dressed in Lincoln green appeared less than impressed.

However, it was too late; whoever it was had come in only minutes before the gong sounded and the butler filled his lungs to announce that dinner was ready to be served. Eliza Smythe, a grey, gaunt woman in a grey, gaunt dress and a friend of his father's was to be his partner. By the time Sharland found her and offered his arm, the library was emptying. Afterwards, though, there would be dancing in the great hall.

✳

"Perhaps one more, just one after the interval. Yes?" Sharland touched the hand on his arm as if to hasten her reply and led the way back to the yellow silk sofa. The drawing room was hot and they had chosen the far corner where what little draught there had crept in from the window. As she turned and smiled, his eyes were drawn once more to the tiny black spot she had placed near the corner of her mouth.

"Perhaps, kind sir but only perhaps. I'm quite exhausted. Can we not sit for a while? Just for these next two...I mean, nobody can possibly dance a waltz so soon after dinner and *then* a polonaise." Sarah fanned herself but allowed him to keep hold of her arm. "Let us sit, I beg you...but I promise I will not accept any other offers. Look," she held up her dance card. "See here. It has been filled, and mostly by yourself. Lord Sharland Preston," she read. "And here, and here also."

"Then some refreshment, I insist." Sharland beckoned a footman before turning and holding her other hand as she sat. "So, Hartland Abbey has been blessed with a new and radiant governess who brings not only a sparkle of intellectual sunlight to the household but who can also dance with the gods." He lifted his tails and sat beside her. "And you will be present tomorrow evening as well, I trust? Duty calls in the strangest of ways, does it not? Yes?" He peered forward and frowned in mock severity. "And those of us who are so commanded have no option other than to obey. You...will...dance. Yes?"

"Indeed, indeed." Sarah adjusted the panels of her dress and raised her eyebrows. "Oh yes, I have been invited tomorrow rather, as you say, it has been required of me, even if only to make up the numbers for such an occasion."

"And you are much in demand...allow me to see your card again." He counted quickly. "Apart from me there are three, no four others...well, a clear cut case of beauty for duty if ever there was." He was annoyed that twice, when she was waltzing with Henslowe Debroan, she had glanced his way and caught him watching them. She appeared to be enjoying her partner's company and he hers. They seemed well matched and it irritated him. In fact it irritated him quite a lot and she must have seen the look on his face for she smiled mischievously and glanced back over her shoulder as she wheeled away from where he was sitting. Now, though, they were together again.

He took the drink from the silver tray and sat back, allowing himself to take in the slender neck and fine, full figure. She looked back, her eyes searching his and, once more, it was he who averted his gaze. He was a fine enough looking man she thought to herself. He held himself well and the figure was trim. The longish nose and square jaw gave off an air of authority but the untidy mop of fair hair and his hazel eyes belonged more to those of a rebel, or of a younger brother trying to keep up. She was pleased to have him beside her.

"That, sir, is too much, but a fine compliment, nonetheless. Your attention flatters me."

"But only *flatters*? No more than that?" He raised a hand to feign exasperation. "The merest flutter of recognition, is that really all my presence commands? How can it be that such close and diligent attention has so little effect."

"Oh, come, sir. Come, now. You tease...you are trifling with my emotions." Sarah half turned on the sofa and faced him. "You do indeed flatter me but whether or not that is all, I hesitate to disclose. There are some matters concerning one's emotions about which it is best not to speak."

"And, pray, why not?" Sharland's arm was along the back of the sofa, his fingers close to her shoulder. "Does my concern for you merit no more than that?"

"That I could not say." She shrugged and moved away from the hand. She did not move far but it was enough for her message to be clear. "And, in any case it is my turn now. For more than an hour, you have quizzed me relentlessly about this and that, about who I am and where I have been. My answers alone, quite apart from the dancing, have left me confused and my head quite giddy." She touched her brow. "And so, good sir," she caught his eye and lifted her head, just enough to show whoever might be watching them that, for her, this gallant held no fear. "I, too, am just as curious about you so, pray tell me, if you will...tell me about Blagdon and about Whitechapel. And about yourself and your family...and your papa, too."

She had noticed that the Duke and his companion were talking about them and met his stare, when she smiled disarmingly before looking down.

*

"Who d'yer say?" The Duke of Northborough inclined his head to hear better.

"Jocelyn's new governess." Eliza Smythe raised a hand to her mouth in order to direct her voice. "A pretty creature, don't you think...as Sharland seems to have found already. Your boy had little time for his poor old partner at the dinner table."

"A racy little wench, I'll be bound." The Duke rose on his toes.

"*Oh*, now listen. That's quite enough of that, Herbert. Don't be so pompous...you're quite insufferable. The child's as pretty as a picture and all you can say is that. You're impossible...jealous of your boy, no doubt."

"Hmmph. Out of the hills, you say? Mmm?" The Duke shrugged nonchalently before emptying his glass and holding it out for a footman to replenish.

"Her mother apparently...she was in service with the Knights for years. Came as a waif, so they say, and finished up at Filleigh."

"Hmmph. The Knights, eh?" He looked across at Sarah, half closing his eyes as he studied her more closely. "Funny lot, they are, those Knights...mmm, a bit odd. Father used to take us there for holidays when old John Knight was around. They live way up in the hills on their own, surrounded by bogs and a handful of locals for company. All very strange...and as primitive as you can get." He wrinkled his nose then pulled on it. "So she's from there, is she? Mmm, interesting. She'll be wild and woolly, no doubt, just like the rest of them." The Duke glanced at Eliza Smythe and rolled the brandy in his balloon. "And out to give me boy a damned good run for his money, no doubt. They're all the same up there."

Chapter Six

Elizabeth-Jane came into the drawing room by herself, a little ahead of the others, leaving the three men at the table. Even as she and the others were leaving, Freddie had taken the port decanters and the three had huddled together at the far end like conspirators. Durnford had begun a cigar and Wilmot, his right leg as painful as ever, lounged back in his chair with his coat open in an attempt to ease the discomfort. If she knew them well enough, it would be some time before they rose but, no matter, Portland Place intrigued her.

She looked round admiringly. Florence had certainly decorated the house with taste and she smiled at the sight of the mementos from Rome. Freddie had insisted on bringing home the marble of the young Dionysus which he and his father had bought together. He, John, had likened the grapes and vine leaves around the god of wine's head to hazel nuts from the grove at Lynton and she remembered how, time and again, the idea had reduced them all to helpless laughter. And then the beautiful yellow silk and metallic Kashan Freddie had bought in Firenza. Florence had hung it cleverly on the dark plum-coloured silk of the back wall where it dominated like a splash of bright sunlight. Outside the front door, mounting watch over whoever was passing up Portland Place, there was the pair of marble Verona lions. It was sad in a way but lovely to think that all those happy memories were being passed on like this. She turned as Rebecca and Florence joined her.

"What do you think, Elizabeth-Jane?" Florence motioned for them all to sit and nodded to the green-liveried Maynard who bowed and left to fetch the coffee. "D'you think Wil is going to accept? We do." Her eyes were wide in expectation. Talk at the table had been about the offer Wilmot had been made by the London and Pacific shipping line. They had approached him two weeks ago with the request that he should join them as chairman. It was tempting but would mean leaving The Bristol Steamship company just as it was beginning to do well. Durnford Morgan had advised them, in his usual concerned and brow-furrowed way, that the London and Pacific were expanding fast by building successful trade routes to several countries in the orient. It was, he suggested, a huge enterprise and Lombard Street knew they were set on further rapid growth.

"Well, I'm not leaving North Molton, so there." The two others laughed at Rebecca's stubbornness. "It's all very well living up here in the lap of luxury talking to shipping people the whole time…and Wil's seen a lovely place in Cranley Gardens, but I miss Exmoor. The wonderful clean air, the curlews, the heather…everything. And the children love it too…ponies and things."

"But you *can* to and fro, you know." Florence, Elizabeth-Jane could see, would be happier running her life from here, the other way round. "The railways are through to Barnstaple now and it's much, much quicker…and far more comfortable than the stage. Honestly, coffee and a French breakfast at Waterloo and lunch at The

George…well, almost. Oh, go on, Rebecca, do persuade him." Florence clapped her hands excitedly. "You'll love it up here. There's masses to do…theatre, opera, ballet, everything. Really, you'll have the best of both worlds and Wil's going to need you."

"That's if he takes it." Rebecca raised a finger in warning. "Oh, he's such a stubborn devil," she shivered. "Sometimes I could scream as he ponders over something, sniffing about here and there, humming and hawing every which way. But yes, I know he'd love it."

"And what about Bideford…the new shipping business there?" Elizabeth-Jane looked at Rebecca. She could see her father in the younger woman and remembered when Piers Deveraux had ridden out to ask John about this young Wilmot Tucker who had asked for his daughter's hand. Sharp as a knife, had been John's response and the next thing they knew he had joined them at Bristol. And as for her, Rebecca, she was a country girl. Somehow the mass of frilled skirts and the wide, flared sleeves of the bright evening dress swamped her comfortable figure. Her hair always looked as though it had been set in a hurry without enough pins or as though the wind had taken hold of it. She was rosy-cheeked and bonny and Elizabeth-Jane could see at once that Rebecca Tucker and her children would never be happy in the gilded London society.

"Bristol have asked him to look after it for them. I know it sounds awfully patronising," she shrugged. "But it's small enough and Wilmot's thrilled…says it will keep his feet on the ground and something to do when he's at Court Hall. Honestly," she laughed shrilly at a sudden thought and put a hand to her mouth. "He's supposed to be relaxing when he's there but he never does…so there we are."

※

"And that's from the man himself." Frederic stood with his back to the mantelpiece. "I don't know how he gets hold of all this but when you're Leader of the House, I suppose you've got your spies everywhere. And if I know William Gladstone, he'll have his eyes and ears open all right." The three men had re-joined the ladies and talk of Wilmot's offer persisted, but now politics had come into it as well.

Elizabeth-Jane looked on. Her son stood just as he always had but the figure of Frederic Knight was now fuller she noted. The scarlet and gold patterned waistcoat was doing what it could to hide the evidence but was having to struggle. The face had become a little too jowly, she thought, and the whiskers a bit more whiskery than hitherto. But perhaps it was age and he no longer had the time to ride and hunt as he once did. She smiled warmly nevertheless, proud that her son had the confidence of such powerful men.

"Really, Wil," Frederic continued. "Just as we were saying at the table, the government's pushing shipping as hard as it can. Let's face it, successful overseas trade is about the best foreign policy there is...and it's vital for England, for Heaven's sake." He tugged at the cuff of his shirt. "And in any case, there're the French to think about and the Dutch...*and* America. Everyone's out east and after as much of the cake as they can grab and we've got to keep ahead of the field. That's the policy anyway."

Suddenly the room fell silent. It was as if somebody had decreed that the talking should stop and it was time for the decision to be announced. Rebecca bit her lip. She knew everyone was waiting on her husband's word but it was Florence who spoke first, rising as she did so, diminutive and dark in her cream dress. "Oh, poor you, Wilmot. It's not fair what with everybody looking at you like this and waiting for your answer. I think we should all leave it alone...let Wil make his own mind up."

"No, no." Wilmot climbed to his feet and eased his leg. "That's too kind, m'dear. Bless you for that. In actual fact I've already decided. My mind's made up and I'm going to accept...it's just too good an opportunity and a wonderful challenge." The others rose but he held up a hand and wagged a finger. "But we'll be staying in North Devon, that's for sure. Bideford's going to be fun and I'll need it. If my head's going to be up in the clouds here in the city, I need to be reminded of what's going on down at the dockside. And then there're the farms." He looked at Frederic and Durnford Morgan, then at his hostess. As he did so, he steadied himself and winced, putting a hand on Florence's shoulder. "Now then, we haven't just been talking about the high seas in there, madam. Country matters have come up as well...under the eagle eye of my learned friend from Esdaile's here." He grinned at Durnford who leant back on his side of the sofa with both hands clasped round one raised knee. "But it's your call, Freddie," he waved his glass at Frederic. "I think you're the one best placed to explain."

"The farms?" Frederic questioned and Wilmot nodded. "We-ll." He paused, pulling on his chin. "Perhaps there was something in that splendid claret and a bit more in the port but, once you ladies had left us to our own devices...well, we started to talk."

"You don't say." Elizabeth-Jane laughed out loud and sat back. "You men never *stop*, for goodness sake. You'd be in there all night if we let you. Oh, come on Freddie. Get on with it, dear. What have you been plotting?"

"You, Durnford." Frederic laughed bashfully. "You were the arbitrator...the great guru and the man counting the shekels. You oversaw it...and everything else for that matter."

"Ha, the devil on you 'Young Knight.' Ah dear. Let me think now." The banker gazed thoughtfully into his glass. "All right." He looked up and surveyed the faces looking at him. Suddenly he smiled. "My goodness me, what a sight," he laughed. "Never have I seen such a circle of gloom." His face fell mournfully. "Well then. It's simple really. We've been discussing the Exmoor farms…Freddie's estate. It's just that he cannot hope to do everything he's got on his plate…and not likely to be able to either. Westminster's pulling him in one direction, and pulling hard while the iron grip of Rugby and Corby pulls the other way. It's a question of something having to give. *So.*" he glanced at Wilmot. "Along comes our good Mr Tucker, here, and the three of us converse together. Now then…." He glanced at Frederic.

"Three farms," Frederic interjected. "Emmets, Wintershead and Horsen. The three new ones behind the high ridge above Sherdon where Jack is. I have to announce that ownership changed about an hour ago, under the careful scrutiny of my banking friend here." He nodded towards Durnford Morgan then turned to Wilmot. "Permit me to introduce the new owner, Farmer Wilmot Tucker."

2

Sarah was alone. It was April yet she had wrapped herself well against the strong breeze coming off the sea. The clouds were high and broken, racing one another across the face of the sun while their shadows chased over the ground beneath. After a while she turned and sat with her back to the cliff edge, pulling up the hood of her cloak, even so she had to keep sweeping back locks of hair that broke free. Sitting like this was better: she would get the sun on her face and would be able to see him coming.

It had been almost two months since Thomas Preston had all but killed himself out hunting. The Hursley had met near Blagdon Park for one of the last meets of the season and it had been wet; apparently the ground had been heavy. She never heard the full details but there was a fence and a ditch and another horse had been involved. Only the boldest had been mad enough to attempt it and Thomas had been thrown. He had broken a hip but his skull had been fractured also and it had been a month before he even sat in bed. Twice Desmond Orchard had gone up to see him and it was only after the second time, less than two weeks ago, that the news was better. He was walking again but slowly and with the aid of a stick. Almost a week ago, Sharland had come down to escape from the dismal business and the melancholy atmosphere at Blagdon.

He had seemed cheerful enough at first but looked tired at the end of each day, his fair complexion accentuating the deep shadows under his eyes. Once, when she came out of the nursery, she chanced upon him in the long upstairs corridor. He looked exhausted but returned her smile and they began to talk. She found it surprisingly easy and had even felt a sudden tenderness towards him. Obviously the two brothers were close and the worry had delved deep down within him. Without thinking she had half reached out to put a hand on his arm, but had checked herself in time. The following day they talked again and it was then that he asked her to meet him at the folly on the cliff top. He would be here soon and the sense of occasion thrilled her.

She thought about the last time they had spoken. It was the morning after the shooting party ball when they had danced and danced. She had enjoyed his company; his wit and repartee had made her laugh. His looks, though not necessarily wildly handsome, were certainly pleasant enough. But he was of noble birth, a Lord in his own right and the younger son of a Duke. Who would not be excited, she asked herself, that one of such blood should desire her company, and alone like this? She bent down to pick at something on the toe of her boot then rose from the stone seat and walked to the cliff top, standing as near to the edge as she dared.

The sea today was azure, doing its best to mirror the spring sky. Far out, white horses twinkled as the wind ruffled the wave tops. Closer in, and beneath where she stood, the swell had somehow been gathered together and line upon line of breakers rolled in with spray blowing from their crests until, one after the other, they thundered against the rocks as though determined to break down whatever lay in their path. One hand held on to her hood, the other pressed back the hem of her cloak which the wind had blown up around her waist. His call, almost lost on the wind, made her turn and she staggered against the force behind her. As she raised her hand, a sudden gust caught her cloak again and she half ran towards him, pushed on by the wind.

"Oh, I'm sorry…sorry I'm so late." He seemed out of breath but it had been a steep climb up to the folly and she could see he had been hurrying. "Desmond…Mr Orchard kept me and I was unable to get away." He shrugged and grinned boyishly, altogether more cheerful than she had seen him earlier. "Magnificent…the view, that is. There look…Lundy Island." His words came hurriedly as though he was embarrassed at the short silence. "Could do without this wind, though…you must be cold. How about further down?" He nodded over his shoulder. "There's a seat just beyond the stile. Come on. It's out of the wind down there and there's a grand view of the Abbey."

*

"No, I'm fine. It was a blow though…we're very close, y'know." Sharland took in the view of the park and Hartland Abbey beyond: for a moment, he was silent. "Damned fool…he'll never learn to steady up. It'll be the death of him one day, you wait." Sarah sat forward with her hands clenched in her lap. She had pushed her hood back and tried to tidy her hair but to little effect. He looked dishevelled also and the wind had made his eyes water. She sensed his vulnerability and nodded sympathetically.

"Yes…I understand. But, pray tell me, sir, why have you asked for me to meet you like this? I mean, you must have much to do, much on your mind…and you're leaving tomorrow morning."

"Oh…to talk. I suppose I just wanted an opportunity to talk." He shrugged, put his arm along the back of the seat and smiled ruefully. "Jocelyn and Desmond have been wonderful but they try so hard, too hard almost and everything seems to be on edge just now. I had to get away and simply thought it'd be nice for us to meet and converse for a while, to relax." He glanced at her.

"And do you believe you can relax with me? That is a rare compliment indeed, but why so? We scarcely know each other and, in any case, it would hardly be right for you to be seen seeking solace with *me*...the family governess...and away up here like this. People will read all sorts of things into such behaviour."

"Let them," he laughed. "But why you?" He shrugged again and pulled a face. "Yes," he murmured. "Why you, eh? Well, I have to confess that I've been thinking about you, Miss Kingdon. The shooting party last winter...and the dance. Remember?" She nodded, not knowing what to say but felt her heartbeat quicken. "It was all such fun and we laughed so, did we not? I teased you and you teased me back...and we laughed again. It was silly but it all came so easily...a happy, jolly occasion, and I felt drawn to you."

"What are you telling me, sir?" Sarah tried to catch his eye. "If you're saying what I think you are then I must stop you. You, we...we cannot possibly conduct ourselves like this. I've told you of my humble upbringing and I am aware of your background. We're so different, far, far *too* different. You are...you're a man of great power and influence. You, you'll..." She threw up her hands, unable to finish but she knew she had to say it. It would have been expected of her to be overawed by even his most casual attention. She should have been flattered or embarrassed, or simply afraid but she was not. She had to pretend she was but her emotions were quite different and she saw more than a hand reaching out for her: she saw his arms, both of them, opened wide and outstretched. "You must remember who you are, sir – you are Lord Sharland Preston and I am simply Miss Sarah Kingdon. The very sound of the two names spoken in the same breath tells its own tale."

"I couldn't care less." He removed his arm and reached for her hand. "Look, Sarah, it may seem unusual but it is quite within my rights to be so familiar when we are alone. Why not, for goodness sake? We are but two people. It may be difficult but can we not try...try to meet from time to time, when business or pleasure brings me here."

She felt him take her hand but made no move. Her mind was racing. What was on his mind? Was he simply desolate after his brother's terrible accident and looking for succour or was he stalking her? Had he been watching her, determined that she should be his next prize? It had to be; there was no other explanation. He was after her and it was as simple as that: anything more was out of the question. And what about all this secrecy, what was that about? *He* might not care less, as he claimed, but there were others who could and well he knew it: his father and his family most certainly would.

"And for what purpose, might I ask? Hardly to take me by my hand and lead me gaily into your world. I should say not. You are, sir, disconsolate over the fate of your brother and you seek companionship with one to whom you may talk freely. Of that I have no doubt and I am honoured, but you must put any other thoughts out of your mind. The very walls themselves at Hartland have ears. We would never be able to see each other without the whole world knowing. And then what? For you, it would be no more than a moment's embarrassment, but for me…why, I would be shown the door and be sent on my way in a trice."

"Well, I would like to see you all the same." He squeezed her hand. "Look at me." She held his gaze. "I *am* being serious, you know, believe me I am. Could we, would you consent to such an arrangement?"

She shook her head but remained silent. If he was persistent now then he would continue to be so. In spite of his position, she was attracted to him but had no intention of submitting to his advances. Not yet, anyway. She had heard from Olive what his valet had said about him and, exciting though the thought of such an assignment might be, she had no desire for him, or for anyone else, to impose themselves upon her. "I really cannot see how? For you it is no more than a game, and you know it. It is played all the time and it is so easy for you and those like you where the risks are non-existent…and good sport I am sure. But for me, I cannot agree." She paused to choose her words carefully. "No, I really cannot agree…not now."

"Not *now*, you say. Then I will be patient."

"Maybe you will." She looked at him. "Maybe so, but from what I have seen patience does not come easily to Lord Sharland Preston. But patience it will have to be." Sarah rose and as he looked up at her before rising himself she noticed his anxious look, exactly what she wanted to see.

3

Jack glanced at Kitty then back at Tod. The boy was barely eighteen, yet he had come to them with *this*. It had taken them by surprise and, as he studied his son, he leant back against the rough stonewall surrounding the hearth. "The *church*? he whispered. "*Holy Orders*? Why? How come, lad? 'Tis unknown for a Tucker…we've never had a man of God in the family."

"You're not cross, father? Or ashamed are you?"

Kitty looked at the tall, slim youth standing in front of his father. It must have taken courage for him to come to them with the news. Goodness knows what struggles he had had at Blundell's. But here he was…so young and yet so sure. "Oh, Tod. Dear, dear Tod." She crossed the hearth to Jack and took hold of his arm. "It's wonderful, reely wonderful. What a man you are, isn't he, Jack?" She glanced from one to the other, her eyes shining with delight. "And why not, says I? You've done well, dear one, an' we've all missed you back here. 'Tis lovely to hear, Jack. Real lovely."

Jack took his son's hand in both his, then drew him forward before enveloping him in his arms. "Aye, lad." He patted his son's back. "'Tis real wonderful and I'm proud of yer, as proud as proud can be." Tod Tucker stood back. There were tears in his eyes as there were in his father's, and Kitty's too.

He told them how it had come to him slowly while at school. How gradually he had been drawn to the great story, studying everything he could and listening to those who came to preach at the chapel. Eventually he went to the chaplain and told him what had been tormenting him. There followed weeks of discussion and consultation. Time and again he had slipped out of his boarding house and gone to the chaplain's home where, sitting closely together around the peat fire in his musty and book-lined study, they had talked at length. It had to be done, the tall, wizened pastor advised, in order to determine whether it was truly a calling or simply a passing passion that came temporarily to many. His housemaster had been informed, then the headmaster.

It had not been easy, he told them. The teasing and taunting in the house had been his own wilderness when he was forced to examine his conscience. But then had come the visit to the theological college and the instruction. It left him more convinced than ever and, in a month's time, he would be setting out for St Anselm's.

While waiting at Sherdon he wanted to help his father, but rarely had time. Instead he helped Kitty in the house and each afternoon would go down to the cottage and spend an hour with Charlotte until Victoria and Anna rode back from school. The gulf between Kitty and Charlotte had grown wider. Tod saw it and it pained him, not so much for himself or for them but for his father who, he knew, was deeply saddened. The girls, too, were confused, Victoria preferring to stay at the farm while Anna spent what time she could with their aunt.

❋

"Let me take the bucket, aunt. Here." Tod held out his hand but, instead, moved quickly to help Charlotte. The plate in her hand, full of scraps, had tilted and the contents spilled over the floor. As she bent to scrape at the mess with her hands she stumbled and lurched against the door sending it crashing open. Sliding to the floor, she sat where she came to rest, propping herself up with one hand and wiping her brow with the back of the other which still held the dripping plate. Tod knelt beside her. "Come on, aunt. Come on...let me help. There's a seat, here by the hearth."

Charlotte grunted noisily and half rose then staggered again, this time against the boy. "Sorry, dear...I'm sorry for the mess." Tod knew that the meaningless ranting and guffawing he had heard earlier had now passed. Next would come the remorse, the mumbled apologies and, finally, the weeping. He had seen it in the mill cottages at Tiverton when he accompanied the school chaplain and the rector of St Peter's. At first the squalor and human filth sickened him. He had often turned away hurriedly to throw up at the stench or at the muck that had coated his hands, as they tried to clean the hovels of those who had taken to drink and who had lost themselves.

Now it was here in his own family. It grieved him to see how his father worried so much for his sister. Sometimes he could feel the anger boiling inside him as he struggled with the dirty, useless woman who had thrown away her life, but then he remembered her past. His father had told him enough about her earlier days in Tiverton. There had been the beatings and then Davey had gone off to the wars never to return. He had been just nine when his cousin left home. The memories were fading but he remembered plainly his aunt's agonies when the news came through. Bamber Heard had been her saviour but he, too, had gone. Lottie was left with nothing and now, whenever anger and revulsion rose in him, his sense of shame forced them back. That he could even think like this, chastened him.

"I'll make some broth. Would you like that? Eh?" He knelt beside the figure in the chair. At first, she had slumped forward and tilted to one side. Her mouth had lolled open and she had begun to dribble. Now she was holding her head and he could hear her moans. "Come, aunt, don't weep." His arm went around her shoulder. There was no one else to see, nonetheless he tried to mask his grimace at the rancid smell of stale sweat. Her neck, fat and unwashed, was damp with cold perspiration and her hair, now grey and cropped shorter still, reeked of wood smoke. Her body, where she had not been able to help herself, stank the worst of all. "Come, come, aunt. We'll be all right. I'll make something up for you and you can sit while I tidy a bit. There's no hurry and nothing to fear. I'll not leave you…don't worry now."

"Thank'e, dear. Thank'e truly." The hand that reached out for his was rough and grimy and wet with tears. Tod held it and shook it gently to re-assure her. "Don't know why I get's like this…dunno." She shook her head and sniffed but her nose was running and she tried to wipe it. Tod closed his eyes in a moment of prayer. "I'm sorry," she moaned dribbling again. "Sorry…real sorry." She held her nose, turned and blew then began to weep unashamedly in deep, baying sobs like some huge overgrown child." Tod remained on his knees cradling her head in is arms until she quietened.

He stayed until it was dark. The meal he cooked was not much and he tidied what he could, reminding himself to chop more firewood tomorrow as he would need extra hot water. He would bring some rags from the farm and a broom and Kitty's scullery mop. Somehow he would see his aunt through, but he would be going in a month and then what. He would speak to his father and see if they might find somebody to help. She couldn't be left like this. As he walked back to the farm he worried over the problem for he could see no way ahead. That night he prayed deeply.

✳

Kitty stood in the open front doorway. The August sun bore down heavily. Everything and everyone, it seemed, had hidden themselves away from the burning midday heat. She lifted a hand to shield her eyes and looked across the valley towards Sandyway. The heat, rising from the parched meadows, shimmered and danced, blurring the view even when she squinted to see through the haze.

Somewhere, down by the pond, she could hear crickets. A yellow hammer trilled its plaintive song as if to tell the world that somebody, at least, was pleased to be alive, but that was all.

She took the sharpest of her kitchen knives and some string and walked across to the well. The flagstones in the house had cooled her bare feet but here, in the sun, the stones were hot to the touch and she hopped and skipped her way across the yard. For the last two days the support to the windlass had become loose, moving alarmingly as she turned the handle to lift the heavy buckets of water. She suspected it was something for the men to see to but, first, she was determined to try to rectify it herself. Nobody else was about. Tod had gone to Withypool and would be seeing Lottie on his way back. Jack, Stan and Frank were digging stones from the streambed to repair gaps in the hedges on sixty acres where the sheep had broken through, and the girls would be at least another hour until they were home from school.

First she lowered the bucket until she felt it float on the water. The handle and windlass with the rope coiled round were secure enough but one of the metal supports, where it was fixed to the side of the well, had worked loose. Even as she tested it with her hand a trickle of loose stones fell into the well, hitting the water with a deep, echoing splosh. She would have to tell Jack but decided to look further. Leaning over as far as she dared, she shielded her eyes and began examining the stonework. Satisfied there was nothing amiss, she moved around the wall and leant forward again, and then a third time. It was then, just before she levered herself back, that she saw the loose stone.

Stretching down, she took hold of it with both hands. For some reason she pulled at it rather than pushing it back and it came away easily. It had never been fixed with mortar and behind it there was a hollow space. She reached down and pulled out a second stone, widening the gap as she did so. Now curious, she leant further forward and felt around the space until her fingers made contact. She cried out in alarm and pulled back hurriedly, thinking it must have been some animal. Then, cautiously, she reached in again and took hold of the cloth before pulling it carefully. It came effortlessly and seemed to contain something. As soon as she had moved it to the lip of the gap, she used both hands. It was the bottom of an old flour sack that had been cut in half and there was definitely something inside.

She inched her way back from the edge of the well, clutching the sacking by its neck so whatever it was could not spill out. Once safe, she stood unsteadily then turned and sat on the low wall surrounding the well. Looking down, with her long, auburn locks half covering her face, she reached into the sack. There was a second piece of sacking inside which had been wrapped carefully and tied. She cut the string and lifted out a leather bag with a drawstring, smaller than a penny loaf, then untied the cord at the neck and looked inside. One hand flew to her mouth and she froze as a thrill of excitement coursed through her.

*

"Dear God alive." Jack shook his head then buried his face in his hands before looking once more at the table in front of him. When Kitty had told him earlier about the find he found it difficult to believe and it was only her insistence that they would have to wait until they were alone that convinced him. Katherine's jewels, her share of the fabulous Northborough collection, had lain hidden all these years. He had seen them only once before, at their wedding in Molland when she had dressed herself so beautifully. He had no idea what had become of them after that, suspecting that they had perhaps been returned to the family. But they had not. She had brought them here, hidden them away and taken the secret of their location to her grave. It was just chance, pure chance that Kitty had come across them.

Kitty's hands were at her mouth. Only her eyes moved. "What are they," she whispered eventually. "What's this, look…a crown or summat?" Even in the dull glow of the lamp, the diamonds and saphires glittered and flashed as she turned the tiara in her hand. "And here, look…a bracelet, and another…and that's gold isn't it? An' look at this necklace. What's us to do, Jack? Whatever's us to do with this lot?"

He took his time, picking up and fingering each piece in turn. Gradually, and with his mind racing, he nodded to himself. "Nothing," he muttered finally. "We'll hide them away where you found them and think about it quietly, just you and me, Kitty. We won't go rushing about anywhere or tellin' anyone. Just ponder on it all for a while."

"But there's a fortune here…a real, real fortune. An' to think they was all tucked away by Katherine. Aah, dear. Poor dear, loverly Katherine. She'd put them away fer the chillern, bless 'er…gave 'em all up fer them, so she did." She looked at Jack. His face was impassive, devoid of expression and he was staring at the gleaming, tangled pile of gems and precious metals, each one coiled around the next as if holding on to one another, terrified of being separated. Suddenly she was uneasy: it was the same nagging doubt returning again. For a while they remained silent then, slowly, her hand reached out for his.

"'Tis 'er, isn't it, Jack. 'Tis Katherine…'er's still here or 'ereabouts. This lot 'ere have brought it all back again." She watched him purse his lips. It was like watching a child about to cry and she put her arm around his shoulder. "'Tis all right, my love. I knows how you feel. I understand." She stood and moved behind him, then put her arms around his shoulders before bending down and pressing her face against his rough cheek. "Try not to be sad, dear. 'Spect it would have been her wish for these to come back to yer one day. Can't see Katherine not wantin' you to have hold of them."

"No, Kitty." His eyes remained on the jewels. "No, I'm not sad. It's funny really, strange and weird but I don't feel sad. Not at all. I can see Katherine here all right but I can see the happiness in her face. It's as though she's bin wanting to hand them on to us, you know, just like you said. It's as if she's saying 'right, here you are, they're yours and the children's." He turned to look up at her. "That's it Kitty.

'Twas fate that you were fixing the well today and fate showed you where they were. Can't be anything else." He paused and returned to the jewels.

"She loved you dearly, she did," he continued. "'Twas terrible that at the end she had to believe what she did about us but I know she thought the very world of you. You're in her place now...now 'tis you that's looking after us. This here, these jewels are Katherine's way of giving us her blessing. It's her way of telling us that...that we're right for each other." He looked up at her and nodded encouragingly. "Honest, my love, that's as I see it. There's some things in life us can never understand. See here." He reached out and picked up the ruby and pearl necklace, carefully lifting other jewels away from it. "That's yours. If Katherine ever really knew, that's what she would have wanted."

"*Jack.*"

"No, I mean it, my love. Katherine was ever so fond of yer. I know she was and none of us can ever take that away. If she were here now she'd be smiling down and sayin 'Yes, Kitty, that's right. That's for you, for all you've done'."

"No, Jack, no. I *can't*. I could never...'tis not right. I *couldn't*."

"Listen you." Jack turned and pulled her round to face him. "If I told yer that that's what I want more than anything else, then what would yer say? Eh? No, Jack, they're not for me. Is that what you'd be telling me? Eh?"

"I can't, Jack. They're yours and the chillern's. You can't go giving them away like that. Not to me, anyways. Honest."

"Shhh. Enough of that. They're mine as you say, an' I can do what I like with them. I want yer to have this an' I know that she would, too. You've bin wonderful to me...I know I'm a bit slow an' that an' there's been lots to think about just now but it doesn't mean I take yer for granted. I don't, you know." He paused, silent for a moment. "I couldn't do without yer, Kitty and this...this here...well, it's just to show what I think. P'raps now's the time...time fer us to be as one."

"Oh, Jack." Kitty picked up the necklace then looked at him. She held his gaze while, slowly, a hand went to his cheek. "Jack," she whispered. "Jack, I do love you...reely, I do." She buried her face in his neck. "Honest I do," she murmured, her voice barely audible. "You won't never leave me, will yer? Her arms tightened around him. "I'd die if yer did. Honest, I think I'd die."

He swallowed and blinked. "No, my love. I'll never be leavin' yer...not now, no matter what." He rose carefully and took her into his arms.

Chapter Seven

It was Tod who realised it first, but not until sometime after his father's marriage. In fact it was he who encouraged Kitty and his father to have a church blessing. The ceremony took place quietly in Withypool where The Reverend William Thornton took the service and asked Tod, now in his second year at St Anselm's, to assist him.

Jack insisted that Charlotte should be there and arranged for Frank and Wally Heard, one of Bamber's sons, to look after her, remarking later how muted and well behaved she was throughout. Victoria had offered to help Kitty prepare for the day and it was only when Anna asked if she could also help did Tod notice how his sister, now twelve, had begun to warm towards their step-mother. It was the little things that told, such as how her eyes now dwelled affectionately upon her rather than looking away when they were speaking, how she smiled more in her company and how she seemed happy enough to be on her own with her.

Kitty noticed it too. She and Tod talked about it but decided to say nothing until they were sure. The girl, still timid and as wild as a wind-blown leaf, seemed happier around the house, more so than down at the cottage with Charlotte. She even asked Kitty to show her how to make Granny's pudding and Crotchy pie where Kitty used meat off the bones to mix with vegetables and apples, leaving Anna to knead the flour and dripping. She loved it and the others watched in amusement as the two of them, both covered in flour, laughed happily as they worked together. Then at last, after her bath in a tub by the fire, she allowed Kitty to do her hair and sat prattling away gaily while her step-mother brought a semblance of order to the mop of unruly golden curls.

✳

"Don't say nort, dear. Just watch and yer'll see what I mean." Kitty was sitting on the stone mounting block just where the stable wall joined the shearing barn. She and Jack had been working together securing the walls of the poultry house where a fox, or it might have been a badger, had attempted to gnaw and scratch its way to the hens. It was a dull day with a gusty, unsettled wind that blew corkscrews of dust into the air forcing everyone to shield their eyes. "Tod see'd it first and 'twas only when I'd settled her up in my old room that I saw what 'e meant. The maid's settlin'…seems calmer now an' happier than I've known."

"Not before time. Cuh…when you think what you've done for the girl." Jack turned from the wind and blinked at something in his eye. "D'you reckon she's sensed something about Lottie then? I mean it'd be a mite strange if she hadn't." Kitty shrugged. A week earlier Dr Collyns had ridden out to see Charlotte as the family had asked. When he finished, he rode on to the farm with the news.

Jack knew in his heart what the doctor would say but was stunned by his verdict nonetheless. For several months he had watched anxiously as his sister's health deteriorated. Her drunken bouts had become worse and ever more frequent, but several times recently he had noticed a more sinister trait. They had tried to find the source of the drink but failed. Twice Jack and one of the boys had hidden themselves by the cottage but saw nothing. Tinkers and gypsies passed occasionally and they could not prevent her from going down to the village. The possibilities were endless and they could hardly confiscate Wilmot's allowance.

Sometimes she remained broodingly silent but on a number of occasions, she became quarrelsome and threatening. Twice it had turned to violence when he had been shocked at her strength and her ferocity when she fought like a man, and a strong man at that. There had been no sign of drink then. It had been her mind and the doctor only confirmed his fears.

She had, Dr Collyns explained, now succumbed to drink to the extent that her mind had been affected. Damage had been done, brought on, no doubt, by the hard, sad life that had been her lot. She was not going to mend, he advised, in fact the condition was likely to worsen and, furthermore, the mental disorder was likely to bring about more abnormal or increasingly violent behaviour such as they had seen. It was over two years ago, he reminded them, that Jack had come to him about his sister. It would be his recommendation that she should be committed. They talked and, reluctantly, had agreed.

"Dunno." Kitty shrugged again and stood, brushing the dust from her dress. "She's not right, Jack. Even when there bain't no drink about 'tis easy to see 'er's crazy-mazed. The way 'er looks at you and all this nicherin' and cacklin'…tain't right. An' if Anna's seen summat or summat's told 'er to stay back then I'm glad fer the girl's sake." Kitty felt her heart beating faster. The mere thought of the heavy, brooding woman frightened her. "An' there's another thing, Jack. Summat else…."

"Aye, go on. Daresay I know what's on yer mind."

"She's so strong, Jack…an' big. I'm afeared of her. Y'know that? I know she's yer sister an' that but I can't help meself…she scare's me."

"Aye…Victoria, too. And Frank's wary of her now." Jack pulled on his chin. "Can't be sayin' what changed little Anna though. She used to love'r, she did. Always playin' around down there and helpin' an' that. *Summat's* changed the maid. Perhaps she can sense her place is up here with us…p'raps the others have said summat, or Tod even. But then, maybe 'tis you m'dear." He caught her eye and smiled tenderly. "P'raps the maid feels more at home with you. Eh?"

Kitty pulled a sad face. "Aye," she mused quietly then turned, hitched her skirts and placed a boot onto the block where she re-tied the lace. "Aye, but what's to do wi' Lottie, then? 'Tis…well, 'tis scary havin' 'er down there. I'm afeared for the chillern. Bain't right havin' 'er so close."

"Next week," Jack sighed. He had hated agreeing to his sister being taken away but there was nothing to be done. He had heard about the asylums and wracked his brains to find a way out but had come up with nothing. Poor, dear Lottie would have to go but it hurt, and hurt deeply. "Doctor's found a place in Dulverton. Said to keep her here until then and they'll come for her. Can't abide the thought really…them takin' her away in a cart like that."

"Will she *go*? I mean, when she know's summat's up, she'll not want to, will she? She'll struggle an' holla an' that and…oh, my dear soul." Kitty shook her head and took his hand. She could see the look on his face. "'Tis awful, Jack…poor soul."

"There's no other way," he muttered. "We've tried everything, everything we can. I told them I'd go with 'er, to help them along but it's not goin' to be a happy day. Aye, love." He stood beside her and put a hand on her shoulder. "The quicker 'tis over the better an' that goes for the young as well. Best leave thing's be as they are right now but if Anna's up here with us then that's all for the good."

✳

The dogs began barking some time after midnight. It wasn't their usual bark for warning off a prowling fox or even the louder one they reserved for trespassers. It was a savage, desperate Babel of noise and Kitty, by now wide awake, lay listening, puzzled at the anger in it all.

Then she heard it. At first she thought it was another dog somewhere. But it was not; it came from further away, across the water meadows and it didn't sound right. The chill, long howl floated thinly across the night air. As soon as they heard it the dogs started again. She shook Jack. He woke and they lay listening together. Then it came again, rising slowly out of the valley, a long, eerie wail that hung mournfully before fading. A sound to ice the blood. Jack tensed and caught his breath. Kitty froze: she could feel her scalp tingling. "What is it," she hissed, panic in her voice. "'Tis strange, Jack. Creepy…and I'm reel flaysome." As Jack threw back the bedclothes she half sat. "Here, let me come with you."

"No." He had to force himself to stay calm; if she knew she would be terrified. "Best go an' check, that's all…else they dogs'll wake the dead. I won't be long…reckon I know what 'tis." His mind was racing. He knew, or at least he had a good idea and, as he dressed, Luke Harper's words came back to him. The old smuggler had repeated them time and again when he had taught him to fight. *'You'll always need yer boots, lad. Can't do nort without summat proper on yer feet…an' always take summat to look after yerself with…once yer there, face to face, then's too late.'* A gun would be no good, he thought as he descended the stairs, nor a knife either for they were too final. It would have to be a stout stick, or a club like the one he kept by the fire irons at the back of the hearth.

For a moment, he stood in the front doorway testing the night air. The wind sighed gently up the valley, barely ruffling his hair. The copse, for that is where he was sure the noise came from, was downwind. He would have to circle around, using the high ground, and come up with the wind in his face. But it was the moon that worried him. Not quite full, it was still high in the clear eastern sky, lighting up everything until it was almost bright enough to read. He would be forced to use cover. Then he heard it again. The howl rose eerily to a pitch then stopped momentarily before descending slowly, the last of it lost to him as the dogs threw themselves against the dog shed walls.

It took him longer than he expected for he had to keep to the hedgerow ditches. The last bit, from the edge of the fir plantation, was the slowest of all but he crawled through the gap by the gate and crouched at the side of the lane. The beech copse was on the far side, just in front of him. By now he was sweating and breathing heavily. His mouth was dry. He paused on one knee and listened again with his ear turned to the ground. It was not until his breathing had calmed and his sweat cooled that he heard it.

At first he thought it was the steady, harsh 'chuuk...chuuk' of an angry cock pheasant that had been disturbed, but then it changed. It was coming closer and he could hear the soft chuckling in between. Then it stopped. Silence. He crouched, this time on all fours in order to see better. He could feel his heart beating and he moistened his lips. But there was nothing - neither sound nor movement. He rose cautiously and moved, one step at a time, his body now tense and ready. He paused again to listen, then moved on once more.

Suddenly the crash. He spun round, club raised and ready to fight. Whatever it was had been stalking him and had burst through the hedge. The figure was coming for him. What forced him to strike out were the guttural snarls. But he was too late: he knew it at once for he had struck too high and the figure was on him.

The face that was trying to reach his was distorted by a wild fury, the eyebrows were puckered into a scowl but it was the mouth, wide open like that of a snarling dog and with the lips drawn back that made him duck. The body when he grappled with it was hard and muscular, the feet kicked out and they fell heavily, locked together until he forced it away. The creature was on its feet in front of him and he watched as it turned and looked down at him.

It was then, against the moon, that he saw her. As fast as the savagery had risen, it had gone. It had vanished in an instant and he saw the outline of her face. It was Charlotte, his sister, just as he knew her. She half opened her mouth in a silent sneer but before he could call out or get to his feet she had gone. Running heavily and with her body swinging clumsily she disappeared down the track to the cottage.

Jack pulled himself up and leant heavily against the bank. Once more he was sweating and, this time, his lungs were fighting for breath. The terrible, mad strength had momentarily beaten him. Tomorrow, he told himself. Tomorrow and not a day later, he would ride to Dulverton and tell the doctor to come for her. He would go with them to see her away but she would have to go and, once gone, she could never return. Until then, he would have to keep this dreadful business to himself.

*

Early afternoon at Sherdon was always quiet. Today was quieter still. Jack was in Dulverton and the children had yet to return from school. Those out in the fields still had several hours labouring ahead of them so Kitty, as had become routine, used the peace as best she could either in the house or the kitchen garden. Sometimes, and when the weather allowed her, she tidied the rose bed under the parlour window and the border of herbs outside the kitchen. Then, if there were enough of them, she would pick a posy of flowers and leaves from the hedgerow to arrange in the jug on the kitchen table.

Charlotte, too, knew the Sherdon routine. The knife she took with her was the small, sharp paring knife she kept by the slop bucket in the scullery. She set out walking quite brazenly up the farm track. She even sung to herself in her sad, tuneless way. When she reached the point where the beech copse and fir plantation met she stopped and searched the hedgerow. Suddenly she dropped into a crouch and sniffed, casting about urgently like a dog, where the grass had been flattened the night before. Then, and just as suddenly, she rose and set off again. As soon as the farm came into sight, she turned down into the valley and ran crouching towards the thick cover by the stream.

Humming quietly, Kitty took the wicker trug and paused to lift open the narrow gate at the end of the kitchen garden before stepping onto the lane. She was happy and had good cause to be for Anna had started her painting again. Having lifted the gate back into place, she paused. Above her a thrush was singing and she looked up to catch sight of the bird, raising her arm to shield her eyes.

Charlotte circled the house warily then stood motionless watching the back door. Twice she stooped low to see better then rose again, her body alive and ready like an alert animal. The two women were now less than fifty yards apart yet only one knew it. Once satisfied, Charlotte made her move. For one so heavy, she made her way easily, slipping inside the house and bounding silently up the stairs as if bent on some mission. Having reached the landing, she paused again, uncertain at what to do next; yet all the while listening and looking.

Kitty reached up to cut some sprigs of rowan then crossed the lane to find the last of the honeysuckle she had seen the other day. She took what she could, checked her basket then turned back towards the house. Stan Bawden saw her. He waved and called out but she walked on. He called again, louder. This time she stopped, saw him and smiled before lowering her basket and waiting for him to catch up with her.

Charlotte knew exactly where she was: it was her brother's and Kitty's room. She pushed open the door and took in the scene before tiptoeing inside. Everything she touched, she picked up and sniffed before placing it back exactly as it was. Some things she sniffed and licked, others she shook and squeezed, checking herself only momentarily before moving on, circling the room in her mad, crazed way yet her eyes and nose missed nothing.

Twice she got down on all fours, once she climbed on a chair to see better. She took a thimble of Kitty's and a comb belonging to Jack. She picked up the Bible by the bed, opened it at the marker and studied the page. She sniffed the candle and flint, fingered Kitty's mob cap, then shook the lamp to check the oil in the bowl. And it was when she was lifting Kitty's clothes one at a time from the chest of drawers with the blade of her knife that the leather bag fell from the blouse in which it had been hidden. Slowly, gently, she picked it up. After untying the string at the neck she took out the necklace and examined it by holding it up to the light. She tasted the pearls carefully like a horse mouths the bit, and then the rubies before going to the mirror with it dangling from her mouth. Then she placed it in her apron pocket with the little leather bag and the thimble and comb.

It took her no time at all to find the box of dried peas in the scullery. She scooped out a handful and ran to the back door where she mixed them with a handful of loose pebbles. With the peas and stones inside twisted tight and folded carefully, the blouse looked just the same. It felt the same also and, as she tossed it lightly in the palm of her hand, she knew it weighed the same. Carefully, and remembering how each item of clothing had lain, she replaced the clothes, smoothing them down with the blade of her knife.

Kitty hurried back to the house. Stan had kept her and now the children would be home from school. As she placed the basket of flowers on the table a sudden gust of wind billowed the curtains, knocking Anna's box of pastels to the floor. The back door slammed. Frowning, for she was sure she had shut it earlier, Kitty went through the scullery to secure it. As she did so, the figure behind the hedge that had paused to check dropped down and out of sight.

✳

The two girls and Frank asked if they should go and see Charlotte the night before she was taken away but Jack forbade it. "Leave her be," he ordered. "Disturb her now and there'll be trouble. I'll be down there in the morning before she goes. Bamber's boys'll be there to sort her things that belong to Brightworthy Farm…Bamber's bits an' pieces and that. It's best not to go near."

Stan Bawden heard the two ponies first. The girls had ridden off to school but got no further than the cottage. As they drew close they could see the door was open and that the fire was smoking badly. Victoria pulled up and the two of them called out. Their aunt always called back in reply but this morning there was no sign of life. Rather than dismounting, they rode up to the door. She was lying inside the open door with an arm outstretched. Around her head there was blood. The table had been pulled over. A chair had been broken and drawers from the dresser pulled out. The contents were everywhere. The girls remembered nothing more for they turned and fled, urging their ponies on as they galloped back up the lane.

Jack took Victoria's pony from her. The girls were jabbering hysterically. As he left the yard he shouted for Stan to follow and to bring Ralph, then rode hard for the cottage where he found his sister exactly as they said. Whoever it was had beaten her down then ransacked the place. It was mayhem but he went straight to his sister and knelt by her side. She was alive but the club marks around her head were already turning blue and she was bleeding from the ears. Her breathing was weak and her blotchy skin had turned grey. As he lifted her head, it flopped to one side and her mouth fell open.

It was not until he turned her gently that he saw her other arm. The leather bag was tied to her wrist. The cord had bitten into her flesh and he could see the bag had been cut. There had been a struggle for it: perhaps they had beaten her down first then slit the bag to get at whatever was inside. Whatever there was had gone. He picked it up to examine it more closely and his eyes narrowed. It was made of dark leather and it was quite small. He had seen it before, a while ago now and he remembered at once. It was, as Kitty said, a little smaller than a penny bun.

2

The rain had stopped. Sarah walked slowly across the park. She was wearing her purple cloth overcoat with shoulder capes and her white satin bonnet decorated with matching ribbons and dark blue plumes. Edwin had run on ahead to watch the acrobats but Jocasta held on to her hand. The girl, still small for her eight years, gripped tightly as she skipped by her side. She was dressed in her favourite pale grey, layered dress striped in deep pink with a large black bow at the back. "What's a soothsayer, Miss Kingdon?"

"Somebody who tells you what's going to happen to you by looking at the palm of your hand."

"What d'you mean?" she queried, looking down at her own hand. "Can I come in, too? Mine's different from yours, I expect."

"No, you'll have to wait outside. Only grown ups are allowed in."

"Why's that?"

"Because their hands have stopped growing and the soothsayers can see what's going to happen. Look." She bent down. "You see, yours're too young and they wouldn't be able to see anything."

The Orchards were hosting the Hartland Christmas Fair and already the park was filling with tents and stallholders getting themselves ready for the occasion. The ox was going to be roasted where the stone bridge crossed the stream over by the wood and they watched as two cooks, dressed in their aprons and hats, set up the spit. Men dressed as knights and their squires were going to parade with heralds and troubadours. There was going to be mock jousting and a falconry display. Tumblers and jugglers were practising already and, later that day, the circus was due to arrive. Everywhere there was bustle and the children begged her to take them to have a look.

It was Jocelyn Orchard who had told her about Madam Tissini. She came every year and always began by telling whoever it was about their past. Somewhat unnerving, Mrs Orchard explained, especially as she seemed to know so much. At first Sarah had laughed but the idea intrigued her. In fact, now, she too was nervous; nervous of what might be revealed about her past but anxious also to hear what might be foretold. The butler had alerted them to Madam Tissini's arrival and they watched as one of the gardeners helped with her blue and red striped tent. Edwin had seen the first customer go inside and they all waited until he emerged. He seemed to be happy enough but it had taken ages and now it was her turn.

"Just tell me if I'm wrong, my dear." Madam Tissini had Sarah's palm in her hand. The governess, now not quite so sure of herself, caught her breath. Her past life had been uncovered, literally. Her home, Filleigh, Mary, her mother, school, everything, even Danny Heslop, her first boyfriend. Madam Tissini had got the last bit wrong, but only just. He was a year younger than she said and had dark hair but that was all.

"No, go on," Sarah whispered, stretching out her other hand to warm herself on the small coke brazier beside them.

"Now, let me see, let me see." Madam Tissini, her round, over-rouged face frowning in concentration, pulled Sarah's hand towards her. There were no gypsy earrings nor any coloured bandanna around her head, simply a homely face with the grey hair tied neatly in a bun. She was a jolly person with a friendly smile, unlike some Sarah had heard about. "Wealth will come…but be patient, my dear. It will be hard at first. Two children, three perhaps and a boy first. Now then." She peered more closely, lifting her hand towards the lamp. "There's something here…but I can't be sure."

"*Can't* be sure or you won't tell me?" Sarah laughed hesitantly and leant forward to study her hand where Madam Tissini was rubbing it gently.

"No, no…no, no. It's just that there's *some*thing here. Fire…a beautiful, glowing fire and then something from the deep. You'll be safe enough, I can see that but there's somebody else…someone close to you and I sense danger…a strong wind and troubled waters. Not your children, but a man…a brother, but you don't have one…a cousin, perhaps or your own…your husband or your lover, even." She caught her eye and smiled mischievously. "There's danger but I cannot see anything more. But for you," Madam Tissini sat back. "Walk carefully, my child. Pick your way carefully through life and you will walk tall."

＊

Sarah stifled a yawn: it was late and she decided to excuse herself. As soon as she entered her bedroom she saw the note. One of the parlour maids must have left it on her bed. It was sealed but not with the Orchard crest and it had not been scented. She walked across to the lamp she had placed on her dressing table where she broke the seal. Her mouth opened then her eyes shut before opening again and staring in surprise. She clasped the paper to her chest before reading it again and sitting weakly on her bed. So she had been right. Sharland Preston had indeed been as eager to see her as she had perceived he would be.

Hartland Abbey
Monday 15th December
Dear Sarah,
It is with great sadness that I learn of your departure for South Molton the day after tomorrow. Try as I might, I have been unable to arrange for us to meet alone. The weather, the very devil itself, has played its knavish tricks thus preventing a rendezvous outside. Furthermore, and exactly as you explained, to see each other alone inside the Abbey is not possible. You remain so elusive.
But I have to see you and I entreat you to consider us meeting tomorrow night, after the charades and musical games. There is much I wish to say but now is not the time. Do not deny me your company, I beseech you. It will be my privilege to be with you, believe me, if only you will sanction our rendezvous. I sign this bon mot in anticipation and remain yours most affectionately.

Sharland Preston

＊

So, Gloria Newcomb had been right. The Smythe family had been invited to stay for the fair 'en masse' as Jocelyn Orchard put it. Eliza Smythe's son and daughter-in-law, had brought their three children and their governess, the last mentioned being Gloria, a petite, jolly and bright-eyed young woman from Guildford. Somehow she always seemed to be smiling. Her eyes, the darkest of brown, twinkled merrily at the world from underneath a mass of prettily curled black ringlets. She was a flirt, so Sarah had immediately convinced herself, but she would be fun and she took to her immediately. She, too, had been to see Madam Tissini and, even then, came away bubbling with laughter and holding her hand aloft as if in triumph, declaring it was nothing but a lot of tomfoolery.

It had been Gloria, two days before, who had warned her that Sharland Preston was anxious to see her. Henslowe Debroan had told her so when the two sat out the last of the quadrilles the night before last. But it had been Sharland's father, the Duke himself, who had taken Sarah's hand when they had been paired together for the lancers and then the slower, gentler gaillard. There were those who thought it no more than a chivalrous gesture, but he only released her to his son when he was too out of breath to continue. 'Too damned cooked', he had chortled, as he brought her hands to his lips before waving her away. Only then had Sharland asked her to meet him, but it did not seem possible for the Abbey was full. Every room was occupied; children were running everywhere and the staff quarters had been packed to capacity with the visitors' own house servants. "Can you not come and see me?" he had pleaded.

"But how…and when? I can hardly come to your rooms during the day time and if you are suggesting after dark…I…it's not possible. I mean, whatever would anybody think if I, the governess, was seen promenading up and down the main corridors? And to be caught sneaking about would be immeasurably worse…and, in any case, it would be singularly undignified. And then, good sir," she shrugged as if she really did not know the answer. "And then, pray tell me how you would expect to find me attired for such an adventure…would you see me dressed as for the evening or for the following morning perhaps?" His look made her smile then they both laughed out loud together. "I doubt that my mistress would be much impressed by such behaviour."

"But I *have* to see you. I must." He had turned himself away from those around him so as not to be overheard. "Look, might I, in that case…d'you suppose…why don't I call on *you*?" Sarah held his gaze but her pulse quickened. For a moment her face was expressionless then she raised an eyebrow and inclined her head in mock surprise. Such a reaction puzzled him: either his suggestion had been dismissed or else it was receiving due consideration. He could not tell

"*And?*" She glanced at him out of the corner of her eye.

"Just to see you…simply to talk and, well, to be alone with you."

"I shall be leaving for home in a few days from now, sir. Really, time is against such an assignation." By now she had recovered her composure. If he wanted to see her then she would force his hand. Sharland escorted her through to the drawing room where they sat on the ornate chaise longue.

His features had matured since she had seen him last and she wondered if the light brown stubble just appearing on his chin at this late hour would be rough to the touch. How, she wondered, might it feel against her own skin? He had a tiny fleck of cigar tobacco at the corner of his mouth and she had a sudden desire to moisten her finger and wipe it away. It irritated her but she didn't know why. He was far from unhandsome and the fact that he still maintained such a close interest in her she found both intriguing and exciting. She warmed to his advances, her mind dwelling eagerly, then lingering shamelessly, on every possibility that came to her. "But I *have* to say," her eyebrow was raised again. "However one might wish to regard such a request, it cannot be construed as anything other than a *most* improper suggestion. Really, sir, I am quite taken by surprise." She was not.

"But allow me nonetheless, I beg of you. Do not suppose for one moment that I would impose myself. I would never, under any circumstances, seek to take advantage…I consider our association far too precious and, in any case, I desire to keep it that way."

"Sir, you flatter me more than words describe but, in answer to your request, I cannot say. I simply do not…" Henslowe Debroan was at her elbow. He bowed and offered his hand. "Thank you, kind sir. Yes, most certainly. Pray forgive me, Lord Preston." She stood, curtsied and was away: never having had time to tell him more. She knew exactly how she *should* have replied and what would have been expected of her, but that was far from the answer she wished him to hear. So, fie on you Mr Henslowe Debroan; you swept me away from my words.

Later, and with the lamp turned down, she lay awake considering what might have been. He was a calculating, cynical man, of that there was no doubt. She had observed him dealing with others and there was a hint of arrogance in his manner, many had been dismissed from his presence as soon as he tired of their company. But, there was more to him. There was a steely virility about the man, an element of flintiness that thrilled. He had not demonstrated this in front of her but she could sense it was there, lurking ready to be drawn like a knife. He exuded power and she felt her body warming to the thought; of giving and taking from him, of writhing and coupling. A sensuousness swept through her body, warm and tingling; a desire for the man she had so nearly had won. But then had come his note.

✴

Sarah sat at her bow-fronted dressing table. Even though she and Gloria had been among the first to retire, it was later than she expected. As she attended to her hair, she kept glancing at the small kettle, set deftly on the ledge in front of her coal fire, waiting patiently for it to boil so she could wash her face. The kaolin and rouge had been removed but it was the kohl around her eyes and the grease she had yet to deal with that irritated her. She had taken off her evening clothes and had just her red housecoat over her white cotton nightgown.

Five minutes and it was done. She took the lamp to her bedside and turned the wick down low. Then, having removed her housecoat and nightgown, she slid naked between the sheets, still warm from the stone hot-water bottle the maid had placed there after dinner. Gradually the house settled. Occasionally a door shut loudly: once she thought she heard raised voices. Something somewhere fell heavily but there was little else.

Twice the floor of the landing creaked and it was only when she had convinced herself he was not coming that the door opened. She knew it would be done quietly for she had left it ajar, nevertheless his stealth surprised her. He was dressed in a midnight blue velvet robe and held a finger to his lips as he turned to close the door. "You surprise me," she jested, moving enough in the bed for him to sense the invitation for him to join her.

"And for why?" he whispered conspiratorially. "I suspect you considered my entreaties all patter and bluff. Is that not so?" As he sat, so his housecoat opened: underneath he too was naked. "Did you doubt my word?"

"Your word, no. But your resolve…I cannot say, rather I could not be certain. But you are here and it is now for me to imagine how you would suppose I should behave at such an intrusion." She took hold of his hand. "Should I cry out, perhaps? Feign horror over some damnable fate? What would you wish?"

He bent forward to kiss her. "What's that…what are you wearing? That perfume?"

"Eau de jasmine, from the Cote d'Azure. My uncle…mmm," she murmured, lifting and turning her head slowly as his lips caressed her throat. "But be patient, my good sir. Remember how I upbraided you once before."

"Come, I'm cold." He rose and let his housecoat fall. She could see him clearly in the soft glow of the lamp. His lean, muscular body was ready for her so she wriggled away, making room in the bed for him to ease his way in beside her.

"You are outrageous…how dare you." She tried to sound angry but the words meant little. "Goodness me. What if…."

"Dreadful, I know." She felt his breath on her hair. "I could wait no longer. Sarah…come." He pulled her towards him and their arms closed around one another. She felt his hands reach up her back to catch hold of her hair, then gasped as his tongue flickered slowly down her body. Turning slowly, she rolled onto her back, feeling his mouth moving ever lower to where her breasts were now cupped in his hands. She groaned quietly and arched herself before reaching out and pulling him on top of her. For a moment he raised himself, one elbow either side of her, and looked down. They smiled and she laughed silently as her fingers caressed his face before he lowered himself once more. She felt him, all of him and raised her legs wide to close around his body. For a while she lay supine, allowing his body to take hers but she could no longer hold herself and their moving began in unison. Her hands entwined themselves in his hair and she cried out softly before pulling his head down so that their mouths came together, each one tasting the other. Gradually her body tensed and their movements became ever more urgent until, at last, their lovemaking was done. It was over, suddenly and finally, and they lay together.

He was spent and his body seemingly dead as though it had been driven through. Gently, and as she lay beneath him as though they had been lovers for years, she allowed her fingers to trail up and down his back, now quite still save for the rise and fall of his breathing and the thumping of his heart against hers. When he rose, she kissed him tenderly once more before turning away and curling her body, allowing him to lie behind her, for his arms to envelop her and for his body to wrap itself around her own. Like this they slept.

Later they made love again in the chill hour before dawn but, already, they could hear sounds beneath them as the great house came to life. He rose quietly and looked down at her huddled under the bedclothes but she turned and saw him. They said nothing, there was no need and he left with just a smile and a gently blown kiss to pass between them.

3

It snowed that Christmas and Sarah could not return to the Abbey until well into the New Year. It then snowed again, after which it froze and Hartland, like so many isolated communities, was cut off from the rest of the world.

At first life continued as usual, or as usual as the weather permited. Sarah took the children tobogganing in the park and they skated on the pond behind the sawmills. Wild geese and eider duck came in from the north while flocks of fieldfares and redwings arrived to feed in the meadows under the wood. One of the woodmen, the tall one with the greased pigtail and lazy eye, reported that he had seen deer in the woods when he was carting logs up to the house and Jake Bennett, the shy second keeper, told them that foxes, now close to starving, were tearing live rabbits from the gins.

About mid-January Sarah started to worry. But she did nothing. She felt well enough and her complexion and her hair positively glowed yet a month later she knew for certain and a visit to the wise, owl-like Dr Spears in his surgery at Stoke, confirmed it. Everything, he assured her, was in order. He would like to see her again in two months but, all being well, the baby would be joining them in September. Virgo, he suggested, patting her hand, or perhaps Libra – but around the middle of the month.

✳

She did not go straight home; she needed to think, although the doctor had done little more than tell her what she already knew. For two months now her body had begun the long, mysterious process of preparing another being to come into the world. She had detected the subtle changes and it had hardly been necessary for him to confirm what she suspected. It would take time, but time would move inex-orably on and in another two months, three at the most, her secret would be revealed.

By now the harsh grip of winter had eased. The snow and the long weeks of frost had gone and today was one when nature set out to reassure the world that there was hope. In the hedgerow by the church, just across from the thatched surgery, daffodils and primroses had appeared as if to defy the recent past and were boldly proclaiming the approach of Spring. As she lifted her skirt to step into the road, she paused for a moment to watch a flurry of sparrows squabbling in the grit, their little minds fussing angrily over something or other. And she could hear the rooks claiming forks in the boughs for themselves high in the elms beyond the graveyard.

It was mild, even warm in the midday sun, but the breeze had an edge to it - after all, it was still only late February.

The latch to the door of St Nectan's had to be forced and she used both hands. When it opened it did so with an echoing clatter as if to warn anyone inside of the new arrival. She closed it behind her and, without knowing why, tiptoed her way to the Orchard pews behind the choir stalls. The pew where she usually worshipped was in shade so she moved to where the sunlight had warmed the seat opposite and sat, tucking her coat under her before looking around at the silence. It was still, very still and somehow it seemed right that she should be here just now. It was as if her Creator had asked her to come and talk to Him. And it was only then, as she bowed her head in supplication, that she allowed herself a moment of weakness for, as she began to pray, she felt the tear.

Her first reaction, a month ago, had been fear; fear of the talk and the pointing; the humiliation and the loneliness that would surely come with her news. At Mrs Patterson's they had talked about such things. Several of the girls knew of others who had suffered a similar fate. Men, they assured one another, wriggled and twisted, ducked and lied, when confronted with the situation. They were no help. You were, they said, on your own when even your family would be minded to turn their backs and shut the door. Better to get rid of it rather than face a life of shame and financial ruin was the considered opinion. Very few men ever gave a second glance to a woman who had borne a bastard child. And a bastard child it would be: as cruel a label that could be tied, but a tag that could never be removed. It would be there for life – stamped, emblazoned and burned deeply as if by a branding iron. The mother of any such child would be an outcast, or a skell as they said in Devon.

Never, they convinced each other, would they allow such a fate to burden *them* for the rest of their lives. There was, above the chandler's shop in Barnstaple's Boutport Street, a woman who dealt with such matters and there was another, a doctor's widow in Instow, who would, for a price, see to any young woman so encumbered. Yet, in spite of the mocking and the bravado, she remembered how they had all listened to the stories with far more care than their laughter and tittering suggested. It had been, and still was, a salutary lesson about life; something to be considered carefully and tucked away should fate ever play that particular card.

And so she had been determined – at first – to seek such a solution and had grimly prepared herself to face the ordeal which, so she heard, sometimes went horribly wrong. There would be pain and bleeding, perhaps days of retching and vomiting as the evil concoctions were swallowed, as well as the suffering of damnable indignities as unknown fingers prodded and probed. But then, and as the weeks went by, her mind changed, prompted perhaps by such lurking fears.

Why surrender, she asked herself? Why give up what God Himself had decreed was to be hers? The world was there to be faced and she, Sarah Kingdon, had faced it already. Why should she give up such a priceless gift? A boy, Madam Tissini, had foretold. A boy who would grow up and wax strong, whose eyes would sparkle and laugh, whose voice she would be able to tell from all others and then, one day, he would become a man who would always love her, his own mother. And *her* boy, the child she was carrying, would be one whose life was destined to inherit his father's share of great wealth, of estates and titles, the likes of which the rest of the world could only dream.

No...she would not give up this child, rather she would see it into the world then love and cherish it for as long as there remained breath in her body. And if the world turned its back on them, she would still make her way, just as she had done before. And if the father should reject his child, she would face him and face him again until she received the acknowledgement she knew must be due. Lord Sharland Preston, whether he chose to admit it or not, had sown the Northborough seed. In his moment of desire, he had passed on to her his family coat of arms for her to safeguard and that she would surely do.

And even now, this tiny morsel of life deep inside her womb was preparing itself and growing day by day. It was hers, her very own, nurtured by her blood. It was a gift so wonderful and so precious that she would never, ever cast it out. The boy child was destined to live; it had been predicted and she would see to it. Nothing and nobody would persuade her otherwise. She would not even dwell on the subject: not now, not ever.

She sat up with a start, her body stiff from bending her knee in prayer. She had no idea how long she had remained like that with her eyes closed but she had to get back. Mrs Orchard wanted her to join her for lunch and there were afternoon lessons for the two children.

Jocelyn Orchard would have to be told. It was going to be hard, not because of facing her eye to eye. That alone would be difficult enough but because they had grown close, as close as a mistress and her governess could be. Once she had been told she, Sarah, would hand in her notice. She would leave Hartland Abbey, and leave before the world knew why. There was yet still time, but by Easter, which would be late this year, the women would begin to notice. She had seen for herself how, after four or five months, the hard, boney stays, the rings of crinolines and the tight bodices had to go, replaced by softer, billowy, more comfortable clothes. When that time came, there would be no hiding. So, she would go, and go well beforehand.

As she made her way back to the Abbey, Sarah contemplated her situation. She walked slowly, stopping every now and then to gaze at nothing in particular, or to stand prodding at the path with the tip of her parasol. She would not, she decided, put her mistress in the position where she would be forced to ask her to leave. It would be cruel and the gentle, shy woman who had befriended her would suffer agonies. No, she would tender her resignation as and when she told her, thereby saving the other from making such a hard decision. She would explain her situation, then announce what she intended to do before her mistress had a chance to consider it.

And the father? She suspected that her mistress might have some idea, perhaps a very good idea, but she would not reveal his name. If she were asked then she would allude, perhaps hint, but not disclose. That would be seen as a cry for support. It would be giving away too much and, in any case, she might well need to keep the name to herself. It could only be revealed once and she wanted to retain control over that moment. If she was going to have to fight for the parentage of her child then she would need every advantage at her disposal.

Gradually her pace quickened. There would be the family, of course, and her mother, she knew, would be mortified. All her life she had upheld the virtues, impressing upon her two daughters the values expected of a lady. There would be tears and recriminations but they would be for herself, her mother, more than for her daughter. Her father would stand by her. He had always done so. It was *he* who had defended Mary when her mother had resigned herself to her sister's fate and it was *he* who had spoken in defence of Charlotte, her aunt, when she fell from grace. It would be difficult and painful but she would see them first of all, and soon. After that she would let her mistress know.

As she crossed the lawn, she waved her parasol mischievously in reply to Jocasta's shout, then waited with her arms outstretched as the girl left her mother and ran to her. The child leapt into her arms and the two of them swung around, laughing delightedly. Then they hurried, hand in hand, to where Jocelyn Orchard stood smiling happily.

Chapter Eight

As he rummaged through the frieze drawer, Frederic could not help smiling to himself for the mahogany kneehole had seen better days. One of the draw handles was loose and the top badly scored, but the old desk was a favourite of his father's and he had brought it up from Wolverley. He bent down further then stood and gave up, unable to find what he was after.

He had left the others talking in the drawing room. Wilmot and Tennyson had been arguing at dinner about where his father's boundary wall crossed the River Barle at Ferny Ball. Wilmot and the poet, now better and stronger after his long illness, had known each other since their Cambridge days. Talk had been about his last visit to the Tuckers at Court Hall a year ago when he decided to reshape 'The Idylls.' It had been on their walk upstream from Landacre Bridge, he explained, that he had decided to expand the whole great panorama into a tribute to Prince Albert. It would take him an age and he wanted to come down again where, so he told them, he could escape and feel life as it should be.

William Gladstone made up the party. He, too, had known the Poet Laureate for some time. Indeed he had even publicly criticised 'The Charge' and 'Maud' only to change his opinion later. Frederic had been involved in the nonsense and had helped to calm matters. They were good friends, all of them, and the Chancellor had been particularly keen to see Tennyson and to see him at Portland Place, hence the gathering.

✳

"Can't see how it can go on." Gladstone, deep in his armchair next to the fire, raised his hands and looked round as if appealing for support. He glanced up as his host rejoined them. "It's almost four years now, for Heaven's sake, since they started slaughtering each other. Last year there was Gettysberg and now...now all this in Atlanta. They *can't* go on...the Confederates are having their very life squeezed from them."

"So what to do?" Wilmot was sitting in his usual uneasy fashion with his right leg extended awkwardly. His maroon smoking jacket had fallen open. He looked either worried or angry but was neither; as usual, his mind was racing and he was concentrating, frowning intently. "There's nothing we can do to stop it now, surely?" Gladstone had been explaining that the governments of Europe had become increasingly distressed over how the civil war had broken America apart, a situation exacerbated by the fact that the anti-slavery movement was gathering pace. The Union forces were pressing on remorselessly and trade with the Old World had been badly affected, in particular with the southern states.

"Desperate...quite, quite desperate." Tennyson, his gaunt face a picture of gloom even from behind his thick black beard, shook his head. "If the business really is over...I mean, if the game's up, then it's got to be stopped. All this terrible warfare...." He rose, as tall as ever but now slightly stooped, and swept an arm expansively. "For mercy's sake, Gladstone, cannot we...cannot *you*, Palmerston and the government do anything. *Four long years* and they're *still* at each other like mad things."

"Phwww," Gladstone blew, shaking his head. "If only we could. We've tried everything." He appealed to his audience again. "We really have...even suggested they consider forming an independent confederation but, they won't listen. And as long as Lincoln's got Grant and Sherman winning his battles, why should he?"

"Well, *we* have." Wilmot sat up and eased himself before finishing his brandy. "As the Union's naval blockade has crippled all trade with the Confederate states, we've signed a declaration refusing to export anything out there to the north that could be construed as warlike material. Metals mainly, but worsted cloth, processed food, optics...anything that could fuel the fire. And anyway William, the cotton business has had it, has it not?"

The Chancellor nodded. "Indeed, I'm afraid so, and for that we thank the blockade. Just look at that dreadful mess up in Lancashire...a complete cotton famine. Mill after mill collapsing. The whole wretched place is on its knees and the poor devils are having a hellish time."

"What amazes me is that there're still some shipping lines who're trying to cling on to business that's just not there any longer. It's gone, doesn't exist." Wilmot smiled grimly and pulled a face. "There're several of these companies along the Welsh coast that're really struggling. Two, no *three* in Bristol and some smaller ones down in the west. They just can't see the evidence in front of their eyes. They're blind...or mad."

"More misery, more misery." Tennyson looked at Wilmot's face. It had hardened. *"'Gorgonised me from head to foot, With a stony British stare.'* There you are, Tucker, 'Maud', you remember. That'll be your very epithet."

"Well, I'm not going to run around advising them. It's up to them." Wilmot pushed back his lock of hair. "Shipping's a cut-throat business at the best of times and particularly now, what with the markets ebbing and flowing like this. If people're going to risk their necks stupidly...or in desperation, then that's their business. And if companies are going to become vulnerable as a result then...." He looked at Frederic and shrugged.

Tennyson gave a sudden laugh. "You're the same rapacious brute as ever you were, Tucker." His hoarse, deep voice boomed across the room. "Like a vulture over there, all black and cooped up behind your feathers and ready to swoop on the weaklings. Why you..."

"Order…order." Gladstone, still deep in his chair, tapped the arm. "Gentlemen, listen. I must be away, but…." He struggled to sit up. "Look, I have a missive here. Sent as a messenger by my masters so I was, and told to catch the laureate by his beard. Here look." He half turned and rummaged in his inside pocket. Here," he coughed. "Now gentlemen, your attention." He glanced at the three, then offered the letter to Tennyson. "You're a wanted man, Alfred, and here's the summons. It's the one from the Palace I told you about. From the Queen, herself, no less and it's for the second time of asking. Here, open it, open it up…we, the House, will need your answer 'ere too long."

"She'll not be seeing me, William…no, no. I could not…" He broke the seal and read. "*I am commanded by Her Majesty to inform you that it is her express desire for you to attend…*" The others watched as the poet read in silence." He groaned, then mumbled quietly to himself as he read on.

"I might have guessed it…but she really *does* want you to accept, Tennyson. A baronetcy's not to be sneezed at, y'know, and that's twice you've turned it down now. I've deliberately broached the subject in here this evening, not to force your hand but so that the four of us, we four, can think about it and speak again." Gladstone paused, glanced at the others then watched Tennyson read it again. "Can I report back that you'll, at least, consider it this time? Mmm? What say you?"

Tennyson's shoulders slumped. Wilmot knew what his answer would be for they had spoken of it often enough at Court Hall. Tennyson, as sensitive as ever and prone to bouts of deep uncertainty, had been horrified at the thought of such an accolade. The Poet Laureate hated publicity and remained deeply suspicious of those who commentated publicly on his work. He caught Gladstone's eye. It was cocked inquiringly and remained so until Wilmot's shake of the head told him what he feared.

The poet handed the letter back, his face more melancholy than before. "I cannot…simply cannot," he muttered. "There's too much to be done. My life's so full. Emily and the children hardly see me and if this came along…were I to accept, why they'd all be baying at my door, morning, noon and night. No William, my dear fellow…my answer's no, it has to be."

"But you'll *think* on it, Alfred? Yes? Let me tell them you'll at least think about it…I must give them some hope. It is a signal honour, unique…when Her Majesty, herself, comes chasing along for a second time."

"Then tell them that, if that's what they want to hear." Tennyson put a hand on Gladstone's shoulder as the two walked towards Maynard who had just opened the doors leading into the hall. "But I'd have to be ready and I'm not, old thing. I'm not. There's too much…far, far too much to do just now." He turned to let Maynard place the red-lined cloak over his shoulders then took his top hat from the butler's hand.

*

Wilmot left soon after Gladstone and Tennyson, but what he had heard from Gladstone intrigued him. Frederic had heard it, too, from the Commons tearooms and corridors. The long civil war in America was coming to a head and the government had determined that there was no hope for the confederate states. What was more, there was little anybody could do to stop the bloodletting. But once the wretched business had run its course there would be a commercial vacuum, which would only be filled by whatever shipping lines could take the merchandise across the Atlantic. Now was the time for London Pacific's future markets to be identified and for the competition to be eliminated. Frederic had seen it too and already his metal works and foundries were gearing themselves to offer what was required after the war rather than what was needed to fight one.

As Wilmot went on his way, the chairman of L & P, as he now was, turned over in his mind the areas of likely competition. Bideford, he decided, they would keep. Wholly insignificant though it was in the grand design of things it was, nonetheless, useful to have a small port so far west. The much heralded Atlantic cable was proving to be of little commercial benefit and its successor was still some way off. Communications with the markets was still by sea and he needed immediate access to them.

Bideford, therefore, was fine but he wouldn't want anyone else around there. They had considered Ilfracombe and the man, Northborough. Jack had spoken of him as well and there was little love lost between the two of them. And anyone who had the mind to treat his brother as this fellow had done would now have to deal with him, Wilmot Tucker. Furthermore, Emma, his sister had told him that young Sarah had come across the man's family at Hartland. Herbert Northborough, Wilmot decided, was a man with whom he should become acquainted.

2

Dinner at Whitechapel had been difficult. In fact it had been very difficult and they barely supped at what had been placed in front of them.

Sharland walked slowly across the lawn. The June evening was still warm and dusk yet an hour away. As he walked, so he half listened to the ewes calling to their lambs in the meadow behind the stables. The birdsong from the thickets at the bottom of the walled garden, where the nightingales and chiff chaffs were competing to serenade the end of another day, passed him by. His head was down. His hands were thrust deep into his pockets and his face wore the frown of a man wrestling with his conscience.

His father had come down from Blagdon yesterday and, this afternoon, Sarah's letter had arrived. It had all happened at once and the row had been inevitable. Sarah was with child, his child so she claimed, and the birth was due in September. He would be able to calculate for himself, she had written in her remarkably fine handwriting, that the child was his. There had been no other before him, as well he knew, and, most certainly, nobody after. He alone had been, and remained, hers. So what, she had been minded to enquire, were his thoughts on the matter. And more to the point, *what*, and here she had been unequivocal, *what* did he intend to do about it. Should his response fail to satisfy her or should he choose to ignore her questions, she would be glad to see him.

Almost at once, and before he had changed, his father sensed something was amiss. The truth came out at tea and again at drinks in the drawing room before dinner, when the subject became heated. His father had dismissed the staff from the dining room telling Cockram, the tall, white haired butler, to wait on the bell. Their conversation had been a stop-start affair. He had tried to reason, but his father had been adamant. In the end it was he, Sharland, who had excused himself from the table, complaining that he needed some fresh air and that he wanted to think.

He kicked savagely at a twig on the lawn, then at another before walking to the edge of the ha-ha. The gardeners had cleared the ditch and he could smell the freshly cut grass. He was angry with himself and, for the first time in his life, with his father.

*

"It's not as though there's anything wrong with the girl." The Duke, a whisky in his hand, was staring into the fireplace now filled with an ornate display of silk flowers. "She's an attractive enough creature an' she's got a head on her shoulders...bold as brass. Nothing wrong there. The Orchard's are lucky enough to have her about the place."

"*Were* lucky, father. She's left."

"Mmm?" He turned. "Jocelyn's given her the push, eh? Had to be done, of course. Can't have the staff waddling about like cows in calf...not the single women anyway. Well, she's got herself in a pretty pickle an' I'm damned if you're going to be dragged down with her. Soon as yer get involved, the whole family's into it and I'm not having any of *that*." Sharland could see he was determined. The jaw was out and the eyes were bulging as they sometimes did. "As I said, we'll set her up. See the thing through that way...get a roof over her head and see that she's looked after."

"But the child's *mine*. Whatever we like to think about it, and I can't get it out of my mind, it's mine...my own flesh and blood."

"How d'yer *know* for God's sake, boy? Just because she told you in her letter." The Duke waved his hand dismissively. "She'd be bound to say it anyway, wouldn't she? Say anything to pin it on you and then come running along, cap in hand.   I mean, all...."

"Because I saw it, father. Saw the evidence as I've told you. I was the first...it was there. No mistaking it."

104

"Oh, poof to that…all that romantic nonsense. You were the first maybe, but so what? There was a second, that's fer sure. And a third and a fourth as well, I'll be bound. Who's to say there wasn't some Romeo up in the village? Eh? Someone of her own ilk…a groom or one of the footmen? Mmm?" The Duke drew on his cigar. "Once a woman's on her way like that then there's no telling who's next and they all go back to their own kind sooner or later. You know that as well as I do. And then…and then when the goddamned carriage loses a wheel and she falls flat on her face, she comes running. Seen it before, so we have. And *you* should know that, my lad. What about that tangle you got yourself into at Ampfield? Eh? The girl was happy enough with what we did for her…so what about this one? What's the difference?"

"She, Sarah's the difference."

"Rubbish, they're all the same."

"No…she's different. It wasn't just a night on the tiles as you keep saying. Its…."

"Then what the devil was it, then? A mistake? Eh? 'Sorry, but I didn't mean it,' or something? Mmm? Who're you trying to hoodwink, for Heaven's sake? Be yer age, boy. It was a damned good evening, plenty of jollity, dancing and the rest of it…and a nice warm bed waiting for you…sheets pulled back into the bargain. Hmmph."

"All right, all right. I'll admit to all that but it wasn't exactly the first time I'd set eyes on her, y'know. It's been almost two years now since we first met. She's a bright, amusing girl. Gay and lively. *Fun*…she's got a mind of her own *and* can hold herself up in company as well. She's leagues away from the usual sort of thing. I've got to know her…I like her and, well…"

"And that's far enough. That's as far as it's going to get. None of this nonsense you were hinting at before dinner. You aren't ob*liged* to take her on and I'll not be having another thought on the subject, d'you hear. It's dead in the water. Dead…Amen. Good God Almighty, *we*, the *Northboroughs* getting caught like that." The Duke walked to the night tray and served himself. "Think on it, Sharland, and think carefully. I know you're not my heir, you're not Thomas…and mercy for that, but it's bad enough. You've a lot coming your way y'know, and there's our reputation to safeguard. Even the second son must ensure that the line remains pure. And you'll be passing it on one day, remember. I'm not having any of the Northboroughs tainted with common blood."

Sharland was silent. "There's plenty of good stock about," his father continued. "And plenty of time…you're barely into your thirties but it's time yer started looking around…and looking in the proper places. You've got to seek out a family of substance to marry into. Look around you…there're the Boscowens from Truro for instance. The Trowbridges…a couple of gals there. The Meynells and the Seagraves from Stanhope. They're the sort you need…not this, this little frippit of a thing."

Sharland knew he was right and was beginning to doubt himself. "Father, I hear you. I hear everything but I do need to be sure."

"Well, you're sure now, my boy, I can tell you. And *damned* sure at that…we both are. Use your head and think." He brushed back his grey curly hair. "Think of what you've got to offer the world and step away from this nonsense. You're the second in line to a great dynasty that stretches way back. You're in a spot right now but 'tis nothing we can't put right…but there's to be no more of it. This is the seond time and that's enough of it."

Sharland sighed and shook his head. Well, yes, it could be done, he supposed. And it was a situation that would never have worked. Never. Better to back off now than let it drag on. After all, he would be free of any responsibilities and that appealed. He looked up and laughed self-consciously. "Yes, you're right, father. Of course you are…we'll see to it as you said."

3

Sir Durnford Morgan lowered his copy of the 'Exeter Flying Post.' It had to be one and the same man that they were writing about. He dabbed at his mouth, adjusted his glasses and read again.

The papers, a small luxury he allowed himself while staying in Exeter on banking matters, had arrived earlier. Mrs Salmons, the rotund and motherly landlady at his comfortable Southernhay lodgings, had brought him his haddock kedgeree and coffee. There had been her usual fussing and flapping at crumbs on the table and he had just agreed with her that the weather was indeed turning, and that it was certainly about time too, when the article caught his eye.

> *'A Mr Samuel Masters and a Mr Tom Hall, both from Friar's Gate and having been convicted of sheep stealing by His Honour Judge Horace Thomason at the Assize Court, breathed their last at the new County Gaol on Friday the tenth instant. The two men were comforted in their final hours by the parish priest of St Thomas's and were duly repentant as they met their fate. After they had been taken down, the bodies were sent to a surgeon, Mr Truman Crandle, for dissection. Two others, by the name of William Bennett and Harry Tucker, both convicted of the same crime had been spared the 'New Drop' due to the clemency of His Honour. Their sentences, originally as that of the aforementioned, had been respited to transportation. The two will, in due course and in conjunction with others, be removed to H.M Prison Hulk 'Leviathan' standing off The Custom's Quay in order to await their transport.'*

As he ate, so Morgan read it again. It was the name Harry Tucker. It might have been a coincidence but he feared it was not and the more he thought about it the more certain he became. It had to be the boy he knew. Jack, poor man, would be at a loss as to what to do for his son, if it was indeed him. Wilmot would know, but he was in London and time was short. He had no idea as to what the procedures were for transportation but suspected they were straightforward, if merciless. But he would have to try to save the boy, whose face he could vaguely remember from a visit to Sherdon. There was nobody else and if he could help the family then he would.

He hurried from the gloomy, heavily wallpapered dining room and went to collect his coat and hat. He had never been near a prison in his life and the thought of having to do so appalled him. He had no idea who he would have to see, or if indeed he would be able to see anybody at all. Somehow, though, he would have to prevent the boy from being taken away. Simply talking about it or pleading would fall on deaf ears. Gold was the answer. Thirty years of banking had taught him that, of all the talking the world over, it was gold that spoke the loudest. And it would speak here, too, in this filthy sordid den. There would be those who held sway in there whose eyes would sparkle and glitter at the very sight of it. It would be gold that turned the keys but he would have to hurry.

He would go to the bank, he decided, draw up what was necessary and postpone the morning's two meetings. Then he would begin at the beginning. The New County Gaol was situated in Howell's Lane, an unenviable and charmless spot. But the whole wretched business into which he was proposing to delve, Sir Durnford Morgan concluded, was going to be singularly unpleasant, from start to finish.

✳

Harry sat against the wall. His head, resting on his knees drawn up to his chin, was half hidden by his arms. His flannel uniform, once grey, was damp. His spiky brown hair had grown into a wild mat that covered his ears and half his face. He had lice, like the rest of them and he stank. His swollen right ankle had turned red and yellow where the leg iron had bitten into the flesh, causing him to carry the chain whenever he moved. When the Recruiting Sergeant had come in earlier, the latrine bucket had been spilled in the rush to the cell bars. The floor was awash with human filth. He had been one of the first to rise and tried to walk normally but the state of his ankle forced him to hobble and he had been pushed to one side.

Two or maybe three, for there were a dozen in the cell, had started a fight. Others had tried to separate them but not before the breakfast pans and kit boxes had been knocked all over the floor. Everyone was covered in the muck and the one who was now sitting next to him picked at his teeth and scratched. Only one of the lamps remained alight and the wick was smoking. It was indeed the devil's parlour as one of those picked out by the recruiters had shouted as he shuffled out of the gate.

Harry forced his head further down in despair. If only he had not been so greedy that night when Snakey and Tom had told him their plan. A guinea a sheep was good money but not good enough to be worth the risk. It was easy, Snakey had boasted. No farmer would be about at that time. They weren't, but three gamekeepers were and their second shot had caught Tom. After that there had been no chance.

The figure on his other side, a boy of barely fourteen, began to whimper. Two others, a sinewy quadroon who had stolen no more than a pair of cord breeches from a washing line and the other, a Scot, started to sing hymns. Others tried to shout them down. Another two began to argue over what was left of the dry straw. But suddenly they stopped.

Harry raised his head. The sound of keys, rattling and echoing in the locks as the door at the far end of the corridor was opened, had alerted them. Visitors meant that something was about to happen and the inmates, like dogs in a shed, fell silent and listened. At the sight of the lantern several of them pushed forward for a better look. Harry half rose but sat back. His ankle was weeping pus and the swollen, red skin burned as he tried to move. And, in any case, what was the point?

"Tucker…Tucker…238 Prisoner Tucker." The guard, bearded and red faced, with his prison cap on the back of his head, rattled his cane along the bars while another, a step behind him, held the lantern high to see better. *"Prisoner Tucker, on yer feet."* Harry looked up. Others were staring at him. One inmate, an older man, thin and balding, pressed forward claiming to be him. Harry watched as the guard checked the tag on his irons and pushed him back. "Will Prisoner Tucker step forward and identify himself. *Tuckerrrrr.*"

Harry rose warily. He picked up the chain between his leg irons. In this way he would keep the heavy, sharp metal ring away from his open sores. He half stood and began to hobble, trying to push his way through those between him and the door. "Come on, move yerself…I said bloody *move* yerself." As the hand grabbed his hair to pull him through the gate, he dropped his chain and yelped in pain. One of the guards hit him while two more were beating back those trying to force their way out.

"That 'im, sir?" The warder's teeth were bad and his breath was rancid. His cane prodded Harry roughly in the ribs, forcing him to catch his breath. Harry looked at the tall, well dressed figure standing back who was holding a yellow and black-spotted silk kerchief to his face.

"Here, sir." Harry's hair was grabbed and his head jerked back. "That better? Get a good look at his face." The tall stranger nodded and Harry was pushed towards the door at the end of the corridor.

*

Sergeant Crocker had had his bit of luck for the day and was feeling pleased with himself. He even kissed the silver top of his black regimental cane. As he waited in the whitewashed processing room so he rose on his toes and stroked the waxed ends of his moustache. He was short and he was portly but he was doing his job just as it should be done. He lifted his left foot and rubbed the toecap of his boot behind his right calf. Then he lifted his chin and adjusted his heavy, felt collar.

Yes, he thought to himself. Oh yes, they could fit an extra one on the cart, all right.
No problem. They would bleedin' 'ave to, for the two sovereigns in his pocket would
see to it. Just wot the gent wanted him to take this extra one for, Sergeant Crocker had
no idea but, at two sovereigns a fellon, he would go on cramming them onto the cart
all day...all bleedin' day if 'e wanted. He shook his head in wonderment and turned
as the party re-emerged at the top of the stairs leading down to the cells.

"You're Tucker, eh?" Crocker preened himself and made a point of looking the prisoner up and down. Harry blinked and stood awkwardly. He was still holding his
chain and he nodded. "*Sir.* That's wot you call me, my lad. *Sir*, or it's back darn there
where you've come from. Now then, sir." The sergeant turned to Durnford Morgan
and smiled respectfully. His Nibs, he could see, was looking a bit white. His eyes
were watering and he was, believe it or not, shaking. Cuh, dearie me. "That's 'im, is
it, sir? 'E's the one you're wanting?" Morgan remembered him now and nodded.

"Right, come 'ere, you, an' listen to me. Gennelman 'ere says 'e knows yer family.
Speaks highly of yer so 'e does, an' persuaded me to take yer into the army – The
Devonshire Regiment...The Bloody Eleventh, as we're known. Right?" He saw no
reason to wait for an answer but continued to hold forth and, by now, was looking at
Morgan again. "This's agin the rules, I'm afraid, sir. Strictly speakin' that is...we can't
be goin' around doin' this all day. But anyways," Crocker turned back to Harry and
rose on his toes. "Seein' the gennelman spoke so well of yer, 'tis on my recommendation that you be taken off deportation. Ahem." He rose on his toes again and coughed
once more, nodding deferentially and watching as Morgan reached for his purse.

"Ahem, yes. Thank 'e kindly, sir." Sergeant Crocker saluted and turned back to the
business of the day. "Right, lad. Seven years it is. Seven long years with the colours
or you're back darn there. What's it to be now?" Harry said nothing. "Well...the
Colours it is, my lad. You're in and that's it." Sergeant Crocker winked at Durnford
Morgan. "A soldier of the Queen, Gawd bless 'er. And a mighty close call it's been,
sir. I'll say." Sergeant Crocker had made sure the third sovereign joined the others
in his pocket. "Imagine, if it weren't fer that I'd left my little regimental cane be'ind
in 'ere, an' had not come back lookin' fer it, well then. You an' I would never 'ave
met, sir. An' then wot, eh? Cuh...dearie me."

Morgan nodded once more. Harry, it seemed to him, was marginally better off now
than he had been before Mrs Salmons had brought him his 'Flying Post.'
Marginally better off, he thought, as he glanced at Sergeant Crocker, but not much.

4

As Sarah had forecast, there had been tears and recrimination at Church Street. Her
mother had wanted nothing to do with it. It was, as far as she was concerned, the
end of the world.

The neighbours would, and for a while did, chatter and point. Sarah could feel the
eyes following her across the square and into the shop, as her mother had warned.

Business was bound to fall, her mother announced but it made no difference at all. They would be shunned, cast out from her circle of friends, she complained. Some did, others did not. Yet one by one those who had turned away came back and, when they did, there were smiles and more tears. Mary would laugh if she knew, but she never appeared. Uncle Wilmot would die, her mother insisted. In fact when eventually he heard he was remarkably sage. And as for Lady Frobisher, her mother, didn't know what to say. But Lady Frobisher knew exactly. It was, she opined with one hand on Emma's who was holding a handkerchief to her eyes, it was the way of the world and the world would survive; which it did.

Her father, meanwhile, had gone quietly about his business. He had always been the one to calm the heated household. Sarah could talk to him and usually she listened to his advice, but this time they disagreed. Troy Kingdon had, in his wisdom, surmised that nothing would ever come of it. He had seen it before. Life as a butler in one of Devon's great houses had taught him the ways of the world. It could never be, he declared. The great lived with the great, and that was that. They sought each other out and they married into each other's families. They might play around elsewhere and most certainly did but, should a mishap occur, then it would be quietly seen to and the great would go on their way.

He would, he remarked wisely, be minded for his daughter to accept the conditions Lord Preston had offered. But Sarah did not. For once in her life she spurned his advice. Even when they walked arm in arm through the park by the parsonage and he pleaded with her, she refused to hear of it

*

She drove herself. Her father had offered to come with her but she preferred to go on her own. Earlier it had rained but the clouds had broken up, leaving the cool west wind to play with the tips of the beech branches now heavy laden with the dark green leaves of July. The wild grasses by the roadside had overgrown and then blown over in wet tangles, leaving the dark brown dock stems standing proud. The thistles had grown taller, too, and had begun to seed. In spite of the breeze, clouds of midges hung in the air, causing Sarah to raise the hood of her cloak.

The piebald her father had borrowed for the day pulled well and it was only when she reached the puddled ruts of Whitechapel drive did she slow the dogcart to a walk. She knew he would be there. Arthur Mason, the elderly second gardener with the bad hip who had worked at the manor for years and whom her father knew well, had confirmed it. His Lordship would ride out in the mornings and sometimes again in the evenings but every afternoon, invariably so far as he knew, Lord Preston remained at home.

She pulled on the heavy bell lever and stood back, adjusting, first, her beige cloak and then her bonnet of green silk with white lace trimming. No matter how she now tried, her seven months was plain for the world to see, as it was for the footman who came to inspect what was at the front door. He paused, momentarily, to hear her business then withdrew to report the matter to the butler. He, too, saw her condition and listened to her tale yet still she was not invited inside. Eventually, and after twice refusing to be told that his lordship was not there, the housekeeper appeared and asked her to step into the hall.

"Lord Preston will be with you presently. He has been busily engaged." Sarah ignored the woman who had tried, unsuccessfully, to look down her nose at her condition. She had glared back and the housekeeper, a starchy, thin faced female, had been forced to look away, muttering to herself in a manner that could be over-heard. The morning room, for that was where she supposed she now was, felt gloomy. The Elizabethans, she noted, had never used light to its best advantage. The heavily mullioned windows and the tiny, diamond-shaped leaded panes kept out too much and, on a dull day like today, a house needed every bit of light it could get. She turned as the door opened.

Sarah looked at the proffered hand before deciding to take it. "You received my letter, I assume?"

"Indeed I did," he replied. She could see he was uneasy. His voice sounded tight and he was flushed.

"And?"

"And what?" She made no reply but savoured the silence. Already she knew what the outcome would be but she was going to face up to him until the end. If he was going to desert her then she would make him aware that he had forsaken a woman of some substance. "Why is it that you have come here? Were you not satisfied with the conditions I offered in my reply to your letter?" He moved to where he could see her better. "I thought they were more than generous, and my sentiments cordial enough."

"No they were not." She held his gaze but his eyes moved to her body as soon as she removed her cloak. "Look at me, Sharland." He did but his eyes dropped away again. "Behold your child. And what you have offered me in return was no more than you would pay that wretched female who had the gall, just now, to look with such disdain upon what is yours?"

"Who says the child is mine?" His voice was raised but his eyes had answered his own question. They were guilty. And, just as she thought, he was wriggling and twisting. "You're not trying to tell me that I was the first to lie with you...or the last for that matter. I've accepted the possibility that the child might be mine...and only *might* be, hence my offer of assistance. But I could never accept that it's mine for certain. Don't expect that of me."

"You saw. You saw the evidence on the sheets with your own eyes after we had lain together: you were the first. And as for afterwards, *well*, if that is your opinion of me then I will leave to your imagination what mine is of *you*." She took a short step closer. "But then...and in case there was any doubt, the doctor at Hartland...the very same man who attends the Orchards, confirmed that the dates made it thus."

"*Possibly so,* maybe, but not *certainly*...nobody can be certain."

"Then why, might I ask, have you chosen to woo me these last two years? Have you *really* been wasting all this time pursuing a woman who takes one man after another in such quick succession? Is that how you regard me, Sharland? Really? As some strumpet who flaunts herself around the very home and grounds where she is known and respected? And how do you suppose I have been regarding *you*? As just one more in a long queue, with others before and after? Lord Preston tonight, perhaps", she mocked. "The butler or bootblack tomorrow, perhaps." She could see he was taken aback. "*Come,* Sharland. Such talk of yours might fool the world and appease your father's wrath but it doesn't fool me. And neither, by the look on your face, are you fooling yourself."

"I'll hear no more of that. Say what you like and do what you will, I'll never accept the child is mine."

"Then he'll grow to haunt you, my lord. From the very first moment our son draws breath...for a son is what it will be. From that very moment, he will haunt you...and haunt your line. D'you realise, Sharland Preston, d'you realise that what you are seeing now in front of you is your own son and heir? Here," her hands moved to the child inside her. "Here lies a Preston, the next Lord Preston. Here, feel for yourself." She held out her hand to take his but he stepped back.

"Lying here, within me, are two tiny hands that, one day will carry your banners and your name forward." She paused to catch her breath. "No, Sharland...there is no doubt, no doubt at all. The child here is yours. However, worry not for I'll not stoop to argue about a matter we both know to be fact. No, I'll accept your offer. I need to for I have no choice. And I shall take it upon myself to care for and to love our child as any father might wish the mother to do."

She turned to arrange her cloak. "Here, allow me," he offered. Without waiting for her answer, she felt him straightening her hood and she froze. For no more than a moment, his hands rested lightly on her shoulders and the two of them stood as they were, he behind her. Her heart quickened and she wanted to turn. His fingers were beginning to tighten and she felt his eyes on the back of her neck. But the moment passed and she moved away, lightly shrugging him off.

"Farewell, Sharland. No, don't worry," she raised a hand. "I'll see myself away." At the door she turned. "I'll bear our child with pride. Never fear of that. He'll grow and, as he faces the world, he'll wish to know who his father is. And I shall tell him. For all you've said and done just now, there was a time not so long ago when his parents loved one another as every child would wish their parents to do. All I ask is that you never forget what is yours." She turned and, feeling his eyes following her every step, strode from the house.

Chapter Nine

As Frederic Knight crossed the bridge, so he lifted his collar and leant forward into the light drizzle. August 1864 had been a wet month, almost a disaster as far as the late haymaking on Exmoor was concerned and today was no different. At this time of the year Sherdon Water should have been little more than a trickle but it was running high, pressing flat the summer grasses along the banks.

Disturbed by the clatter of hooves, a dipper flew out from under the bridge and perched on a hump of wet rock over which the water was trying to break. Frederic watched as the little white-bibbed bird bobbed and dipped before hurrying on its way. Somewhere, far off in the mist, a crow called out but, that apart, it was eerily silent. The moors had wrapped themselves in a thick, grey-white cloak and hidden themselves away from the world. He wiped the rain from his face and kicked on up the lane. Jack, he knew, would be waiting and there was much to discuss.

*

"More, Mr Frederic?" Kitty took his earthenware bowl and ladled in spoonfuls of her rabbit and vegetable broth. Then, wiping her hands on her newly washed pinafore, she opened the bread oven and slid the scoop under the baking tin before lifting it to check the potato cakes. They were hot to the touch, making her flick her fingers but they had crisped and she put them, one at a time, onto the flower-patterned plate.

Frederic smiled. Never was he happier than when here at Sherdon and nobody meant more to him than Jack. He had known him, literally, for as long as he could remember and, whenever they met, they wasted hours recalling old times, such as when Jack first let him go from the leading rein at Castle Heights, or the time when he was head lad at Simonsbath and took Frederic, his brothers and the Acland boys out hunting with Jack Russell. It was he, Frederic, who had given away Katherine at Molland and he who had shown them Sherdon when it was no more than a builders' shell. Katherine had gone but the fond memories of her still lingered in his mind and, most probably, always would. Jack, it seemed, had found happiness with Kitty. He needed somebody out here with him and she was doing him well. She was an attractive, neat little person and they seemed right for one another.

But it had not been easy and Frederic knew that his own problems, mainly financial, paled into insignificance. Charlotte, too, was no longer there. They had taken her away and it had been a dreadful time at the farm. And then there was Harry.

Durnford Morgan had told him the story and they had sworn that Jack should never hear the truth. He had simply run off to join the army, they said. Durnford had seen him in Exeter and he was fit and well. Jack's fears had been placated but he remained saddened by his son's wild ways. It was not all bad news, though. Tod had been ordained and was at Simonsbath with William Thornton. The boy, now twenty-one and tall like his father though fairer, had been a great help when the new school opened. Victoria would be leaving also. Next year she would be going to Molland to live with the Quartlys at Great Champson. That left Frank and Anna who both seemed happy enough.

"Thank you, Kitty...and goodness, *woa*, that's plenty." There was enough on his plate. "That's marvellous. My thanks, again...cuh, no wonder you're all looking so well." He returned her smile and turned back to Jack. "You were right, you know, about the ponies. That cross breeding we tried never really worked but I can't make out if it was the blood that was wrong, the cross we went for...or the weather up here. What d'you reckon?"

Jack sat hunched over his broth. He had tipped the bowl towards him and frowned as he chased what was left with a crust of bread. "More like the keep, Master Frederic. Since they've gone and put sheep on most of the pastures now, they've had to turn the ponies out on the higher ground. Weather's bad enough up there but they little mares need good keep when they're in foal. Got to remember they're not bringing a pure bred Exmoor into the world but a cross...and one half of it doesn't know what it's like up there. You can't expect good results if they're kept out all year round. I'll only have pure-bred Exmoors here...and I've told Wil that."

Frederic nodded. "I know, I'm cutting back on the numbers. I've got to, really. As you say, the sheep are taking all the decent pasture...they're the real money-spinner and when we turn them out on the commons in the summer they clean the place right out. Those Cheviots and Black Face we brought down from the north are doing well. Especially that very first lot...better than we ever expected."

"Aye, dare say." Jack broke off another corner of bread. He had known it all along and had warned them at the time, but would never make reference to the fact. He took a swig of warm beer and went on chewing. "Our hornies do best down under." He swallowed hard. "Simonsbath'd be all right, y'know, sir. You're down below the worst of the weather there." Frederic was silent, wondering whether or not the moment was right. He glanced at Kitty. He could see she had made an effort for his visit. Her clothes were freshly pressed and the green ribbons in her hair suited her. Right now she was burrowing into the oven for more food. Apple turnovers they were: his favourite. Jack must have told her.

The man would be sixty in a couple of years. He had worn well, wonderfully well, but the hard, remorseless slog had taken its toll. His face, still as handsome as ever, was drawn and the hair, still as long as he could remember it and still tied back, had greyed. The hands, he could see, had become gnarled and several knuckles were swollen. The suppleness had gone and there was an air of age about him. He could not last for ever, perhaps not very much longer, but his knowledge of farming on the high moors was absolute. The man had been the very first on to the forest and had stuck it year in year out, through blizzards and drought, through bereavement and sadness, yet he had never complained. His name was a byword with those who knew the moor and Frederic was proud to have him as a friend. If ever he had felt love for a man it was for him.

"Simonsbath's coming along well, y'know."

"Aye, so I've heard." Jack leant back, wiped both hands down his shirt front and reached for the plate of apple turnovers Kitty was offering.

"The school's up and running." Frederic closed one eye in concentration. "Twelve children, I think it is so far, and more to come. And young Tod has settled well…William Thornton's very pleased with him." Kitty turned at the mention of his name and smiled affectionately. "And six of the cottages we finished are now occupied. *And* we've begun work on the church at last. It'll be a year or two yet but when it's there we'll be a proper village."

"So you're staying then, Master Frederic? Us've heard word that London an' that's taking your time." He chose not to mention they'd heard his wife, an upcountry lady, had little time for the moors.

"Mmm, London? Yes, for certain. It does indeed, my friend, but the more I'm away the more I long to get back here. No, I'm staying put at Simonsbath and they'll be burying me out there one day, you wait. Up in that new churchyard we're building. I feel part of my soul's up here."

"Glad of that, sir." Jack grinned at him boyishly, still chewing.

Frederic took out his handkerchief and wiped his mouth. "But listen, you're getting no younger, you know. Life's bin good to you in some ways but you've had your knocks…my goodness you have." Jack never looked up. "One day, some time, Sherdon's got to come to an end. When the day comes, I want to use you, Jack." The farmer remained motionless. "I've got the farms up and running but I need somebody to see to them…somebody who knows the moors and the way things are up here." Frederic patted his thigh then bent to lift up the grey tabby. The old cat had left the hearth after stretching and was now rubbing against his boot with its back arched and tail raised.

"An agent, sir? You've got one of they, surely…what's his name? Smith, isn't it or Hawton, the new fellow?" Jack sat back and folded his arms. "Bain't no room for another, y'know. We'd start falling out afore long and then where would we be?" He paused and raised a hand to his mouth to stifle some wind. "Pardon. And, in any case what you need is a man of books…an' I'm no man for books and that."

Their eyes met. The answer was as Frederic suspected. "Up to a point. But you can get any number of those sort of people. It's the wisdom I'm after, knowing what's what…and your knowledge is second to none. What you've got up there," he tapped his head, "is priceless." Jack tasted a flake of crust he had picked from the table. "I mean, just look what you've been saying about the sheep and the ponies…and breaking the land. Nobody knows more about it and I was hoping that perhaps you might be able to work together. But you'll never budge, will you?"

"Aye, and my thanks for that, Master Frederic. 'Tis really kind of you, sir, but I reckon me an' Kitty are best off here at Sherdon…eh, love?" He reached out and pulled her towards him playfully. "Times can be hard, right enough, but I daresay we're better off here at Sherdon where I knows what I'm about, than up at Simonsbath telling others what to do and getting in the way of things."

"I knew it, you old devil" Frederic leant across the table and put his hand on his friend's shoulder. "You'll be here until they carry you out. Eh?" They laughed and settled back, each knowing that their time together was precious. Frederic would have to be away and he had told Jack about how he was fighting for the Yeomanry in the House of Commons. Cheap at the price had been his cry. Cheap, yet loyal and patriotic as the ranks of the regular cavalry would testify. It was from the ranks of the Yeomanry that so many regular cavalrymen came yet they, the government, were paying them a pittance and turning their backs on requests for better equipment and conditions. He was doing what he could but it was an uphill struggle.

How old Sergeant Fanshawe of The Royal North Devons would have approved. They threw back their heads and laughed out loud at the memory of the man and they laughed at other things. Frederic explained why he had left the Royal North Devons and that they had made him a Colonel in the Worcestershire Yeomanry. So I can shout louder in the House, he said and they laughed at that. They then talked about the things they loved and feared, things that worried them and about others they knew. They talked on, just as two old friends always do, until the light began to fade.

By the time Frederic came to go, the mist had thickened and the rain was coming down harder, but it worried him not. The ride home, up the Barle valley past Wheal Eliza, would take him and his man little more than an hour. Their parting was hard; it always was. As he rode down the lane and left the farm in the mist behind him, his thoughts drifted back down the years; almost half a century now.

2

Troy Kingdon could see that she was exhausted. It was finally over but the last three days had taxed them all, Emma in particular. He tiptoed from the room, leaving her asleep in the chair and made his way into the square and across to The George where he had agreed to meet Arthur Mason.

✳

It had been back in June when Emma first admitted that she might be wrong. Everyone in Church Street and many from further afield knew about Sarah's predicament. There had indeed been the usual tittle tattle that unnerved her, but her friends had rallied. Even Mrs Hebditch, the gossip from the haberdashers, the one who always used to stop at the shop and pass on endless nonsense, had fallen silent. Probably because there was nobody left to discuss, Troy pointed out.

Three days after Sarah returned from Whitechapel, she took the piebald pony and dogcart and drove herself into Barnstaple. She was away all day and when she returned it was late. What she had to say made her mother bite her lip but, to start with anyway, Sarah stood her ground. "Oh, mother, *please, please* stop worrying so. I've made up my mind and that's that. The Mother Superior was very understanding and they're going to take me in when the time comes."

Emma was horrified. "But they're *nuns*, dear…they don't understand about these things. They can't, they've never been married and people only ever go there to hide themselves away. You can't go there…what'll everyone think?" It was her father who persuaded Sarah to change her mind. She knew she should have taken his advice earlier about going out to Whitechapel and this time she listened. And there was another thing. Mrs Bootle, the midwife from one of the whitewashed cottages in New Road, behind the market, had told her mother it would be best if the confinement was at home. No place like home, she declared, and she should know for she had been delivering children for thirty years. She knew her business, she assured them, and wanted to see the mother-to-be at least twice beforehand: just to make sure. Mrs Bootle, tall and upright and dressed in her usual long black dress with a clean white apron over the top and wearing her black woollen shawl, settled the matter. There was peace, so father and daughter walked out together, arm in arm. In fact they walked out together every day until the twenty-seventh of September.

✳

At first she thought it was her back but the pain went away. Twenty minutes later it returned and then it came on again. They had just finished lunch and Troy went immediately for Mrs Bootle but she was nowhere to be found. She should have been back the day before, her neighbour announced leaning against the door with her arms folded, but nobody had seen her. Granny Warren came instead, short, jolly and with a whispery grey beard. Although she had had thirteen of her own, as she told Troy when she tried to straighten herself to look up at him, it had been a long time ago, but she would come along and see what had to be done.

An hour later she ordered Sarah to bed and they took it in turns to watch. At dusk they could see it would not be long, but it was and, by eleven o'clock, even Granny began to worry. Yet the pains were getting closer until, suddenly, Sarah struggled and cried out. As she pushed so her hands gripped the side of the bed, then her mother's hand, then the bed again, throwing her head back with her face screwed up in pain. It seemed to go on…and on, until at last, and with her mother holding her up, at last, at last as she pushed and pushed as she had never pushed before she saw Granny Warren reach down. She was gulping for air and crying and throwing her head back and pushing and then suddenly she was there. The tiny cries of freedom she could hear serenaded the triumph and she fell back hot and exhausted, drenched with perspiration.

As Granny Warren attended to the babe, so Emma washed her daughter and it was only when she looked round to see the child for herself that she saw the midwife's face. The crying had stopped and the child was still. For two hours they struggled. Granny blew air into her mouth as Emma pressed two fingers onto the chest. Granny picked her up and swung her, they rubbed her chest and massaged her back but to no avail. Just after midnight, little Charlotte Katherine Kingdon died. She died in her mother's arms. Her eyes were closed but the tears of her mother's grief washed over her tiny face. Her hair was as black as the night but, the nose and the chin, Granny Warren whispered, were those of her mother.

Granny did not go for some time. She wanted to, to leave the family alone together, but there was something not right. They had taken the babe away but it was Sarah that was causing concern. Granny Warren knew twins, she had had them herself, and was certain there was another one there. She waited until dawn but there was nothing and, shaking her head, she finally went on her way.

*

Arthur Mason, the Whitechapel gardener, got on his grey, bob-tailed cob. It seemed strange that his master, Lord Preston, had asked to be kept informed. Troy Kingdon had said nothing except that His Lordship and his daughter had met one another out at Hartland. But it made him wonder, perhaps…after all everyone knew she had come back the way she had. But no, and it was none of his business anyway. His Lordship had asked him to let him know, straight away like, and that is what he would do. He couldn't help but to wonder, though. Couldn't help it.

Sharland saw the gardener from his bedroom window and knew, by the way he was urging the old horse forward, that he brought news. He hurried to dress and it was Blackman, his valet, who knocked on his door. "Beg pardon, m'lord, but the gardener, Mason's, down at the back."

"Yes, yes…tell him I'm on my way. No, wait, I'm ready now…come on, come on." He brushed the man aside and strode along the landing and down the back stairs, taking two at a time. The man would be at the scullery door and the servants would be all over the place but Sharland had to hear. He'd see him right away so he shut the door behind him and the two stood together in the yard.

"What news, what news, Mason?" Sharland caught his breath. The gardener was standing with his cap in hand. For some reason his shiny, bald head looked a strange marble-white compared with his ruddy-red face that was always blackened by stubble. He was a short, wiry man and, like many of his age, still wore the old fashioned smock. "Tell me…tell me, man. You've come from the town, yes?"

"Aye, m'lord. Right away, sir." The sad face was impassive, almost dog-like.

Sharland could see at once. "Well, what is it? What have you to say?"

"Beg pardon, m'lord but bain't good news, I'm afraid...no sir. A little girl, m'lord. Born last night but...but, I'm afraid...afraid her didn't live, sir. I'm sorry, m'lord, ever so sorry."

"Dear God alive." Sharland paused. "And the mother? What of her? She's all right...tell me she is. Quickly now."

"Oh aye, m'lord." Mason's face brightened and he allowed himself a toothless grin, one more of relief than humour. "The mother, Miss Sarah, that is...her's fine, sir. Tired mind, but fine." The questioning went on until Sharland realised he would learn no more and sent the man on his way.

✳

Now Sharland leant over the gate. Since hearing the news earlier he had been walking. First up through the oak woods behind the manor, then down to the lake they had made for wild duck by damming the stream. There was a seat, no more than an old moss covered oak bench, but it was good enough and he had sat for a time. Sometimes his head was in his hands, sometimes he got up and walked about and then came back again. All day the same thoughts kept returning. Sarah had survived and he had thanked God for that without realising why he had done so. The child had gone and it saddened him. *If* it was his, *if* it was then he had indeed lost something precious and the more he thought of it the sadder he became.

But it was the mother that held his mind: he did not know why and was confused. He felt the loss of the child as if he was her, imagining her feelings after carrying it so bravely and for so long. Such sentiments surprised him. He should not have cared less. He thought he had hardened himself to be *un*caring, to dismiss the situation as inconsequential and to move on. But he could not. Furthermore a joyous surge swept through him every time he reminded himself of her survival, that she was alive and would soon be strong again.

So why all this? Was he sad about the child because he knew it was his? And could it really be that if she, too, had succumbed, he would have actually grieved for her while now he was *rejoicing* for her? Was he elated, not simply because the woman had lived but because it was *her*, Sarah? Could it be so? Well, yes. It had to be...it really did. Then shame on him and the devil take him for rejecting them like he had, for allowing himself to submit so weakly to his father's hectoring, and for degrading her by trying to buy her off. Once he had been fully prepared to leave her and the child to find their own way, but not now.

All day he wrestled with his emotions, trying time after time to reason with himself. At last, he could stand it no longer. He had to go and see. He knew well what her reaction would be, and who could blame her. She would, he surmised, turn her back on him, denying him the opportunity to see the grief that would be scarring her face and, for certain, she would want nothing of his commiserations or his attempts at any form of reconciliation. But he could only try. He deserved

119

nothing more than to be shown the door but he would go in the hope that, afterwards, she might at least feel somewhat less ill-disposed towards him.

*

He had had to knock twice and when she answered the door, the tall, grey haired woman in the long black dress with a white pinafore, looked as though she was busy. "My pardon, madam, but I've come to enquire about Miss Kingdon. I heard the news this morning and I have come to offer my condolences…to say how sorry I was to hear the news and to offer my best wishes."

"Thank you, sir. I'll pass on your sentiments." Mrs Bootle had to admit she was surprised at the sight of this finely dressed stranger and the groom holding his horse. "Er…she'll not be seeing anyone for a while yet, sir, and, right now, they're both asleep."

"Both?" Sharland leant forward. "Did you say *both*? But I thought…I was told that the child did not live."

"Well, no, and you're right…in a way, so to speak." Mrs Bootle noted the concern on his face. "The first one, the little girl, she died but her brother, the twin, he's a fine little man."

"Twin?" Sharland stared and the midwife stared back. "Oh, right," he stammered. "Well, my man said nothing of that when he came with the news. Nothing at all. He said that they had waited and…but, when they were sure there was no other…they assumed the firstborn to be the only child."

"I know, I know." Mrs Bootle sighed but allowed herself a smile. "You see, 'twas Granny Warren, sir. I was s'posed to be here but was called away out to Rackenford and only got back when the little girl had been born. Granny Warren, she had had twins of her own but they were *identical* twins, you see, and they always come along quick like…one behind the other. But not these two, here. Why her second waters weren't passed for a good twelve hours after but then, when he came, he came easily enough. And praise be for that.

"But," she wagged a finger. "There was nothing identical about these two, though. Very different they were and when it's like this they can be a whole day apart sometimes. The little maid had dark hair, dark as a chimney she was, but the boy…Isaac, he's to be, why he's a fair one. Right fair little mop he's got." She bent forward to look up at the side of his head and frowned in the light. "'Bout like yours, so 'e is, sir…proper little chap."

3

Wilmot learned of his knighthood in the spring of 1865. The messenger from the Prime Minister's office came by handsome cab to Cranley Gardens with the letter.

Later, that day, he lunched at The Reform with William Gladstone and a small group of friends. He was fifty-four, he had been chairman of the London Pacific for three years and, apart from his lands on Exmoor, he had amassed a considerable personal fortune through his banking interests with Esdaile's and other business dealings. The citation *'for services to international trade and industry'* seemed particularly apt. His contacts in the worlds of commerce and politics were capital.

Rebecca, Lady Tucker, would, he knew, loathe the publicity and take it upon herself to hide away in North Molton more than ever. It mattered not to him, in fact it was an advantage as her presence there would draw him away from London whenever he could escape. Road and rail links to the west country had improved immeasurably although North Devon remained gloriously isolated. Lionel, now fifteen, was doing well at Sherborne while Jessica had inherited from her mother a charming and sunny outlook on life and to all those around her. In short, Sir Wilmot Tucker was content; or nearly so.

If he was honest with himself there was, hidden away at the back of his mind, a concern for his wider family. Jack, who he revered, had had his problems. They had moved poor Lottie from the asylum to somewhere where there was at least a measure of comfort. Durnford Morgan had mentioned to him about Harry and now there was Sarah. Rebecca had told him what Florence Knight had passed on. It was scarcely believable. "She's a remarkable girl," Rebecca had commentated. "Florence saw her and she was quite open about it. There had been this affair, the usual fly-by-night sort of business, and the wretched fellow had all but denied any responsibility."

"And accused her of being a scullery wench into the bargain, no doubt." Wilmot's face had been grim.

"In about as many words. But at least he has had the good grace to put matters to right…to look after her."

"*Huh*…some grace, and guilty as judged by so doing. If that lot stoop to putting their fingers into the purse then it's as good an admission as you'll get." Wilmot had gone white. A vein on his temple was throbbing and she could feel his rage rising. "How dare he? How dare the man treat a girl like that. And our Sarah?" His anger was deep. The Northboroughs and others like them had ridden roughshod how and when they chose. Young serving girls and female house staff were there to be used, to break-in the young blades and to oil the wheels. Picked up, trifled with and discarded; it had always been the same. But not with his family.

∗

"You're looking well, m'dear…in the pink if I might say so. And that goes for the young gentleman, too." Wilmot peered into the wooden crib. It would not have been the way he would have chosen to become better acquainted with his niece, nonetheless it had done the trick. She was indeed a positive and fine looking young

woman. 'Ems', his sister, was there in the girl: he could see it in the fine bone structure and the complexion. But she seemed so self-assured. "And you're happy
enough with the way things are…I mean it's difficult, I know, but you're not having
to tuck yourself away?"

Sarah laughed. It was a bright peal of laughter which caused Wilmot to smile. "Oh,
uncle, goodness no. There have been problems enough and moments, too, but
no…life goes on. It has to. We'll see it through."

"And what about the father, Lord Sharland Preston? Denied it all I suppose? Out
came the purse and away he went." He had to know for certain.

She shrugged. "More or less. But uncle, look." Sarah put her hand on his arm. "I'm
not going to go begging. I *know* he is the father…and so does he, of course, otherwise he wouldn't have paid alimony. But the child will grow and we'll see what
will be. He'll be given a good life, a fine one at that, so I'm as content as I could be."
She paused. "And my thanks to you also, uncle, for your generosity." Wilmot
looked down at her hand. There was certainly something determined about the
girl. He bent down, took her head in his hands and kissed her forehead.

"Yes," he said quietly. "We'll see, and we'll give the boy every chance there
is…every chance."

4

"Aha. Good evening…good evening, your grace." Wilmot nodded to Steer and
limped briskly across from the fireplace to take the Duke of Northborough's hand.
"And a very warm welcome to Court Hall, sir."

"Tucker." The hands clasped and the eyes met momentarily but already Wilmot
had assessed his guest. The body language spoke volumes and the man was just as
he had heard. Herbert Northborough, he thought, looked pompous and bluff, in
fact ideal for what he had in mind. Once his questioning became direct, such overt
self-importance would never conceal the true character that lay beneath. A man like
this would not last five minutes in the city; those around the boardroom table
would eat him alive. Such efforts to create a presence invariably hid weaknesses.
Wilmot was well satisfied with what he saw. It helped him to smile.

"A pleasant drive out, I trust? Folly Lane or the South Molton road?" Wilmot
ushered Steer forward with the salver and watched as his guest raised his glass
briefly in salute then sip thirstily before pausing for breath.

" Folly Lane," he gasped. "It's quicker and time was agin me…I was working late."
Wilmot said nothing, simply let the silence run its full course. Such uneasy
moments, he knew, were advantageous. They tended to draw out those not at
peace with themselves. "Congratulations are in order, I hear, Tucker. You must be
very pleased, and the family as well, no doubt."

Wilmot inclined his head. "A great surprise and, yes, we're all delighted. Very flattering, in fact. Something we must learn to get used to." He laughed drily. "Tell me, sir, you're comfortable at Whitechapel, I take it? It's a marvellous part of the world and the house lies easily, tucked away like it is. It's a wonderful position you've got there." The small talk continued until Steer indicated that dinner was ready.

The Duke made no comment on the fact that he was the only guest, not bothering even to enquire as to the whereabouts and health of his host's family. However, by the time of the call to dinner, Wilmot considered that his visitor should have realised he would be on his own for the evening, a matter which might, in part anyway, explain his diffident manner. And he might thus be wondering, perhaps a shade concerned, as to why it should be so. If he was, then Wilmot was happy enough to let such uneasiness brew quietly until the man felt compelled to comment.

It came as Steer was carving the beef and while Tabor, the fresh-faced and somewhat overweight second butler, was serving. His Grace, so his host observed tartly, had an uncommon regard for both the dry Baron Briare and the Burgundy '38 he was offering. Steer noted it also and twice caught his master's eye, once after the visitor had pushed forward his empty glass impatiently. The butler rose on his toes and frowned at the ceiling. "Well, my good man," Northborough began. "We are quite alone, and seeing as we've not had the pleasure of each other's company before, I feel bound to ask why this is so. I have to say that I'm intrigued and not a little surprised at such...such surreptitious arrangements for our first meeting." An eyebrow had been raised inquiringly.

There it was again. Wilmot smiled to himself at the character of the man. Such boors, he was of the firm belief, always had something to hide and the bigger the bluff the more was hidden. He fingered his glass, speculating as to whether the one opposite knew of his relationship to Sarah, his niece. If so, would he be wondering if he, Wilmot, was aware that his own son, Lord Preston, was the cause of her predicament? Perhaps so: thus the masquerade. Perhaps not, but it was interesting to speculate.

"Aha." Sir Wilmot Tucker lifted a hand in horror. "How remiss of me, sir, and my apologies...my apologies indeed. Of course and I should have explained earlier." He smiled disarmingly and sat back with his elbows resting on the arms of his chair and with his hands clasped together. "You see, as I have become aware, you and I are moving in the same direction...as far as business is concerned, that is. Ilfracombe and Bideford lie not too distant from each other. Yes?" He cocked an eye and leant forward in a show of eagerness. "And it appears that we might have similar interests...in the maritime world. I thought, therefore, it might be prudent for us to consider each other's enterprise quietly and by ourselves. Harmony in such matters is so much more desirable than conflict."

"But now, listen here." The Duke dabbed at his mouth. "What I choose to do from Ilfracombe is entirely my own affair and really, in spite of your excellent hospitality this evening, I see no reason to declare my hand." He sat back and threw an arm over the back of his chair. His look might have been devil-may-care or it might have been from one whose authority had been challenged unexpectedly. "And why so, might I ask, are you taking this line? What is all this about?"

"Well...first of all let me say that it is indeed your prerogative to remain silent. I respect that, of course, but do you not think that, by combining our ideas, our visions for the future perhaps, that we might be able to assist one another." It was nonsense but the bait on his hook had to look tempting.

"Or compete." The Duke's shoulders shook as he chortled at the idea. His eyes were wide, frog-like, and Wilmot saw the look. *'Who is this fellow?'*, it was saying. *'Who is this man here suggesting working with me?'* "I've ideas and plenty of them," he went on. "Some of them are good, too, and I have to say that I'm happy enough the way things are."

"But America's dead." Wilmot cut in sharply.

"Poof, and who says so? One would have to be very naïve to think that...remarkably short sighted." Wilmot shrugged, eased himself and pushed back a lock of hair. Now the Duke leant forward. "Is that what you *really* think? Once you start talking like that, my good man, it's nothing short of scaremongering, y'know. Not trying to frighten me off by any chance?"

Wilmot raised a hand. "Indeed not, sir, but that is the word right now. You've an excellent concern going for you, that I do know, and I'd hate to see it founder." He was again sitting upright with his hands together. "There'd be no need, for there's room enough for us both on the high seas...literally oceans of room. But right now there's the war *and* the blockade. It's just that I've been advised to look elsewhere for the time being. America will come back, for sure, but I thought you'd like to know." He shrugged then looked down and adjusted his cuff.

"That's the word from Bideford, eh? From the Bideford docks?" The chuckle might have been genuine but Wilmot suspected it was contrived. A glance confirmed it.

He inclined his head, feigning surprise. "Now, there's a thought. But no, goodness me, no. Dear old Bideford doesn't pretend to look any further than the bar across the mouth of the estuary. They're doing me well, down there, and proudly so. However I wouldn't want my dockside to start telling me what to do and where to go. But there're others...the City, the House, those that know...or should."

"Hmmph." The Duke was silent but Wilmot sensed the mood had changed. The bluffness had gone, as had the desire to bear down, but he remained as one spoiling for a fight. His guest was trying to fathom him out, trying to get a fresh line on this upstart who had asked him all the way out to dine alone with him and who was now preaching from the head of the table, telling him how to run his business. That was how his mind would be working. But he was less sure of himself than before.

✳

The dessert came, and the cheese, and the fruit, and the port and canary. They walked through to the large, deserted drawing room, Wilmot limping half a pace behind his guest yet courteously stepping forward to show him the way. They sat and they talked on, and it was only when Wilmot spoke of his own household that conversation turned to family matters. The Duke spoke proudly of his own and it was after listening to the praises heaped upon Lord Thomas that Wilmot enquired about his guest's second son. "The boy'll be following you no doubt...into business, that is?" His question came innocently enough.

"In time, in time." The Duke raised his chin and fingered his collar. "He's fiddling about just now. Can't make up his mind what to do with himself. Like so many, today."

"Yes...like so many, indeed," Wilmot mused quietly. He nodded and inclined his head knowingly then turned to the butler asking for the night tray to be left and for the staff to be dismissed. "Thank you, Steer, that will be all. My thanks to you and to Tabor...and to old Crang out there." He lifted his hand in acknowledgement as the butler bowed and withdrew." Now he was ready.

"Well, he's young enough just yet," the Duke continued. "And he's still enjoying himself." Wilmot nodded understandingly. He rose and took the other's glass. "And who can blame them, eh?" the older man went on. "Life gets serious enough soon enough these days. But I expect he'll knuckle down one day...I'll be needing him around in a year or two."

Wilmot returned the Duke's glass, now re-filled. He then sat and pulled his chair round so he was facing his guest like a partner across the card table: it was then that he struck. "Well, I'm glad to hear it...very glad. You see I, or rather *we*, will be needing him around, too."

"Mmm?"

"Sarah?" Wilmot raised his eyebrows and lifted his head. "Sarah Kingdon? The governess at Hartland. Does the name mean anything?" The Duke's frown was shortlived and his face began to empty. "You've heard word, I'm sure. In fact I know you have...you see, she told me."

"Mmm? Told you? Who told you what, might I ask?" By now the mouth was half open, the look one of incredulity. "I'm not sure that I ..."

"Then allow me." Wilmot's voice was quiet and he moved himself away from the lamp, so the Duke could see him better, and he him. "You see, young Sarah Kingdon's my niece. She's a Tucker by birth, daughter of my sister Emma and a niece of Jack, my brother...a man whom I understand you know well from the past." He checked his nails then looked up again.

"She, Sarah, worked for the Orchards at Hartland, a family you and your son know *also*. And know well, as it happens, although the circumstances are somewhat different." He raised a hand as if to dismiss the comparison as insignificant. "You stay there quite often, I believe. So," he paused to study the Duke's face. "Whilst there my niece had a brief encounter…she conceived, became with child. Naturally she had to leave. She returned home and eventually the child was born. Well two, twins as it happens, but the first, a girl, died. However, the second, a boy…young Isaac is very much alive and doing well.

"What are you saying?" The words were barely whispered. "Are you trying to suggest…why, if you are…."

"I'm *suggesting* nothing, sir. Everything thus far is the truth, albeit perhaps a touch bitter." Wilmot was staring at him intently, only his eyes moving in order to take in everything. For a moment the Duke glared back then his eyes dropped. "You see, Sarah swears the father of her child is your son…Sharland *and*, my dear sir," he raised a hand to discourage interruption. "Before you dismiss this as either some scandalous outrage or mere trifle of no consequence, perhaps you can explain why your boy took it upon himself to visit my niece the very morning after her confinement. Hardly idle curiosity, I would suggest. Hardly the actions of one who should, under normal circumstances, be totally unconcerned about the fate of some mother and her child. In fact, hardly the actions of anyone but those of the father himself."

For a moment, the Duke was silent; his one free hand clenching and unclenching. He glared at Wilmot. By now his face had coloured and his eyes were staring as if unseen hands had him by the throat. "Why you *devil*, Tucker."

"Oh, no." Wilmot cut in decisively. "Before you dispute anything at all I suggest you think very carefully as to what I have just said." He spoke slowly and deliberately. "Up until the time of the confinement there may have been *some* grounds for dispute, *perhaps*…or even a bold denial, but *since* then the actions and attitude of your son have, I would suggest, placed the situation beyond any doubt. And I speak, of course, of the alimony he has offered. Right now is hardly the time to begin an aggressive defence of a matter which is quite indefensible."

Herbert Northborough slumped in his chair, one hand clutching his glass. The fingers of the other eased his collar as Wilmot continued. "I would suggest, sir, that neither party has emerged with credit from this. Problems have been created that will not go away as I am sure you would wish. This will *never* go away…for I will see to that. Might I suggest that, far from allowing the situation to run away with us, that we, you and I, discuss the matter calmly and…if possible, amicably."

But it was not to be. Lord Herbert Preston, The fifth Duke of Northborough had been humiliated. He had been outmanoeuvred, not by the facts, though they were bad enough, but by an up-jumped, young whipper-snapper. It rankled and it hurt, and he took his leave.

Chapter Ten

As soon as she saw him coming into the yard, Kitty built up the kitchen fire. Now he was inside and standing almost in the hearth itself. Sometimes the flames drew well and the logs crackled busily, on other occasions a layer of blue smoke hung dispiritedly in the kitchen air, as if unwilling to face the outside. Today she was lucky.

Before he came in Jack brushed what snow he could from his hair but it had matted with ice. His coat was heavy and so cold were his boots and leggings that the ice only began to melt as his body warmed. She watched as he stamped his feet and blew on his hands. He must have sensed her standing there for he looked up and caught her eye. "How's the chest, m'love?" he asked tenderly. "Still coughing?"

She shrugged and took his hand. "Still there...more or less." He could see she was having to draw in her breath. "Oh, it'll be a day or two yet, I expect. But...come on you, Jack Tucker." She grinned impishly and reached up to pinch his cheek. "Away with yer questions and get yerself sorted. Supper's ready and's still too hot to touch...just as you like it."

*

It had been the worst blizzard for years and yet it was March. The snowdrops had come and gone already. Early daffodils were in bloom and now primroses were appearing in the hedgerows. Jack had heard the first curlews; they had come up from the estuaries to check on their nesting grounds and it was their long bubbling cry that told him spring was not far off. Arthur Fisher from Ferny Ball and Wally Sexton had both swaled the high common, burning off the dead bracken and old heather, yet winter had returned with pitiless cruelty.

This time he had seen it. Almost a week ago the weather had started to change. He remembered how, overnight, the wind had gone out to the northeast and when he had gone up to Sixty Acres it had blown with a remorseless, stinging blast. Twice his hat had been torn from his head and his old cavalry coat had tugged at his body when he turned his back to the wind. The fields were bare; there was not a blade of keep to be seen, just a few hardy clumps of rushes standing defiant against the weather. Even the dogs had cowered with their backs hunched and heads down, barely able to work, and it had been a struggle to get the stock down from the hill.

At first there had been little snow, a mere powdering that was blown like dust into corners. But the ground had frozen hard with water in the puddles icing so quickly that pockets of air crunched underfoot as they walked across the yard. The following day it tried to snow and it was then that Jack and Stan Bawden saw the hinds in the bracken down by the large sweep of Sherdon Water. "It'll be with us proper, shortly," he predicted as they watched the deer move away. The creatures scarcely broke into a trot before they stopped together and looked back with their heads high, sensing carefully yet more curious than afraid. "When the hinds are in like that, they know what's coming. 'Tis late for such weather though…badly late an' we're going to pay for it."

The first snow fell the following evening. It was the lambing flock that had worried him, but they were now in the shearing barn. What cattle had not been pressed into the shippons they penned in the rick yard. Jack opened up two of the lower ricks, but it was water that was important so they filled the troughs from the well, bucket by bucket, and watched as the animals drank thirstily.

Earlier, Kitty and Anna had ridden into Withypool for provisions with Anna leading the pack pony. They needed more lamp oil and wicks, flour, salt and lard for the house. Kitty wanted knitting wool from Mrs Spanner and vegetables from the market before going on to pick up Frank's boots. Jack had asked them to collect two sacks of grain from the mill and to see Newcomb, the saddler, about the old work harness. It was the usual weekly run but there, in the middle of it all, Kitty felt her breathlessness come on again.

Twice on the way home they had to stop. Every time she coughed she felt the sharp pain under her ribs where, before, there had been no more than a dull ache. That evening she felt tired and listless when, for her, the day should have been nothing. Supper was an effort and Jack could see she was not right. For two nights he had lain awake listening to her breathing, easing himself away from her as she tossed restlessly. She dismissed it all, as he knew she would, brushing aside their concern and telling them that it was no worse than she had had before. There was work to be done, she proclaimed, and, in any case, there was nothing anybody could do; not out at Sherdon. That was three days ago. The bad weather had taken Jack away from the house and it was Anna who told him that Kitty was getting weaker and her cough worsening.

As he stood warming himself with his back to the fire, he watched carefully. Even when she had pinched his cheek just now, he could see she was struggling for breath. Her chest had been heaving at the mere effort of putting a few logs on the fire and there had been little of her usual bubble. She had tried a brave smile but it had been an effort and, as she carried supper through to the table, his eyes followed her.

It was her cry that brought them running. They found her bending half over, one hand to her side the other clutching the table for support. Each time she coughed, she cried out. Anna had been right.

✳

Doctor Baillie closed the bedroom door behind him. He paused and pursed his lips while one hand pulled at his chin. He then frowned and scratched at the back of his head. Edgar Baillie, a shortish, rather plump man, with a shock of red hair and pince-nez spectacles perched on his pointed nose, was the same age as Jack. It was he who had officiated at the duel when Kenton Knight was killed and he had never got over how fiercely Jack had fought. Now that Dr Collyns had retired, Baillie visited Sherdon more frequently. He felt easy in their company, and they in his. He always enjoyed staying on for a chat and bowl of soup, but this morning was going to be difficult.

It had not taken him long to see what a state she was in. If only they had called him earlier; but that was typical. Time and again he had warned them to come for him as soon as they were worried about something but they never listened, only hurrying along at the last minute when they could no longer cope. He shook his head and moved steadily down the stairs, his boots clumping noisily on the bare boards.

"I have to say that I'm none too happy." The faces looked up at the sound of his high pitched voice and he could see their concern. He would break the news gently but would have to leave them in no doubt. "There're two things, Jack." Baillie joined them at the fireside, leaving his bag on the table and rubbing his hands, glad to be down from the cold. "Pneumonia's there for sure, I'm afraid...and that's what's brought the girl right down. Her lungs are infected, the left one in particular. And it's *that* that's brought on the fever...she's running a high temperature." He said nothing about the blueing of her lips, or the blood in her phlegm which was worrying him.

"But then there's the pain when she coughs...even when she breathes in. We call it pleurisy and the pneumonia often brings it on." He saw Jack's frown. "It's not so bad on its own but when the girl's struggling for breath she can do without the pain and the added infection. It's the membranes around the lung. Here...see." He demonstrated by running his hand around his chest. "It gets inflamed and that's where the pain is. Put the two together and we've got ourselves a very sick patient up there." The doctor looked at them from over his spectacles as if inviting questions.

"What's to do then, doctor?" Jack pulled out a chair and sat, motioning the doctor to another. Taking his seat, Baillie saw the look on his face. "D'you reckon...I mean, d'you think that...."

"She's very sick, Jack, but there're a number of things we can do and I had it in mind it might be something like this. Your lad described it well enough over at the surgery. Now then." He leant forward and tapped the table. "The first thing's warmth...the girl needs to be kept warm and it's like an ice house in winter up there. You'll have to bring her bed down here by the fire...and it's to be kept going. Right?" He nodded at Jack's glance. "And as for what's to do..." Baillie reached for his bag. "I'll be leaving these with you. The first, here look." He rummaged clumsily before producing a small brown bottle. "Laudanum, you've seen it before...three or four drops every afternoon and again at last thing. It'll help her to sleep, stop that coughing for a while and it'll give things a chance to settle."

Edgar Baillie took his time. Jack, he knew, would look after her but there was the iodine, the licorice root then the mustard plasters. He went through what had to be done, how Kitty should be kept and what she should do and not do. He hated leaving the household like this, but there was no other way: they had to know. Jack accompanied him to his horse and held the reins of the bay as Baillie strapped his bag to the saddle, then watched as he hopped clumsily before clambering aboard. "She's bad, isn't she."

"Yes." The doctor looked at him. "She's not at all well but," he held up a finger, "I'm hopeful…there's a strong will there and that's half the battle." Jack's eyes closed. "But there's something to remember, y'know. These things leave their mark. She'll be weakened by it and will always be vulnerable to another attack. You'll have to think on it, Jack. It's a wonderful place out here but not if you're susceptible to this sort of thing."

The doctor's handshake was firm and Jack watched him until he had disappeared from view. The news was bad; he could sense it. The doctor had not said as much but the signals were clear enough. Kitty was very ill and, even if she recovered, she would be weakened. He took a deep breath and blew disconsolately. His Kitty…oh, dear God…the one who had come to his side and stood by him throughout all his days, months…his years, of hardship. Now it was her.

He never felt the chill breeze that cut through his shirt as he walked down the lane. Following the doctor's horse seemed sensible enough but it didn't matter where his feet took him. He had to clear his head of the thoughts racing through his mind. It was fate again: black, evil fate. What on earth had she done to deserve being struck down like this…and why him? Not again, surely. Surely to goodness he was not going to lose her as well. Not after everything else…after Katherine, Lottie and Harry. Was there a curse on the place after all?

It was what Kitty had said last night. He remembered how she had woken him, how she had shaken him roughly and how, in an instant, he had been alerted by what she was telling him. It was the sound of her voice. She had had this dream. It had been about Charlotte and Katherine. And there had been that ruby and pearl necklace. It had been there dancing in front of her eyes, she whispered fearfully, and while she was looking at it, she had seen the others. Their faces had been frightened and their arms were waving as if they were appealing for help but she had done nothing. Then, slowly, and as she watched, they faded from sight leaving only the necklace, by now lying snugly back in the leather pouch.

It was an omen, Kitty had declared. She was sure of it or she would never have seen it like that. It was the curse of that family, the Northboroughs, and she had thrown her arms around him and held on before her body began to shake with her husky coughing. Eventually she calmed and fell asleep, her small body curled up and turned away from him.

At first he had dismissed it, but what she said kept returning and he had lain awake thinking about it. Now it was here again. Was there, he wondered, something there after all? Was there something evil out here that went after those he loved and which was now stalking the one who meant so much to him? He turned and walked slowly back to the farm and when he reached the yard he looked up at the house. He saw her figure at the middle upstairs window, dressed in her long, white flannel nightgown. She had been watching him and raised a hand in a wave which he returned. He then waved again and lengthened his stride, suddenly aware of the fading light and how cold he had become.

2

"I *don't* like it...don't like it at all. It's a scandalous business from beginning to end."

"Father, I know." Sharland Preston sat uneasily in the deep, red leather, library chair. He looked more comfortable than he felt. "But I have to say it again, the whole thing is of my own making. Sir Wilmot Tucker can *not* be blamed for fighting his family's corner. We can't do that."

Father and son had met at Blagdon. The Duke was beginning to feel trapped. On one side there were the Tuckers, not the least of whom was the mother of his son's child...his own grandson. And now his own boy, the father, was making overtures towards the woman. The other day he had even spoken of marriage. There had been another row but it had got them nowhere. Now he was irritated about it all, as well as being worried.

"That Tucker fellow's far too full of himself and anyway, look at him...common as dirt from the neck down. Too clever by half, but a common little man. If it wasn't for him sticking his oar in like this we'd be shot of the whole damned business by now. Wretched man...won't let go." The Duke walked to the library window only too well aware that, years ago, he had been summoned to this very room by his own father to witness a similar family dispute. His sister, Katherine, had walked out...and for another Tucker. It was simply unbelievable: the great Northborough dynasty brought to its knees twice and by the same family. "And this is what makes you start talking like you are, I suppose." He looked down at his brown and white check trousers, then bent and flicked angrily at something.

"No, not at all, sir. I had become fond of Sarah before I knew her uncle even existed. It really is nothing to do with him. Nothing whatsoever. In fact you told me that when you dined with him at Court Hall...you said he even offered advice and help over Ilfracombe. Well, if that's so, a bit of charity's in order, is it not? Come, father." The Duke's back was turned but he knew he was listening. "That's hardly the mind of a common little man and certainly nothing to pillory him for. I know you were angry with him, but *why*? What had he done to deserve that?"

"He shouldn't start meddling in other people's affairs and certainly not mine. Should keep that nose of his *out*." The Duke half turned. He remembered it well and, even now, the way the man had taken the battle to him over his son's conduct grated. And he had been clever, too, the slyboots; the way he produced the evidence like he had. Tucker had done his homework, all right, and there was nothing much to be said in reply…and that hurt.

"Look father. You may well dislike the man intensely but I repeat it again, you can't blame him for this. And, besides, as far as business goes he *is* very successful…and well connected. He knows his way around the City backwards and his political connections are strong…on both sides."

"Damned Liberals…they'd give the nation away if they'd half a chance."

"Damned Liberals, maybe, but they *are* the government and Tucker knows them all…Gladstone in particular. He's Leader of the House and his card's clearly been marked. After Russell, so they say, and Palmerston's no longer a fit man. William Gladstone could be there or thereabouts sooner than we think and Tucker's close to the man. Like that." He crossed his fingers. "But the Tories too, y'know. Frederic Knight's his man there and *he's* the one with Lord Derby's ear."

"Damned Knights."

"Father, *look*." Sharland rose and walked over to his father. He half pulled him around and placed a hand on each shoulder. "It's *me*," he said. "You've got to accept it's *me*…*my* fault. You can't go on blaming the whole world and damning everyone left, right and centre. Try to accept it. Don't you think I've been agonising about it all, wondering how on earth I'm going to live with it."

"And all you can think of is *marrying* the girl." He scowled darkly at the thought. "I mean, look where she comes from. Mmm? Who is she? She couldn't cope, wouldn't know how to behave. She, she…." He waved his arms. "What would everyone think, for God's sake?"

"Father stop." Sharland was surprised at the strength of his own voice. "You're sounding just like dear mother used to. Sarah's not a disgrace to anyone…far from it. The Orchards thought the world of her. Jocelyn's been to see her twice and the children have been screaming out for her. They hate the present woman and even Desmond admitted he missed her…come on, it was *you* that told me that. Blue blood there might not be but the girl can stand on her own two feet. We've seen it, all of us…even you told me so." Sharland let his hands fall and the two stood in silence.

"Can't be right," the Duke muttered. "It still can't be right." He turned to the window again, both hands sweeping at his tight curly hair in frustration. "Damned good job your brother doesn't go around behaving like this…what then, for Heaven's sake?"

"I was not blessed with primogeniture."

"And a merciful blessing *that's* turned out to be…I know you're the second son but it still leaves us in a devil of a predicament. Any formal union would still be a blight on our line."

"Maybe it's not perfect but the alternatives are far worse. I couldn't bear to walk away from it all, just leave her…and my son. I *could* not, and *would* not go through life without seeing him. And as for paying to keep her tucked away…father, it's degrading. It's humiliating and if we went on doing that then our Mr Wilmot Tucker would indeed climb on his high horse…and who could blame him." Sharland paused. He looked past his father and on to the lawn where three peacocks, one of them white, were feeding. "Father, listen. You must believe me…I've spent the whole winter thinking about it…almost with nothing else on my mind. Paris and Rome were disasters and life here's been…well, not much fun."

"Have you seen her…seen the boy?"

"No. I tried twice as soon as I knew but she didn't want to see me. Then I wrote a number of times from here and from Paris but…nothing."

"Well, it's hardly your fault then." He looked round, his face suddenly brighter. "I mean, if she's going to turn her back on you, bite the hand so to speak, well, that's her affair. You simply can't go tying yourself up with a situation like that. When the woman won't even acknowledge you. Mmm? It's mad, bizarre. What sort of life is that?"

He replied slowly, a word at a time. "Father, I'm going down to Whitechapel and I'm going to see for myself." He paused. "I want to see this son of mine and I want to see his mother as well."

"You really are serious aren't you?" The Duke looked at his son, then walked slowly to the round centre table and stared down, fingering the edge as if studying the ebony parquetry. "All right, my boy." He said eventually. Sharland watched the shoulders sag. "You know my feelings and they'll never change. I don't like it and I never will. But I can't forbid it; as you say there's the boy to think of. And if his mother's half the girl you're telling me she is then…hmmph." The grunt and shrug were lifeless and he shook his head. "It's just that…oh, I don't know. There could be the very devil to pay for all this, y'know."

"Well, let us see. It may not be this way at all. She may close the door on me and send me on my way back here?"

"Hmmph." The Duke shook his head again.

3

Sharland continued to agonise over what might be. As his father said, there could be the very devil to pay. If he was honest with himself, he hardly knew her and to whisk her away into the world of Blagdon and Hartland, of Filleigh, of Arlington and London was a frightening risk that could so well end in disaster.

High society was cruel and unforgiving. She would be deemed to have forced her way in and there would be those who would set about her with relish, watching her every step, listening to her every word. Her dress, her manners, the ease and confidence she exuded…all would be dissected minutely and every tiny morsel examined by eagle-eyed society matrons. And their daughters were no better, *worse* often, with the tittering and gossiping behind the fans, the scowling and frowning and tut-tutting at the cut of her silks or the grace of her offered hand, or anything, anything at all. Any excuse to comment, to smirk or to carp…they would love it and feast off it. No, it was not going to be easy.

And yet the very mention of her name filled him with a sense of longing to see her again. But, then, suppose she *did* keep her back turned? Suppose she *did* dismiss him and send him on his way? Perhaps her uncle had warned her about the way things should be. His father, of course, would be delighted. The prodigal son would be welcomed home and the fatted calf killed. But what about himself; life without her and never a sight of his son? The mere thought chilled.

He kicked on, his black cloak swirling behind him in the spring breeze. Arlot, his groom, was no more than a couple of lengths behind and, as he glanced round, he noted that the grey was more dappled than he remembered. The sunken eyes of the older man, tucked away behind the black beard, saw him looking back and smiled cheerily in return. Above them, skylarks were singing. The blackthorn was out and the long, cold winter seemed a while ago.

*

"Perhaps I might be allowed to wait?" Sharland had already detected the coolness in her glance. For a moment Emma had panicked. All her life she had been taught to curtsey and step aside when those of such noble birth came her way. "*My lord,*" it should have been. "*Of course, sir, and if it pleases you…I'll see to it right away, sir.*" But what now? Standing in front of her was the father of her daughter's child. In an instant the tears and recriminations of last winter came flooding back. Here was the man who stole her daughter's innocence, then denied it and then tried to buy her off. And here he was *now*, standing in her parlour asking if he might wait until she returned.

"That might not be wise, sir. I have to say that my daughter is not well disposed towards her present situation. Neither she, nor her father…nor do I consider her treatment to have been…well…."

"Forgive me, madam." His voice was contrite. "I understand, only too well. Believe me I do."

"I think not, sir. How can you possibly understand how this has changed our lives." Emma had begun to find her confidence. "It has been a terrible time for us all…made more so by the fact that *you* sir, the father, have chosen to ignore our situation."

"Madam, please." Sharland held out his hands. "That is the very reason why I am here today." He saw her look of bemusement. "I assure you that the past has also dwelt heavily upon me and I could not continue without coming here to see your daughter...and my son. You see...in spite of what you might think, Sarah does mean a great deal to me."

"Enough, sir." Emma raised her hand and looked over his shoulder. "She comes directly, here. Now let her have *her* say. Pray, allow my daughter to decide for herself whether or not she wishes to continue any form of association. I cannot speak for her...." Sharland turned as the door opened. For a second and while she frowned into the gloom to be certain who it was, Sarah held the door, then she turned and closed it slowly before entering the room. He could tell she had recognised him.

"It's Lord Preston, dear."

"Thank you, mother." She glanced down as she unbuttoned her blue-grey cape then up at Sharland. Her face was flushed because she had been hurrying home and because of the fresh breeze. A lock of fair hair had fallen to her cheek and her eyes were shining. "A surprise, Sharland...but perhaps not the most pleasant, I have to confess." She was still breathless and her chest was rising and falling.

"Look, dear...it's best if I leave you. I'll...."

"No, stay mother. Lord Preston will not be long. *So*," she sighed and laid her cape over the back of fireside chair then tucked back her hair. "What is your business here? To what do we owe this unexpected pleasure?"

"Sarah, as I said to your mother, I had to come...I just had to." Sarah noted how his side-whiskers met above the striped, silk neckcloth. His face was fuller, the pinched look had gone. For a moment she wanted to reach up and brush back his hair where his hat had flattened it against his forehead, but then she remembered. He was on his guard but his hazel eyes stayed with hers. "I came down from Blagdon last night. The whole point of my journey to North Devon was to see you...and to talk." Both turned as the door behind them closed. They were on their own. "But first, might I enquire if you are well?" he stammered. "And the child, also?"

"Very well, thank you. Yes, we are both in excellent health...and excellent spirits. But come, Sharland, why this and now? It has been six months since the child was born and well over a year since you knew I was carrying your son. Why this sudden desire to come here, to..." she waved her hand, lost for the right word. More, she could feel herself getting angry. "You made your intentions plain right from the start," she continued. "You denied everything, you fled from the situation and you deserted me. I am no longer employed. My status, my lively-hood...everything is lost, and all you could do was to try and buy me off which, incidentally and now that you are here, you can stop. I have a family, you know, and I need neither your concern nor your support." For a moment he did not move, then his eyes dropped and he lowered his head. "Well?" she continued. "Well, Sharland? What *is* this all about? What have you got to say for yourself?"

"I want you. You and your boy…our son. I want you both to be mine." He swallowed. The words had come tumbling out. He could not have said anything else for it was exactly what had been on his mind.

Sarah turned, gathered her skirts and sat. "Oh, do you? Well, a greater change of heart it would be difficult to imagine. Just six months ago, you were wishing me out of your life. So, pray, why this now? *Why*, after all this time have you suddenly come back? Mmm? *Why?* If I was a fool, a complete fool, someone who was blinded by your position in life, I might believe you *meant* what you have just said. But whatever I am, I am certainly no fool. My supposition is that your one desire is to legitimise your son and heir. Yes? The future Lord Preston; it's him you are after, not me. That's what you want, is it not?"

"Of course I do," he blurted. "Your assumption is correct. I'm desperate to see my son but not only him. Sarah, do please believe me." He took a step towards her but she looked up sharply. "Believe me…you, too, have been constantly in my thoughts. I have tried to live without you, tried to forget you knowing that it might be easier for us all that way, but…I could not." He shrugged dejectedly. "You have been constantly on my mind. If you agree to nothing more, today, will you accept that what I have said is the truth…honestly and sincerely…the whole truth."

She was silent for longer then he expected. When she rose, he stepped back. "I cannot answer that. How can I possibly believe what you say, *anything* you say, after your behaviour? And then…even if I did believe you and tried to accept what you have done. Even if I could manage that, I would have to ask myself if I really wanted to become part of your life. Right now the answer is *no*. I am content where I am, here with my son and my family…and, to be honest, good sir, I find it difficult to give what you say any credibility whatsoever. You hurt me grievously…it was a dreadful, loathsome way to be treated and I doubt that I could ever put my trust in you again." She could see she was hurting him.

"All that I accept…all of it," he replied. "And I am only relieved that you did not ask me to leave the moment you set eyes upon me just now. Might I, therefore, ask one thing of you…if I have not asked too much already. And that is this." He paused to catch his breath. "Might I ask you to consider what I have said. Do not, I beg you, reject me out of hand this very instant. Allow time to run its course and to temper your thoughts. I can imagine how you must be feeling. Angry, no doubt, bitter and aggrieved as well. I…I will not even attempt to apologise…no matter how eloquently expressed, such sentiments would seem wholly insincere."

"They most certainly would. But, yes." She sighed wearily and inclined her head which then shook slowly as if she was in two minds. "I'll *try*. I'll do my best to consider it, that is. It will be difficult to reason coherently with my emotions but I *will* try." But already she knew.

"Then might I call upon you again, say in a week or so when you have had time. And I would dearly love to see my child…might I ask if that will be possible."

"Yes, but in my own time. I will write to let you know when I am ready…*if* and *when* I can ever be so. Never fear, Sharland, I will let you know to your face." Suddenly her tone had become decisive. "You will not find *me* turning away and running from this situation however difficult it might be. I will find you…where will it be? Whitechapel or Blagdon, which?" Her eyebrows rose impatiently.

"Here at Whitechapel. I shall wait here." She could see his relief. "But now I shall take my leave. You have shown me more consideration than I dared hope and more than I deserve. My thanks indeed…permit me." She allowed him to take her hand and watched as he lifted it to his lips, then nodded in acknowledgement as he bowed before closing the door behind him.

Her heart was pounding. She was furious with the wretched man. How *dare* he…the heartless creature. But, in and amongst the anger, there was a surge of excitement. His eyes, his voice and his fine features still attracted. For all his ways, he remained a handsome devil. He had behaved like the veritable King of Hell but it had taken much for him to come back as he had. He was contrite, he was humble…and he was sincere. She could see that and had felt it as he stood beside her. If he were not then his desire to see them would have long since evaporated. And, if he was prepared to do that then…well, she would consent. But it would be her, Sarah Kingdon, who would say when. And it would be she who would say how and at what price. When she was ready, and only then, she would summon him and give her reply.

*

The letter arrived a week later and, true to her word, Sarah would be pleased to see him at Church Street when she would give him her considered reply. Sharland had agonised at what he might take with him. In the end he decided to take nothing; one way or another her mind would be made up and the mere thought of arriving bearing some offering appeared gratuitous in the extreme. In the event it would have been wholly inappropriate. Church Street was narrow and cobbled, inconvenient for a groom to be waiting with two horses, so he decided on the phaeton. Grainger, the young Whitechapel coachman, could wait in the market area behind The George and it was only a short walk across the tree-lined square.

She received him coolly but the kettle was on the maid. There was no sign of anyone else and no sign of the child. He had no idea what to make of it. After placing his top hat and cane carefully behind the door, he fumbled with his short, grey overcoat, grateful and surprised to feel her helping him and thankful of her offer of a seat.

"I accept." He had barely sat and struggled to get up but she raised a hand. "No, wait," she demanded. "This is by no means an ordinary situation, it is really quite *extra* ordinary. Love and affection, the cornerstones of any marriage, may or may not come into it, only time will tell. But there are conditions to which you and your family must agree." By now, Sarah was sitting calmly with one elbow on the arm of her chair. Even in the half-light of the cottage and accepting the situation, Sharland was taken by her looks. Her cream coloured silk dress was hemmed with a woven flower design. The wide neckline was similarly embroidered and her red bonnet trimmed with flowers and ribbons. Her skin was soft and there was no more than the slightest hint of rouge or kohl. "Strange though it may seem, Sharland Preston, I do have feelings for you...*some* feelings and very mixed they are at the moment, as you might expect." She could see the expectation in his face.

"My present circumstances, my financial situation, and I hate to bring this up, are secure for the present. You may not be aware of it but I am well supported by my family." She half rose to ease her skirts. "That is no problem...it is the future of my child and, indeed, my own position in whichever life I choose to live that has been of most concern, and it is to our son that I have attached my conditions."

"Of course." Sharland sitting opposite her, leant forward. One hand came to his mouth as he cleared his throat. "You must understand that I, too, have been considering the situation."

"But there is more to all this. I mean, what about your family? There must surely be hostility...outrage at such a proposition. Who on earth will hear of a humble governess being swept into such a society as you are proposing to do. And your *father,* what about him? Knowing him as I do, I cannot believe he will ever accept my becoming part of his family. The very idea must appall him."

"Yes...and no." Sharland laughed self-consciously. "You are very observant. My father is a difficult man and when I first told him he was indeed, how shall I say, moved to protest. But he has mellowed and now more or less accepts the situation. But he is a man of the old guard, I'm afraid. It matters not so much to him that his titles will not come to me, rather he would have preferred me to have scoured the land for one that would satisfy his approbation." Here he paused. "But it was the boy, your son...*our* son, that changed his mind. I told him that I would never desert the child, or indeed you, no matter what. He saw I meant it. Initially he tried to dissuade me but I made clear that this was the way it was going to be."

"And me? What about me? How will he accept *me* and what about his family and the society in which he lives...what are they all going to think?"

"It will not be easy, I admit to that. But we will face whatever we have to, together. I would not be here now if I was not prepared to do that. It would be madness for me to come here today, to seek your hand and then to fight shy of what others may think. And, in any case, every new member of any family comes under merciless scrutiny...for a while...and after that some other poor soul arrives to be judged and tried, and the world moves on. A pattern of relationships is set one way or the other and I am more than happy that this shall be of little consequence to us. As it so happens I *know* you will be a success, and for certain with those of concern." The two were silent.

Eventually Sarah spoke. "No matter what you have said and no matter what we imagine the future might hold, our relationship is still untried. We have yet to get to know one another like any other couple who, of course, will have had the advantage of time. Circumstances have thrown us together and I have to know that Isaac, our son, and I are secure."

"Isaac? Oh yes, of course. That is to be his name…Isaac, the son of Sarah."

"Yes. Isaac, the one who laughs, so they say. The one in whom God delights. That is his name."

 For a moment he was silent. His mouth became a line and he looked down at his hands. "Indeed," he whispered. "Yes, indeed…and these conditions, what are you suggesting?"

"That we are married in church and that only those who support and have faith in our union bear witness to the occasion. Society, if that is who they are, will have to wait to find out about me. I want only those who respect us to be there and *none* for whom this is some cheap drama. *But,* and this is important, before I agree to anything, *anything* at all, I insist that Isaac is recognised as the true heir to the family line. You will have to go back to your father and insist that this is made clear so there can be no possible chance that our son will be forsaken." She saw him purse his lips. "There is no alternative, Sharland, no alternative at all. If you want me to accept, I need to know where I, and our son, stand, and not just live in the vain hope that somehow everything will fall into place. And finally, I shall need further financial security." She saw his look.

"Oh, yes," she continued. "Anything can happen. Anything, as you and I well know. My family are providing for me most generously at present but, if I accept your proposal, all that will cease. Then I will need my own security and one commensurate with my new-found position. Do not think for one moment that I am one who is prepared to come begging every time I need a new dress, or a horse…or a lady's maid. I am expecting nothing less than full financial independence, no matter what might be said or thought about it."

She touched the corner of her mouth and took a deep breath. "I am content enough with your proposal Sharland and once you have persuaded me that you have accepted my conditions then I will accept as I have said. But I shall never be able to forget the past." As he rose and stood over her, she looked up at him.

"Allow me." He took her hands and steadied her as she rose. They were close. She could feel his clothes touching hers and his breath on her face but made no move to distance herself. "Really? You mean that?" She nodded and smiled before dropping her gaze.

4

Thursday the twenty-eighth of March dawned wet and half a gale was blowing. But it mattered not for today was the first day of Spring staghunting and Lord

Thomas Preston had been up before daybreak.

The meet was to be at the gates on the moor above Molland and it would take an hour to get there. From time to time as he moved about the stable yard, his old back injury caused him to wince, but this morning nothing could dampen his spirits. Elsie Summerfield, slimmer now and far more fetching than hitherto, would be riding out from Filleigh with Gertrude Frobisher. He had not seen her since the New Year's ball at Blagdon and the idea of her company was appealing.

The ball had been a success. His father had taken the opportunity to introduce Sharland and Sarah to those in Hampshire who had not been invited to the small wedding party he had given them before Christmas. Elsie had remembered Sarah from Hartland and he was cheered by how the two had got on; even his father appeared to have rejoiced in the company of his new daughter-in-law. Once, and Thomas was sure of it, the Duke held her rather too close, close enough for her to admonish him mischievously, tapping him on his chest with her fan.

Thomas chuckled merrily. It was just as his father had always been: one rule for him and one for the others. Tonight there would be dinner at Whitechapel followed by dancing. The Frobishers and Elsie were staying for the weekend and, in spite of the rain and his hip, the world was a happy place. Yet three hours later he was dead.

∗

A number of riders had left the hunt early, wet through and frozen to the bone. The pack had been laid on and hounds were running well when the accident occurred. It was a stack of freshly cut peat bricks that made the two horses shy. They had been riding hard into the weather and neither Thomas nor the other rider had seen the trench just to the left of the track, half hidden by heather. As it swerved so the other horse bumped Thomas's and his mount never had a chance. Edgar Frobisher spoke later to others who had seen the animal somersault into the pit then crash down heavily, trapping his rider underneath. Thomas Preston's back had been crushed just below the neck.

Sharland left his father shortly after tea. The Duke had taken it well at first, remarking that it was the way the boy would always wanted to have gone. Later, when they had been alone together, he had broken down and Sharland sat helplessly while his father wept beside him. But he had recovered and it had been the Duke who had brought up the matter of succession.

Sharland had thought about it already and was surprised at how he felt. It was while they were waiting out on the moor in the pouring rain for the dogcart to come for his brother. It was as though a hand had reached out and touched his shoulder. Where the fingers had rested, he felt a great weight bearing down on him. He had stumbled as he tried to stand, without knowing he had done so, half slipping in the mud beside the body lying on the ground now covered by coats. The thought that he was now the heir to the dukedom, to be followed in time by his infant son had all but overwhelmed him.

＊

"Dear God." Sarah stood in her mother's parlour. Both hands were at her mouth and her eyes stared wide in horror. It was only hours since she had wished her brother-in-law well, allowing him to kiss her affectionately as he took his leave from the breakfast table. Then she, too, had left Whitechapel, making the short journey with her groom to Church Street in order to see her father who had not been well. "Oh, dear God," she whispered.

"I'm so sorry." Sharland lowered is head. He had barely been able to get the words out. "It was the way of the dear fellow," he muttered. "Always the same…always the same wild, madcap rider to hounds. He was never going to learn, never. It was his destiny."

Sarah watched as he covered his face. "Come, Sharland, my dear," she murmured, placing her hands on his shoulders and easing him gently towards the chair nearest the fire. "Wait here while I collect my things. Mother," she turned and called. "See to Sharland, will you. He's all but done in. No, sit," she commanded, holding him back as he struggled to rise. "Just rest a moment…I'll not be long."

It was half way up the narrow stairs that she realised. It came with a suddenness that took her breath. She stopped dead, started to move on again then paused once more, this time to gather her skirts slowly before continuing on her way. It was something the soothsayer had said at Hartland…something about danger, about a man close to her and how, if she was careful, she would walk tall.

She collected her coat and bonnet from the bed and turned towards the door. The reflection in the dressing-table mirror caught her eye and she stopped. Slowly, as if afraid of what she might see, she raised the lamp and bent forward, frowning slightly to check herself in the soft light. The shadows under her eyes made her look sad. Barely conscious of what she was doing, she drew up a chair and sat, her eyes still on the face that stared back at her but the sadness had gone. Instead, the figure she saw was now sitting upright, the head held proud and erect. Sharland, the man she was to marry, was now his father's heir. One hand went to her throat, the other to her hair where the coronet she had seen at Whitechapel would rest.

She leant forward again and peered at herself, this time looking directly into the sea-blue eyes. Slowly, and cautiously at first, the face in the mirror nodded then gradually it broke into a smile.

PART TWO
The Ruby and Pearl Necklace
1868

Chapter Eleven

In the end Jack had to admit that Wilmot was right. The girls, his brother had convinced him, needed far more from life than Sherdon could offer. It all began when Wilmot rode out to see them, bringing with him his son, Lionel, now seventeen, and Jessica, just a year younger. The four cousins had done little more than sit together awkwardly until Frank came and joined them. At first he, too, had been somewhat tongue-tied but Lionel had taken to him immediately and the two had gone off together.

"I know it'll be hard, Jack, but they can't stay tucked away out here for ever, y'know. They're growing up fast…almost exactly the same age as my two and it's high time they saw something of the world." The brothers were standing together discussing the Exmoor mares and foals in the field below the shearing barn. It was hot, even for August, and already the swallows and martins had begun to gather on the rooftops where they sat chattering. Wilmot had come out to see his farms before going back to London. On the way they had stopped to pick whortleberries on North Molton hill and it was there that Jessica found the white heather she had given Kitty. Later, Martin, their new groom, had spotted wild strawberries in the hedgerow where they were half hidden by moss and fronds of fading bracken and they had stopped again. It had become a lovely family day.

"But they're happy enough, Wil." Jack was staring into the distance. "London and all that's not for them. Can't be, they're country girls through an' through."

Wilmot turned and leant back against the gate, hooking his elbows over the top bar. "Of course they are and I can see they love it here but they haven't seen anything else. There's a lot in them, y'know…all their mother's wonderful charm and character. *And* you - you mustn't forget their father. I mean, look at us, we were blessed with fine parents ourselves…it's all there hidden away in your youngsters." Jack was silent. "There's so much in them, Jack. We've got to give them a chance to see what they make of life and what the world can do for them. Mine are happy enough with it all, love it so they do…and look at Sarah."

"Oh, aye?" Jack glanced up sharply. "And Mary? Look at her, Wil. What's the world done for her then? And my Harry, an' all? They've not done so well." He paused and shook his head. "I'm none too sure of all this worldliness an' that. Doesn't always pay, y'know. There's summat to be said for stopping home an'

142

being happy with what you've got. Bain't a bad life…hard at times but not so bad."

"But let them have a *look* at what's out there. Let 'em find out for themselves and if they don't like it then they can come back. See here, Jack." He turned and faced his brother. "Victoria's a young woman now…a pretty little thing and clever, too. You should have seen her at lunch telling me about the stitching and sewing she's bin doing at school. She's a charmer really she is and, to be blunt, there's a fineness and dignity there that's just wasting away." He put a hand on his brother's arm. "Let me help, old thing. We needn't rush them. You're coming over to Court Hall tomorrow and I'll mention it then. Just see what she says…and Anna as well."

Jack wasn't so sure. Sarah had shocked him. He had seen her in South Molton and there was a haughtiness and arrogance about her he had found distasteful. Whether it was the money and finery or the titles or what he could not say, but she seemed to have forgotten that he had known her since she was in a cradle. It was as though she was trying to make out she was somebody she never had been, as if she was ashamed of her roots and was hiding them. He didn't like it. And then there was Mary. Wilmot had tried to help there as well but the poor soul had gone, and it had broken her mother's heart. For all that his brother said there was something deeply secure about life at Sherdon, something that gave an honesty to the character of those who lived there. Once Victoria and Anna had come into contact with her brother's wonderful world, they would be changed and changed for good but he was far from convinced of the benefits of the proposal.

✷

At first the two girls were hesitant about going to Court Hall but Kitty managed to persuade them. They left early with Jack and Frank, Wilmot having begged them to make a day of it. Frank had declared that he would drive as it was to be his father's day out. He took the dogcart and after he had stopped to set them down, he went on into South Molton with the spare horse tied to the hitching rail, trotting on behind.

Steer met them at the door. The butler had told his master that he had heard word of 'Mister Jack' and that he was much respected. He could have mentioned also that his name was known throughout the mining community for his part in bringing the murderer, Burgess, to justice years before and that the duel at Simonsbath had become the stuff of legend.

A butler such as Jacob Steer would not normally show respect to a mere farmer from the hills but he was intrigued: he was also a mite wary of the man about whom he had heard so much. The gnarled hand that took his so firmly and the steady gaze of the grey-blue eyes that looked down at him confirmed what he had heard. The man might have called for beer rather than take his master's wines; he might even have tipped his plate to wipe the rim with bread, and his hair might have been tied back as it was, but there was something about him that stirred the soul. Perhaps it was the way that, when he came to bid them farewell, the man gripped his shoulder and insisted he thank those who had done them so well.

There was a strength about him; Jacob Steer saw how his master looked up to his elder brother and he was impressed.

Later, on the way home, they talked about what they had seen. Anna confessed that she thought all the servants were other guests and that her Uncle Wilmot was very grand and rather serious. That was until he started to tell them about his time at Cambridge, and what went on down the mines when he was an engineer. She liked him and her sister felt the same but it was she, Anna, who had talked so easily with Lionel. When they had gone to look at his mother's paintings the two had laughed helplessly together after she had asked him about the tapestry in the hall. Even now she blushed when she told them she had thought it was a carpet they had hung to cover something on the wall.

Victoria had been left with Jessica. At first they had made small talk but it soon tailed off. In many ways Jessica seemed to be so worldly and spoke loftily about London and her fine clothes and the dances she went to. It was as though she was trying to impress her country cousin, her airs and graces in no way anything like the manner of her father or brother. Rather than reply, Victoria chose to keep her counsel but she felt her younger, mousy-haired cousin was a boast and a show off. What was more she knew nothing of life, of the real life such as how the land was farmed or how to harness a workhorse, even how to trim the wick of a lamp. And, as for sewing and making clothes, she knew precious little and tried to cover her ignorance by dismissing it as no more than trade for the working classes.

Victoria had said nothing to her father but he noticed how quiet she had become and it worried him. He had half listened as Wilmot talked to her about London and his offer for her to come and stay. He had hoped she would have been encouraged by what she had seen and heard but had a suspicion her reticence was more than mere shyness.

As for himself, he had seen what Wilmot meant. His daughters, he now knew, were not getting the best of chances. It was his own fault. He had done what he could for them but he should have seen this years ago and spoken to his brother. Had she been alive, Katherine would have done so for she knew about these things. Now he would have to harden his heart and send them away : the thought hurt. Even now he could see the look on Victoria's face; she would not take kindly to the idea. She adored Kitty and they would miss each other. There was much of her mother's softness in the girl and he rejoiced in her presence around the place.

He glanced at the two of them. Anna, still chatting to Frank, would survive when it came to her turn. She had the spark and sense of adventure but Victoria was sensitive and shy. Even as he watched her she stood. With one hand on her brother's shoulder to steady herself and the other shading her eyes, she rose on her toes to look over the hedge and catch a glimpse of Sherdon on the far side of the valley. She loved her home and he, her father, loved her dearly for that.

✳

It was Tod who brought news of the Quartlys. Only two weeks after the Suffragen Bishop of Taunton had ridden out to see William Thornton, bringing with him a letter signed by The Bishop of Exeter, Tod left Simonsbath. The elderly parson at Molland had been taken ill and it had been agreed to send Tod to take over his duties until a replacement could be found. The appointment would be for three months initially, the Bishop explained, but he should be prepared to extend his stay.

He had been surprised at his reception from the village. There were many who remembered his father and some even his grandfather. Mabel Quartly had been a Rumbelow and there were the Loosemores of Luckworthy and the Thornes and the Hawkins, also the Cockrams and Darts and the Vellacotts of The London Inn: it was almost as if he had come home. Old gran'fer Quartly of Great Champson had first bred the Red Devon cattle almost a hundred years ago. His son, Henry, had followed him and now, Joseph, *his* son, was running the manor farm. And it was Joseph who remembered the Tuckers best. A year younger than Jack, they had played together after school when Grace asked him down to Mill Cottage. The farmer had heard tales of how Grandfather Tucker had been killed at Waterloo and he, Joseph, had been one of those who ran up the road behind the cart when his father and Emma left home.

Joseph Quartly looked the prosperous yeoman farmer that he was. Slim and of medium build with close-cropped, steel-grey hair over his round face, he always appeared well turned out. As he walked with his hazel thumb-stick so his body rolled in order to spare his hip. No matter what the time of year, he dressed himself in the same green, three-quarter length tweed coat and red waistcoat, complete with a ragged, cream stock. Below his heavy cord breeches he always wore a pair of brown leather boots and matching gaiters, all polished to a shine. He had built steadily on what his father had handed down and was proud of it. Never a man of words, he would simply lift his head and beam politely in greeting to all who came his way then leave most of the talking to Mabel.

It was easy that way for the words came tumbling and gushing out of his wife. Tod had first met her one morning in St Mary's when she came to change the altar cloth. He, and later Victoria, was taken aback at first by the ruddy face under her fierce dark eyebrows but it was the eyes themselves which gave her away. They were soft and kind and lit up whenever she smiled. And when she smiled, which was often enough, her whole body would wobble and shake with mirth. She was round and jolly, a motherly sort.

Sunday lunch at Great Champson had been a success. Nobody there had been to Simonsbath and they listened intently as he told them about farming on the high moors. Three of those sitting round the long refectory table were Mabel Quartly's pupils. For years the accomplished fingers of the farmer's wife had made fine lace and now she ran a small school, passing on her skills only to the ones she thought able to master the craft. In return for learning the lace maker's secrets the two girls, now living in the house, worked on the farm.

It was only as he was walking back through the village that the thought occurred to him, for it was there, at Great Champson, that his sister might be happy to take her first steps away from home. His stay in Molland had been extended for a further three months so he would be in the village with her. Joseph Quartly, like so many of the villagers, remembered their father and, in any case, the farm was no more than a day's ride from Sherdon by pony and trap. And so it came to be.

∗

Her pupils were concentrating on their double and treble crochet stitches so Mabel Quartly slipped away. She went up the broad oak staircase and along the high, wide corridor where she opened the bedroom door quietly and looked in.

In the room, where the ceiling had a long, jagged crack, there were three iron cots arranged side by side on the bare wooden floor, each with a pine clothes' box underneath. It was a sunny room and the lace curtains, made by previous pupils, were fastened back. The window was open. On the chest of drawers by the window, and where they had probably had too much sun, the flowers Victoria had put in the chipped earthenware pot had died. As she moved to collect them up, so Mrs Quartly saw the head of the rag doll peeping out from under the down pillow. She stopped and peered closer, now thinking about the new girl. Picking up the doll, she smiled briefly but then pursed her lips.

She had sensed it herself but it was Joseph who remarked that the two older girls, the heavy, flirtatious Lisa Tregowan and Nan Bulled, a mean girl whom nobody really liked, had turned their backs on the newcomer. Joseph had nicknamed her 'Queenie': it was obvious and the name had soon stuck. The small, red-headed girl with her green eyes and the band of freckles across her nose had blushed to her roots and beamed with delight, but the happiness had not lasted.

 At first Mabel thought it was homesickness that had extinguished the brightness but in the lace parlour, when she was out of the room, there had been words. The other two, she could see, were an inseparable pair and either sat together or walked into the village arm in arm. Come the end of the day it was always Victoria who was last to leave the parlour. She would bring in her lace work and sit sewing quietly, looking up every now and then as she listened to the fireside chat. Invariably she would stay to the end as though she was loathe to join the others in the bedroom until they had settled for the night and the lamp was out.

Nan Bulled was the worst and took it upon herself to torment the small, shy newcomer and it went on mercilessly. First it was her name, her size, her voice or the way she dressed and did her hair. Then, once they found out who her mother was, the taunts and jibes cut deeper. "Teeny, weeny Queenie," she would hiss, her face inches from Victoria's as she buried her head under her blanket. "An' yer ma'am were a lady an' all that was she? All namby pamby like, I'll be bound. Bet 'er never got 'er hands dirty. An' you're just the same...don't know what a hard day's work's like, you don't. Me dad says your ma'am must've bin maized to run off with the likes 'o they Tuckers. An' now look at yer…our precious little Queenie darlin', lying there an' cryin' out fer dada." Then came the water, and the dirt in the bed. And then the tales in the kitchen about why she was late when they had held her down and messed her hair.

It was Edwin, Mabel Quartly's son, who told his mother that he often heard voices raised late at night. Only the day before she had found Queenie crying alone when she should have been working in the stables. She was a sweet child and Mabel Quartly was filled with a sudden anger that this should happen at Great Champson. But this morning it had been worse. Victoria had not come down to breakfast. The others said her bed was empty and it was an hour before they saw her with Tod who had brought her back from the vicarage. The girl was unhappy and Mabel Quartly was determined to get to the bottom of it.

2

Almost two years had passed before Sarah returned to Hartland. Then Isaac was barely a year old but the boy, fair-haired and tall for his age, was now three and little Amelia almost one.

 To begin with it had been strange rather than difficult. Some of the staff had moved on. Tedder the butler had gone as had Bilson the footman, whose eyes used to follow Sarah everywhere. For that, she was glad. Desmond Orchard, so she perceived, found her presence a problem initially but he had always been rather distant and aloof. Jocelyn and the children, though, had welcomed them, in partic-ular Jocasta who was now thirteen. The girl threw her arms around her neck and smothered her with kisses before suddenly standing back, confused and embar-rassed. Time had moved on and things had changed, yet she had missed her governess and wanted things to be as they were.

Since then the Orchards had twice been up to Blagdon where Sarah helped her father-in-law run his house parties. He, the Duke, had become ever more amenable to her company and once, last Christmas, she had scolded him for his over-atten-tiveness. In three days time he and Sharland would be joining them at Hartland but, for the moment, she was on her own with just her maid, the nanny and the two children. Jocelyn had invited her to come early…*begged* her would have been a better way to describe it, in order to make up the numbers.

✻

"My dear Lady Preston, were you my wife I could not bear the thought of you being in such rapacious company as you now find yourself. I would be compelled to deploy the most diligent and trustworthy of escorts to remain by your side. Nothing less would appease my concern nor soothe my fears."

"But I'm *not* your wife, Captain Barclay. In spite of which, you have, as I am being reminded constantly, paid me the most assiduous attention this evening. I could

147

not have asked for more, so how is it, might I ask, that your sentiments have been captured thus?" Sarah was enjoying his vivacious company.

Cardew Orchard, now exactly twenty and an ensign in the Life Guards, had arranged a house party to coincide with his birthday. Marcus Barclay, swarthy, heavily moustached and with dancing black eyes had arrived two days ago with no less than four brother officers and their ladies. He was tall, beautifully dressed and possessed of a sharp wit: he was also an incorrigible flirt. Glanford and Fanny Frobisher were also here as was Charles Bamfylde with his new belle. The Abbey was packed.

"The price of my answer will be the pleasure of a dance after dinner...no *two*, in order for you to secure the truth." The Captain leant towards her but his back was half turned and he spoke out of the corner of his mouth as if nobody else should hear. As he spoke so she felt his leg reaching out to explore her skirts. "Promise me that and I'll tell you all...everything. I will declare my heart."

"Promises, promises, gallant sir, are made to be kept but when one speaks of dreams..." Sarah paused, sensing the footman behind her and was immediately irritated that she had no time to parry the captain's advances as she would have wished. She watched as Jocelyn rose from the table and caught her eye before rising also, aware that the two scarlet-jacketed officers on either side of her stood at once. "I'll have to see, Captain Barclay, and my thanks for your company." The ladies were withdrawing and she had been asked by her hostess to help entertain the guests in the drawing room. Desmond, Jocelyn assured her, had been instructed not to dally over the brandy and port. The young men would want to dance, prefer-ring by far the company she had assembled who, by now, would be waiting impa-tiently.

The officer stood aside and bowed. "It's been my pleasure, dear lady...indeed it has." Sarah smiled and inclined her head. If she found the gallant Captain Barclay so appealing, his wife so she considered, was equally un-appealing. Jocelyn Orchard had warned her about Lucinda Barclay. Already Winnie, Sarah's lady's maid who had come down a day earlier from Whitechapel, had wanted to know if she was to do as Mrs Barclay had bidden. "I told her she should see you first and ask, m'lady, but she said it wasn't to matter and I'd be best do what she wanted."

Sarah had seen the captain's wife. Words were said, quietly but icily and that had been that. Mrs Barclay, a tall, ungainly and down-at-the-mouth looking female, certainly had a nerve and Sarah remembered how she felt her anger rising. The ire was still there, but now smouldering resentfully, however she was alert and wary. If Lucinda Barclay's husband knew of her feelings he gave no indication but it mattered not. The situation had now developed and had become rather interest-ing...intriguingly so.

Sarah waited on the main landing for the ladies to reappear from their rooms. Lucinda Barclay was the last and, for a moment, the two stood regarding one another. "How kind." Mrs Barclay held out a hand then let it fall. "How very kind of you…to wait like this." Sarah noticed the carmine-red cochineal around her lips. Too much and too red, she thought. 'More like a wound than a mouth,' the old Duke would have grumbled.

"Jocelyn asked me to see you all down." Sarah found herself smiling easily for the other's attempts at airs and graces were bumbling and clumsy. The woman was jealous, and blatantly so.

"Mmm?" Lucinda Barclay was taller than Sarah and made the most of her height, coming as close as she thought necessary to make the point. "*How* kind. But then, you're used to it, I believe…waiting on others, that is. Isn't that so?" Both women knew they were on their own and would not be overheard.

"I wait for nobody, Mrs Barclay…nobody at all."

"Not even your husband I see. Mmm?" She paused at the top of the stairs, caught up the hem of her midnight-blue dress and turned sharply, causing the ribbons and flowers in her hair to flutter and bob. "A cleverly arranged seating plan, I would say, Lady…er…Preston. My husband, the Captain, seemed to be enjoying himself…encouraged, no doubt, by your close attention."

"I'm not surprised, Mrs Barclay." Sarah was two steps behind her on the stairs. "His company was indeed a pleasure. He was in great heart…as a prisoner might be whilst on parole for a while. We…all of us around him much enjoyed his presence."

"But don't believe a word he says, my dear." The older woman turned once more. "He likes to think himself something of a scoundrel…a lady's man, if you like, but he's not. Believe me. Tempt him if you must, but please do *try* not to make it quite so obvious…somewhat inelegant, you know. And you will find nothing there of what you seek. He knows where he stands…and so should you. It would do you well, my child."

The music, serenading those who were gathering in the hall, had started and Sarah watched as Mrs Barclay strode across the hall to make a fuss of Jocelyn Orchard before sitting and sweeping her skirts to one side with a flourish as Desmond lifted his tails to sit beside her. She felt the hot coals of rage inside her and her chest was heaving. The woman was awful. It was not only what she said that angered her but the tone of her voice. It was meant to sting. It had done so and the woman knew it: her gauntlet was down.

She started suddenly at the hand on her arm. She had no idea how long she had been standing alone at the bottom of the staircase like that, but realised at once that there would be those who had noticed. It was Captain Barclay. "Forgive me, dear lady, but I come to claim the first part of our bargain. Will you allow me the pleasure?" He bowed slightly and indicated the dance floor with a sweep of his arm which he then crooked for her. "The dance? Yes?" He inclined his head. "And it's to be a waltz...my special request, you should know."

"I would be delighted, sir." She took his arm and they moved on to the floor. She had forgotten how tall he was but there was something about his voice. It was deep and mellow yet, hidden away, was the trace of an accent: French perhaps, but foreign most certainly. Fascinating, she thought: a trifle more spice. His right hand moved to the small of her back. His touch was gentle but, as the music for the dance began, his fingers slipped further around, hidden from view by the silk trails of her dress. As he pulled her towards him, she could feel him tightening his hold. She was trapped and it was delicious.

He moved easily and she with him, turning and turning again and again, his eyes on hers, hers sometimes on his or else glancing about her as they moved together round and around until the dance was over. As they drifted apart his other hand should have let hers go but he held on to her fingers just long enough to squeeze them firmly. Even then he waited as if to elicit her reply, which duly she gave before allowing her hand to fall away. Their eyes met and it was all that was needed. Both knew instantly and, for a moment, nothing was said. "Lord Sharland Preston is either a very brave man or a fool and I cannot but for the life of me determine which." Captain Barclay did not look at her as he spoke, rather he fingered his collar and took her arm once more as he led her away from the floor.

"I beg your pardon, sir." Sarah laughed coquettishly. "Pray what do you mean by that?" She knew exactly, of course. They had paused in the wide archway between hall and salon. Two couples were standing there talking and they were unable to move on. "Well, no...perhaps I do have an idea." They moved aside to allow a footman with a tray of iced drinks to pass.

"Of course you do," he half whispered in her ear. "You're beautiful, quite the most beautiful creature I've seen and you're all on your own." He turned towards her, his head bent low to avoid the fronds from the ornamental palms. "And you realise that...what I think of you, I mean? Your body's alive and as we danced it spoke to me...cried out. I sensed it and you know I did." He paused. "And it did not speak in jest, did it?" He paused again, his eyes searching her face. "Do you realise how I feel about you?"

"Well," she breathed. She could feel herself trembling. Behind this wickedly handsome man she saw his wife, humourless and spiteful whose remarks earlier had been calculated to wound so cruelly. Before she could reply further, she felt his hand reach down for her fingers. Her back was to the plants and there was a sudden melee of people passing to and fro. As she inched backwards to make way, she felt her body against his. His hand felt for hers again. Now, suddenly, she was breathing more quickly. She ran her tongue over her lips then dabbed one finger at the corner of her mouth. "And so?" she replied huskily then cleared her throat. "What are you proposing, might I ask?"

"Allow me to show you." Sarah froze, catching her breath but then, and she could not help herself, she found herself smiling. She glanced up; his eyes were waiting for her answer but he knew already, that she could see. So, why not? She looked away. He was an elegant man, her own warm, earthy desire for him told her so. And as for his wife, the wretched Mrs Barclay? What would she ever know? And even if she did, even if she knew all about it, it was no more than her just desserts. She deserved every bit of it. And, what was more, had she not initiated just such a challenge? Tempt him if you must, the woman had taunted, but not too obviously. So, why not indeed? The parlour maids had turned down the beds and the fires had been set. The curtains were drawn and the rooms left ready. Winnie, her maid, would have long since gone to her quarters.

"Ten minutes," she murmured. "I'll need ten minutes. You know my room? Should it not be convenient then a silk glove will be outside my door...as if dropped accidentally." Without looking at him she moved away, excusing herself as she made her way between the small groups standing together, fanning themselves and talking amicably. Captain Barclay moved also, taking a flute of champagne from a footman's tray before strolling casually across the salon to where Cardew Orchard and two other officers were in earnest discussion by the fire. He joined them for a few minutes then danced once more, this time with Fanny Frobisher. They stopped by the door and he was about to ask his hostess to accept his arm when she was called away.

✳

He had unclipped his spurs yet, even so, the floor boards creaked under the soft leather soles of his mess Wellingtons. At the top of the stairs he paused and listened carefully. The lamp at her end of the corridor had been turned low. He paused again at the corner but he was on his own and could barely hear the hum of voices and laughter coming from the hall below. There was no silk glove. The door opened easily and, even as he entered the room, he could detect the outline of her figure in the bed.

3

Edwin Quartly looked up at the sound of girlish laughter. Usually, at this early hour, the shippons and stable yard were peaceful places where men and animals prepared themselves quietly for the coming day. Apart from the clatter of hooves on cobbles or the lowing of cattle from across the way, there was rarely much noise. Like the others, he had been up long before daybreak and, even now, he needed a lantern to see his way into the back of the stable block. The day would brighten but dawn had brought the first autumn chill and he could see steam rising from the dung heap where the fowls were already scratching.

He watched as the two of them, both wearing white milking caps and dressed in their bulky working dresses, walked towards the house, each carrying a full pail of milk. As they walked, they continued to laugh. One of them, the smaller and slimmer Nan Bulled, lowered her pail to double up with mirth while Lisa Tregowan waited, giggling with one hand to her mouth. Edwin frowned. Deciding to wait until they had gone into the scullery, he rested his dung fork against the wall.

＊

At first he could see nothing; the row of heavy, red-brown Devon cattle stood waiting patiently. The only sounds to break the silence were the sound of cud being chewed. Every now and then a neck chain would rattle as one of the beasts threw up her head and occasionally one would stamp down hard to deal with some irritation but that was all. Edwin walked down the line of strong flat backs towards the hay stall, his hand moving from one flank to the next. Apart from swishing their tails at his touch, the cattle barely moved.

Then he saw her. She was alone and standing by the far lime-washed wall, leaning against the open sill. Her head was buried in the crook of one arm and he could see she was crying by the way her body was shaking. He spoke quietly so as not to startle her, yet just loud enough to let her know he was there and to reassure her. "It's me, Queenie...Edwin. Only me." Eventually she calmed but he remained where he was, giving her time.

Nobody could really call him a handsome man. His eyebrows, like his mother's, were rather too dark under his floppy brown hair; they and his beaky nose gave him something of a puzzled look. He was not particularly tall either, nor was he well built or muscular and he would never stand out in a crowd. But none of that mattered for the quiet and sensitive Edwin Quartly lived for his animals and the farm life into which he had been born twenty years ago.

There was one brother and two, much younger sisters. The problem was that Daniel, three years older than Edwin, was mazed. He was here at Great Champson with them but lived with Mrs Grainger, his nurse, in two rooms at the back of the house. He was quite harmless and they saw him every day as he walked around lippetty-lapetty with Mrs Grainger. His head would be in the air and his knees would knock together as he jerked along on tip-toe with one arm twitching and the other tucked into his side. As a result, Great Champson Farm would one day come to Edwin. He was mindful of the fact but never let the strange ways of the Almighty affect him. If anything it made him more understanding than ever about the plight or misfortune of others.

Victoria remained as she was with her back towards him, shaking her head slowly. Edwin knew she would be embarrassed at having been found like this but knew also that she had been hurt and he wanted to comfort her. "Here, come now." He approached silently then paused for a moment, before placing a hand on her shoulder. "Come on, Queenie...I've a mind at what's bin upsetting yer. 'Tis all right now, maid, there bain't nobody else here, just me."

She made to shrug his hand away but he kept it there, suspecting her half-hearted effort was because she would rather he stayed. Her white cap had been pulled away from her hair and he could see where her auburn curls had been tied by a green ribbon. He noticed, too, how large and rough his hand looked against the whiteness of her neck, then saw the mess on the floor beyond. Her milk pail had fallen or been tipped into the gutter, its contents little more than puddles of greeny-white sludge where it had seeped away into the dung. "Here, come on...no need for that. They've gone." He took her shoulders in both hands and pulled her gently away from the wall. At first she resisted but then turned and fell against him, starting to weep again. Years ago, when he was small and awkward, he, too, had suffered like this from others in the village.

"It was nothing really...nothing to worry about." Victoria had composed herself and the two were leaning against the shippon wall. For a moment he was silent. "It was partly me, I dare say," she shrugged dejectedly. "Anyway, it doesn't matter."

"Oh it does, I'll say it does." Edwin could just imagine the two older girls. Victoria had finished first, she told him, and had got up from her milking stool when Nan Bulled tried to put some dirt in her pail. There had been a struggle, the milk had spilled and she, the smallest, had been pushed and slapped by the other two.

"But don't say anything." It was the first time she had looked at him and he could see the tear stains on her face. Her nose and mouth were wet. "You won't will you?"

"Here, you'm a proper mess...a right old state." He lifted his chin to take off his ragged blue necktie then handed it to her. "'Ere, look. Bain't much but it'll help clean you up." She smiled, then laughed and sniffed loudly. Suddenly her face brightened and he wanted to stroke her hair.

"Thank you," she whispered, handing it back before wiping her eyes with the cuff of her sleeve and looking round. "Oh no," she groaned, her shoulders sagging. "The milk, look at it." Her head shook and she bent down to pick up the pail. "Your mum'll be right gnarled."

"No 'er won't. I'll tell her and I'll be telling they two girls summat an' all."

"No, please." Her voice was stronger and she took off her milking cap then shook her hair free before making an attempt to tidy herself. "Don't say anything, Edwin. Please." She looked at him. "I'll say I slipped, then it'll be all right."

"Hey, come on you two." They started at the voice and turned. Molly Carter was in the shippon doorway. She had been sent to find them and had both hands on her hips. "What's goin' on? And at this time of the day, an' all. Us have bin lookin' up an' down all over for 'e, so us have."

" 'Tis all right, Mol. Queenie's bin a mite upset, that's all. We're coming. Bain't nothing like you s'pose 'tis." He smiled gamely then grimaced at the serving girl just to let her know.

✳

Mabel Quartly put her hand on her hips. "Whatever've you got there, child. Where's all the milk to? An' look at the state of that milking bucket." The kitchen was silent. The two older girls sat side by side eating their breakfast. Their heads were lowered. Mol Carter looked at the farmer's wife then at Victoria before lifting her skirts and hurrying into the scullery. "'Ere that's the second time, that is. What be going on out there?"

Victoria opened her mouth but it was Edwin who spoke first. "'Twas I, mother. I'm sorry an' that but it got knocked when I went to see they calves." He tried to sound convincing and looked from one to the other as if he was appealing to them to believe him. He tried to continue but had nothing to say and his face reddened.

"More'n two gallons o' best cream milk. I dunno…just mind what you'm up to out there, all of you." She wiped her hands on her pinafore then took it off and hung it carefully on its hook by the fire. "On you go now, Edwin…yer dad's bin waiting." She paused then rounded on him. "Gid on, boy, stop standing there," she scolded, tidying her bun of hair and scowling as she watched him leave.

"Now then, come on you lot. Clear away, an' up to your rooms to tidy. I'll be back shortly." She glanced at the wall clock. "No more'n twenty minutes, mind."

Victoria was last into the bedroom. She had missed breakfast but did not feel hungry. She was now late and anxious, and felt ashamed at not having spoken up about the milk. The other girls had noticed her silence and stared spitefully at her when Edwin took the blame. She was grateful but had no idea why he had done so as the milk would have to come out of his wages like it always did when anything was broken or lost. She hurried up the stairs, half tripping on the way and was well into the room when the door shut behind her.

"Take her, Lisa. Go on, hold her fast…grab hold of the little toad." She cried out in surprise and at the sudden pain as her arms were pinioned behind her. Lisa Tregowan was holding her and she could hear her grunting with exertion. Nan Bulled stood in front of her. "So there we are…little Queenie Tucker," she jeered. "Creepin' an' crawlin' around them all are you now? Grovellin' your way up to Edwin, askin' him to speak up fer what you'd let go to waste. Eh? Cum'ere you."

Her head was jerked back forcing her face up and making her gasp. "Look at me you whining little lickspittle. Bain't got your mum…our loverly Lady Katherine, nor yer dad here neither, have yer now? Look at me," she shrilled. She glanced up just as the other spat. She felt the spray but the great glob of spittle struck her cheek and slid towards the corner of the mouth. She tried to blow it away and shake it off but Nan Bulled spat again and again, each time forcing her head further back.

"That'll larn you to go licking and sucking up to all they lot. Go on then, Lisa…drop her."

She half fell to the floor but managed to support herself on one hand then watched as Nan Bulled came up to her. Before she could begin to wipe her face the other girl walked slowly across the back of her outstretched hand. Again she cried out in pain and tried to pull away but the wooden clog rolled back over the fingers then forward again. "Oh, my dear soul. Oh, dearie, dearie me, whatever have I done. Oh my, oh my," she sneered. "My humble pardon, Miss Queenie Tucker…and 'tis your little lace fingers as well…oh, dearie me…my pardon, my pardon." Only after the door opened and shut again and their laughter had faded as they made their way down the stairs did she allow herself to collapse on to the bare wooden floor where she lay prostrate.

It was just after lunch the following day and shortly before they were due to start their lace work that Victoria found her rag doll. It was under the bed. She and Kitty had made it together before she left home. She had bought the wool at Withypool and crocheted the head, then made the eyes and mouth while Kitty made the clothes from scraps of her father's old shirt and breeches. It was a silly little thing really, more suited to a child half her age, but it was a keepsake from home and she treasured it. When she pressed it against her cheek she was convinced she could smell her father's hair and the smoke from the kitchen fire at Sherdon. It brought them all closer and it was this same ugly, tatty little doll that reminded her of all the things she missed so much. Now it was in pieces. Somebody had pulled off the head and the arms and legs had been cut away.

*

Edwin had an idea where she might be and took the larger and stronger of the two shepherding ponies. The track up to the high ground behind the house followed the course of the stream that came down from the moors. It was little more than a drovers' path but it was the best route for the stock and, as far as anybody knew, had always been the one they used. The hunt used it also and the young farmer knew it well. The weather was about to break and he was worried that she might get lost up in the hills.

High above the village, some way between Molland and Twitchen, a great post, higher than the beech hedges behind it, had been set in the ground to mark the spot where beacons used to be lit. It was a wild and desolate place from where the countryside fell away in folds right across Devon until it rose up again towards the craggy peaks of Dartmoor more than forty miles distant. The cliffs of Hartland could be seen as could the beacons of Dunkery, Blackdown and many others. Cussacombe, it was called: a place where highwaymen were once hanged. Now it was a haven for wild ponies and ravens, for deer and blackgame. But it was never a place for a girl to be on her own when the autumn winds brought in a chill from the sea as they swept across the moorland .

And there she was. He caught sight of her as he came over the crest; just a small figure a few hundred yards ahead of him struggling through the heather that was up to her waist. "*Queeenie*." He stood in his stirrups and shouted into the wind. "*Queeeenie…stop*. I'm coming."

"Leave me. Let me go." She tried to push him away but, even with one of his hands holding the reins, she was no match for him. She tried to run, taking a few stumbling steps before falling just as he caught up with her. "Leave me, Edwin…please leave me."

"Stop it. Listen, Queenie. I know 'tis hard but come on back home with me. The others have gone. Father turned them out as soon as mother heard what happened. They've gone an' won't be back…honest they won't."

"No. I can't go back." He was still holding her but she had stopped trying to wrestle herself free. "I couldn't, Edwin. You've bin kind, all of you but…no, I can't." She was looking down, ashamed to face him and she shook her head. "I just couldn't."

"Queenie, listen. It's for father, I've come."

"*What?*" She looked up.

"Aye, honest." The wind was rising further and Edwin brushed the hair from his eyes. "Soon as he'd seen they two away he began to worry after you. Said he owed it to your father to see you happy at Champson. Said he could never look him in the eye again if you were to run back to Sherdon all sad an' flayed like you'm be…an' yer dad were to see you like that. Do anything, he would, to see yer back along with us an' happy. Honest, Queenie, that's what he said." He paused. One hand held her arm, the other moved to her shoulder. He wanted to pull her to him but dare not in case she drew back. "An'…well, I'd like you to…an' mother, as well," he added hurriedly. She didn't move. He waited patiently, still holding her, the two of them alone and together. "Well?"

"I'll try," she whispered. "But…" her voice hesitated.

"Aye?"

"No…nothing, it doesn't matter. Yes, all right. I'll try." Edwin lifted her on to the pony. There was no saddle for there had been no time, so he sprang up behind her and held her with one arm around her waist before easing the pony round.

4

Lord Sharland Preston walked briskly up Bedford Street and turned into Cathedral Yard. Exeter, he thought, was looking and feeling autumnal. The first yellowy-brown leaves of the limes in the Close were fluttering down, swept on their way by a brisk northerly wind that collected them, only to pause briefly before moving them on once more. The sudden change had all but put paid to the summer. There were two hours before the mid-morning train to Barnstaple. The coach journey to Hartland would take longer but, never mind, he would be with Sarah and the children before dark. He increased his pace, humming cheerfully to himself while his heavy Inverness billowed out behind him. A sudden sharp gust made him snatch at his pale grey bowler.

The visit earlier to the Northern Bank in Summerhayes had been a success and they had been delighted at the figures for the rates and the summer income from the Blagdon estates. They had exceeded even the optimism shown by his accountants last week. It was Thomas Peàrson, the bright and good looking young assistant manager, who had told him about Bruford's, the Exeter jewellers. The conversation had turned to investments and Pearson had suggested, somewhat audaciously, that the excellent figures in his accounts merited some form of recognition.

At first he passed the window by. His eye had been taken by the tall young woman in front of him dressed in an exquisite sealskin coat trimmed with light-coloured fur. Her hat, wide brimmed and of blue velvet with ribbons and plumes added to the image, but it was the light veil over her face that fascinated him. He lengthened his stride, determined to overtake her and to satisfy his curiosity as to whether or not her beauty would match her sense of fashion. It did not and he stopped, disappointed yet amused by his own indiscretion. Only then, and with his spirits still buoyant, did he realise he had walked too far.

It was the clever way by which the mirrors accentuated the light that made the jewels shine like they did. The three featureless female busts of grey velvet had been decorated from head to throat as had the matching hands and wrists and he waited while those closest pointed and peered with their heads pressed against the window and their hands raised to shield their eyes. It was only when the couple in front of him left that he could see properly.

They were exquisite, quite, quite beautiful and he stood for some time looking from one to the other before moving on, pushing his way back through the press behind. Suddenly, a few yards down the street, he stopped and turned back. Once again by the window, he stood briefly on tiptoe to see over the heads of others now in his way before stepping down and bowing through the low door.

"Unique, sir. We've never come across anything quite like them before." The short, wizened director of sales looked up. He had withdrawn the jewels from the window and they were laid out on a green baize cloth that covered the glass counter. The jeweller had donned white gloves before handling them and stood back reverently, like a priest who had just administered Communion. "The only other we've heard about that's anything like this had the rubies drilled…to form a continual string with the pearls. But not here. We understand they're Flemish. The middle of last century, possibly slightly earlier, but we've nothing to compare them with."

"And what's their history?"

"We've no idea, sir." He caught Sharland's look. "I know, I know...we all know what they say... 'no history , no purchase'...but if we don't know where they come from, then we most certainly know what they are. Here, look." He lifted them carefully from the baize and put a glass to his eye. "See here, the setting of the stones. White gold, and we've checked every one. And the stones themselves, they're perfect...beautiful, all of them, that is, except two...the first and the last." He cleaned the glass then passed it to Sharland. "Take a look, sir. You can see that those two are very slightly flawed...a slight opaque cloudiness and what looks like a small internal scratch." He paused while Sharland examined the two stones. "You'll notice that those two stones are identical and we believe that's been done quite deliberately...a sort of trademark that could never be forged or erased, and to remove them would alter the whole balance of the piece."

"So?" Sharland removed the glass and blinked. "That diminishes the value, surely?"

"Oho no, sir. To the contrary." The jeweller smiled. He had the air of one about to impart a morsel of salacious gossip and bowed theatrically before continuing. "No, no. We had our suspicions that this might mean something special and Van Damens of Bruton Street confirmed it. One of their men from Amsterdam came across to verify what London told them we'd found. Apparently they were made in Ghent by a little known craftsman...a Mr Jan Kuypers...a hundred years ago or more. His works are much sought after and are recognised simply by this trademark of his. Most odd...unique."

"And the pearls?"

"The same quality, sir, but all perfectly matched." He watched as Sharland checked them one by one. "It was one of our contacts in Plymouth. He saw the piece in a pawn shop in Devonport. Heaven alone knows where or how they came by them. We dread to think and the constabulary have no idea either. They held them for six weeks but heard nothing, nothing at all. They became Crown property then came on to us after the inevitable Court deliberations." The jeweller picked up the necklace. "As I said, sir, stones like these set between pearls...and each pearl strung independently...it's very, very rare." Sharland looked down at the man who stared back before smiling encouragingly.

They talked and they bartered, then the jeweller locked the shop door. His eyes had taken in the fine clothes, the heavy signet ring and the diamond in the cravat pin. And Sharland, as they spoke, took heed of the cold small eyes behind the wrinkles and the tightness of the mouth. It was the bank note that helped clinch the deal. Lord Preston was happy enough for he had driven the man down by fifty guineas no less. Schlomo Einfeldt was equally satisfied for he had still made a profit of one hundred guineas, one third of which would be his commission. The handshake was warm, as it usually is when both sides consider they have had the better of the deal.

Sharland had to hurry. It had all taken far longer than he expected and, after walking as quickly as he could into Bedford Street, he broke into a run, those on the footpath standing aside at such a sight. Were a footpad or sneak thief aware of what he was carrying they, too, would have to have hurried. He had no idea when he would give them to his wife, but it was in his carriage on the way to Barnstaple that he took out the receipt he had been given by the treasurer of the Northern Bank. *'Taken into safe keeping on behalf of Lord Sharland Preston, one ruby and pearl necklace consisting of forty-one set rubies and forty pearls, each strung individually. Valuation attached and as given on this the twenty-fifth of October eighteen hundred and sixty-eight by Mr S. Eindfeldt of Messrs Bruford's, Cathedral Lane, Exeter.'*

One ruby and pearl necklace indeed, and it had all been so easy.

Chapter Twelve

"Ghastly isn't it." Wilmot, half smiling in disbelief, glanced across the compartment to where his friend was gazing out of the window. "Look at that one over there, that great big fellow." He lifted a finger and watched as Tennyson eased his tall frame around to peer solemnly at the clouds of steam escaping from the green and black engine.

"Awful," the Poet Laureate muttered, turning back. He reached up and pulled hard at the chintz curtain in order to shut out the scene. "Like some great primeval beast in the very act of expiring." The recent addition of a further six platforms and the domed roof had turned Waterloo Station into a cauldron of hissing and snorting steam within which whistles shrieked and blasted, and everybody rushed madly about. The air was foul with bitter soot and, within minutes, a thin layer of grime had settled on faces, hands and anything remotely clean. Eyes watered and throats stung. The two friends had been driven straight on to the concourse where Maynard, who had been sent on ahead, was waiting with a porter. It was the butler who then led the way to their reserved compartment before seeing their luggage safely into the guard's van.

Last night they had dined at The Reform. William Gladstone had been Prime Minister for little over a year and, since Christmas, rumours had been circulating the House that he had a reshuffle in mind. Frederic knew of it already for Sir Thomas Acland, Liberal Member for North Devon, had arranged the dinner in the Cabinet Room and warned him that he would be approached.

Why, Gladstone had asked, did Frederic not cross the floor and join him where his well known sympathies for the poor would be appreciated? After all, one good turn deserved another and the hand that fell on Frederic's shoulder pressed home the point. Wilmot had been intrigued, well able to imagine the outcry and what the other Tory members for Devon would have thought had they any idea that Young Knight was even to consider entering into such a discussion. No wonder they had slipped into the small dining room through the club's back entrance.

"Y'know...going back to last night." They had started to move and Tennyson crossed his legs, pulling impatiently at his grey worsted trousers. "Freddie played his hand very well, so he did. That fellow Clarendon, the stout, redheaded one with the funny eyes...he really had a go at him."

"The Foreign Affairs man?" Wilmot unbuttoned his coat. "Yes, he's persistent all right...like a puffed up little bantam cock, but he was the first to realise that Freddy's not for persuading. I can't blame him, Freddy, I mean. They'd murder him up in Worcestershire and in any case, just as he told them, he can hammer away at these issues just as effectively from where he is on the back benches."

"And escape from the place more easily when he's not tied to a specific job."

"True, true," Wilmot nodded. "But Lord Derby's not a fit man...pretty poorly, I believe. Gladstone and his Liberals fairly knocked them around during the election and he took his defeat very personally...quite a drubbing, so it was." For a moment the two were silent as the train slowly gathered speed, winding its way through the smoke-grimed suburbs of Battersea and Clapham. "Freddy's going to let the dust settle then have another go at the Poor Laws. Reckons they're still far too discriminatory. The Prime Minister's well aware of that...and Freddy knows he is. Gladstone didn't really press him but...oh, I don't know, but it was quite an accolade nonetheless."

"And a very good dinner too." Tennyson's eyes were smiling. "I didn't mind singing for it."

Wilmot chortled and looked at the poet. 'Enoch Arden' had taken him years, a struggle no doubt prolonged by his two visits to the sanatorium at Netley. Sometimes his friend looked haggard and downbeat to a degree that alarmed him but then, as now, a shaft of light would flash out from behind the eyebrows and beard to show the world that all was well. Nobody else he could think of would have had the Prime Minister twice calling for silence and begging him to honour the company with a recitation. It had lasted for half an hour and Tennyson had explained that it was inspired by a visit to Bideford with Wilmot. The two had ridden out to Appledore for lunch then visited the church where Tennyson found the name on some half-hidden, moss-covered gravestone. It was later still, when they stood together on the wind-swept point watching the ebb tide struggling over the bar, that the idea of the lost mariner came to him.

✳

Wilmot read but Tennyson dozed fitfully until the attendant knocked. He took their coats away to brush while two boys, dressed uncomfortably in tight fitting liveried uniforms and with their pill-box hats tilted almost over their left ears, stood with hot water and towels. As they washed and tidied so their spirits rose for Exeter was, by now, less than an hour away. They would take lunch in The Central Hotel before embarking again to descend slowly through the recently completed tunnel to St Thomas's where they would change once more, this time for Barnstaple.

The closer they got, the more Tennyson, fresh and alert again, quizzed his friend about Exmoor and the family. Wilmot had told him about his niece. "Titania," the poet growled, pointing a finger at his friend in emphasis. "Titania, that's her...that's who she'll be. Diana, daughter of the Titans, just as Ovid told us. But then the Bard's Fairy Queen was her own mistress as well, y'know." He paused, chewing on the corner of his lip. "You've done her well, Wilmot...well indeed. So many I know would have cast a girl like that aside yet the love of a family must always shine through...no matter what." He pulled slowly on his beard. "What was it Titania said to the dear old weaver...near the end, in the woods. *'I am a spirit of no common rate...and I will purge thy mortal grossness so.'* Eh? Ah, yes...Titania. She'll be fine, your Sarah...a survivor if ever there was."

"Aye, but the fellow she's found is no Bottom the Weaver, nor any of the fairies either."

They both laughed. "As long as she's happy, Wil. And as long as the family's there with her."

"Her uncle was non too pleased, I'll have to say."

"Jack?"

"Mmm." Wilmot lifted his chin thoughtfully.

"Surely he's not thinking this is some other burden he's going to have to carry?" Tennyson frowned. "The man's got enough to worry about...too much as it is. We're due up there this week are we not?" He fingered his wing collar and stared at the countryside as the carriage rocked and swayed. "Dear old Jack, he'd carry the world on his shoulders if he could. Anyone out there in trouble or grief and your brother's reaching down to help them back on to their feet."

"You're right, Alfred, but he's not finding getting up on his own two feet quite so easy now." Tennyson cocked an eye. "You'll see a change...and he misses his young more than ever he admits to us. Tod's not far away but little Victoria's off the moor and he longs to see more of her. And then there's Harry."

"And Kitty? What of her?"

Wilmot shrugged. "We thought she was better but there was another turn before Christmas. Not a bad one but enough, mind you, and Jack sees his staying on at Sherdon as the root cause of it all. As usual he blames himself. Freddy's worried for him as well...even suggested it might be time to give up the farm altogether."

"But he won't hear of it. *Ha!*" Tennyson gave a sudden shout of a laugh then shook his head. "Don't tell me, it's typical of the man. I can just see it. 'No thank you, Master Frederic, my place is here. Here's where I belong.' That's your brother, I'll wager." He looked across at his friend with his eyes now wide, expecting the other to agree.

"True." Wilmot nodded. "It's his life and there's nothing any of us can do. Anyway he'd have it no other way."

Tennyson rested his elbow on the window ledge and scratched at his tangle of hair. "I'll have him ride out with me...that's if he'll spare me the time. I delight in just hearing him talk. I've done something on Landacre...Landacre Bridge and I'll see if he and I can't get away for an hour or so. I always see him there, y'know. Every time I pick up the folio and start to read it, I can see him by the bridge, looking up towards Withypool hill."

"He'd like that, Alfred. He's always talking about the times you spend at Sherdon. They all love it."

"And Katherine's still there, of course." Tennyson looked up from underneath his eyebrows.

"Yes," Wilmot sighed and stared back at his friend. "Not so much now, perhaps, but he often talks about how she used to look forward to your visits. They were happy times...I don't think he was ever happier." The two were silent, swaying to the movement and rhythm of the carriage.

2

Mordaunt Bisset handed the glass back to the footman and leant further down from the saddle, his hand on Jack's shoulder. The huntsman and his whipper-in had the pack held in the meadow by the cross tracks below Simonsbath manor but the field and foot followers had spilled out onto the road. As the big bay lifted his head so the Master of The Devon and Somerset Staghounds let the reins fall and bent forward.

Everywhere, almost as far as the eye could see, traps, dogcarts, chaises, broughams and carriages had pulled into the sides of the road, many tilting alarmingly where they had parked too close to the ditch. Draft horses reached down to pick at the roadside grass, some pulling their carts with them as they inched their way forward greedily. A great swathe of people had collected around the hounds; even as he glanced up more were hurrying towards the gathering, impatient to be part of the scene. It had taken 'Missa Bisset,' as he was known, more than a dozen seasons to develop his pack but now the hounds were running well and giving tongue once more, their music filling the deep Exmoor combes.

"Tell me again, Jack. Two big fellas, you say, and a number of prickets?"

"Aye, sir." Jack stepped back as the horse pushed his muzzle against him. "Just up in the brake under Barkham, where the river bends. There's a largish patch of old gorse on the higher side. South facing up there. They're there, bin there for weeks now. One of them's a master great chap...three atop either side."

"Oh yes, I know. I know exactly," the Master mused. "Look, we can get up to you in a couple of weeks, three I dare say. We'll meet at The Sportsman's. Grand." He settled back into the saddle, collected his reins and looked round. The sharp nip in the September morning air reminded him that the autumn rut was not far off when the stags would be getting restless and starting their search for hinds. Time was against him. "We'll get up there before the end of the month, anyway. I'll get Ned along to see you. Waaayup." He scolded his horse as the animal swung round impatiently. "I'll be away now…their lordships, look." He nodded to where two grooms were holding their charges steady. "Lord Frobisher's got visitors I see."

*

It seemed ages since he had last been to Simonsbath. Kitty had urged him to take a day away from the farm and he had ridden up the valley with Anna who wanted to hunt. Wilmot's groom had taught her to ride side saddle and, where the high bracken forced them into single file, he had ridden behind her and watched carefully. She had a natural seat and rode gracefully, a fact not lost on those already waiting for hounds to arrive.

They had gone up to the rectory for breakfast with Tod but even then several had gathered for the meet and, on the way past, they stopped to chat to those he knew. The presence of his daughter had been noticed as had her shy acknowledgement of their greetings. Once, when Arthur Scriven called his two sons forward, she had blushed coyly and lowered her head. She was only seventeen but looked older and more worldly in her dark russet jacket and matching long skirt. Her neat top hat with it's curved brim and plume of feathers gave an elegance of which her father was justly proud.

Tod had been waiting for them. "Come, father, Anna…here, dearest, let me show you the way." Earlier he had taken Communion and Jack started at the sight of his eldest son in his long black preaching gown. It was indeed a young man of God who embraced him warmly as soon as he had dismounted, yet the face and voice was that of the boy he knew so well. Again his heart was filled with pride.

The meal was brief: a bowl of eggs beaten into an omelette with soda bread, a plate of cold meat and hot broth. But they had time to talk and the young, fair-haired curate with the gaunt features told them news of the Knights' village. It had grown, he explained; there were now nigh on twenty in the school. More cottages were planned, a sawmill had gone up next to the flour mill and a shop had been built just down from the inn. It was amazing. Fifty years ago, Jack recalled, there had been nothing, nothing that is except for the old manor house where he had spent his first night away from home.

"So you're not lonely then?" His question was hardly necessary and he smiled at the look of surprise on his son's face.

"Not enough time in the day, father." Jack nodded, now concentrating on what was left on his plate. "William Thornton's away to Challacombe just now but it's usually me that rides out to the farms. Then there's the school and Miss Brack asks me to take scripture and prayers twice a week.

"Miss Brack?" Anna leant forward.

"The school mistress, from Taunton."

"What's she like?"

"Oh…fair enough." Jack glanced up. His son's voice had faltered and he smiled mischievously. "Yes," Tod continued, sensing what was on his father's mind. "She does a good job…strict enough yet the children have taken to her."

"Fair enough, eh? So that's all the young vicar has to say about the maid?" Father and son regarded one another. Jack grinned again and took out his fob watch.

"Is she nice, Tod?" Anna's eyes searched her brother's face. "I mean do you like her? D'you get to see her…out of school, I mean?"

"Yes, of course," he sat back and laughed. "Hey," he shook her arm. "Why're you looking at me like that…and you father? What's this inquisition for?" He wiped his mouth on his white napkin. "There's nothing more to say, certainly there's nothing…"

"Just ribbing you, lad." Jack patted his son's arm and rose. "Nice, you've got company up here. Now then…best be getting on or they'll be moving off." The chairs scraped and suddenly there was bustle. Jack stepped aside to let the maid pass then followed them out into the cobbled yard. Tod was happy, he could sense it and it lifted his spirits. He looked at the sky then half turned to see the clouds coming over from beyond the river. They were broken and high; rain later, perhaps, but not now. The courtyard where they were standing was still in shadow, but the sun had already touched the tips of the beeches on the road down to the river. They barely stirred in what little breeze there was yet the first of the leaves were falling. Scent would be good.

✳

Jack had seen Anna on her way. He was going to accompany her but, last night, had decided against it. His back was playing up and he had promised to call in at the cottage behind the manor to see Jenny Squires once the crowds had gone. The old lady was over eighty and nearly blind. Most of her teeth had gone as well, but her mind was still alert and she could talk for ever in her hoarse whisper about 'them days'. He nodded to Lord Frobisher's coachman then paused at the roadside to let a number of riders pass. They were hurrying to catch up with the field and he stopped again to let even more press through the crowd. It was only when he had started to cross the road and was looking out for horses that he bumped into the two men who were coming his way. They, also, were not looking where they were going.

"Uh." Jack put out his hands and caught the other by his elbows. "My pardon, sir." He smiled apologetically. "I should have seen you."

"I do beg your pardon, sir. I did not…" The heavier of the two men turned. He was finely dressed; his grey top hat, his black cloth coat with his grey trousers and white spats cut a dash among the drab country folk. His tightly curled grey hair, well cut and scented, lay neatly above the collar. But it was the eyes that gave him away and Jack recognised him immediately. They were round, almost staring as if the man was surprised. The face was smiling politely but, even as he began to speak, it seemed to drain of life. The eyes narrowed and the figure remained still, unmoved by those jostling him from behind. "I know you, don't I?"

"Aye, sir." Jack's voice was steady. He had let his hands fall but otherwise made no move. "Lord Preston, I believe."

"Yes, I do know you." His companion had continued on his way but Herbert, the Duke of Northborough, remained motionless and, for a moment, the two stared at one another. "Yes...by Heaven," he whispered. "*Tucker*...isn't it. *Tucker*...you're, you're..."

"Aye, sir, that's me. Jack Tucker of Sherdon Farm."

The Duke straightened himself and took a short step backwards. "Why...what...what the devil are you doing here?" Jack's chin rose but that was all. The Duke's face had coloured and now his chest was heaving as though he had come running from somewhere. "Damn you, Tucker...God damn and blast you, man," he whispered before turning and hurrying on his way.

3

Elizabeth-Jane stood as her husband came into the room. She could see he was still angry. Usually a hand was raised in greeting or a kiss blown as he came in, but this time he frowned and pushed the door shut behind him. "Was it *that* bad, dear? You looked very cross out there."

Sir Durnford Morgan shivered involuntarily, rubbed his hands and came over to where she was standing by the drawing room fire. Only then did he bend to kiss her forehead. "I had to send the wretched man on his way. The lawn's a dreadful mess. November it may be...and windy but the grass still needs to be tidied and look at it." He took a step towards the window. "Just look at it, will you. A whole mess of leaves...old molehills, weeds, everything. He peered forward awkwardly with his hands on his hips. "I'm seeing Greenway in the morning and I'll put him in charge of the front of the house." They were silent for a moment and Durnford glanced at his wife as she made a face, as if telling herself that she thought little of the idea.

"I suppose you have to, dear?" Elizabeth-Jane looked up sadly. She had changed since coming back from South Molton and was dressed in one of his favourites. The dark blue bows and accordion pleating of her promenade dress stood out from the pale grey poplin. Even here at Bremridge on such a dull and cheerless autumn afternoon she looked radiant. "Dismiss him like this, I mean. The Bowers're a large family, y'know...and there's not much chance of any other work around here."

166

Durnford lifted his hands in exasperation and let them fall again. He sat heavily, tugged at his collar and winced. "Phhhw." His brow was furrowed as though the idea worried him. "I'm afraid I had to," he muttered. "I've tried and tried with the man but he's just not up to it. Oh, dear…what a day it's been."

"Frederic you mean?" He had mentioned earlier how her son had come to seek his advice about his financial situation. They had been closeted in the library together for more than two hours and, even then, he had declined the invitation to stay on for lunch, having to hurry on his way instead. She put down her embroidery. "It's not very good is it."

"No, I'm afraid not…but it could be worse, I'll say that. And it seems as though we might have worked our way towards a glimmer of hope. There're one or two problems, you see, the most important of which drags on from when those wretched mining companies upped sticks and pulled out. That was bad but the High Court supported him. I always thought they would in the end but you can never be sure." Elizabeth-Jane shook her head. "Yes, I know," he continued. "It was bad enough as it was but if the courts had pronounced against him then we really would be in trouble. It's the family involvement that won't let go."

"Who?" Now she stared at her hands. "Oh, why don't they leave him alone? He's working so hard."

Durnford Morgan shrugged. He had seen both sides of the dispute and while he wanted Frederic to be free from the burden, he knew he had to be fair and the others had to be paid their share. "Well, we've managed to re-arrange his affairs that will ensure they all get their dues in *time*. Here again, dear, the courts were sympathetic. Alex Major, the man we got to put forward Freddie's case, did well. It'll mean we're going to have to sell off one of the Corkley smelting works but," he lifted his hand. "It'll keep everybody happy."

"And when's all this going to be over…when's the poor boy going to be left in peace?" Durnford turned at the sound of the door opening then signalled the mob-capped maid to bring in the tea. They watched in silence as she set out the plates and cake stands on the mahogany dumb waiter, before standing back and looking from one to the other. Durnford smiled and nodded in reply as she bobbed before leaving the room.

"Five…five years or so, unless he starts looking for gold in those hills again and I've warned him against that. And farm prices are down, I'm afraid, so he's got to do away with his pony herd. That hurt but he has just too many overheads…and he's taken on so much…all these other matters."

"And did you talk to Wilmot?"

Durnford was on his feet and gave a short laugh. "No luck there either, I'm sorry to say." He remembered how Wilmot had declined his offer to join Esdaile's board.

167

"He was absolutely honest about it though...said he thought there could be a difficult conflict of interests. We thought he was talking about our involvement in the shipping business but he wasn't at all. He felt we were getting too involved in agriculture in this part of the world and that could clash with his own interests...inevitably, so he thought. Fair enough, and we couldn't argue."

"And what about the other business? The Kingdons and Herbert Northborough's family?"

Durnford caught her look. "Yes...well, we touched obliquely, but he said enough to give me a pretty shrewd idea that the blood between them's not exactly healthy. Herbert's such a fool...an oaf of a man. One minute he makes out it was all the girl's fault, the next he's singing her praises to the rafters and not in a particularly tasteful manner either. A bit of an old lecher in my opinion."

"I always thought he was rather too pleased with himself, ever since the days when he and Kenton used to get up to all manner of mischief in London." She stopped suddenly. "Oh, goodness," she whispered shaking her head.

"Mmm?" Durnford's cup was poised. "What's that, dear?"

"Kenton's name always reminds me of Jack...Jack Tucker. And I've just remembered...this girl, Sarah's his niece, and Wilmot's too, of course."

"I know. I'm afraid it's all a fearful tangle and we're not out of it yet...not by a long way." He sipped quickly and placed his cup and saucer back on the waiter.

Elizabeth-Jane sighed then her shoulders sagged. "And now, if all that's not enough, Freddie tells me that his Sebright's getting involved. As soon as he's up in Simonsbath he's away down to Sherdon."

"Oh yes?"

"Anna, would you believe. Little Anna Tucker, Katherine's baby."

"Well...stranger things have happened. But come, my dear, the child's only what...seventeen."

"Exactly. And at that age, I'd been married for nearly two years and so had Florence. Seventeen's seventeen, y'know, and she's a lovely young thing. *I* don't mind; not at all. Goodness, to think of a daughter of Katherine joining the family...and Freddie's pleased enough as well but I'm afraid Florence does *not* see it like that."

"Oh, dear." Durnford smoothed back his hair. "Another little problem."

"Well, perhaps, but it could turn out to be quite a big one. Florence is not a country girl, you know. She knows nothing about farming and, well, farmers to her are just the working class…the peasantry as I've heard her say."

"Jack, you mean? Hmm." Sir Durnford paused. "The girl's mother's fine, I suppose. The right stock and all that but the poor old father, Jack's just not good enough. Breeding they call it, don't they? Isn't that it?"

She noticed the hard edge to his voice. "In a word, yes. Yes, that's exactly what she thinks. She's got her plans for Sebright and they're all a very long way from the top of Exmoor."

"And what has Freddie got to say about that?"

"He really doesn't know what to do. If Florence wasn't there then he'd be de-*lighted*. He adores Jack…there's a fineness about the man, something very special. And look at Wilmot, for Heaven's sake. They're a marvellous family and that's before you even think of her mother. And you know his thoughts there." She paused. "But no, poor Freddie, I really do think he'd love to see something come of it."

"But it's *very* early days…very early and far too soon for anyone to start getting excited."

"All except Mrs Frederic Knight that is." Elizabeth-Jane raised her eyebrows and pulled a gloomy face. "Our good Mrs Knight is not happy at all and wants to put a stop to 'any such nonsense' as she describes it."

"Oh dear."

"Exactly." Elizabeth-Jane rose and straightened her skirts. "It's not going to go away, I'm afraid…not yet anyway."

4

Victoria pulled the dark cloak more tightly around her shoulders, leant forward and patted the pony's neck. They had come down from the highest ground but still the east wind had a cruel bite. Christmas would be in less than a month when she would be going back to Sherdon.

At first she had been thrilled at the idea; it would be wonderful to see home again. Her father had been over to Molland when he stayed with the Loosemore's at Luckworthy. She had been given a day's grace and accompanied him everywhere, even to The London Inn where she sat beside him with one arm through his as he chatted to old friends. Later, he told her she reminded him of his younger sister, Hannah, the one who died. She used to sit like that, he said, with an arm through his and her head on his shoulder.

Great Champson had changed. Another girl had come to do lace work. Jenny Parker, tall and dark with a mass of black curls was as easy as the others had been difficult and she enjoyed her company. Mr and Mrs Quartly were almost like a mother and father, well almost. The trouble was that he, Joseph, so rarely said anything. She was sure he was nice but could never say that she knew him. Mrs Quartly though was lovely and the two of them would sit for hours together with their lace work.

And then there was Edwin. Thinking about him, even looking at him now as he rode behind the sheep brought a flutter of excitement. He had been so kind, but then he was kind to everyone, in particular to his brother, Daniel. She marvelled at his patience as the cripple would gurgle and shout and wave his arms about as he tried to say something. Sometimes Edwin would take him by the arm and the two would walk slowly around the garden, stopping every now and then to bend down and examine something. Daniel would stumble and trip but his brother never let him fall. There was something warm and kind about him and Victoria knew that if she went back to Sherdon she would miss him; even for a week or so.

She reached down from the saddle, half lifted the gate and, using the pony's body, eased it open far enough for the sheep to run through. Then she turned to watch them as they scampered passed. "Thirty-eight," she cried, still counting. "Oops, no, forty-one." Edwin laughed as she included the last three that hurried through the gateway, two of them jumping high in the air as they rushed by.

"Still another ten." Edwin, his eyes watering from the wind, sniffed and wiped his nose on his sleeve. "They'm further up the combe." He stood in his stirrups, half turned and whistled shrilly for the two collies. "I'll get on after them, Queenie. You'm froze, you are...get on back down, it'll only take an hour or so."

Victoria shook her head causing the hood of her cloak to fall over her face. She pushed it back and both laughed at her tangle of hair. She, too, sniffed and wiped her eyes. "No, come on. It's not that bad...I'll come with you."

"Sure?"

She nodded and swung the pony round then stopped and waited as he closed the gate. She felt happy: everything, at last, seemed to be easy and fun. She loved shepherding and when it was with Edwin it was better still. He had a quiet way with the dogs and the sheep, and his presence gave her a sense of security. "I'll miss'ee when you're off back to Sherdon...with two horses and two dogs like this, 'tis a mite easier." He wheeled away from her. "I'll get up on the top," he cried over his shoulder. "You stay on the lower path and we'll drive 'em down."

"Edwin." She had to call again and only later realised that it might have been better if she had not blurted it all out like she did. He stopped and turned, frowning as though something might be wrong. "Will you come with me? Come back to Sherdon...for Christmas, I mean, and meet papa, and Kitty and Frank...and Anna?

Will you? D'you think your father would let you?" She stopped suddenly, one hand to her mouth. They were still a few yards apart and she realised with a shock that she must have been shouting all this into the wind. For a moment he did nothing but then urged his pony slowly forward and came up to her.

"Up to Sherdon?" The cold had made the stubble on his chin seem darker, black almost, and his face was red from the bitter cold. "Is that what you said? Sherdon?" Once again, the wind had blown his hair across his face.

Victoria nodded, watching him brush it back, her fingers still covering her mouth. Suddenly she felt foolish. Her words had come tumbling out telling the world what was on her mind when they had no right to do so. He had heard her all right, she could see he had and he thought it was a silly suggestion, she could see that as well. How could he possibly come away for a week and over Christmas at that? He was needed on the farm: his parents would wonder what on earth was on her mind. What could the silly girl be thinking about? Up to Sherdon…what ever next? And now it was too late. She studied him closely, now suddenly afraid of what he might say.

"D'you mean that?" He had come alongside her pony. He wasn't smiling but he wasn't angry either although his dark eyebrows had furrowed. His eyes were searching hers and she could see he was thinking of what to say. "Eh? D'you *mean* that, Queenie…reelly?"

She nodded again and felt her eyes beginning to fill with tears. It was not the wind this time for they were still in the lee of the hedge.

"Well." He was stumbling now, scowling as he sought the right words. "Well…'tis not quite so easy as that. I mean…but yes." He paused again and looked away. "I'll have to see father…an' mother'll have to know. But yes…aye. Us should be able to do summat, all right. Daresay father'll manage, p'raps just fer two three days, like. There's Ted Small an' Luke…Luke Windsor." He was talking as he was thinking but then he turned suddenly and looked her. "Aye, Queenie. That's if yer mean it, like. Reckon I'd like that."

She smiled and sniffed again. It had to be the cold and she wiped her eyes. It was just as she dared hope. He would like Sherdon and he would get on with Frank, she knew he would. And he was bound to like Kitty, everybody did. They could both help her father and she could show him how they had made the farm out of nothing for it was so young in comparison to Champson. Her father had built it up with his hands. She would show him Sixty Acres and they would ride up the Barle together, perhaps even up as far as Simonsbath to see Tod. Then they would gather holly from the copse in the valley and strip lengths of ivy from the bark of the older trees.

"Yes, of course." She smiled then laughed out loud at the look on his face. "Yes, of course I do."

Chapter Thirteen

Milton Brodie sat on the edge of the ornamental fishpond and gazed at the house. The lower walled garden of Whitechapel Manor was hot and he allowed the fingers of one hand to trail idly through the water. It was also bright and, as his mind wandered, he blinked in the midday June sunlight. Somewhere over by the Virginia creeper that clad the kitchen garden wall a cock chaffinch trilled earnestly. He could hear the gardeners working beyond, and beyond that again a cow was lowing for her calf. That apart, it was quiet.

Herbert Northborough, he mused, would never change. He had got so much going for him including this beautiful place yet there was always an element of danger about the man, as though trouble was never far off. There was this shipping business at Ilfracombe. Successful enough to be sure, but where was it going to take him? The newspapers were awash with reports of the smaller companies folding as the mackerels began to devour the sprats. And now there was this family drama he had talked about last night. And his daughter-in-law: that she was alluring and sonsy there was no doubt. Once, no twice, this last week at Whitechapel, she had let her intentions be known. On the first occasion he had not been so sure but when she had joined them on the fishing picnic she had made herself clear, as clear as the cut of her sun bodice.

Ever since they had fished the Test and Itchen together as schoolboys he had admired Herbert for the way he diced with life. Covered by the Blagdon fortunes life had been easy, but Herbert had always played fast and loose and he could remember the times when the two of them, with Kenton Knight, Godfrey Bolun and others, had tilted at the devil in London. It had always been the young Herbert who led the way.

Milton Brodie, his best friend's confidant, smiled to himself. They had talked about it last night and he had warned him but the wretched fellow, now almost sixty-four, heavy and not so fit as he was, was as bad as ever. He rose and flicked his hand dry. There would be eight for dinner tonight and Sarah would be playing hostess for her father-in-law. He smiled again. The girl *was* exciting. She was alive, bright and she fizzed like the bubbles in good champagne. If half what he'd heard was true, then Lady Sarah Preston led a merry life herself. No wonder her father-in-law enjoyed her company.

He grinned and hooked his jacket over his shoulder. Tomorrow, if the promised clouds came over, he would be fishing the Mole down by the Junction Pool and it was Sarah, the good lady herself, who would be joining him for lunch.

✳

Jessie Painter shrugged and turned the basket upside down to shake out the

172

crumbs. "'Ow do I know?" She glanced at Fred Buckingham out of the corner of her eye and chuckled. "He's handsome enough, mind. 'Andsome as sin, all us girls can see that, but goin' with her like 'e is…I dunno." The small, bony parlour maid with lank hair had been sent out with the picnic. Fred Buckingham, one of the under coachman had driven her to where the brougham was parked under the oaks just off the bend in the road. There was nobody about and they waited until they saw Collins, the driver, the one who had gone to look, step through the hedge by the river. He was fat but he ran nevertheless, hanging on to his hat and puffing heavily. His eyes were wide with excitement and he had a finger pressed to his lips that demanded silence.

"'Tis true, I'm telling yer. Cuh." Collins wiped his mouth again. He was steadier now but still panting hard. "They'm down along the bank," he gasped. "Just through the next hedge…nearly fell over 'em, so I did."

"Did they see yer?"

"Nah." He looked from one to the other. "Too 'ard at it, they was. Could'a fired a gun an' they wouldn't 'ave stopped."

"Well, there you are then. Winnie Cook, 'er maid, said she was one of they sorts." Jessie Painter pulled a face, flicked the napkin and lifted a second, heavier wicker basket from the cart. "Well, gid on then. I'm having nort to do with it. If you wants to go peepin' an' that then away with yer…I'm getting lunch. They'll be back shortly so make haste, mind."

"What's the matter wiv you, maid? Frightened you'll see summat that'll make 'e all 'orny. Eh? Can't have that, can us, Fred? Cuh, can't have Jessie Painter getting' all goaty, watchin' Lady Preston havin' 'er bit o' fun." Reggie Collins jumped but not before the maid pushed him, sending him staggering over the picnic hamper.

"Ere, 'e bugger orf, Fred Buckingham. Just 'cos nobody gives two farthings for the sight 'o your ugly face." She watched as the two men made their way back through the long grass, then stood on tiptoe as they ducked low and crept towards the hedge. She saw Reg Collins take the other by his arm and point towards a bent sapling then point again. He was describing what lay the other side. The closer they got, the more slowly they moved.

Fred Buckingham eased his way onto the bank. Sheep had broken through some time ago, wearing down the turf until, in some places, the bare earth had been exposed. He leant forward, his head half through the gap then inched forward again using the toes of his boots to push himself. Reg waited until he slipped back. The two of them crouched together. "Five yards," he mouthed, barely audible. "'Ere," he grabbed the other's arm. "Go careful mind. They'm there all right…'bout five paces out in the grass. Shhh." A finger to his mouth urged caution.

Suddenly a cock pheasant clattered its way out of the brambles nearby calling out angrily. One froze, the other dropped to the ground but it was Fred who moved first, signalling that he had heard something by cupping his ear and pointing at the bank. He wriggled his way through and all but disappeared into the long grass. Minutes later he backed out, turned and slipped to the ground with his back against the bank. The coachman rolled his eyes then grinned and moved aside for his friend.

"I'll be damned," he gasped. They had run half way back to the carts before stopping. "That were they all right. 'Er and that Brodie, the one all the wimin talks about. "

"Told 'e, didn' I? Eh? Right locked up together so they were."

"Cuh," Fred Buckingham shook his head. "*Cuh*, I'll say. Just like anyone else, eh?"

"Us is all the same, buiy. Don't matter if you'm Mister this or Lady that, 'tis all the same down there underneath." Reg Collins wiped his mouth. "Right bit 'o fancy though, she be."

"Aye, that's what they say, an' all. If Her Ladyship takes yer fancy well…"

"Cuh, an' to think His Lordship knows nort."

✳

"Here, let me ask you something." The Duke of Northborough turned slowly. His face wore a sly, conspiratorial look and, for a moment, Milton Brodie quailed. Then he relaxed for, in his hand, the Duke held a dark green, oval jewel case. He walked purposefully across to the window where his friend was sitting, pushed his legs to one side and sat. Milton Brodie lowered his paper. "Think back, will you…quite some time if you will, back to dear Katherine at Blagdon." Brodie frowned. "It's a difficult one this but I want to know if you can remember any of the jewellery she used to wear."

"*Jewellery?*" Brodie's frown deepened and he looked askance. "I'm afraid I can't, well not specifically." He shook his head. "How on earth d'you expect me to remember anything like that?"

The Duke looked at him and shrugged. "Oh, all right…it's no matter. But here, take a look at this." He shifted to a more comfortable position. "See here." He opened the jewel case and allowed the rubies and pearls to spill into his hand. Brodie sat up and whistled quietly then lifted the necklace to have a better look. "By the saints, Herbert, what's all this about…where did you get this, it's beautiful?"

"Right, let me ask you something else. Keep hold of it a moment and take a closer look. Look at the two stones either side of the clasp…let me know what you think." He watched, waiting patiently. "Take your time."

Brodie held the necklace to the light and squinted, checking the rubies one at a time before staring at the two in question. "Imperfections...both appear to be flawed. Only just though. Come on," Brodie laughed nervously. "What on earth's all this about?" He held out the necklace. "Why all these questions if it's something that used to be Katherine's?"

"Pheew." The Duke blew and shook his head as he tidied the necklace into the case and closed the lid. "Just before Sharland left last week he gave these to Sarah. Right?"

"Sharland? But what's so wrong in that? Perhaps Katherine bequeathed them to him....."

"No. She did not and that's the whole point." The Duke smiled grimly. "When Sarah first wore them, we were having dinner together, just the two of us and I couldn't take my eyes off them. I knew at once that I'd seen them before and then it came to me...I recognised them. I hadn't seen them for years. Their mother passed most of her jewellery on to Katherine and Lizzie and among them was this." He tapped the case. "The point about it all is that Sharland did indeed give them to Sarah but he *bought* them...bought them in Exeter a few months ago, would you believe."

"But what I don't understand is how you know they were ever Katherine's. I mean, they *are* beautiful but I'd've thought there would be others about. Rare, I admit, and something that'd need a ransom to buy...but why not? Or is it something to do with those two stones?"

"Exactly!" The Duke slapped his thigh. "As soon as I saw them I knew I had to check, and I did just that. I took it upon myself to go into her bedroom and find out. There was nobody around, nobody at all and there they were...absolutely no mistaking them. They're unique. Mother and father told us that they came from Flanders. They used to visit a jeweller over there and that was his mark, his trade mark. They were Katherine's, sans doubt."

"But are you sure they weren't left to Sharland?"

"Absolutely not."

"Then how on earth did they get to Exeter? Somebody sold them on?"

"Right again." The Duke rose and began to pace the room, his hands now clasped behind his back. His head was lowered. "We never saw them again after Katherine left home. She must have taken them with her and when she died they must have been up at that farm of hers. *Somebody*, and I'm damned sure I know who, decided to get rid of them...sell them. Sort out a few farm debts, wouldn't they just?"

"But who? Her husband?"

"I'll wager," the Duke replied. Brodie could see his friend was hurt. He looked angry: angry and brooding. The idea of it had got to him. "Yes...that God forsaken husband of hers," the Duke continued. "It was him, I'll be bound. His hands are in here somewhere, that's fer sure. But now the necklace is back where it belongs...back from whence it came. Ha...damn him, Brodie, damn the man. The wretch haunts me."

"Not only back with the family but, from what you've told me, right into the hands of his very own niece...and in this house."

"And there's the pain, Brodie." The Duke of Northborough bent over his friend. "That's what hurts like hell. It's as if the damned thing in there won't leave us alone." He picked up the case again. "It's here, this necklace, plaguing and taunting me about all sorts of things and all because of that sheep stealing beggar up in the hills." He straightened himself and shivered then looked down again, his eyes staring defiantly. "But I'll not let it rest."

"Do they know anything of this? Sarah and Sharland?"

"No, nothing," he snapped. "Nothing at all and I'll bide my time."

"But Sarah? You can't lay blame on her. She's innocent...you can't drag her into this."

"No, no, of course not," he mused. "I'd never hurt the girl. As far as she's concerned they're a gift from Sharland and that's that. But those Tuckers, they're different...very different."

✳

Sarah leaned back against the rose pink velvet of the high sofa and looked at her father-in-law. She smiled slowly; it was an affectionate smile but she was also amused. They had dined alone and she had noticed him looking at her even more than he usually did. The three central leaves of the mahogany dining table had been removed but he remained a distance from her and had to peer through the central candelabra. She was used to it and didn't mind but tonight his eyes had strayed constantly. They had dined well and left the table early.

Tomorrow the Duke would be returning to Blagdon. Sharland had left already and had been at Hartland for almost a week. In a way she was looking forward to seeing him again and Jocelyn had arranged a birthday party for Amelia. She would be two and, even now, her daughter had learned to stamp her foot when she wanted her own way. Her grandfather said she got it from her mother and Sarah smiled again, this time catching his eye. He was looking well, she thought, the bottle green smoking jacket suited him and his hair was shorter, taking years off him.

As it was their last night together for several weeks she had dressed for the occasion. The pale blue silk and cotton evening dress with the low neckline and short sleeves was the one he liked best, the one he said was his favourite. Winnie had brushed and set her hair into long ringlets, tied at the base with black silk ribbons. As she sipped her canary, she touched the corner of her mouth then the beauty spot on her cheek and glanced up at the French bracket clock.

"You're good to me, y'know, Sarah, m'dear." The Duke struggled up in his chair, put his glass on the floor and held out his hand. "Come over here a minute, there's something I want to see."

"Really, Bertie...that's no way to win my compliance." Isaac, as soon as he had begun to talk, had, for some reason, insisted on trying to call his grandfather Bertie. The Duke had been flattered that he should be seen as one so young and the name had stuck, its new owner demanding that the mother of the child should refer to him likewise, but only when they were alone. "Anyway, I'm too, too tired and my feet hurt. Look" She had taken off her shoes and now hooked one up on to her toe and dangled it provocatively.

"Then I'll do as I believe I've bin commanded to do...or is there a request hidden away in that stubbornness of yours?" He rose heavily and came over to where she sat. "I've been admiring your necklace, my dear. Here...am I allowed to?" He reached out and took hold of the ruby pendant.

"It's beautiful, isn't it." Sarah sat up and pushed her body forward making it easier for him to see more clearly. Their faces were close. She could see the heavy, red-rimmed lids to his watery eyes and the bloodshot web of veins on his cheek. But he was still an attractive man and she watched affectionately. He sensed she was appraising him and turned his head slightly to catch her eye.

"What're you looking at me like that for?" he grinned raffishly. "Mmm?" She watched as he wiped some grains of food from the corners of his mouth. "You're very beautiful, y'know, Sarah...I'm a lucky, lucky old man to have one so young helping me. Everyone says so...everybody." She tensed at the sudden feel of his hand cupping her breast. He was kneading her flesh and now, as he did so, he watched her closely.

"Stop it, Bertie. That's very naughty," Sarah caught hold of his hand, forcing it away. "Go on," she gasped. He half turned and sat heavily beside her. "What did you do that for?" she scolded, smoothing the rushing and flowers on her neckline. "Testing me again, I suppose."

"Mmm? Come on, m'dear. You've got them all eating out of your hand. Take Milton Brodie; you sent him on his way happy enough. What?" He rested his hand on her knee and leaned towards her. "You're a wicked little minx, that's what you are. A wicked, mischievous little minx."

"*What?*" she cried, louder than she would have done had it not been for what she had just heard. "Me? Now now, sir. Come, come. Get thee hence this instant." She lifted his hand and placed it on his own knee. "That from you, my dear Bertie, is as rich as the darkest of Jamaican molasses. Here we have father and son, why barely a week passes without me hearing this about one, or that about the other and now…now you dare to suppose that I should be so Rabelaisian as to give chase to those nearest to you."

"But you did…you little Delilah, you." His hand returned.

"No, never Delilah. She was beastly. I'd never be like that. I want to make people happy, to see them laugh and clap their hands. Titania, that's me, that's who I am. Titania the Fairy Queen, so says my uncle's good friend Alfred Tennyson. And any more such outrageous suggestions from you and you'll be my Bottom." She pushed a finger on to his chin and giggled helplessly, unaware that his face had hardened at the mention of her uncle.

2

Parson John Froude moved his two sticks one at a time then took a faltering pace before repeating the exercise. Eventually he reached the wooden seat where they had put cushions for him. He turned slowly, half lowered himself, then sat clumsily and sighed. Slowly, as if it were really an effort, he lifted his wide-brimmed straw hat, mopped his brow, and leant back.

The guests had gone and they would be coming for him tomorrow, but today Sunday, they had left him alone to recover. Edward and Millie Samuels, the present vicar and his wife, had been wonderfully kind and would be joining him shortly for tea. He tried to turn to check if they were coming but his neck was stiff and he had to force his whole body round. There was nobody, just the old spaniel lying on her side in the shade, half of her under the wisteria, the other half on the terrace. He twisted further round to glance up at the rectory he knew so well, then turned slowly back again.

It had been really splendid to see Jack Tucker and all the others again and to think that he and Wilmot, now Sir Wilmot of course, had asked him to assist at Victoria's wedding. It had been so kind of them. Dear Molland hadn't changed at all and the village had taken to the girl in the two years she had been there. He had been back to the church from time to time but it had been almost twenty years now since he had been forced to retire. One tumble too many whilst following hounds was the doctor's verdict, and they had found him a little cottage down by the bridge in Dulverton.

He was glad to see the boy looking so well and his new wife looked happy enough. A frail little thing though, who had been ill so they said. A nice enough girl but very different from Katherine. John Froude smiled to himself as he remembered how, when they were standing in the porch and talking of old times, he had got Jack mixed up with his father. Now there was a man, but Lionel had gone all too soon and that had been the start of the adventure. Later, at the feast, young Frederic Knight spoke warmly of the family. They had decked out Great Champson for the occasion and the Quartlys had been there in force. Joseph had done his boy proud. The lad and little Victoria looked splendid…just a happy loving couple, exactly as it should be. It had been a marvellous day, marvellous; they could have done with a bit more sun perhaps, like this afternoon, but at least the rain had held off.

The old parson's head dropped forward, jerked up then settled slowly once more until his chin was on his chest. As his grip relaxed, so one stick fell to the ground. Without realising it, he let the other one drop too, then eased himself deeper into the seat until he was comfortable. It had, indeed, been a wonderful day…there were so many friends…so many he knew…they all seemed to be so happy…and the bride and groom as well…and the singing, and all the children…yes, a marvellous, marvellous day. Quite marvellous…mmm.

3

Desmond Orchard looked out of the drawing room window and up at the sky. The cirrus clouds were riding high in their endless columns and seemed to be thickening by the minute. Last night the glass had fallen faster than he could remember but it had been Jed Davey, his shepherd, who had first mentioned it yesterday morning. Lundy Island had been far too clear, the man claimed, and the grey seals had been hunting right on the cusp of the cove beneath his cottage. "They fish know summat's up and 'tis they that bring the seals in like that." The storm was coming.

Earlier that morning Sharland had taken Isaac out in the lobster boat. He had decided to go as soon as the tide would allow so they could get at the pots more easily. Even then the burgeoning swell had made handling the dinghy difficult. There had not been a breath of wind but the steady rise and fall, coming from a point almost due west, had pushed them close into the shore until they were tucked under the towering cliffs. High, high above them, no more than specks against the sky, an occasional seabird wheeled while all round them lines of exposed black rocks, still wet and speckled with barnacles lay low and menacing in the water.

The swell did not break, it simply rose further and further against the rocks until it could climb no higher then fell away, gurgling and sucking as it went. Sharland felt as though they were being shepherded unwittingly into some deep and sinister tomb. Isaac laughed when his father called out, shouting at the walls around him then standing with a hand to his ear waiting for the echo to return. The boy tried it too, his shrill cry fading to no more than a small pip in the distance.

The child demanded to hear it again and again even as his father was pulling hard to clear the headland. They shouted together and laughed out loud as their voices floated back to them. Once round the point, Sharland relaxed to let the flood tide and the deep, rolling swell do his work for him. They sat facing one another, for a moment the only two people in the world: the little boy in his sailor suit and his father in an open shirt. Sharland shipped oars and took the child onto his lap then ruffled his soft hair before pulling him close to his chest. The boy reached up and felt for his father's face.

But all day the wind had risen steadily and now, as Desmond looked on, the trees, still heavy in summer leaf, bent alarmingly to the wind, the underside of the branches exposed like heavy skirts that had been lifted suddenly. Green leaves, torn from the treetops whirled through the air. Even as he watched a garden chair toppled over. Caught by a sudden gust it tumbled over and over along the terrace. Behind him a door slammed then a further gust made the windows rattle angrily.

*

Jed Davey leant forward. The afternoon air was hot yet he had put his coat on half expecting rain. He had spent all afternoon bringing the ewes and lambs down from the cliff top pastures that rose either side of his cottage. The storm, and it was going to be a big one, would be on them by nightfall and he wanted the flock down. His long black hair blew wildly about his face. A man still in his prime, his body was lean and sinewy, kept that way by his bachelor life and the steepness of the land around him. As he climbed he scowled with effort; his heavy eyebrows and sharp nose giving him the appearance of the peregrines that ruled the cliffs around Hartland. He half closed his eyes to the wind yet they missed nothing as they searched the countryside around him.

Almost at the top, he paused and looked back down at his squat, lime washed home. The cottage had been there for as long as anyone could remember. Perched some hundred feet above the high water mark and set cleverly in a dip just above the stream that ran down from the Abbey, it seemed to be standing watch over the cove. The tide would not peak for an hour or so but already it seemed higher than usual as the breakers streamed in one after the other to break untidily among the pebbles and boulders that made up the beach. Most though were caught by the cliffs beyond the cove, sending great spouts of spray whirling high into the air as they crashed against the towering black walls. As each wave subsided and was drawn back out to sea, he could see the foam seething angrily where the jagged rocks that ran out from the shoreline were exposed. Lundy Island had almost gone, the spray from countless wave tops having formed a low mist across the horizon. Two ships, one a heavy barque, the other a ketch and closer to shore, were running before the wind towards the shelter of Barnstaple Bay, the larger of the two with no more than half-reefed topsails set. Jed turned back into the wind.

Two hours later it was dark but the shepherd was restless. The wind, he knew, had veered round to a few points west of north and increased further still. Anything caught out there where the tide was ebbing fast across this wind would be facing terrible seas. The crew would be beating landwards on shortened sail tempted to come close in to seek whatever shelter there might be. But there was none. Unless they could clear Hartland Point and find shelter, the mighty coastline was unforgiving, each year punishing more of the careless or unwary. Once aground there was little hope as the churchyards at Stoke and Hardisworthy testified.

He had to force his door open against the gale. Now the darkness was filled with the roar of the tempest as it tore through the furze and the stunted oaks above and behind him. He could not see the shore but heard the crashing of breakers. It was as if the sea was trying to battle its way towards him, and that was just in the shelter of the cove. He lifted his lantern high as if in a salute to anything that was out there on a night like this. As he turned back towards the warmth of his cot he felt the first heavy drops of rain on his face.

*

"Who is it...I said who's there?" Sharland heard the voice from his bedroom. It was Clements the second butler. Then the knocks came again. He threw on his coat and, as he stood in the bedroom doorway, felt the sudden pressure of air as the front door opened. It cannoned shut with a boom and he could hear several voices raised in concern. He saw the lamp in Desmond's room but ran downstairs ahead of his host. The two visitors were talking excitedly to Clements and one of the house boys. "She's a schooner, m'lord." Clements turned. "Failed to make the point and she's turned back and started to run...but then she tried to stand off. No hope, sir, not in this."

"And where is she now?"

"Driftin', m'lord...in under Damehole Point. Lost her foremast and she's coming in beam on." The older and more heavily built of the two men, both of whom were sodden with their hair plastered flat, pointed vaguely towards the sea behind them. "Most likely off your beach, sir...down the bottom of the valley...by Jed Davey's place."

"Ye Gods...those rocks, and both sides of the bay. They're monsters."

"Aye, m'lord." The man glanced at Sharland. "There's nort much to be done. There's a party up on Dyer's Lookout and more back down by the quay, in case her drifts back but us reckons she were too close in. Reckon 'er'll be in tight to the shore just down the bottom there."

"Has anyone gone down there?" Desmond Orchard was adjusting the belt to his gown. "We'll need to get a party there with ropes and lights." He looked from one to the other, scratching at the back of his head. "Clements...wake up the stables and you, you boy, run to the gardeners' cottages. I want everyone assembled here, right here in the hall...everyone, d'you hear." He turned to Sharland. "Best if you get on down there with these fellas." Then he turned to the visitors. "Lock, isn't it? Lock and Bawden from the village? Good...good men," he nodded in greeting. "You go on, Sharland. Throw on some clothes and I'll come on with the others. I'll wake the cook and send somebody for the doctor. They'll be needing him…if they're lucky. If not…" he left the sentence unfinished.

*

The storm lanterns were not required for even as they reached the cove dawn was breaking into a heavy dull grey that brightened only reluctantly. The tide was ebbing fast but even so the gale had whipped the wave tops into a thick spray. The schooner had failed to make the cove and was aground on a line of half submerged rocks about a hundred yards off shore. She had swung beam-on to the cliffs but the wind was driving her in one direction and the tide pulling her in another. She would never last. Even as they watched a great breaker picked her up, slewed her round then dropped her again before racing on to the cliffs.

"Best wait until the tide's down." Sharland glanced at the man who had spoken. It seemed sensible.

"Her'll never last." Another broke in. "She's startin' to break up right now. There look…her mizzen's down. Two hours an' she's gone, let alone six. Break 'er back soon, so she will."

"And if we do wait?" Sharland had to shout above the wind. "How long before we could get across to her?"

"Two hours, three, p'raps." A second man had joined them. "But there's a deep channel this side o' where she's lyin'. Bain't no way you could reach her 'til low tide."

Sharland calculated quickly. No matter what they wanted to do, time and the ebbing tide were against them. Yet something had to be done. The crowd was getting larger, carts were arriving with ropes and lights yet nobody knew how to set about it: nobody was in charge. By now people could be seen on the listing deck, somebody shouted that one of them had jumped. Further delay and the ship would be lost. He stepped forward and clapped the nearest man on the shoulder. "Get a rope. You, quickly, get that line over there…it look's better. I'm going for them."

"Don't be bloody daft, man." Several heads turned his way.

He waved the remark away. "I'm not standing here watching women and children jumping to their deaths. See here, the tide's ebbing fast and we can already work our way along the rocks under the cliffs. Over there look." He pointed and they turned, following his arm. By now everybody was listening. "Almost opposite the ship, there by that big square-shaped fellow. And the ship herself, look at her. The rocks she's on are sheltering the landward side of her. It's only a hundred yards or so and I can do it…the seas're quieter there and I'll be with the tide."

"But the size o' they breakers…you'll never do it."

182

"Don't fancy getting' caught down there on they rocks…not for a coupl'a hours or so."

"Look." It was Sharland again. "I'm going and that's that. I'll need three of you at least to pay out the line. I'll take it around my waist and, once aboard, we'll haul out a stronger rope. The rest of you follow on behind. Come on…who's coming?" For a moment there was silence. "For the sake of Jesus Christ," he yelled. "Are the whole damned lot of you going to stand there and watch good people die…well, are you?"

Still nobody moved and he was about to turn away when a tall, fair-haired young man stepped forward. "I'm with 'e, sir." Another followed him, then a third. Soon there was a band of able men. Sharland lead the way down to where the rocks met the base of the cliffs. One by one they followed him, clambering over boulders and scrambling along what might have been a path.

✳

The water was surprisingly warm. He could see the ship clearly now. Every so often a larger wave lifted her and she would settle further. They could see figures on deck, three women and what appeared to be two small children with a number of men. Ten in all, perhaps. There was no stopping now; he would have to get out to the poor souls or they were certain to perish.

He pushed himself away from the rocks thankful for the rope-soled canvas shoes. They were the ones he had bought for shrimping on the rocks with Isaac. The sudden memory made him smile, even now. He gasped and spluttered as a wave lifted him, filling his mouth with salt water. As soon as he struck out again he could feel the weight of the line behind him. It was holding him back like a sea anchor and he turned to call for more line but already the current had taken him too far.

Those on deck were waving to him, shouting soundlessly into the wind and pointing to where the rails had broken and ropes were trailing. She was lying further over on her side now, listing heavily towards the shore. Rather than lifting her, the smaller seas were grinding her against the ledge while they waited for the next big wave. He stopped for a moment to catch his breath and tried to pull in the line but it was too heavy. The warmth in his body was fading and he could feel the cold creeping up his legs. His arms were tiring. Another ten yards or so and he would try to find a spot to clamber aboard. He stopped again, staring in amazement as the ship was picked up by another giant roller then thrown down like a toy. He could hear her timbers groaning and splintering below the water line. She was dying.

He knew he was weakening yet slowly, yard by yard, he was closing on her. The trouble was that the tide was swirling madly around the ledge and he could feel the current sucking him away from the wreck. A wave washed over him making him choke then another, a bigger one, swept past and he was ducked again. He stopped, treading water once more as he coughed, but his body was getting lower.

Another wave washed over him. The bow, leaning at a crazy angle, was the nearest point and he was almost under the bowsprit when the ship was again picked up and thrown forward. He tried to catch hold of a rope that was hanging down but he was too weak. Then, suddenly, he was alongside.

Clawing his way along the slippery timbers he reached out for another rope but that, too, eluded his grasp. The men leaning out were gesticulating and shouting with their hands cupped but he could hear nothing. He looked around frantically, scrabbling at the side of the ship that now loomed high over him but there was nowhere for him to catch hold. All of a sudden, he felt himself being dragged back towards the bows. He was helpless, then the whole ship was picked up again.

The hull rose high above him. He lifted an arm in a futile gesture to protect himself but the four hundred tons of the 'Bristol Rose' crashed down, twisting and driving herself against the rocks below. He felt himself being forced down and down then winced in agony as his legs were crushed against the rocks. He tried to push himself free but nothing moved. He was trapped, his legs held fast, pinned by the ship.

He pushed again and watched the green seawater foaming around him. His hair was floating in front of his eyes and when his mouth opened he saw his breath bubbling its way to the surface. He gulped, for there was no choice. Water flooded into his mouth and down to his lungs and, just for a moment, he tasted salt. Then his mouth was forced open again and he clutched at his throat. His head rolled from side to side but he was weakening. His mind was spinning dizzily and the light was beginning to fade. Once more his mouth opened in a last desperate gasp but it was no good and instead of life darkness came instead.

*

Jed Davey watched the gulls. It was the following day after he had checked the sheep that he walked over to the cliff edge. Beneath him and now almost stripped clean by those working on her were the bare bones of the 'Bristol Rose'. They had managed to save four. Four more bodies had been recovered and three were still missing, two from the ship and Mr Orchard's friend, the one who had tried to save them. He stood for a moment looking down on the scene, wondering what mighty hand had ordained such a thing.

Yet today nature was smiling again: it was as though there had never been a storm. The sea was cornflower blue. What few white clouds there were, were broken and the late summer sun had returned to his valley. The cove was a tangle of timber and flotsam and he watched as those who were still picking along the shoreline made their way. But it was the gulls out near the point that caught his eye. They had been attracted by something in the water, something white that was floating like a sack. He lifted a hand to shade his eyes. Two or three birds had alighted on whatever it was while others fought and quarrelled for a place. He knew at once for Lord Sharland Preston had been wearing nothing more than a white dress shirt and a pair of thin cotton trousers. It had to be him. The shepherd turned down the hill and broke into a run.

*

His father decreed that he was to be buried at St Mark's in the village of Blagdon and the journey was to begin the following day. The doctor had prescribed laudanum to help her sleep but Sarah refused. She felt strong, proud he had died in the way he had. The villagers had come up to her and taken her hand one after the other expressing their condolences along with their admiration. Even in the milliner's shop in Hartland where Jocelyn found a hat and veil to go with her long black dress, she found herself able to smile and thank them. Her father-in-law was being brave but the shock had aged him; both his boys had now gone and gone violently. Isaac was all he had and the boy seemed to draw them closer together.

It was on that last night that she began to remember. In the hall earlier she had heard two maids talking about the fair that would be coming back to the Abbey in a few months and, with it, of course, would be Madam Tissini. It was six or seven years ago that the soothsayer had taken her hand. She could see it now, as clear as crystal, when the neat, friendly little woman had looked up and talked about danger, and that it was about a man in her life and to do with the wind and troubled waters. It had all been so horribly, horribly true but there had been another thing. She had spoken also about a beautiful glowing fire and something else as well, something from the deep. But that was all she could remember. Whatever it was had gone from her mind, hopefully never to return.

Chapter Fourteen

It had been raining hard during the night but by mid-morning most of the clouds had lifted and the sky had become broken. Now, though, a bitter east wind was feathering its way up the Barle valley reminding the inhabitants of Simonsbath that it was late November. Such was the chill in the air that there was even talk of snow. Sebright Knight ducked and looked at his reflection in the hunting painting by the front door. He tweaked at his cravat, patted his tidily-cut brown hair back over his ears then stood and straightened himself, just as his mother started to come down the stairs. He knew it was her by her footsteps on the landing; he knew also that she was unhappy about him visiting Sherdon and it rankled. They had talked after lunch yesterday and it had almost developed into an argument until his father intervened.

It was his first visit home for three months. While in London he had written to Anna on a number of occasions, but had heard from her only twice, and that was since last summer. In spite of all the distractions around him, he found himself living in hope of receiving a missive in her bold hand. It was a poor substitute for seeing her but a letter brought her closer nevertheless.

The first year at Esdaile's bank had been a challenge for the tall gangly young man but he had survived and was heartened by the fact that Sir Durnford Morgan had told his father they were pleased with him. Exmoor was a perfect antidote to the hurly-burly of London life, exactly as his father said. Here nobody could chase him for lists of returns or balance sheets, nor last minute briefs on clients and their complicated financial affairs. And the wonderful peace was made better still by the presence of Anna Tucker. Nobody, not even his mother, was going to deny him that.

"You're not really going out in this weather are you, dear? You'll catch your death…it's a beastly wind." Florence Knight stood back from her son, one hand on the back of the armchair. She was still irritated by the way he had chosen to ignore her request to spend a little less time at Sherdon. What was more she found this sudden interest of his most disquieting. "And the Chichesters will be here by six…you haven't forgotten have you?" She glanced at him quizzically. "You really should be here to greet them, you know."

"Mother, listen. I have made up my mind. I'm going to call on the family and pay my respects, that's all. Yes, yes, I know," he saw her look of disbelief. "Of course, I'm going to see Anna…take tea with her, I sincerely hope, and perhaps arrange to see her again. I shall take Nathan Harper with me in case I don't get back until after nightfall but I'll be here for the Chichesters. Fear not." He could see she remained unconvinced.

"Very well, dear, but do not allow yourself to become too embroiled down there. There're other…we've a number of other engagements arranged and you're only here for another week." She moved closer to the fire. "Your father and I would like to see something of you as well, you know."

He could feel his exasperation. Inside he was beginning to boil. His mother had come down stairs quite deliberately just to make this point. She had chosen her words cleverly but they were too transparent. Perhaps they were meant to be, but her sentiments were clear. She did this far too often, as though he was still a child that had to be kept on a tight rein. The last thing he wanted now was for her to be snapping at his heels all week about who to see and who not to see. For Heaven's sake! He had been living in London for a year with high society on his doorstep in one direction and every whorehouse and gaming den a mere cab ride away in the other. What on earth did she think he was going to get up to further down the valley?

But he knew exactly. It was Anna Tucker. In his mother's eyes, the tall, lovely fair haired girl was not good enough, seeing that her father was but a mere farmer from a far-off village. One whose hands were rough and who deferred to his own father in his Devon burr.

"Don't be like that, dear. It's not very nice." She had seen his scowl and was piqued that he should be so demonstrative to her face. "I was only pointing out that there's a lot in the diary and, well, I wouldn't want you to get too tied up. That's all." There was a look of his grandfather about him when he was like that. He was slimmer and taller than she remembered John, but the heavy eyebrows, the frown and the picture of defiance in his face were all pure Knight. The fact that he was dark like his father made him seem angrier still.

"Mother." As the hall door opened, Sebright glanced over his shoulder. "Mother, look, I'll be back by six…at the very latest. I know exactly what's on your mind, you were plain enough yesterday. But fear not, I'm not going scouring the Barle valley in search of a spouse. All right?"

"I know," she began but checked herself for his abruptness surprised her. Suddenly she saw her son to be the man he was. "Very well dear."

"Beg pardon, Mr Knight, sir, but Harper's out front with the horses."

"Thank you, Tarr. I'll be right with you." He smiled at the elderly butler. "I'll take your leave, mother, and I'll be back as planned…you have my word." He bent to kiss her cheek.

✳

Jack stood straight as the dogs rose growling from the hedge. The two riders had made their way over Horsen Hill and had come on to his Sixty Acres through the top gate. He had just finished checking the pen of ewes and was about to release them so he stretched out and reached for his jacket. Warm enough when working with the sheep, but the wind had an edge today so he threw the larger of his two

sacks around his shoulders as well. He had it in mind that the lad might be down.
Anna had been talking about it for sometime but had not said much over the last
few days. Shy perhaps or a mite nervous, but Kitty had told him the girl wasn't
quite so sure about the young man's intentions. He shrugged to himself, wiped his
hands on his breeches before raising an arm in return.

"Very, very good to see you, Mr Tucker." Sebright dismounted hurriedly and left
his horse. He strode forward and took the hand, his face beaming in genuine
delight. "Father said I'd probably find you up here. Start on the high ground he
said, and…sure enough. How are you, sir? How are you? Cold enough, no doubt."

"Aye, Master Sebright, well thank you, sir, and grand to see you. 'Tis a chill wind,
that's for sure." Jack walked over to Nathan Harper who had remained mounted
and was holding his master's horse. The young visitor watched as he took his
groom's hand before turning back. "We've been half expecting you these last
coupla days, mind. And to what do we owe this pleasure, eh…or need I ask?" Jack
went to let the sheep out and glanced back over his shoulder.

"You know I could never come down to Simonsbath without paying a call. It's been
so long and if Anna would care to see me I would be more than delighted. I was
hoping, perhaps, that I may take tea with her."

"To be sure. She's been expecting you, and that's for Kitty as well. They'll be
more'n pleased to see you and they've a good fire in the hearth right now." He
reached down for his workbag. "Anyhows, you best be getting on down. I'll be
there presently…there's just the bullocks to see." He took hold of the sack around
his shoulders. "We're keeping them out 'til just afore Christmas this year…that's if
this weather don't keep up. I'll see'e directly, then."

Jack watched as the two made their way down to the farm. Anna would be nineteen in three months and she needed someone in her life. Young men such as
Sebright Knight did not come riding along every day and it'd be a foolish girl to
show him the door too quickly. Her mother would have been delighted. But then
Kitty might have been right: usually she was.

✳

"Yes, I do get bored. Of course I do." Anna sat up straight on the edge of the worn
armchair. The small fire she had lit before lunch had stopped smoking but a blue
haze remained in the room. Her feet were crossed and tucked under her long,
floral-patterned skirt. She dropped her eyes shyly, balancing the chipped saucer in
her hand. She was unsure how he would take her answer and felt his eyes on her.
Sebright waited. Apparently she used to have the same straw-coloured hair as her
father but it had grown darker, as had the long lashes that swept up from the hazel
eyes when she glanced up at him. There was an elegance and a dignity about her
he had noticed before, something to do with the straight nose and the high, intelligent forehead.

Sebright cleared his throat. "I mean, if you would allow me, I would find it a pleasure to introduce you to a number of good friends I have here. There's Polly and George Chichester, their parents are staying for a few days. They would be delighted to make your acquaintance...and Cecil Luttrell, and then there're the Aclands...and several others."

"It's not that bad." She laughed, still coy, and looked up before tucking a thick wave of hair behind her ear. "I've seen my cousin, Lionel, a number of times. We get on well and I've met some of his friends."

"Were they agreeable? To your liking, I mean?"

"Oh yes, for certain." This time she held his gaze, again wondering exactly why it was that he was showing such interest. Did she really take his fancy and, if she did, how could he be so certain? He hardly knew her to be talking like this. More probably he was bored at Simonsbath. It would be like the inside of an empty church compared to what he knew in London. And, if he was bored then she could find little satisfaction in being seen by him as some temporary plaything.

"Well perhaps you would not be averse to my introducing you to some of those I know. Maybe we could arrange for Lionel and Jessica to come up to Simonsbath. Perhaps we could have a house party some time in the New Year? Would you like that?"

"But of course," she lied. The very thought of standing alone in the great hall of Simonsbath manor among all these rich and worldly people, all of whom knew each other and who would be laughing and talking among themselves, was terrifying. "I'm afraid I haven't got anything to wear for such an occasion. I'm...we're not," she pulled at her skirt and let her hands fall as if to emphasise what she wanted to say. "I'm afraid I've got nothing to wear," she laughed self-consciously.

"Don't worry." Sebright was on his feet and standing by her. "Honestly, Anna." He placed a hand on the back of the chair close to her shoulder and bent forward. "We'll find a way," he said reassuringly. "I'm sure we'll find a way but you will come if I can arrange it. Say you'll come."

She shrugged and glanced up, smiling shyly, then looked away again. It would be too easy to say yes like that. She wanted to but the idea was daunting and she was not going to allow herself to be rushed. "I'll have to see...I'll have to ask father and see what he says."

"I do hope so, Anna. It would make for a wonderful party and I know you'll enjoy the company. Lionel and Jessica will take good care of you. And so will I of course," he added hurriedly. "We'll make sure you're not left out...I'll see to that."

They had not yet brought a lamp into the room and the light had begun to fade. He walked over to the curtainless window, wiped the condensation with his sleeve and peered out at the farmyard gloom. Then he turned and drew out his watch. "Uh, I thought so and it'll be dark soon. I should be on my way...but I shall leave here in hope." He turned back to her, smiled and held out both hands as she rose. "My thanks, Anna, for allowing me to take tea with you." He wanted to hold on to her but dare not. He simply looked at her, just long enough to catch her eyes.

"It was a pleasure...."

✳

Florence Knight looked at her husband. The last of the guests had retired and even the staff downstairs appeared to have finished for the night. The house was quiet. Frederic stood in front of his wardrobe. His chin was raised and he was struggling with his collar stud.

"It's not that at all, dear," she replied, ruffled that he had brought the subject up again. "There's nothing wrong, nothing at all. I just want the boy to take his time...he's only twenty and he's got the whole world at his feet. There's no need to rush into anything like this."

"All right," he growled, leaning forward and grimacing into the mirror. "*Argh*, that's better." He stood back and began to undo the studs down the front of his dress shirt. "As long as that's really the reason for your caution...or hostility as sometimes it seems to be. As long as that really is why you've taken this line. For me, they're a wonderful family. Young Tod," he turned and waved his arm towards the church. "Take him for a start. William Thornton's forever singing his praise and he delivers a sermon like a man twice his age...you said so yourself, last Sunday. And then there's Wilmot...God's truth, if only I could do a tenth as well as he's done."

"Yes, I know, Freddie," she sighed. I know, I know...so you keep telling me. They are a very talented family. I'm not denying it but it's just that...well, there're other young things around."

"Now don't even begin on that...I really do think you're getting yourself into a state about Jack. Come on, admit it...that's it, isn't it? That's the truth, Florence."

"I must say it would be easier." Florence tilted her head and began to brush out her hair. "I do find him rather difficult...he's always so formal and rigid and...well, oh come on dear, you know exactly what I mean."

"Yes, I do." Frederic shrugged on his dressing gown. "I know exactly and all that you're saying is nothing more than skin deep: it's all so shallow. Underneath these so-called social shortcomings you keep pointing out there's a remarkable man. Ask anyone...Durnford Morgan, Tennyson. Ask father if he were here. My goodness I know what he'd have to say. Put all that's good about him with the girl's mother and there's a fine, fine combination."

190

"Is that it, dear? Katherine? Is that why you're so anxious for such a match to succeed?" She caught his reflection in the mirror. "She's still there, isn't she, Freddy?"

Frederic's shoulders sagged. "Oh, for goodness sake...please, please don't start on that. Yes, of course I remember her and very fondly, too. Just as you have your own memories and faces from the past...James Henslow's one that comes to mind. You're always talking about him as though he was some icon of manhood in your coming-out days. But do please believe me that, as far as little Anna Tucker is concerned, if Sebright ever went so far as to seriously consider asking her for her hand, I'd be delighted...thrilled."

Florence Knight got up from the dressing table and came up to her husband. "I know dear, I know you would be. I'm sorry. Please don't be cross." She stretched up and kissed his cheek. "You're right...let's just see."

Later, long after the lamp was out and she could hear her husband's breathing, she lay still, staring up into the darkness. It was all so nearly right, but it wasn't: not quite. Sebright was their only son and if he was going to marry and secure the family line then it had to be exactly so. The pedigree had to be complete. Her mother and grandmother had insisted on it and so would she. No matter what Freddie or the others thought, she would find the perfect match.

2

Corporal Harry Tucker leaned over Landacre Bridge. The old grey gelding that Billy Westcott had lent him had seen better days and the donkey that was carrying his two boxes was an obstinate little cuss. But he was getting there slowly and the thought of the kitchen fire and hot broth cheered him. He cracked his knuckles and reached back to unsheath his bayonet. Then, and using just the tip of the blade, he addressed himself to the business of exploring under the nails of his left hand. It helped him to think. Eight long years it had been since he left home. Cuh, he was a lad then and he looked up, his eyes narrowing as he tried to remember the place further downstream where the bailiffs had caught him.

Harry Tucker had a barrel of a chest and a voice to match. His huge red-black mutton chops and even blacker beard made up for the bald patch in the middle of his thinning brown hair. His nose had been broken in the ring by the bare knuckles of an artilleryman. Then it had been broken again, and one of his cheek bones too; all that before the Marquess of Queensbury came along and spoiled the fun. The heavyweight champion of Gwalior Garrison was still undefeated, but his seven years with the colours of The Devonshire Regiment, the old 'Bloody Eleventh' were up. He had taken time to reach corporal for there had been a number of misunderstandings along the way as he put it. But all that was back in Cawnpore and Fyzabad, and now he was home recruiting.

He had settled up the little business in Exford. Neither Lewis nor Eric Denholm remembered him, until he had shut the door behind him and told them who he was. 'Black' Richards recognised him all right and had got out of The White Horse in time so he gave his brother the slapping instead. Nothing much, mind, but he'd squealed like the little runt that he was. Harry smirked to himself, bit on his lip then got the tip of his bayonet working again. He hawked, hawked noisily again and spat. He had to admit that his scarlet jacket with its six brass buttons and the regimental badge on his high green collar looked a bit out of place up here on the moor. And the same went for his white belt and black forage cap, but that's what the orders were. Recruiting meant 'on parade', even out in the wilds.

He clambered heavily back into the saddle then kicked savagely at the grey for trying to bite him. Sherdon was a mere half-hour away and the light had started to fade. Harry rolled his shoulders and began to hum. It was a mindless, stupid little song that soldiers sang and it went on and on for ever. He couldn't sing anyway but it was all about 'time-expired troops' and it reminded him of the ones still back at Lucknow. Huh…and the very best o' luck to them an' all.

✳

It was Frank who saw him first. He called out to Anna and the two of them stood watching. At first they were deceived by his beard and his cap and his white clay pipe but as soon as he raised his hand and waved, they recognised him. It was his round shoulders and the way he sat hunched in the saddle that gave him away. Anna shouted to Kitty who came to the front door wiping her hands. Then, one by one, the dogs started to bark and Anna ran for her father.

There was an extra Granny's pudding under the sieve in the back pantry and a haunch of smoked bacon to go with the crochy pie and potato cakes they were going to have that night. They hurried to finish-up early outside then gathered in the kitchen while the meal was being prepared. At first they were shy, none more so than Kitty who remembered him as he was but the questions soon came and the more they heard the more they laughed for his voice was so deep. His brother and sister sat with their eyes wide, Kitty busied herself at the sink but kept looking round at something she heard. Jack said little; he simply sat back and smiled, his eyes rarely leaving his son.

He told them about the journey home from Calcutta and then about the barracks at Fyzabad, about the sights and the sounds and the smells; about the native bazaars, about the colours of the clothes, the spices and mangoes and paw paws; about the pi-dogs and monkeys and the hump-backed brahma cattle roaming the streets. About the elephants and camel-trains; about the dhobi and charpoys, the punkah-wallahs, the saris and the pugarees and about the Devonshire Regiment and the West Kents, the Gordons and the Fusiliers and the lines and lines of native sepoys.

He could have told them about the dust and the searing, blinding heat and the monsoon rains, the dysentery and cholera, the mosquitoes and flies, snakes and rabies, the dirty filthy water and the gut-wrenching stenches. About the bullying and fighting, the sodomy and the native women in cages in the shanty town behind the market; the floggings and field punishments and the awful mind-numbing boredom that went on day after day, week after every other deadly, interminable, never ending week. He could have done but he didn't.

However, he told them a bit about the train journey and the long, hard march up to Fort Wellington at Landi Khana where they were stationed for a whole year. And he said a little about the lean, hawk-eyed warriors who lived by the rifle up in the mountains, who were a law unto themselves and whom they had been sent to bring to heel. Hmmm. But he said little about what a soft-nosed bullet does to the head of the man standing next to you and nothing at all about what happened if you fell wounded and the women of the hills got to you first.

They begged him to go on but he was tired and one by one they left him with his father. Jack moved from the table. He hung the lamp from the beam over the hearth and pulled up a chair. The two of them sat in silence. Harry had undone his jacket and leant forward, elbows on knees, staring into the fire. His head dropped and he covered his face with his hands as if he was praying. Jack just watched. He saw way beyond the great rounded back that stretched the heavy scarlet jacket taut, and the tufts of red-black beard that stuck out from between the calloused fingers; way beyond the dark trousers with their red stripe and the heavy, black, studded boots. The deep, booming voice had faded, as had the hard, rasping laugh and the crack of knuckles. The little boy sitting there leaning forward, all tense and waiting was as anxious and as prickly as he always had been. It was just as if he had come running in from outside after a quarrel with the others and was sitting there all fraught and het up waiting for his mother's soothing hand. "It'll take you some time, my lad." He spoke quietly.

Harry looked up, his chin now resting on his fingertips. Then he nodded. "Aye, father. 'Tis hard an' all." He shook his head. "I dunno. Feels though I'm torn in half, that there's two of me, like…one half's back 'ere, t'other half's miles an' miles away, back out there with me mates. Feels though I don't fit nowhere proper anymore." He paused. "I've finished with they lot, yet 'tis all strange back here on Exmoor. I'm a foreigner, y'know that, father?" He half turned and glanced at him. "A right foreigner…folks know me yet they don't. They'm all distant, like, standin' back from me. I just can't settle." He buried his face again, this time shaking his head as if not knowing the answer to the questions in his mind.

"Well," Jack rose and put a hand on his son's shoulder. "*I* know you, m'dear. I've known'e long, long before any o' this…any o' this soldiering and all you've been telling us tonight. Might be difficult for 'e just now but this is where you're from, lad…this is where you belong. It'll take a while for 'e to settle, but your home's right here, that's fer sure." He patted the shoulder gently and his hand moved up to his son's neck which he pressed, kneading gently. "There's a deal tucked away in you that's yet to come out. Just take yer time…take yer time, boy." As he patted again, so his son rose.

He turned to his father, pushing back his chair. He was not as tall but he was broader and deeper. They looked at one another as only those who love one another can. There were tears in his eyes and his father watched as they began to run down his cheeks. He saw his son's brow furrow and his face become all anxious just like it used to do. For a moment he stood there, then he opened his arms.

*

There was still a week to go before he had to report to Ebberley Lawn barracks at the top of Bear Street, and Harry enjoyed himself. First there was Tod up in Simonsbath. His quiet, worldly brother was still the same and they sat for hours in the freezing rectory, huddled together round the fire, talking about themselves and what they had done. Tod had been amazed but he, Harry, listened in silence as his brother told him about St Anselm's and St Luke's parish here on the moor.

They went up to the churchyard to see their mother's grave. Tod had taken it upon himself to keep it tidy but Harry helped him collect some sprigs of holly and evergreen to put in the earthenware pot by the headstone. For a moment they were still, looking down at where the turf remained raised, each with his own tender memories. He helped clean the church, then went with him to the school and watched him with the children before he, too, joined them to tell them about a soldier's life in India.

He had been down to Molland where he found his little sister, now heavy with child. He loved the name 'Queenie' and they laughed about it in the kitchen when they all had supper together. The two of them walked to the shop then on to the church where it was her turn for the flowers. Then, when it was time for him to go, he held her gently, promising to come back and see her with her child. Emma and Troy had been welcoming too. The news of Mary, whom he barely knew, saddened him but he shook his head in wonder when they told him about Sarah. The more he asked the more they told him, and the more curious he became.

*

Whitechapel Manor looked as grand as they said it was. He loosened the girth of his old grey mare, adjusted his jacket and belt then walked stiffly up the gravel path towards the front door, raising a hand in greeting as he passed the two gardeners. Although it was milder today, it was December nonetheless, and he regretted not wearing his short black cape. "Afternoon, my friend." Harry took off his cap and looked at the pink-cheeked footman. "I've come to pay my respects to Lady Preston, if you please." The man stared at him. "If Her Ladyship is at home, pray give her my respects and ask if I may have the pleasure of making her acquaintance."

"And who shall I say is calling?" The footman was looking him up and down not

194

liking what he saw. "Who are you, sir, and what is your business here?"

"Corporal Harry Tucker, sir, and I'll thank'e fer asking, but my business is my own affair." He leant forward. "Now get on your way, boy." He straightened himself and pulled on his beard then stepped back to admire the house. He had counted only half the windows when he heard footsteps and voices in the hall.

"Good day to you, sir." The new face, long and sallow, belonged to an older man. His dark blue frock coat with silver buttons and his white breeches told Harry that a man of decision had come to check on the visitor. "And pray what business do you have with Her Ladyship? She is, at present, indisposed."

"Then I'll wait…I'll bide me time. Daresay she'll be along soon."

"Oh no you won't." The older man preened himself and stepped forward. "There's no business here for common soldiery. I'll tell you that now…so away with you, man." The footman made as if to close the door but the toecap of Harry's boot jarred against the woodwork.

"There's no need fer that, my son." Harry tugged at his collar. "I've come with good fellowship in my heart. Bain't no need to treat no one with such disrespect…not even one o' the Queen's men at that."

"I said away with yer." The footman had raised his voice. "Get yer body away from here." Again he tried to close the door but Harry's boot remained in place. He opened it again and beckoned help from the garden. "Right…if that's the way you want it, we'll rid the place of you ourselves."

"See here." Harry took the man by his lapels, lifted him and walked him backwards into the hall. "This common soldier, the one you're looking at, does not much care for such talk." He lowered the man. "Now then…" he paused but then turned quickly. The gardeners were behind him. "Aha, right then. 'Tis to be like this, eh?" The younger of the two grappled with him, taking him by the neck but he took the man's arms, spun round and threw the youth easily. He saw the footman coming for him so he crouched then hit him in a manner that bare knuckle fighters used to do. The man crashed backwards across the hall table holding his face. A silver salver fell to the floor ringing loudly as it spun while a vase smashed into a thousand pieces.

But then there was a shout. "Stop all this…at once. *At once*, I say." Sarah had come halfway down the stairs. "What on earth is going on? Who are you?" She stopped, surveying the scene around her. "Jenkins help Barrow at once, he's hurt. Then clear up this mess." She continued on her way. "And who the devil are you, and what brings you here? And *what* are you anyway…English, French or what? What's all this?" She waved a hand dismissively and glared at Harry, her eyes moving up and down his uniform.

"Tried to force his way in, m'lady." Jenkins looked up from where he was kneeling beside the footman. "We asked him what his business was but he wouldn't tell us…we weren't having any of that and were seeing him off when he went fighting mad."

"Harry Tucker, ma'am. Corporal Harry Tucker. I'm your cousin, ma'am, your cousin. And my apologies for this. Said I'd wait, bide me time but they wouldn't have none of it. Here…" he pulled the footman to his feet and held him steady. "Should never have gone for a soldier like that, my friend. Here…take a seat. Steady yourself and sit to get your breath."

"Leave him alone," she snapped. "What on earth do you mean, my *cousin*?" Sarah's voice was raised. "What nonsense. It's rubbish. Get out of here. Go on…leave this instant before I have you thrown out."

"Madam." Harry wiped his mouth with the back of his sleeve then adjusted his jacket. "I came here with nothing more than friendship in mind. Believe me, I came in peace to make your acquaintance. You know, m'dear, let me tell you something…'tis bin a long, long time since us played together at Sherdon."

"*Get out,*" she hissed. "Get out and never set eyes on this place again." He could see he had shocked her by the way she was gripping the banister rail. She was breathing heavily and her other hand was at her throat. "I've no desire at all to become acquainted with anybody who conducts themselves like this. A relative indeed. My cousin…coming in here…barging your way in like that." She half turned. "You're no relation of mine," she called out. "Now get out." She lifted her skirts and began to climb the stairs.

Harry watched her go. It was as he had been told. He grinned and shook his head. "Oh yes I am, m'dear," he called after her. "And I'm afraid there's nort you can do about the blood what flows through our bodies…nort at all." He put on his cap and stepped over the rug which had been piled against the door by the struggling feet.

3

Sarah's eyes were wandering; Florence Knight could see that and found it irritating. A younger, tousle-haired man was standing between her and Rebecca Tucker. He was bending over with his back towards her and half blocking her view thus making it impossible for her and Rebecca to continue talking. For the moment Florence found herself isolated.

Arlington Court was looking at its best for the traditional New Year's Eve ball of The Barnstaple Staghounds. Caroline and John Chichester always threw their house open for the occasion and, for a number of years now, it had been held on the last evening of the old year. She glanced up at the net swinging gently above the dance floor, filled with balloons, ribbons and dried flowers. It would soon be time. There would be two or three more dances then the band would strike up the

Post Horn Gallop. After that they would dance the Lancers and after that again they would be called onto the floor where they would all join hands. Hunting horns would be blown, crackers would fizz and, right on time, Soames, the second butler, would strike the enormous gong in the hall thus dispensing with the old year.

Florence watched as Lady Preston dabbed at her cheek and caught her eye. Sarah's eyebrows flashed up in recognition and she was about to resume her inspection of those in the hall when Florence decided to join her. She moved quickly to an empty chair. "I was telling you about Tod," she offered. "D'you remember before the last dance?" Sarah half turned. "We do love him being up at Simonsbath with us. He works so hard, you know, but I'm sure the poor boy's lonely."

"I'm not surprised." Sarah gave a hollow laugh. "There's not exactly much to make the heart flutter out there."

"I know, it's such a shame." At that Sarah turned back to face the ballroom floor and Florence, conversationless once more, studied the figure next to her. There were too many rings on her fingers, she decided. Simply too many…it was pure show, just had to be. And emeralds were never her colour, not with that dress. Sapphires perhaps, but certainly not emeralds: oh dear, what a giveaway. They must have been handed down to her. Her white satin dress with gold metal embroidery was beautiful, she had to admit, but there again she had spoiled it all by showing off too much of herself. There was certainly enough of her to show, mind you, but not like that. It was simply bad taste.

"Tell me," Florence persisted. "How old is he now…must be twenty-six or so?"

The other's back was turned. Either Sarah had chosen to ignore her or her mind was elsewhere, then Florence watched as she raised a hand in greeting. "Oh, sorry," Sarah glanced back fleetingly. "I'm sorry, do please forgive me but Damont Westham's here. They've come all the way from Ringwood," she explained. "Isn't that marvellous?" She lolled back in her chair and held out her hand for the new arrival to take, revelling in his attention and watching admiringly as he presented himself to the others around the table. It was as if she had found an excuse to be relieved of the present somewhat tedious company.

The newcomer took her hand again. "Yes, of course." She rose eagerly, now free from those sitting behind her. But she turned again, if only briefly. "Do excuse me."

Whoever it was who had been talking to Rebecca had also gone and the two were now left on their own. "Shush, I know." Rebecca, suppressing a laugh, raised a finger to her lips. Florence grimaced before turning to accept a glass of champagne.

The footman bowed. "Mrs Chichester's compliments ma'am, but these are for the toast…the New Year, just a few minutes now." Rebecca took a glass also.

"I'm sorry." Florence moved to sit alongside her friend. "But there's just something about her. It's make, make, make all the time and it's not very pretty."

"Wilmot's furious with her." Rebecca scratched at her frizz of red-grey hair. She looked quite matronly in her voluminous apple-green dress that appeared neither to fit nor match anything else. But with Lady Tucker it mattered not. Many years ago she had stopped all the silly nonsense of painting her face and combing her hair as one might do with a pet. Life for her was too short and, wherever she went, her peals of laughter advertised her presence, surrounded as she would be by so many who delighted in her company. "He's determined to take her aside but I won't have it," she frowned. "Honestly, it's none of our business and it would only make matters worse. I told him it didn't matter…it really doesn't, you know."

"And she's becoming something of a painted lady, I fear…more and more goes on as each year goes by. And as for the dress…my dear, she's spilling out of it. It's…it's just so common."

"Well, look at her father-in-law…hardly an example there. But then…." Rebecca caught hold of Florence's arm and threw her head back, neighing with laughter. "He is the paymaster, is he not?"

*

"Thank you, John, dear." Elizabeth-Jane smiled up at John Chichester who had sat talking to her while Durnford was dancing with Flossie Westham. "It's a lovely, lovely party…you really do spoil us, you know." Her host stood and stepped back. She inclined her head in reply to his bow before taking hold of her Malacca cane. Sir Durnford Morgan was returning to his wife, having seen his partner back to her own table and Elizabeth-Jane made to move on the sofa in order to accommodate his presence.

"Oooh, dear me," he panted. "That's quite enough for an oldie like me." He took a drink and joined her. "That cane of yours is the best excuse I've seen yet. One sight of that and no young blade would dare risk you on the floor. Perhaps I might borrow it? Now then, what has our court correspondent been spying out there? What's been going on while I've been gallivanting about? Eh? I've never known you to miss anything yet, my dear." He smiled affectionately and patted his wife's knee. She was seventy-six, looked sixty and had the mind of a sharp and perceptive thirty year old. "Come, now. Somebody out there's taken your eye."

"Young Sarah Preston's making waves again."

"Surprise, surprise."

"Mmm. She was over there with Florence and Rebecca." Elizabeth-Jane nodded across the room. "Something was said. I couldn't say what but as soon as she'd left them, the others put their heads together about her. I could tell by just watching

198

them. It's all so silly." She shrugged and pulled a face.

"Well, she's only got herself to blame." Sir Durnford Morgan wrinkled his nose. "I'd have given her every chance, every chance there is but she's hardly been fair to the memory of Sharland, has she now? I mean…oh, I don't know, a little bit more respect and a little bit of decorum would not have gone amiss. The poor boy had not been gone for a year before the whispering began."

Elizabeth-Jane smiled and lifted a cautionary finger as Frederic and Wilmot walked past to join their wives. "But it's not been easy for the child, you understand…and we mustn't forget that. She's a remarkable girl in many ways and, my goodness, she's done well for herself."

"But over-reaching herself like this isn't very attractive…and everyone can see it."

"Then I blame Herbert. He should have taken her in hand." Elizabeth-Jane lowered her lorgnettes. She had been surveying the room and paused to watch Sir Wilmot and Lady Tucker. Her husband followed her gaze. "He's given her far too much too soon and it's always the same…it goes straight to the head…money and glamour."

"I know." Sir Durnford paused. "And now he's squaring up to Wilmot over something or other. And if that's true then there's a battle ahead. You should hear what Freddie's got to say about them. Come dear." He rose and took her hand. "A breath of air before the jollifications…New Year's Eve or not."

4

"You all right, maid?" Mabel Quartly took hold of Victoria's hand. She had noticed the girl was flushed and restless. She had not touched her breakfast and, just a few moments ago, the farmer's wife had seen her tense. Her time was up for they had been counting the days.

Victoria rolled her eyes. "I think so, yes…oh, I'm not sure." She held her stomach. "It could be the child, what d'you think?"

"'Ave they come reg'lar, like? The pains, that is?" Joseph Quartly looked across the table at the mother-to-be then up at his wife with his eyebrows raised in concern. "Bain't no worry, Queenie, m'dear…if it's time then 'tis time. Bain't nort to worry about."

"I'm not sure." Victoria looked from one to the other, suddenly filled with the realisation that motherhood was upon her. Whoever it was, who for the last few months had been turning and kicking inside her, might at last be delivered from her. "I'm not sure, Mrs Quartly…I don't know." Her mouth was drawn into a brave line. "I don't know," she whispered.

"Come on then, love." Mabel Quartly rose noisily. "Us best get upstairs, just in case, like. Us'll see directly and if it's time then us'll send Poppy fer Mrs Baker. Bain't no worry," she chuckled reassuringly. "Us'll see'e fine, my love."

And that is how John Lionel Quartly prepared to begin his long journey through life. Right from the start, 'Little Jack' or simply 'Littl'un' as he became known showed all his grandfather's desire to be helpful. Some months ago they thought it might be twins, for they were in the family. But Mrs Baker was firmly of the opinion that it was not the case. The child, she decreed, was on its own. It was to be big, though, big enough that she and Mabel Quartly had agreed that the birth might be difficult. However, on Sunday the twenty-ninth of February eighteen seventy-two, just after lunch, the new arrival proved them all wrong.

He was a happy child as all who visited him observed but it was not until three weeks later, after the last of the snow had thawed, that he was visited by his grandfather. They all watched closely. Nobody could remember what was said between the two of them, suffice it to say that 'Little Jack' approved of his visitor, clinging tightly to the finger that was on offer and giving, in return, a delightful but vacuous smile. A firm relationship had been struck up, so much so that when the time came for them to be separated 'Little Jack' registered his extreme displeasure. After all, he had been perfectly content with the situation as it was.

Chapter Fifteen

May at Sherdon had been wet, early June also. It had been fine for the sheep because the flush of young grass kept coming and the ewes had done the lambs well. But it was the fields he had left for hay that had been causing Jack to worry. The third week in June had been very bad and much of the grass had been flattened by rain brought in by a strong sou'westerly. But then the weather cleared.

For the last three days they had been helping Arthur Fisher at Barkham and now it was their turn. The Fishers had come over as had Gaile and Ralph from Ferny Ball. Tod came down from Simonsbath, even Harry managed a few days from Barnstaple. The new horse-drawn mower Wilmot had bought had done its best but the damp grass near the hedges still had to be cut by scythe.

Then, of course, it all had to be tossed to dry, then turned again before the sweeping could begin. Earlier that day Jack had decided where he wanted to build the three ricks, first clearing the area and laying tightly packed wood faggots for the base. Arthur Fisher, the rick maker, was in charge. He would thatch them with the dried rushes that had been cut and collected back in May.

✳

Anna stood for a moment and watched. Sebright, quite untutored in farming matters, was still struggling with his pitchfork. He had ridden down from Simonsbath each day offering his services to Jack, dressing for the occasion in a white collarless shirt and a floppy, wide-brimmed straw hat. He had been sent down to the field nearest the river where the hay, dry at last, needed to be gathered in from the edges for the sweep that would be drawn by two heavy horses. She had joined him after helping Kitty prepare tea.

"Just skim the fork over the ground, like I showed you...here, look." She showed him again then watched before bursting out laughing. "*Se*-bright, you'll never do it like that. You're trying to dig it out of the ground. Just skim lightly...honestly...oh, come here." She walked across and took the fork from him. As she did so he wiped the sweat from his chin and and tipped back his hat. "Had enough? Well, we haven't done badly, have we?" She grinned, nodding to where the hay lay in neat lines. "Arthur'll be down in a minute."

"It's killing me." He took back the fork and stabbed it into the ground, took off his hat and scratched wildly at his hair. "Let's wait for him. Here look...a bit of shade." The ground was hard and he brushed at the grass with his hat for her before she sat as he might have done to a dusty chair. He could see that she, too, was hot. Her face, already tanned, was flushed and he watched as she settled before dabbing at her brow with a bright, flower-patterned handkerchief. He joined her, sitting casually enough yet close. For a moment they were silent.

Sebright pulled slowly at a long grass, rubbed it between his thumb and forefinger then tasted the bitter-sweet juice. "Anna, tell me something. D'you mind me coming down like this?" She lowered her head, momentarily taken aback by the directness of his question. "You don't think I'm imposing myself on you all, or making a bit of a fool of myself...I'm not embarrassing you am I?"

"No, of course not." If truth be known she had been looking forward to each day. Ever since the party at Simonsbath last winter he had been more on her mind than she believed possible. On reflection, it had been a lovely evening in the manor, the most glamorous occasion she had ever been to and he had looked after her as he promised he would. The others had been fun too, all except for Jessica Tucker who had barely spoken to her. Since then she had missed him but had replied to all his letters, never finding it difficult to fill several pages about life on the farm. Only yesterday he had told her how much he looked forward to them.

"You know I love being down here. With you, I mean." He turned towards her and half lay, supporting himself on one elbow. "I told you yesterday how much I missed you in London, didn't I." His hand reached out for her arm. "D'you believe me now or d'you still think you're just my 'Exmoor girl' like you said at the party."

"No," she replied cautiously, sitting hunched with her arms around her knees and peering into the distance. "I only said that to tease." It was untrue and she knew it, blushing at the memory of when she rounded on him after they had danced, accusing him of amusing himself with her because there was nobody else around. As soon as the words were out, she knew what a stupid thing it was to say for the whole house was full of beautiful and sophisticated young women, any of whom he might have chosen instead. And it had been spiteful, too.

"Well you *are* my Exmoor girl. You must realise that. Listen." He gently squeezed the softness of her forearm. "You're my Exmoor girl and every other sort of girl for that matter. There is nobody else, Anna...honestly, and that's the truth."

"I know...I should never have said that. It was silly but I really didn't know what to think. I just had to force the truth out of you somehow." She looked down at him, brushing a curl of her hair back as she did so. "But yes, I do believe you and it's nice having you here." She hugged herself tightly in a moment of pure happiness. "Everybody here enjoys you coming down like this. The boys think you're topping...you make them laugh so."

"Even though I'm pretty useless with the heavy horses and things."

"Yes...all that and the pitchfork as well." They both laughed but, suddenly were silent again, each waiting for the other to continue. Anna glanced down.

"I'm very fond of you, Anna." Sebright searched for her hand. It was soft and he rubbed the back with his thumb while his fingers felt for hers "It's difficult to say exactly how I feel but I do miss you terribly when I'm away. Perhaps it's because

I...."

"Please," she murmured. "Don't say any more. It's too soon, Sebright...we've only known each other a few months...less than a year and for most of the time we've been hundreds of miles apart." She glanced at him nervously. "Don't say anything more."

"But you know what I was going to say, don't you?"

She nodded, then took her hand away and started to rise. "Yes...I think so." She half overbalanced, put one hand down to steady herself and paused, crouching in front of him. "And if I'm right then it's much to my liking but, shush, not just yet. Let's be sure first." Then she stood quickly, took him by the hand and pulled him up after her. "Come on," she gasped. "There's your pitchfork over there, and we've still heaps to do."

"Yes madam...right away ma'am. Just as you say." He bowed theatrically and replaced his hat, laughing in delight at the joy on her face.

*

"But he's serious, all right. I can see that." Kitty bent to lift the pile of plates from the kitchen table. "Wouldn't 'ave wasted his time coming down 'ere just to see me or yer father, would 'e now?"

Anna was silent. She knew instinctively that she had taken his fancy, more perhaps, and that for the moment anyway she was the woman in his life. She was thrilled at the idea. The last few days, when they had worked together or sat at the long table with the others or on the rugs in the hay meadows, had been idyllic. He made her laugh, made all of them laugh about his supposed ignorance of farming matters. But he laughed at himself, too, shrugging off the jests about him being a man of books and top hats. But she remembered also the start he gave her when he asked her if she would like to come to London with him. He suggested that she might like to stay for a few days when his parents were there so he could show her his other world.

At first the idea had excited her but it would mean leaving home and that would not be easy. Kitty had been ill again right in the middle of lambing and it had been Anna who had taken care of her father and brother. It would be impossible to leave them now. Kitty could barely cope and, brave as she was, she needed help. And then there was Sebright's mother. Nobody had said anything, yet she could sense that Mrs Knight thought little of them at Sherdon. His father was so different, a delight to be with, but not so his wife. Perhaps it was the way she regarded her or why Sebright was so protective when they were together but, whatever it was, Mrs Frederic Knight did not approve.

"'E's a lovely young man...reel loverley, that's fer sure." Kitty was breathing hard.

She had stopped clearing the table and Anna could see she was struggling.

"Sit down, Kitty. Here…steady." Anna hurried to where she was supporting herself and took her by the shoulders. "Sit, Kitty, gently now…you've been overdoing it again. Just rest for a bit."

"Thanks, dear." Kitty reached up and patted Anna's hand. "Just lost my breath for a moment."

Anna looked down at her. Her hair, greying now, had lost much of the auburn lustre they all used to admire and she had lost weight too. Her neck and shoulders were thinner so were her hands where the veins stood proud and the fingers looked so boney. What's more she was in pain, almost constantly but sometimes severely so. And Kitty was her father's wife. He loved her dearly and she, in return, had given him everything she had. Suddenly Anna realised how much this frail, uncomplaining little person meant to them all; for without her their father could not have managed to struggle on. The land and the loneliness would have broken him. She was a dear, dear person and, without thinking, Anna lowered her head and put her cheek against Kitty's.

However much she wanted to be with Sebright, she couldn't leave Sherdon. Only an hour ago, when she and Kitty had been talking, she had been agonising about it but now her mind had been made up for her. And, in any case, there were other things about which she had to be certain before any such move. Life with Sebright and his parents might not be so easy and she had to be sure.

2

Malcolm Locke was a North Molton man. There were several Lockes in the village and a number of them had done well for themselves. Lucy, his aunt, had married Jacob Steer, butler to Sir Wilmot and Lady Tucker of Court Hall in the village, and was now running her own tailor's shop in the square by the church.

It was Jacob Steer who had secured Malcolm his job at Whitechapel Manor where he had been promoted to butler after two years. He was doing well, so they told him, and he felt he was right for the position. Lady Preston, herself, said that he had a butler's poker face and anyone who saw him would think he was the sort of person who missed nothing. Others wanted the job including Barrow the footman but he had seen them off and, once there, had made it his own.

And Malcolm did not miss much. It was his obligation to know everything, every single thing that went on; that's what Mr Steer had directed. Malcolm Locke was a tall man, taller than His Grace, and he kept his dark, wavy hair short and neatly swept back. His uniform was immaculate and he walked as straight and as proud as Jacob Steer had shown him how.

The fact was that Mr Steer had shown him a great deal and they had talked a lot, too. The older man had warned him about the bad blood between Sir Wilmot and the Duke and that it was he who had been on duty at Court Hall on the night of the argument concerning Lady Preston. Later he had heard Sir Wilmot and Mr Knight discussing Lady Preston. Things were going wrong, so he heard, and there were supposed to be a number of gentlemen friends about.

If that were the case then he wanted to know everything that went on down there at Whitechapel. If ever there was anything going on that might upset Sir Wilmot then he wanted to know about it and fast. What was more, Lady Preston was related to Sir Wilmot and to Mr Jack so if there ever was any trouble then he, Jacob Steer, would see to it that his master knew about it. It was, as he put it, his right and proper duty. Malcolm was to keep his ears open and his eyes alert. The position at Filleigh would be available soon and if he wanted to be butler in a great house then he had better do what he was told. Simple as that.

Malcolm Locke stood back and surveyed the table. Just the two of them for dinner tonight. He bent down to check for fingerprints on the mahogany where Jenkins had removed the central leaves, then picked up the fish knives one by one and held them up to the light. The setting of the glasses was wrong again and he made a note to tell Blencowe, the new boy. And His Graces' napkin looked as though it had been used before. Otherwise it looked up to standard.

He took off his white glove, licked his finger and ran it along the mantelpiece checking for dust. Next his thumb touched the blade of the carving knife on the sideboard. Then there were the wines, and he glanced at the list His Grace had ordered from the cellar. Finally he drew the curtains, dressed them as Lady Preston had requested, and retired. Dinner would be in an hour.

✳

Sarah was puzzled. She had been so for a while and it upset her, in fact it made her angry. Why it was that people were distancing themselves from Bertie, she had no idea. He used to be considered such fun, the very centre of attraction. She remembered it well, how at Blagdon there seemed to be party after party and if not there then up in London. These rebuffs were not so bad in Hampshire or Park Lane but, down here, things had become very quiet. And that went for Hartland as well. How they used to enjoy themselves yet, last time, Desmond Orchard had been noticeably withdrawn. It seemed so unfair. Mercifully Jocelyn was the same as ever and they would be back there in a couple of months. The children loved it. How could people do this sort of thing? Bertie was such a generous man and he had lost both his boys, poor dear.

The fact that she, herself, had ruffled a few feathers didn't concern her one bit. They deserved it down here, tucked away out in the wilds like this. Honestly, they had no idea what life was about. Take Tamsin Butler for instance; a mousey little thing who had nothing better to do other than sit around and gossip all day, and most of that was pure fabrication, in spite of her ferrety eyes. And Rebecca Tucker, she

205

should know better than to let herself get caught up in it all. Fanny Frobisher was almost as bad, as were Polly Chichester and Florence Knight. They were all like it; cliquey little women, conspiring away and chattering together like magpies. Jealousy would get them nowhere. If that's what it was all about then she would show them she couldn't care less. If they didn't like it, then that was too bad.

It wasn't fair on poor Bertie. He was a lovely, gentle man but, never mind, she would look after him and, in any case, she had to. It had been sometime now since he last mentioned his idea of passing his estate directly on to Isaac; bypassing her in the process. It would have been more usual, he suggested, but in the end had deferred to her objections and let matters rest. It had been a difficult time for her but she had persuaded him that everything would be going to the boy one day in any case. In the meantime she really did need to control the family affairs. It should be up to her, rather than some distant trustees, to ensure that his grandson came into his inheritance and his responsibilities gradually. Too much too soon was never a good idea.

And then there had been the dreadful business of the ruby and pearl necklace. She remembered only too well how, one day after lunch, he had asked her to fetch it and had then told her the story. She had seen the flaws in the two stones at once and remained spellbound until he told her she looked as though she had seen the devil himself. The necklace had to have come from Sherdon after Katherine's death, there was no other explanation. Even as they talked she could see how the mere thought of the heirloom being sold like that had hurt him deeply; sold off like a pen of surplus sheep so he said, rather then being treasured and kept in memory of his sister.

It was then that he confided in her about her uncle and how there was no love between them, how he knew all along that Jack had married his sister purely for her wealth and her status and how this callous act of his only went to prove it. The man had no heart, no feelings for the wife who had given up everything, and who felt nothing for the Northborough inheritance that, one day would have passed down his own family line. The story had shamed her and she felt a growing bitterness towards this uncle of hers who could do such a thing. The necklace, she vowed, would stay with her. She alone would care for it and if she could not have it then nobody would. She promised him that and remembered how it had drawn them close. It made her smile then and it made her smile now. She looked up and caught his eye.

"Very quiet, m'dear." The Duke ducked one way to look past the candelabra then the other. "Not plotting anything down there, are you? Can't see a thing through all these damned candles on the table. Locke, where are you man?" He glanced round. "Ah, there you are. Now then, pull up a chair just here will you. I need to see who I've been having dinner with for goodness sake. Can't sit here all night being blinded by lights?"

"Yes, m'lord." Locke manhandled one of the wide, heavily carved French corner chairs towards where his master directed. He found himself doing this more often now and Lady Preston liked the broad, high-backed chairs the best. They were wider, roomier and easier on her dresses. "Coffee in the drawing room, sir?"

"No, in here. We'll take it in here where it's warmer. Eh?" He patted the chair and glanced up at Sarah who was standing waiting for the butler to move.

"Very good, m'lord. There we are, m'lady." He finished positioning the chair and glanced up. "That about right, ma'am?"

"Bring it all in here, Locke…and you can leave all this." He waved a hand at nothing in particular. "Then fall the staff out for the night. I'll see you in the morning about Blagdon…we need to get to Barnstaple in time for the eleven o'clock train remember."

"Very good, m'lord. And I'll have Mrs Carver to wait on your word, m'lady. Right after breakfast." Locke bowed and withdrew.

"Here." The Duke reached for the decanter. "They call the stuff madeira these days. Just the same as canary so far as I can tell…too darned sweet for me." They were silent as he filled her glass. "Now then," he reached out for her hand. "Just a teeny bit quiet down there, so you were. Lonely, were you? Mmm?" She reached out for her glass, took a generous sip then moved closer in her chair, allowing his hand to stroke her arm.

"No, not really. Just thinking about here, and Blagdon and the fact that we're leaving tomorrow. I'm a very lucky girl, Bertie. You're very good to me, you know." Her head was resting on the back of the chair and she turned it slowly towards him, smiling lazily as she did so. "Ooh, your fingers are tickling."

"Mmm? You like it do you?" He hitched himself around in his seat giving him more room to move further up her arm. "That nice?" He was watching her face. She was still smiling but her eyes had closed and he could see she was enjoying the sensation. Without removing his hand he rose silently and went to sit beside her. She moved to release her dress from under his weight. As she did so his hand closed over her breast.

"What are you doing?" she murmured, her eyes still closed. "You know that's not allowed." For a moment she hesitated, thereby unconsciously encouraging him and his hand moved further along the front of her dress. "Bertie, whoa." Her hand took hold of his. "That's very naughty…and quite far enough." She felt full and too idle to move; in any case what he was doing was quite harmless.

"You're very beautiful, Sarah. You know you are don't you. The way you dress and carry yourself…you've a wonderful figure. It makes me very proud, y'know, just to watch the way everybody looks at you."

"Yes, just to watch, Bertie, and that's all you should be doing." She was lying back in the chair, but lying still with her hand on top of his where it had come to rest. "Oh, you're squashing me…ooof," she gasped, struggling for room. "Give me a little more room, I can't breathe properly." If she sat up she could look after herself better.

The Duke half slid and half rolled from the chair and onto his knees beside her. "There you are…better?" he drawled. His hands moved swiftly, one to the front of her dress, the other behind her. As he did so, he lowered his head on to the soft swell of her breasts. "There, that's better," he murmured. "That's more comfortable." For a moment she lay there. But he was stopping her breathing and one hand went instinctively to his head. She knew at once it had tempted him for he rose on his knees and began to kiss her cleavage, pulling down the front of her dress as he did so. She should not have let him get this far. That was enough.

"Stop it, Bertie," she said, more firmly than before, patting his head as if to admonish him. Suddenly she felt his other hand under her skirts. It was working its way up to her knee. "*Stop it*…stop it at once," she cried, a note of alarm now in her voice. She tried to struggle up in the chair but the weight of his body held her down. His hand was moving higher and she felt him trying to force her legs apart. "That's *enough…stop*. Stop it at once." Still the hand moved on, squeezing the warm, soft inside of her thigh. Now she was frightened.

"No…no…stop." Her shout was more of a scream. "You're hurting me…Bertie, stop it. It hurts. Ohhhh God…..no…..stop, it hurts," she shouted, louder still. It was more of a cry for help and there was panic in her voice. "No…don't *do* that…*no*."

Then, suddenly it was over. The Duke sat back on his heels. His face was in his hands and he buried them deeper. "Oh, Lord," he mumbled. "Oh for goodness sake, whatever have I done." He looked up, his eyes wide and pleading. "Sarah, my dear. My dear girl, please forgive me…that was most improper. I do apologise."

"Yes it most certainly was," Sarah sat up and was adjusting the top to her dress before lifting herself to tidy her skirts. "What on earth d'you think you were doing? Bertie…answer me. Speak to me. What on earth got into you? I'm your daughter-in-law, for Heaven's sake."

"I know, I know," he groaned, pulling himself up to his feet. "Goodness only knows what came over me." He looked down at her. "Do please forgive me, my dear. It was quite dreadful…really, I'm deeply ashamed. I beg your forgiveness."

Sarah rose. "You're very wicked, Herbert Preston. Extremely so…I mean it really was most undignified. Dreadful." She paused, still breathing heavily. "All…right," she said slowly. "I'll let this go, this once, but never, ever again, d'you hear? Never again, Bertie. Come on now, look at the hour. It's time to retire."

Malcolm Locke stepped back quickly from the door. He pressed himself into the shadows, hiding behind the grandfather clock; they would never see him here. He had left the dining room door slightly ajar when he took his leave earlier. As soon as the Duke had sat Lady Preston beside him and dismissed him, he had half expected something like this to happen. When he crept up to listen, he had shut the kitchen door behind him but they would have still heard her shouting like she did. It was loud and piercing and, in fact, the kitchen door had opened once, just after her scream.

Anyhow, that was it as far as he was concerned. Sir Wilmot's niece had been savaged by the old man and a right good savaging it sounded too. Just how far he got or what he was trying to do, Malcolm Locke could only imagine. But Her Ladyship wasn't enjoying it that was for sure; not enjoying it one bit.

✳

"Permission to speak, sir?"

"Yes, of course. Come in Steer." Wilmot turned in his swivel chair. He had been writing at his desk and was quite surprised by the knock on the door. "You sound very formal. Everything all right?" He looked more closely. "No, it's not, I can see by your face. Is there a problem?"

Steer coughed and rose on his toes, then pursed his lips for a moment. "I'm afraid it's something very personal, sir." He put up a hand as if to stifle a cough. "Not quite sure how to begin, sir, and it'll be sounding as though I'm being disloyal...but I'm not, sir," he added hurriedly. "Never would be."

Wilmot frowned. "Well, come on, man. We've known one another long enough. Let's have it...all of it, no matter how tough it is."

"Very good, sir." The butler coughed and retold the story as Malcolm Locke had reported to him. After a few moments Wilmot eased back in his chair. His eyes closed, shut tight at what he was hearing and one hand went to his forehead. Steer stopped, afraid that he had gone too far but Wilmot waved him on, demanding grimly to know everything. When he had finished, the butler took out a handkerchief and wiped his brow. His hand was trembling. Then he swallowed and waited, staring at the picture behind his master's head.

"And who else knows of this." Sir Wilmot Tucker's face was white.

"Mr Locke says he believes the kitchen heard some of it, sir. Two or three of them, down there doing the tidying up." Wilmot's eyes closed. That was more than enough; any one of them would have been too many and word would get out. It had to, that was the way of the world. And it was Sarah, their Sarah that the old beast had tried to ravage. Sarah, ye Gods. How dare the man and after trying to fob her off just a few years ago. How *dare* that ghastly man.

"Thank you, Steer." Wilmot pushed himself up and on to his feet then limped towards the door. "Thank you very much. I can see it was difficult for you and I thank you for your frankness. I'll trouble you to keep it to yourself, of course."

"Of course, sir." Steer rose on his toes. "Beggin' your pardon, sir, but just to say that I went down there meself, sir. Straight after he told me, an' we got the three o' them together. Told 'em straight, sir, so I did. One word, just one word and I'd have the skin off their backs."

"Thank you again, Mr Steer. You've done me well." Wilmot opened the door. "We'll have lunch at the usual time, please."

"Very good, sir"

Wilmot nodded and closed the door. He sat heavily for his leg was hurting, then he picked up his favourite paper knife. For the whole of the next hour he remained there, staring out of the window. He swivelled his chair from side to side but not a paper on his desk was touched. By the time Steer came for him he knew what he was going to do. His mind was made up.

3

"I'm telling you, Wilmot. If Disraeli gets back he's going to actually set about buying a controlling interest in the canal...the whole of the Egyptian stock if he can." Frederic paused. He could see that his point had struck home. Wilmot had asked to see him saying that it was a matter of some urgency. They were due out later together but he had hurried back from the House as quickly as he could. "He's in no doubt whatsoever that our future lies east of Suez...politically, militarily and commercialy. He's set his mind on it and sees the canal as our umbilical cord to prosperity...he'll put his head on the block if needs be."

"Hmmph, I'm not so sure. All right, all right," Wilmot added hurriedly, seeing his friend's expression. "You'll be knowing about all that far better than me. But one minute I hear all this from you Tories and the very next they tell me that Gladstone's going to concentrate on the Americas...and he is the Prime Minister after all. Sees our commercial and political future more in that direction." He eased himself around in his armchair. "And most of the City's following the buzz from Westminster – that the Americas it's going to be."

It had been a torrid week for the chairman of London and Pacific and he had been hard pressed to fend off a boardroom rebellion. The introduction of refrigeration shipping had stunned the maritime world but he had refused to allow himself to be persuaded. One by one they had come to him asking what he proposed to do about it. Mallory and the dreadful little Sir Dennis Speakman had actually started a shouting match. For a week he had deliberated, still confident that the future of the company lay east not west. But he had to admit that refrigeration would open up huge new opportunities in both the Argentine and Australia. Even New

Zealand, thus far out of reach, would be within their grasp. They were now barely dependant upon sail and the latest line of faster steam ships they had ordered were over two thousand tons. East or west, it mattered not. They were well poised but it was essential to know how the government was thinking.

Tomorrow L and P were due to meet again. The tension of last week had subsided but there were still those on the board who doubted his decision. He had to swing them behind his decision; a split board made for an impotent chairman. He would be vulnerable and Frederic, he knew, had been part of Disraeli's team studying the canal.

"Well, let them," Frederic raised his hand in exasperation. "And a fat lot of good it'll do any of them. Let them bring back all the meat they want but there's more to your world of shipping than just meat, for Heaven's sake." He slapped his hand down on the arm of his chair. "And in any case, if you're going to get involved in this frozen…this refrigeration business, you're going to have to start building your-self new ships, after which you're going to have to go out searching for new contracts. Honestly, think about it." Wilmot was silent.

"Listen, my friend," Frederic continued, getting out of his chair and walking briskly over to the fireplace where he turned and stood, hands behind back, like some frock-coated commissionaire. Wilmot could sense his agitation. "You've got your trade routes well established and it's taken you years to do that, ever since the old East India Company. Start fiddling around now with something the other side of the world…and quite untried, and you're entering the unknown. What sort of commercial acumen is that, eh? What sort of chairman advocates that?"

"Aye…aye, you're right, I s'pose."

"Damned sure I am, Wilmot. The way to play it with any detractors who've got mutiny on their minds is to ask them if they're prepared to risk everything London and Pacific stands for. They can't have it both ways, nobody can, and anyone who wants to cut all the old ties and jump had better stand up and be counted. Go on, ask 'em that…ask who's prepared to stand up. Oh no…I'll wager they'll all be sitting there hanging on to the sides of their chairs for dear life, every man jack o'them." They laughed, it was an interesting scenario. "Here, have a drink, we've time." Frederic reached for the bell. "Look, that's it, my friend. That's the way to snuff out any dissent." He grinned suddenly and rubbed his hands. The table for four at Hatchard's had been booked for seven and the curtains were going up at the Adelphi an hour and a half later. Sir Arthur Sullivan's 'Cox and Box' was just what was needed.

Wilmot glanced at the clock. The ladies would be back soon but there was time for a quick aperitif as the French called it before they all assembled again. Maynard took their orders and returned almost immediately. "You know, the best bit about what you've just said, Freddie…and you've convinced me, you old dog. The best of it is that I haven't got to play the agricultural card, all this business about asking them to feel sorry for our farmers."

"Oh yes?" Frederic cocked an eyebrow.

"Indeed. I brought it up on Wednesday and a couple of my board flew at me, telling me that I was a protectionist and that the company was not a charity to those who couldn't cope with market forces. Bang, bang, just like that."

"They just don't understand, do they…haven't a clue."

"Either that or they simply refuse to face facts," Wilmot continued. "The country-side's on its knees. I mean, only a couple of months ago we had this new union…this fellow, Arch, who's pulled all the agricultural workers together." He stretched his leg and brushed back a lock of grey hair. "I asked them what they thought would happen if the country was suddenly flooded with cheap overseas meat and the beggars just laughed in my face…simply not interested in what goes on out there. As long as there's Smithfield and Billingsgate…and Covent Garden, the stuff could be coming in via the moon for all they care. They haven't seen a cow, half of them."

Frederic pulled a face for it had ever been thus. He knew from those members in the House who came from the cities that shipping magnates were not the only ones who showed supreme indifference to the lot of the farmer. Funnily enough it was the Lords who were more in touch. They were the ones, the great landowners, who understood what it was like out there. "Now then, how's Lionel?" Shipping and meat had bored him.

"Oh, well enough. Not sure what he's getting out of Oxford." Wilmot rose, bent and stretched his leg to get the circulation going. "Bit of a dreamer, really. Keeps on about going off on the grand tour as they like to call it these days. When I asked him what he was going to do for a living he just gawped at me with his mouth open. "Ha," Wilmot shrugged. "And what about your lad? Still in love?"

"Oh, God. Don't bring that up. Sometimes I think Florence's gone potty." Frederic shook his head. The two of them had talked about it and Wilmot had been very understanding for Jack was his brother, but it had been difficult.

"Don't worry yourself, dear boy." Wilmot grinned raffishly. "The young all think they run the world. It couldn't matter less…honestly, either the two of them will get themselves together in their own sweet time or they won't, and mothers running around pushing and pulling every which way won't help. Best just to leave them be."

Both turned as Maynard threw open the double doors. They could hear voices coming up the stairs and it was Rebecca's gale of high-pitched laughter echoing around the hallway that was the loudest of all.

Chapter Sixteen

It seemed as though the knock at the bedroom door that morning came almost as soon as the bed-side lamp had been extinguished a few hours earlier. Once outside in the fresh air and with his head clear, Frederic had to admit that breakfast at Fremington Hall had been a sombre affair.

The Officers' Ball, always one of the highlights of Barnstaple's Cavalry Week, had been its usual success, most likely better than for many years since so many Old Comrades were present. It was held on the last night of the week, immediately before this morning's church parade. The Royal North Devon Hussars were holding a joint march with the Devon Rifle Volunteers. Also on parade today was a company of regulars from Exeter, bringing the total to more than a thousand men of whom almost half were mounted.

Grenville Incleton, Colonel of the Hussars, had put him and Florence up for the whole of the festival and two nights ago they had been joined by Wilmot and Rebecca. It had been a noisy if somewhat chaotic house party yet, somehow, the carriages had arrived in time after breakfast on the last morning to transport them to church. The Grand Finale was to be an open air luncheon party in Rock Park followed by the presentation of prizes before the whole contingent marched past the mayor.

They had even managed to persuade Jack to come. It had been difficult but Gaile and Ralph Rudd had offered to keep Kitty company at Sherdon. The fact that Harry had been involved in organising the boxing tournament helped. Sebright was also bringing Anna. They were in the same party as the Chichesters thus, for Jack, it would be something of a family occasion.

*

He was as tall and lean as ever but now slightly stooped. The years of weather had burnished his face oak brown and his grey-blue eyes gave his features a sharpness, almost those of a hawk and especially when he was casting about for something. Nobody who saw him standing there could say that he looked comfortable, in fact one person thought he was lost. Jack pulled at his collar, gazing around to try to catch sight of familiar faces.

He would have far preferred to be on the other side of the park, closer to where the line of tall chestnuts bordered the river. It was here that most of the huge throng of people had begun to gather. He could hear the military band and, above the heads of the crowd, watched the plumed helmets and lances of the hussars as they waited to begin the military ride. The sight and sound brought back distant memories. No doubt the ghost of Sergeant Fanshawe would be there somewhere, he thought; the idea made him suddenly laugh out loud and he shook his head. Behind him and further away was another band, its drummers and musicians sounding curiously flat and off-beat in the distance. Wherever he looked more and more people were hurrying towards the row of flag-decked marquees, most coming from the railway station where special trains had been running since dawn.

Wilmot had attired his brother in a high-buttoned lovat green tweed suit with black braid edging. It was the checked, flannel shirt with its turned-over collar held tightly in place by a necktie, rather than the looser cravat, that irritated him. He pulled at it again, this time lifting his chin to get at it better. In his other hand was the brown, narrow-rimmed bowler the tailor had suggested he wore, but he had refused steadfastly to have anything to do with the silver topped cane that had been offered as well.

Wilmot, himself dressed more for the City in his dark grey cutaway coat with purple silk cravat, stood on tiptoe. "Here he comes, spot on time." He raised his stick at Harry. Even he, bigger than most, and resplendent in his scarlet jacket and white belt, was difficult to spot in the melee of brightly coloured silks and cottons. The world it seemed had dressed for the occasion to the delight, no doubt, of local dressmakers and milliners. Feathers, plumes and ribbons fluttered and bobbed on hats and bonnets as their owners walked this way and that. Children darted about excitedly. Soldiers hurried from point to point and everywhere there was bustle.

Frederic arrived last, having decided to walk on ahead of Florence and the others whom he had left outside the parish church of St Peter and St Mary. He was a little late but they met, as arranged, in front of the Officers' Mess marquee. Here a large area of neatly cut lawn had been fenced off with white railings and decorated with tubs of flowers and shrubs. Between these, several small tables, covered with cloths of white linen, had been set. Somebody had decorated them with posies of garden flowers and already people were taking their seats.

Uniformed waiters, carrying trays of drinks, moved amongst the guests already inside the enclosure where an atmosphere of calm and genteel orderliness prevailed. Nobody rushed and nobody appeared too excited. Voices were barely raised, allowing those who wished to listen to the chamber musicians playing quietly on the flower-decorated podium. Under the blue and white striped awning at the entrance to the marquee, two bearded regimental farriers were standing guard over the colours and guidons of those on parade. Dressed in their ceremonial scarlet jackets and heavy white leather aprons, they stood at ease with their spiked axes slung casually over their shoulders. In front of them the Mess Sergeant, round and ruddy-faced, was keeping a close watch on those entering his domain.

"You're quite right, Jack." Frederic grimaced. "We'd never get poor Harry near the Mess dressed as he is. It's all changed…look at it all for goodness sake." He glanced at Wilmot. "Years ago we might've got away with it…the old days at camp. But now…it's more like Derby day in there." He peered this way and that, even bent his knees to try to see inside the marquee then turned and shrugged, holding out his arms in appeal. "Sorry about that; I should have known better. Different to the days out at Blackmore Gate…eh Jack?."

"Aye, sir…or Tiverton, mind. Grabbin' our food in the saddle like we used to."

"*Ha*, those days indeed," Frederic laughed. "Today this lot have got nothing better to do. They're getting soft." He patted back his hair. "Oh well, there we are…but it's a great shame."

"Look, sir, never mind about this…never mind at all." Jack put a hand on his shoulder. "It doesn't make no odds, really it doesn't. Harry an' I, we'll be keeping an eye on one another out there. Eh, lad?" He had been astonished when, at the tent pegging yesterday afternoon, Frederic announced that they would meet up at the officers' marquee before luncheon and the final parade. He tried to tell him that it would never have worked; junior ranks were kept well clear of the place. Cavalry Week in eighteen seventy-three was very different to the old annual camps when an easy informality prevailed. Here The Royal North Devon Hussars were entertaining the local society.

And, in any case, the idea did not appeal. Not a bit. Few, if any, of the older officers would remember him, and any that did would have moved on in life. He would have nothing in common with the young gentlemen of today who made up the officer corps of his old regiment and who would regard him with no more than mild curiosity. It would be difficult and, inside the marquee, it would be stifling hot.

Once clear Jack stepped out. "Thank the Lord for the man at the gate…the tubby little Mess Sergeant fellow. I said it was wrong…said it to Master Frederic yesterday and I'm pleased enough not to be part of it. Other way round would be fine. For him to come along here with us, that is. Said he'd like it that way."

"'T'was his missus said no, I'll be bound." Harry walked in step with his father.

"Aye. A fine lady, mind…a very fine lady but she keeps her menfolk to heel." He paused for a moment to survey the scene and check their way ahead. "Oh, yes, Master Frederic'd like to be down here all right. Love it he would and there're several here he'd remember."

"But he's not the commanding officer up at Simonsbath, eh?"

"No, sir." Father and son laughed. "Never be allowed down here with the rough necks. His good lady'd have him out of here in no time. Come on then, lad," Jack pushed Harry forward. "Let's see what's what."

The three big dun coloured tents were packed tight. Each of the sides had been removed and the hundreds upon hundreds of soldiers, together with their families and friends, and the friends of their friends, stood or spread themselves around in a great mass.

The air was thick with the smell of warm beer and the smoke from the ox-roast behind the far tent. Jackets were off, white shirts and braces being more comfortable in the August heat than the heavy serge tunics. All around old friends and new had come together. Some were making a noise about it, raising their voices excitedly, arguing even, with fingers wagging or poking. And some were talking quietly with their heads together, nodding solemnly as if serious judgement had just been passed. Yet others laughed and joked, with heads thrown back and bodies doubled up with mirth and when thighs were slapped. Some lay peacefully in the shade, one or two lay where they fell.

Sometimes there would be a great raucous shout from the depths of a tent or a high-pitched shriek. Cheroots were dropped and pipes tapped out. Beer and wine straight from the cask were spilled, dogs nosed about and scavenged hopefully and small children tumbled and fought, or ran wildly between legs. Another band was playing and from somewhere came the sound of singing, causing anyone nearby to shout even louder to get themselves heard. Between them all a white-belted Military Provost patrol prowled slowly.

Even as he took in the scene, Jack felt better. He smiled, filled his lungs and rubbed his hands before a shout made him look round. He turned further, lifting a hand to his eyes then suddenly called out in recognition. Nancy Coward reached him first and he swept her into the air. For a moment he thought she was on her own but Hector was there too, some way behind, having been caught up in the crowd. Even as Nancy was in his arms he could see another man with her husband. "Dear, dear Jack," she cried as he lowered her gently. "*Cuh*...seems 'tis years an' years. Us 'eard you might be down, an' us've bin lookin' all over. Cuh...dear o' dear."

She stepped back to see him properly yet still clasped him round the waist. "And...what's more," she gave him a tug. "Us've got someone 'ere for you today." She grinned, her same dimpled, mischievous grin, and nodded back over her head to the ones behind. Jack's eyes narrowed. "Know 'im, d'you?" she quizzed.

Jack stared. It was the shape of the head and the thickset body. There was a name there somewhere, but where...who? He looked again There was a face, also, but it was from way back and, once more, he was beaten. "Gid on, Jack Tucker...you bain't that blind, y'know." Nancy watched him closely, her eyes searching for signs of recognition, then she pulled sharply at his waist. "Come on, man. Where's yer mind to?" He shook his head again. "Jack...'tis Len, our Len. Leonard Grant, back home again."

He stared. His head shook again but slowly this time, in wonder at what he was seeing. "By the saints," he whispered. "Cuh, dear God, so strike me down. Leonard, eh? By the very saints and angels." Even now his voice was barely audible. "Our Len...Leonard Grant."

It must have been forty years, forty long years since the ride to Taunton gaol after the wrestling match then the desperate race down to the prison hulk moored off the quay at Exeter. The man should never have been taken away, never. It had all been a terrible mistake and the pardon, when it arrived, had come too late; Leonard Grant had been taken from them. But now here he was, back again. Back home in Devon.

For more than two hours they talked, after Nancy had pulled them apart and slapped their backs for causing such a scene. Twice she pulled Jack's head down to wipe his eyes, scolding him for never having seen him in such a state. But between the tears and the long, hard clasps there was laughter, not laughter at what had been said but the sudden, tumbling laughter of pure joy that comes from the soul when close friends meet after so long.

Harry went off to join the parade and many of those in the tents went to watch but, for the four friends huddled close together around the food and drink-strewn table, there was no parade. They never saw another soldier that afternoon nor heard a note of music as the bands marched by. There was so much to say but nobody knew where to begin. Time and again one of them would start but they never got far before stopping and beginning again somewhere else. There would be time enough, all the time in the world but, for now, Leonard was home and that was what mattered: just as Wilmot said when he found them later.

*

Sarah and the Duke were sitting with the Bamfyldes and Frobishers in the officers' enclosure. Lunch was over and the waiters had finished serving iced sherbets and mint tea. One or two tables had emptied already. It was warm, comfortably so, and at first talk had been of the forthcoming Dartmouth regatta. Now Marcus Bamfylde, already a successful owner of thoroughbreds and soon to become famous, was describing the difficulties of the course at Goodwood where he had had three runners the previous week.

Behind them the musicians had struck up a selection of waltzes and polkas. Henry Bamfylde took out his watch. He studied it carefully and shook it before announcing loudly that there were but ten minutes remaining and that they should make their way to the rostrum behind the saluting dais. The final march past, never to be missed, would bring the whole affair to its end.

When the Duke first noticed her, the young woman had her back half turned. It was not her clothes that caught his eye for they were simple enough. Her dress was one of the new fashioned slender variety that he liked but which others considered to be too American. It was cream in colour with brown accordion pleating and offset by a large yellow ribbon behind. The woman, scarcely more than a girl was tall and carried herself well, her brown hat with cream ribbons and plumes giving her an elegant look. But it was the way she moved that held his attention, and he studied her more closely.

As she turned, she glanced at her escort and smiled shyly before taking his arm. Suddenly the Duke was alert. There was indeed a look about her that was familiar, about her graceful movements and the way she turned towards her man; the way she lifted her chin in acknowledgement to something he said. It was halfway between a nod and a glance into the far distance. He had seen it before. They were approaching him now and he caught the young man's eye as they came up to his table.

"Your Grace...Lady Preston." Sebright Knight bowed. "May I have the pleasure, sir, ma'am, of introducing my companion, Miss Anna Tucker." Sarah inclined her head smiling politely. Her father-in-law rose, pushing himself stiffly out of his chair. He was staring with his mouth half open as it was sometimes wont to be.

"Anna Tucker." He held out his hand. "Miss Anna Tucker. We've never met, I regret to say. At least not that I can recall." He took her hand. Then he saw it at once. She had to be the one; there could be no doubt. The longer he looked the more certain he became. The eyes, her nose and the corners of her mouth and the very way she stood, they all belonged to his sister. He paused, still holding her hand. "You are...you are none other...."

"Indeed, sir." She anticipated him, knowing instinctively what was on his mind for she had been watching him closely. "My mother, Katherine...Lady Katherine Darcy before she married my father, was your sister. I am your neice, sir." Anna looked at him expectantly.

"And so...so I can see." The Duke still had her hand. "You are, Miss, er, Tucker...Anna, as perhaps I should say. I have to tell you that you are the very incarnation of your dear mother when she was a young woman, exactly as I remember her at Blagdon, exactly. And I could never pay you a finer compliment than that." He stood back but his eyes remained on her.

"Thank you kindly, sir." Anna blushed but still managed to smile with pleasure. "My father, from time to time, expresses a similar opinion."

"And my father, as well, Anna," Sebright laughed. "Don't forget that. He's forever telling us how you bring back so many memories...whenever he sees you, in fact." Anna glanced away.

"I'll be damned." The Duke's eyes narrowed. "*Really.*" He remembered now how his own parents had talked about Frederic Knight, that most eligible of suitors, and how they hoped that, one day, he would ask them for their daughter's hand. He'd heard also how Frederic had professed to his father how he had loved his sister but that he had been too late. Once she had given her consent to that dreadful man he had stood back. And now this, this lovely young woman, the issue of that union, was standing here, announcing herself so innocently and yet with such composure. That, too, the same quiet authority was so typical of her mother.

"Come on, Bertie." Sarah drained her glass, tilting it high before she rose. She sounded bored but was not, simply she had no desire to sit and listen to such flattery being heaped upon the girl. "We have no time to sit around and listen to you reminiscing about the past. Come, now." She picked up her parasol. "We must be on our way."

Anna turned to her. "When my mother died...your aunt, madam, my father was left on his own with us and times were difficult, very hard no less. But now," she looked from one to the other and smiled. "Now you will be pleased to hear no doubt that your uncle has found true happiness once more...the happiness he so richly deserves."

"I'm so glad." Sarah, having studied the younger woman as she was speaking now turned away as if wholly indifferent, occupying herself instead with moving a chair in order to join the others who had risen also. "I have no doubt but that it is all a most suitable arrangement. Most convenient and I'm sure everyone is very happy."

"And none more so than your own mother, ma'am." Anna again looked from one to the other. She was as tall as Sarah but slimmer and held herself well, looking down at the Duke as she spoke. "You see, sir, my father," she pointed at herself then nodded towards Sarah. "And Lady Preston's mother are brother and sister...but I daresay you are aware of this already." She hesitated. "You see, I am Lady Preston's cousin, as well as your niece." She felt Sarah's eyes on her. "My dear father and his family are very close and nobody was more delighted to hear of his re-marriage than his sister, my Aunt Emma." Anna saw the expression on his face. "It's very complicated, I know," she gave a little shrug of helplessness. "But I'm afraid there's no way that any of it can be untied." She paused. "And as for father...he's very happy with the way things are."

For a moment the Duke stood where he was. The very criss-crossing of all these family lines was complicated enough but there were the relationships that flowed between them as well. Here, in front of his eyes, was his niece he had never met; a quite charming and beautiful young woman who reminded him so keenly of his sister. Yet she was a Tucker. And it was these same Tuckers who, one after another, had come into his life bringing nothing but confrontation and bitterness with them. The girl's uncle, the shipping man from North Molton, was bad enough but her father was none other than the man who slew Kenton Knight. And the one who had taken his sister from them. He had spirited her away, ruined her life and then, on her death, sold off her birthright for his own gain.

"Will...you...come...*on*." Sarah turned to go. "Are you going to escort me, good sir, or are you going to stay here and discuss other peoples affairs?"

"Sorry, m'dear. Yes, of course." The Duke half lifted his top hat but hesitated, with the hat poised above his head. He scarcely knew what to think. For some reason he felt angry, angry that the name Tucker had been waved in front of him yet again. Yet how unfair it was to harbour such sentiments when this girl had had no part in it all. Innocence itself she seemed and innocent she most surely must be. And what about Sarah? There had been a coolness in the air, more than that there had been silent hostility. Jealousy, maybe, or had she, too, had her fill of her troublesome family? Who could tell? Only women understood other women. But that was enough for he had to make haste. "My thanks to you, sir, for affecting the introduction. And to you, too, ma'am." He replaced his hat and inched past them to hurry on his way after the others.

✳

Florence Knight eased herself on her uncomfortable wooden chair. All around her guests of the Regiment were being shown to their seats. In front, and on the raised dais, six empty chairs awaited the Mayor and the Colonel of the Regiment. Beyond them again and on either side of where they were sitting, the crowds had gathered. Wherever possible they were lining the route, many of them already craning forward and waving paper flags.

She had been surprised and a little disquieted when Sarah was shown to the seat next to her. Frederic had risen and greeted her warmly but she had found it difficult at first, remembering the occasion at Arlington. Nonetheless for the last few minutes, Lady Preston, as she made sure she was known, had been surprisingly friendly and they had chatted together amicably, waving to those they knew. She had been most impressed with Sebright, Sarah had said, complimenting him on his fine features and impeccable manners. No doubt, she observed, he found himself in a most enviable position in so far as young ladies were concerned. Florence had hesitated. Sarah, she was certain, would have her own strong opinions about what would be best for the boy. But Florence was curious as to what that might be and mentioned her son's interest in Sherdon.

"And so I saw after luncheon." Her reply was typically direct yet non-committal.

"And does such a companionship surprise you?" As soon as she had asked it, Florence considered her own question had been equally direct yet she had not meant it that way.

Sarah did not hesitate. "No, not as far as Anna is concerned. Any young woman would be delighted to receive such attentions from a son of yours and I congratulate her on her good fortune. She would be foolish indeed not to accept his arm." She was still smarting at the way the Duke had behaved towards the girl. Distant relative or not, he had all but fawned upon her.

"And Sebright? You seem a mite…er…hesitant."

"Yes, as far as he's concerned I think I am rather surprised." Sarah looked at her. "The boy has got everything…everything he wants and there must be countless eligible and well connected young women who would be only too delighted to catch his eye."

220

"But the young lady in question is Anna Tucker…your own cousin none the less. Do you consider her to be not suitable? Is that what you are suggesting?"

"No, not *un*-suitable but the girl knows nothing of the world, nothing at all. My uncle keeps her tucked away up there, slaving at the sink or out in the farmyard and what have you. Really, Sebright should look further, you know…you should encourage him to cast his net wide. The boy would surprise himself." She dabbed at the spot on her cheek. "No…there are better catches to be had, that's for sure." Sarah looked at her and nodded as if to emphasise her point. "Unless, of course, you are happy enough with such a situation. Mmm?" She raised an eyebrow then turned to the scene in front of them.

People were stirring. They could hear the band and the first guard of the Hussars came trotting slowly into view. Florence sat up. The woman was hard. She was brash and outspoken and she was decidedly wary of her but, in a peculiar sort of way, Sarah, Lady Preston was a woman of her own mind. For both of them, it appeared, only the best in life would do, and nothing would be allowed to stand in the way.

2

The Duke of Northborough put the letter down and got to his feet. He sniffed, noting for the first time the musty smell of damp paper. The library at Blagdon, like the rest of the house was shut up for most of the year. He would have to get back more often but this letter from Ilfracombe, the contents of which was about the deteriorating situation within his shipping company, was going to take him away again.

He walked to the window and stared out, pulling a face at what he saw. He hated October, it was always such a depressing month. Summer had gone and most of the flowers with it. All that remained was a mess; the weather challenging the very patience of his gardeners as well as their energies. Autumn had begun already, for he could see the cold wind tossing the branches of the two copper beeches all over the place and the poor things were still heavy with leaf.

Ilfracombe had indeed become a worry and was now exercising his mind more than he bargained for. He turned back to his desk. Only two months ago it had been Minehead. His shipping agent there had written to him and he had gone down to see the man. Bookings had fallen off badly and the situation appeared to be getting worse. Why so? Competition. But where from? He remembered how Cummings, his wizened and frizzy-haired agent in his ill-fitting suit, had spelt out the answers to all his questions between bouts of wheezing and coughing. The more he heard the less he liked the man, but liked even less what he was being told.

"We can only go so far, my lord." Cummings had spread his hands wide over the books open on the mahogany side table and stared down at the evidence. They were in the first floor office and the view from the window overlooked the marshes. It was a dingy little room with a low ceiling and an uneven floor whose boards complained at every step. "I'm sure I don't need to tell you but it's a case of simple arithmetic. On one side are our annual expenses, there." He drew a finger down the yellowing page. "And the income's here. And if there's not enough coming in then...." Cummings shrugged.

"Can't we do *anything* about it? Cut our costs any further?" The Duke didn't wait for an answer. "But how does everybody else manage...and where's our problem coming from?"

"Bristol mainly, sir. Bristol and Falmouth. Up there we've got the Bristol Steamship Company. They're big and getting bigger...and they're being subsidised by London. Have been for years but it's getting worse now and they're simply under-cutting us." Cummings laughed cynically, caught his breath and began to cough. "So easy," he gasped eventually, taking off his spectacles to wipe his eyes. "It's all too easy when you've got the banks or bigger shipping companies behind you. We believe that they're under contract to one of the major shipping lines that's looking eastwards and they'd be happy enough to see that somewhere like Bristol keeps its lines to America open for them." He paused again, turning away to cough into an old and crumpled handkerchief. The Duke frowned: Cummings was an unattrac-tive little man and he wanted none of his germs. "The odd part is," he said at last. "It's only us – rather your good self, m'lord, who seems to be suffering like this...strange, really."

"Go on."

"Ilfracombe seems to be affected, but nobody else. We've been in touch with Watchet and Barnstaple...even Bideford and none of them are feeling the pinch. Order books are as full as can be expected, or so they say...the post-war American boom." He shrugged at the apparent mystery of it all. "It's almost as if we've been singled out." It seemed strange indeed. The other harbours he mentioned and their port facilities were better than his, so it was unlikely that Bristol or whoever it was had eyes on Ilfracombe and was trying to squeeze him out. The markets were spread wide. Most harbours dealt with coastal business moving from port to port, tramping as it was now known. He, Northborough, dealt with America unlike the others except for Falmouth, Bideford and Swans of Exeter.

But two of his ships were currently laid up and that was not good. Seagoing vessels only paid for themselves when they were out on the high seas. Not only was there no business but the overheads, while laid up in harbour, were considerable and some of the crew were still on full pay. Others were on half pay and they had laid off only a few for it would be no good getting a sudden order and having nobody about to handle it. A thousand pounds was a lot of money, a great deal in fact, but the miserable little Cummings had done his sums. If that was what was required to keep the business going then he would have it.

All that had been bad enough but this letter from Ilfracombe now in front of him was talking about crew numbers. Newton, the harbour master there and a good man at that, had been overseeing the crews while the ships were lying idle. All had been well and the two of them had agreed over lunch in 'The Admiral Lord Nelson' that most men quite liked the idea of getting something for nothing, for a time anyway. But now, it seemed, that was not the case. Something or somebody was enticing them away. Two months back, the letter said, six men had gone missing but ten days ago the number had risen to fifteen, and some of those had been on full pay. He looked at the letter again. '…*would His Lordship, therefore, be so kind as to find time to come and discuss the matter at his earliest convenience. I remain, sir, you most obedient servant etc etc.'*

∗

He had to agree that it was a melancholy sight. His two larger schooners were inside the harbour. The tide was out and they were leaning heavily against the inner wall. His third ship, 'The Plover' was lying off Rapparee Cove just beyond the breakwater. She, the smallest and just a little over three hundred tons, had been part loaded and was due to make her run on the evening tide. She was bound for New Orleans and there was not yet much news about a return cargo. Newton had been hard pressed to man her and would find it harder still to crew either of the others…were the agent to find any business.

The Duke dabbed at the sweat on his lip and looked at Tam Newton. He had taken to the man at once when they first met three years ago. Newton knew his business and he knew how to handle men. He was fair but he was hard, very hard in fact and knew a deal about many other things as well. Word was that he had been even too hard on his own crew back in the days when they were running brandy and fine wines. Perhaps he had been too hard here, but then the world was becoming a soft place and men preferred the easy life. "What the devil's going on, man?"

"They're being bought off, m'lord. Simple as that." Newton leaned forward and crossed his hands, not bothering to hide the gap where his left two middle fingers should have been. "'Tis always the same, sir. Human traffic moves faster than any cargo if the money's right…and somebody's paying right good money, and for some o' the best o' them at that." His finger jabbed the table.

"Any ideas? We'll have to find out and put a stop to it."

"Bideford's the whisper. Building bigger ships at Appledore, so I've heard tell. It's a small fleet there, part of a much bigger one…up country someplace." Whoever it was, was costing him dear. The lot of the harbour master at Ilfracombe was not easy and the commission he was being paid to look after the crews was a nice bonus. But, if this went on, there would be nobody left and that would hurt. "Slot the beggars, that's what I'd do. If ever I catch hold of them, I'd slit the beggars' throats. Spill their guts as well."

The Duke looked at him, and believed him. Newton's father had lived by the sword working out of Lundy, and his grandfather had done the same. Tam Newton, a man of today, had other methods, so they said. "I'd run him to ground then take him right out, all of 'em if needs be," he continued with his eyes still on the Duke. "I know it sounds a bit hard an' that but when it gets dirty like this then men's livelihoods are at stake." He looked at the back of his left hand and clenched what remained of the fist. "Once it get's to this then the talking stops."

"Really?" The Duke's face was deadpan but his breathing was coming faster.

"Not me…not me anymore." Newton sat back and laughed. The man didn't look evil. His short hair and lightly tanned, clean-cut face gave him the air of a respectable businessman, which he was…until, and as he had just said, the talking stopped. "But I know who could…and would, if the terms were right mind you." He looked down and paused, one eyebrow cocked expectantly.

"Well." The Duke shuffled uneasily. He had heard that there were those who talked like this but had never heard it first hand. It was chilling and sent a shiver through him. They didn't do this sort of thing in the City of London. They would bankrupt you, of course, smiling sweetly as they did so, then take you to court and hang your name out to dry, but not your skin. This was altogether different and he doubted that he should hear anything more of it. He coughed uneasily. "Well, first we'll need to know exactly what's been going on. I can survive for a while but I need to get it cleared up. I'll keep paying you Newton but I want to know what the devil's going on. D'you hear?"

"Aye, my lord. Don'e go worryin'. I'll find out an' that's fer sure. Somebody out there's costing me a deal of money as well as your good self."

＊

It took Newton two weeks and a rider brought his letter. It was a simple one but enough. *'I have the news you want,'* it read, *'and we need to speak. I suggest our usual lunch on any one of the following days – Wednesday the fourth, Wednesday the eleventh or Friday the thirteenth. Be sure to tell my messenger which.'*

The eleventh it was, but the Duke saw little of his lunch that day. The news Tam Newton brought him took away any appetite he might have had. Bideford it was; that's where his men were going. The small shipping company there was a branch of the huge London Pacific Line and it was still operating to America. New and bigger cargo vessels had been ordered and, three months ago, the search had begun for crew members. The ships were big, relying almost entirely on steam power and they were fast. The new crew would have to be trained up and only the best need apply. Newton pushed the cutting from 'The North Devon Journal and Herald' across the table.

The pay and conditions on offer explained why the best of his men had gone, but what Newton said explained a great deal more. London Pacific – L and P - meant only one thing, and only one person – Sir Wilmot Tucker. And Sir Wilmot Tucker's presence explained another thing as well – The Bristol Steamship Company from whence he had gone on to London. That was the connection. And the fact that he, the Duke of Northborough, was losing his best men in one direction and his most lucrative American contracts in another while nobody else was being touched, meant just one thing also – the hand of Sir Wilmot Tucker was at work. The man had set out to break him.

All that day he brooded. He remembered to book his room for another night but then he walked, and as he walked his mind raced. It took hours for his cold fury to subside. His walk took him up over Capstone Hill and out beyond Preacher's Rock as far as The Outfalls and back again. He dined alone then called for pen and ink. His note was brief. They had to meet again but this time it would be on Broadstrand Beach at midday. Newton must come, he insisted. He could not order him to do so but he would find it very much worth his while. Indeed, very much so.

✳

"Say nothing more than what you have to say, my lord, for I know what's on your mind." Tam Newton was leaning back against the higher side of the barnacle-covered rock where sand rather than rock pools and seaweed made standing easier. He was staring up at the cliffs, his eyes sweeping them casually yet missing nothing. "I've dealt with men such as yourself for more'n thirty years. Most of 'em, all of 'em perhaps, were men boiling with hot coals of rage or else they were half terrified out of their wits. Their faces told me what I needed to know and what they wanted from me…sometimes they were begging for their very lives themselves. I know what's on your mind, sir."

"Well now." The Duke swallowed and changed his gloves from hand to hand. He hesitated further then came and stood beside him, the two of them leaning back together, the Duke with a dark grey cloak about his shoulders. Tam Newton wore a simple cotton jacket as if he had told the autumn chill coming off the sea to stay clear of him. "It's…it's not easy to say but yes, yes I do want to see it through."

"Want to see it right through, eh? To see the villain who's bin dragging you down, out of the way?" The Duke nodded. "It'll be done, but it will not come cheap. Three hundred guineas," he glanced across at him. "Two hundred to me and one hundred to the man at the far end. And then there's the man in the middle, fifty for him."

"Ye Gods man…how many are in this fiendish plot of yours?"

Newton laughed, his eyes following a seagull that drifted between them and the cliff edge. "Only two. The middleman…well, we call him 'the Break'. You see there're some about who're in debt to me, and there're others who never should have done what they did to me. They're the ones we use…that fifty goes to those who deal with the Break."

225

"You use them?" Newton nodded. "And you mean that after they've done your bidding you, you...."

"Oh aye. A trick left over from the high seas when old foes used to meet and prisoners were exchanged. It helps keep order."

"Are you serious?"

"Are *you*, my lord?" Newton pushed himself away from the rock and brushed back a strand of hair. He turned and folded his arms, all trace of deference now gone. "You've had long enough to make up your mind, sir, but now's the time for you to answer your own questions. You cannot sit on this fence any longer...and I can't be waiting for you neither." He paused, waiting for the Duke to look at him. "Well, my lord. Your answer now, if you please."

It was Katherine. This evil family had taken her and destroyed her. There had been the insults and the cunning of this man Tucker and the treachery of his brother over the jewels. And now there was this rotten, devilish affair with his business. It had gone on and on and would continue to do so. There was no way he, Herbert Northborough, would be able to compete against the might of the London shipping world, no way at all and the man knew it. Furthermore the ghastly, limping, scowling creature had made a complete fool of him when Sarah first came on the scene.

He was a powerful, rich and well connected man...and he was up-jumped. An up-jumped peasant from nowhere and now he was throwing his weight around. The fellow had it in for him and was out to destroy him. So, either he could succumb meekly, wave the white flag and creep away or he could retaliate: fight back just as brutally. Tucker had made it plain that there was no room here for both of them and was set on getting him out at any cost. Now he would do the same. Out at any cost it was to be.

Damn them and damn the man...and damn him again. "Yes," he almost shouted. "Take him and the money's yours. Do what you will but get the wretch out of my life."

Chapter Seventeen

"*Sshh*...c'mon, m'lady. Bain't no need fer none o'that." The lady's maid perched on the edge of the bed. "There now...shush." She was half turned towards the figure lying face down and both hands were gently kneading her shoulders and neck. "C'mon, now...that's better."

Daisy Price understood her mistress better than anyone, and they both knew it. The tall, knowledgeable woman had been appointed by Sarah as her personal maid just over eight years ago, in 1865, shortly before the Blagdon Park wedding. She was older than most other members of the staff at Whitechapel and had her own room high at the back of the west wing. Her deep-set, hooded eyes and somewhat mournful look did not endear her to the other staff and she seemed happy enough to keep to herself.

And that was why Sarah liked her. She trusted her implicitly and relied upon her far more than she would ever admit. The bond between them was strong, perhaps both appreciating how close in life's social strata they might once have been. Daisy Price was her confidant, one with whom Sarah could escape from a world she was beginning to find increasingly hostile. Daisy, gaunt and aloof to those who did not know her, saw her life's mission as looking after Her Ladyship and, to that extent, she had not been found wanting.

Her hands remained where they were until the sobs subsided. Eventually Sarah turned over and sat unsteadily, one hand propping herself up, the other making a feeble gesture at cleaning her face. "Here you are, m'lady." Daisy offered the damp flannel she had prepared. "'Tis the drink again, y'know. Isn't it?" She bent down in an attempt to look into her eyes but Sarah kept her head bowed. "Whatever took it upon yourself...and after luncheon an' all?"

"Don't know...I just don't know," she moaned, shaking her head. "Oh God...I really don't." She sniffed loudly and remained staring vacantly at the sheets. "I don't know what the matter is. Why's it got like this? Nobody...nobody seems to like me anymore." She looked at her maid. Her eyes were red rimmed and tearful, her nose and mouth a mess. "What's the matter with me, Daisy?"

Daisy moved up beside her and put an arm around her shoulders. "I've told'e before, ma'am, an' I'll tell 'e again, now." She pulled her mistress towards her. "Look...you'm awful hard on others sometimes, y'know. You don't know you are but sometimes you say summat that bites...an' hurts real bad, all full of spite an' that. I know's yer don't mean it but they don't and either they'm afraid of you or it vexes them sore." She glanced at her. "An' now then, all of a sudden, you've started this drinking nonsense. Gets yerself all worked up, then it comes out in a mess like this."

Sarah took a deep breath and nodded, resting her head on her maid's shoulder. "I know," she whispered. "You've told me often enough and I do *try*...I really do but I can't help it." She shrugged disconsolately then shook her head again and put a hand to her eyes. Her mouth was closed tight into nothing more than a thin line. "When I'm talking...meeting people and things like that, I'm just afraid they're going to be too clever for me and too quick," she whined. "I'm just frightened really, not angry or bitter."

"I know, I know." Daisy let her arm drop. "We've spoken often enough but you must keep tryin', ma'am...and that goes the same for they men, too, y'know."

Sarah nodded. There had been times, several times, when Daisy had tidied or covered for her and that included twice for Milton Brodie. Once they had rowed about it but Daisy had just stood there and opened her arms, as though she was appealing against the tirade. And once she had threatened to leave, but Sarah had begged her to stay.

"I know you're on your own and His Lordship's been gone but they can all see you're lonely, these men...an' they takes your advantage. Trouble is you're still a lovely lady but you go seekin' their attention...go off after 'em, and it bain't necessary...bain't right neither."

Sarah got up and walked hesitantly to her dressing table mirror. She put out a hand to steady herself, sat clumsily and studied the face looking back at her. It was a mess, a red-eyed, puffy mess and the kohl from the eyes had mixed with the tears and run down the cheeks. Her hair was dishevelled, half ruffled, half unpinned and the dress, her lovely lemon coloured day dress with silk bows, was crumpled. "Nobody in the world'd want me like this. See here..." she held up her hair. "And look at this," she pulled at the short sleeves of her dress. "Oh, heaven's, Daisy, I look and I feel a wreck...I just don't know where I'm going in the world." Her hands flew to her face again. "Oh, dear God," she wailed. "I do try...I really *do* try."

"Listen, ma'am." Daisy was by her side. "Bain't no good getting' all maudlin'...got to pull yerself together. Come on now. Us'll talk after you've rested." She helped her get undressed and bathed her before easing her into bed and drawing the curtains. Then she sat for a while holding her hand until the breathing steadied, rising to leave only when her mistress turned over and curled up like a child. Looking down she stroked the long waves of fair hair, now brushed and settled once more, and pulled the sheets over the bare shoulders. It was Sarah's father, Mr Kingdon, who had first seen the signs. He and his wife, Emma, had asked Daisy to tea when they told her about Her Ladyship's sister, Mary, and how the drink had got to her. Daisy said little but listened and agreed that their daughter was lonely.

She tiptoed out of the room, closing the door behind her. Now would come the questions from the kitchen and staff room. Mr Locke would, no doubt, wish to see her and Mrs Carver would pretend that she knew more than she did. But she would say nothing; butler and housekeeper or not, it was none of their business. Daisy took a deep breath and adjusted her mobcap.

＊

For a moment, the drawing room at Bremridge was silent. Wilmot sat with his chin resting on the tips of his fingers. His face was glum. He seemed lost for words and shook his head slowly. Somebody was going to have to do it. Frederic stood leaning against the fireplace. Durnford Morgan was standing next to him while Elizabeth-Jane and Rebecca were together on the deep, mahogany sofa with the scroll end. Florence sat opposite.

"However it's done, it will have to be done tactfully and sympathetically. I insist." Elizabeth-Jane had both hands on top of the Malacca cane in front of her. "The last thing we want is for the girl to believe she's being got at or ostracised." Her hair, now stone grey, was swept back into a tight bun. Frederic looked at his mother. "We know there have been all sorts of unpleasant scenes," she continued, "but I'm of the opinion she's really a rather sad little thing."

"It's not going to be easy." Wilmot looked up. "Time and again the family's been made to cringe by these dreadful antics of hers." He lifted his hands and shrugged in exasperation. "Each time it's more an' more difficult to be charitable, and sometimes she drives me wild...I get absolutely livid. I mean, her behaviour in Barnstaple towards Florence was quite unacceptable and from what Sebright told us when he introduced Anna...that was pretty awful, too." He swivelled himself in his chair and eased his leg. "It's not as though she's a child anymore....she'll be thirty-five in a few months and should have got all this nonsense behind her by now."

"I know, I know...we all know what's gone on, Wilmot, dear." Elizabeth-Jane inclined her head. "But some people just can't cope with things and it tends to get worse. We've got to face reality." She looked at her son. "But I'm not sure I like your idea, Freddie."

"Alfred?" Frederic walked across to the sideboard. He lifted the decanter and nodded his head this way and that. "It was only a very long shot," he mused. "And in any case he's devilishly tied up with his own affairs. He's got appalling family problems of his own, y'know, and I really can't see how we could ask him." He glanced back over his shoulder. "It's pretty..."

"What?" Wilmot looked up sharply. "Alfred Tennyson? Is that who you were thinking of? Absolutely not...it's out of the question. We've got to keep this within the family. Come on, Freddie, that's ridiculous."

"Well, now, wait a moment." Frederic half turned with the decanter in his hand. "Alfred told Jack he knew something was amiss and that he'd help if he could. Jack's been upset by it all, more than most of us; swears blind he saw it all coming way back. And he and Alfred get on so well. He *could* do it, you know...and he'd be very good. Sarah's always liked him and...well, it would get me off the hook."

229

"You're not on the hook, dear boy." Wilmot lifted a hand. "Never have been. Not you and certainly not Alfred." He pursed his lips, looked down at his hands then suddenly up again. "Well...I'll do it myself. I won't enjoy it and neither will Sarah but it's got to be done."

"What about her parents? Surely she sees something of them?" Rebecca lifted herself to straighten her skirts. "Well, does she...in South Molton, I mean?"

"Mother and daughter, my dear." Elizabeth-Jane raised her eyebrows and put a hand on Rebecca's arm. "Like tinder and flame, the pair of them. Hopefully Jessica will spare you all that but when it's difficult it's really very difficult. Look at my Isabella...goodness me." She raised a hand to her head. "No, I'm afraid that poor Emma finds it very hard with both of them; always has, ever since they were little girls."

"You're the one, Wil." Frederic, still standing, nodded towards him. "D'you know that? If she takes it from anyone it'll be you."

"Be careful, dear." Elizabeth-Jane spoke quietly. "I know exactly what you young are thinking but she's very much one of the family. Whatever's happened has happened and I urge you to go gently. There's another Sarah there and I'd hate her to be hurt by it all...it'd be dreadful. She's just as special as the rest of you."

"She's certainly that," Durnford Morgan interjected. "But y'know, for all these tidal waves of hers she's a remarkable young lady."

"No, I'll be fine." Wilmot smiled thinly at Elizabeth-Jane. "I suppose I know her as well as anyone...and Heavens, yes," he shrugged. "I can but try and if I have your mandate then I'll see what can be done." And so it was decided.

2

Sebright lay back under the hedge with his arms behind his head. They were on the higher side of the field, facing south, and below them the land fell away towards Sherdon Water. It was the late May sunshine which had encouraged the bee to inspect the first of the foxgloves in the bank behind him, and he listened as the little creature made its way about in a business-like manner.

Anna sat cross-legged beside him, frowning in concentration. Most of the flowers they had picked were in her lap and she was weaving together the last of the marsh buttercups and red campion to make the base of her garland. On their way down from the farm they had stopped to gather bunches of sky blue speedwell, red campion and daisies. They had even found a half-hidden clump of late bluebells. She muttered angrily at her fumbling before raising a stem to her mouth and biting. Finally she was ready and held out her handiwork, examining it critically with her head to one side. "There you are, my swain, a crown for your queen."

"Let's see." Sebright half sat with one hand raised against the sun. He watched as she tidied the flowers before passing the garland across. "Here," he gasped, reaching out then laughed as he settled further and leaned towards her. "Lower your head, ma'am…there…ooops, stay still…there we are." Anna put both hands to her head while Sebright, now close beside her, pushed back a curl of her hair.

"Here," he whispered, lifting her chin and bending forward to touch her lips gently with his own. "It's very beautiful…like the queen herself."

Anna looked at him and took his hand, then stopped. "Don't move. There's a beetle or something." She bent forward to inspect his collar then blew. "Gone," she cried, brushing the inside of his shirt in case the intruder was still there. Then she bent further, caressing his cheek briefly as she did so. "Thank you, kind sir. There you are…one fine compliment deserves another." He reached for her but she swayed back. "*One* compliment…that's enough for now."

For a moment they were silent, both of them again thinking about what Kitty had said after lunch. Jack and Frank had gone up to Sixty Acres and the two of them were helping her clear away. It was Kitty who had brought up the subject, asking them directly how long they thought they were going to remain like they were. "You mustn't stay waitin' fer ever, y'know." The exertion of clearing the table had tired her and she was sitting catching her breath. "You've got your own lives to lead and you must do as you see fit, not wait around for everybody to agree to your wants…they never will. Not everyone."

"Tell me, Kitty." Sebright had stopped what he was doing and leant on the table. "How on earth do you deal with a mother who likes to lay down the law but only by by hints and suggestions…who avoids being open about it but who's most subtle remarks come crashing down like hammers. D'you know, sometimes it's almost as if she's laying down a list of prerequisites for anyone I'm thinking of befriending. What's a man s'posed to do…when it begins the moment I come in the front door and it goes on for day after day? Mmm?" He stood. "Tell me because I don't know."

"She only wants the best for you, m'dear. Anna an' I've been over it all time an' again, haven't we, love. All your mother wants is the right one for you."

"The right one for *her*, you mean."

"Well, fer you both, the same as all mothers do. I can see it, clear as day. You see, she's afeard that Anna's too tied up here at Sherdon…an' she's right. 'Fraid that she's becoming a right little country maid, all mud an' mools." She turned to Anna. "Trouble is, m'dear, as far as *Mrs* Knight's concerned, you'm still in the nest. Told you that afore an' 'til such times as you spread your wings nobody can see how you'll be flying."

She paused, breathless and looked from one to the other. "'That's what's worryin' yer mother, m'dear. So there'e are." She saw the look on Sebright's face and smiled but turned back to Anna once more. "An' you've got to show 'em, my love, just show 'em you've got they pretty colours on your wings, like you told me you did at Barnstaple. *Cuh*, I can imagine it...Lord Preston, as he were, an' all they lot. What'd I have given to see that. An' if that means Lunnon town fer a while an' fancy clothes an' that, then so it does. Exmoor'll still be here, y'know...it bain't goin' nowhere."

"But it's not just that, Kitty. It's leaving you and father." Anna remembered how she had left the sink and come across to join her. "Look at you, dear Kitty." As she pulled out the chair to sit beside her, so it had scraped loudly on the flagstones. "It's not just a question of walking out of here. We can't all take our leave as and when we like."

"Course ye can. Don't be so daft. That's just what it's all about as far as you'm concerned. Get yerself up an' away proper like, then Mrs Knight and all they lot will see you reelly are Lady Katherine's girl an' not some little flipperty-gibbet with clogs on her feet." And that had been her final word.

✻

"Well?"

"Well what?" Anna glanced at him out of the corner of her eye knowing full well what he was about to say.

"Kitty. She's right, isn't she?" Sebright pulled at a grass. "A wise, wise little person. She had mother exactly right, spot on. She knew precisely what's been going through her mind as if it were her own. And she was so right about Barnstaple, too. They loved you, all of them."

"Except my cousin." Anna picked at a nail.

"Sarah? Phoey...jealousy. Cold, bitter jealousy if ever I saw it. And that just proves what Kitty was saying. You caught all the looks, and the smiles and the nods...and Lady Preston didn't like it. Mid-thirties now, two children...with a waist that's starting to go and far too much rouge an' cochineal. Cruel, but that's mother nature for you." He shook his sleeves free and buttoned them at the wrist one at a time. "But d'you think you will be able to get away for a bit...I mean, d'you *want* to?" Sebright looked at her. "It's no good me trying to persuade you if you're deter-mined to remain here."

"Of course I do." She sounded hurt. "Yes, of course. I'd give anything to come away with you but it's just that, well," she shrugged. "At the moment things aren't easy here. You saw for yourself how Kitty is. She's so frail. I've got to wait a bit and be sure." Sebright nodded. "You do understand, don't you? Just a little more time."

"Yes." She caught his eye and he smiled at the worried look on her face. "Don't worry, I'll wait. Of course, there's no hurry." He put a hand up to her cheek.

3

Tam Newton grunted as he lifted the saddlebag from the table. The three hundred and fifty coins were heavy but they were all there, for he had counted them twice.

It had been a difficult plan to put together because it was going to take place so far inland, yet Mervyn Harper had been confident enough. Mervyn, Jasper's nephew, was a ruthless man even by the standards of those still doing the runs from France. Smuggling had become more risky these days, and often more violent than before because of the cognac. The runs began much further down the French coast and they used bigger boats, better seamen as well, to get back to Lundy Island. Once there, they took their time to bring it across in fishing smacks.

Mervyn Harper never said very much: his reputation did the talking. When the two trawlermen were found washed up last year, tangled in their nets, word was that Harper and another from Martinhoe knew more than they should. But the trail had gone cold and the boatman who found the bodies went missing so that had been that. In spite of it all, Harper still used Ilfracombe.

He trusted nobody and, once his merchandise was ashore, he took it inland himself, just him and one or two others with the ponies. He kept his contacts to himself but he knew the moor, he knew the people up there and he knew how to handle a horse. And he knew how to look after himself as well, of that there was no doubt. Tam Newton thought his long barrelled pistol was a cumbersome weapon but Harper swore by it and, as far as Newton was concerned, that was his affair.

Harper was a small, almost sickly looking man with a longish, grey face and a head of wiry, unkempt hair that might have been either fair or grey. But his body was steel, pure steel, as anyone who saw him working the high cliffs on the end of a rope, looking for gulls' eggs when half a gale was blowing would testify. Other than that it was money, or the lack of it, that brought him to life, just as it had done for his uncle Jasper and old Luke before him.

So, Harper would do the job and Walter Crick from 'The Admiral Lord Nelson' would be the Break in the chain. Crick was a waster and Jemmings the landlord wanted him out. There was no warmth between them so, for certain, no questions would be asked when it was all over. Twice now Crick had crossed Tam Newton. Tam had let it ride. He had gone soft on the man so they said, and the fat, bearded cellarman boasted about it. That was until Tam Newton paid him a visit a week ago. After that there were no more smiles. Whatever Tam Newton and Mervyn Harper wanted him to do, Walter Crick would now be happy to do.

✳

Tam Newton sat back. The most difficult part would be to get the Duke to talk to Crick but he would have to, and talk to him as often as was necessary. He reached into the bag and drew out a handful of coins, pausing for a moment to examine the Queen's head. He bit, rubbing his teeth into either side of the sovereign and then looked at the scratch marks they left. Gold and no mistake, and freshly minted at that.

He placed the first coin half way across the table – that was the Duke. The next was Crick, the fat, little cheat who was now blubbering with fright. The last in the line was Harper. Newton smiled. What a trio they were, but that was how the information would be got from one end to the other. The Duke would pass everything to Harper via Crick, the Break, and any questions from Harper would go back the same way. Everything would go from one to the other like that while he, Tam Newton, stood aside. He placed a fourth coin between Crick and Harper but a little way out. That was him and he, of course, would know nothing. His eyes would be shut and his ears covered – well, almost. And in any case while all this was going on he would be in La Rochelle buying brandy with his sovereigns.

If Walter Crick had double-crossed him twice then he would do so again: his sort always did. But Tam Newton wanted no more of it and bought the services of two others. Constable Morton, a solid enough man, knew about Crick and his ways but he knew Tam Newton better and had known him for years. From time to time money had gone one way and word about the Excise Men came back the other. It was barely a whisper but it worked. Morton would deal with Walter Crick.

✳

'The Exmoor Forest' tavern in Simonsbath is the first inn one comes across when travelling south across the high moors from the wild North Devon coast. For years wayfarers had stopped off for the night before moving on. Shepherds, miners, draymen and carters, Reg Mathews, the landlord, made them all welcome. Were it not for the village that was growing up around it, the inn would have been lost in such a wild and desolate place. Even so, the arm of the law rarely stretched that far; those responsible for maintaining order preferring instead the easier and softer worlds of Dulverton and South Molton.

Years before, Luke Harper had seen this when he heard that the landlords further south welcomed the chance to purchase brandy and tobacco without the nose of the excise men getting in the way. And what better place for them all to meet than The Exmoor Forest? The previous landlord had seen to it that such transactions made on his property were profitable, to everyone involved and to himself in particular. Now Reg Mathews saw things exactly the same way and it was not unusual for Mervyn Harper, the seaman from far off Ilfracombe, to be seen at the inn. He was there in July and twice in August, on the second occasion making the rare decision to stop over for the night. The ostler knew him also, sometimes changing horses for him but more usually taking in his tired animal while Harper dealt with the matters in hand.

*

The Reverend Tod Tucker could not have been happier. Only a month earlier his stipend had been increased and it was then that he learned from the suffragan Bishop of Taunton that he was to be in sole charge of the parish until well into the New Year. He was now approaching thirty and it was Kitty who told him that, with his hair tied back as it had been for a while, he was growing evermore like his father.

In addition Miss Brack at the school had had her contract extended. The school was expanding and she had told them that she would be happy to remain where she was. The farmers had had a good summer and tomorrow, Sunday September the fourth, was Harvest Festival. He found himself humming the 'Te Deum' as he wanted it played but stopped suddenly, embarrassed that one of those helping nearby was humming along with him. They both laughed.

"I think a few more apples and pears in that window, the first down from the pulpit…there look, Mrs Stephens. Can you manage it while I go and see about the corn?" Tod, dressed in his long, black preaching gown and with his hair flowing behind him, turned and ran down the porch steps and along the gravel path to where the cart had backed up to the gate. Albert Clapworthy and his brother Fred had brought the two sacks of corn as promised and, with them, their plough.

"One either side of the choir pews, Mr Clapworthy. That'll be marvellous. And roll the tops down so we can all see the wonderful corn. No doubt the mice'll have a go tonight," he grinned at the two farmers. "Should leave a bit for us, though. That's grand, just grand."

"Aye, vicar. An' the plough? Same place?"

"Yes, yes." Tod scratched his head. "Just in front of the altar, like last year. We'll get the children to bring up their flowers and produce during the first hymn." He was in his element. The Knights were staying in Simonsbath and although the flower show had been a month ago, Mrs Knight had run the usual garden competition and in an hour the villagers were due to bring in offerings of their produce. Lady Morgan, quite his favourite, would also be staying with Sir Durnford. Whenever she was up from Bremridge she always came and took communion with him.

Loaves of bread and two sheaves of oats were coming from Simonsbath Barton and the junior class at the school were making corn dollies to hand out after the service. Len Cockram, Mr Knight's water bailiff, had promised his usual basket of salted and smoked trout from the river and, this year, they would have salmon as well. Cheese was coming from Warren Farm and the honeycombs from Driver, together with two old hives to place in the porch. There was always far too much of everything but it was all going on to the Dulverton Poor House so he took in whatever was brought along.

St Luke's would be full and, after the service, they would walk down the hill in procession for lunch at The Exmoor Forest. For Tod it was to be a special occasion and the family had promised to support him. His aunt Emma was coming from South Molton. Victoria could not come from Molland, it was just too far, but everybody from Sherdon would be there together with his Uncle Wilmot and family from Court Hall.

*

First of all Mervyn Harper had to make sure. Walter Crick had passed on from the Duke what he thought was a fair enough description of his quarry but there remained some doubt. On the first occasion he had been told that the hair was black but then it had changed to grey. Six feet tall was one estimate of the height, but then it was claimed that he was only five feet eight and stooped at that. It was not good enough and he had to be certain.

It was on the second day that he saw him. It was raining in North Molton and for two hours the beggar had been standing leaning up against the church wall with a leg bent behind him, resting on a box. He had had to move carefully when he changed legs but nobody noticed and he was about to change again when the coach and four pulled up. It stopped only briefly before going on its way but the man who got off was the one he wanted to see. Five eight or nine he was but there was no stoop, rather a bad limp in the lower right leg, helped along by a heavy walking cane. As he entered the tailor's shop at the bottom of the square, he took off his top hat and Harper saw the hair. It was dark, once black perhaps, but now peppered grey and it was lank. Just as he went through the door, Sir Wilmot Tucker swept back a lock that had fallen forward. It had to be him for the rest of the description fitted.

He waited for several minutes after the man had come back out of the shop and walked past him through the tall gates at the front of his drive. He never gave him a glance, rather he hurried on with his head down and a worried frown on his face. What was more he never put as much as a groat into the cap he had in the road beside him. The shame of it.

Everything else was set. His horse would be fresh and there would be a spare mount saddled and waiting in the ostler's yard. His weapon had been tested, twice. The little skinning knife he always carried in its sheath at the small of his back had been honed to the touch. Were anything to go wrong and they were to catch him then he would resort to his trusty little friend. It had worked well before. It was going to be a long, hard ride off the moor so, once the service had begun, he planned to set free any horses tied up by the church gate in order to buy himself some of the time he needed. That night he slept well: others were not so fortunate.

*

Whatever was left of the moon that Saturday night was not due to rise until gone three in the morning. A slight, chill drizzle, little more than a mist, came in off the sea as two men wended their way across the shingle and over the rocks towards Wilders Mouth. It was only a mile from Ilfracombe, it had gone midnight and, although they could just about see, the night was at its blackest. But, tonight, Conrad Morton, the officer from the North Devon Constabulary was not about Her Majesty's business, nor was Mat Bright, his companion. They were on their way to square the books for their friend.

"Count it out and count it with care. Here you are." Conrad Morton squatted down on his haunches and opened the bag, spilling the coins into the shallow cleft in the rocks. "Take yer time and count steady, mind, for there bain't no more." As Morton rose, Walter Crick squatted and wiped his hands. Mat Bright moved next. Before Crick's eyes had even seen the gold, his head was twisted round sharply. He tried to call out but Morton had him by the waist. "The pool quick," Morton grunted. The two of them stretched him out and forced his head into the rock pool. It was only a few inches deep. "Twice now and hard...helps him to breathe proper." Bright wrenched back the head and drove the face hard down onto the jagged rocks, hard enough to feel the nose and jaw splintering into the face under his hand. The scream, when the head came out, was cut short as the face was driven back into the rock pool, this time to remain there.

It took them half an hour to wrap the body in the weighted tarpaulin and the same time again to reach the blowhole high on the point. After lifting him up the two stood swaying and gasping for breath, one either side of the crevasse. Far away beneath them they heard the muffled rumble and hiss as the swell from the tide pumped water into the deep cleft. At a nod they moved together and listened again as the body bounced twice against the sides. They barely heard the splash but, no matter for they had dealt with the Break exactly as Tam Newton had demanded.

✳

The first thing that Mervyn Harper noticed was wrong the following morning was that the coachmen had collected by the rail where the horses were tied. They had gathered together under the rowan tree by Simonsbath church gate and there was no way he was going to be able to cut the animals loose. He swore silently but nodded to the two or three who looked his way as he turned up the long church path. He could hear singing up ahead, for the service had begun, but he slowed by the stone bridge to retie his boot. It would give him time to think. As they chatted away among themselves, some of those he had just passed kept looking his way. They were watching him, only casually it appeared but not quite casually enough.

No matter, for the door was near the back of the church and he would make his final check in the porch and out of sight. Somewhere in the first three pews he was told, that is where he would be. Earlier, from the edge of the spinney, he had watched the congregation arriving in their small groups and had seen him. His limp gave him away but it was his pale grey frock coat and checked trousers that were important for it would be his dress that would identify him when the moment came.

The back of the church would be no place to shoot from so, just before he retired last night, he had gone around to the far side where he identified the window closest to the front pews. It was too high so he made himself a stand out of a nearby pile of logs. He tested it and then removed a small diamond-shaped pane of glass from the window. The field of fire was good but he had to go back into the church in order to stack fruit and vegetables around the open pane to shield himself from wandering eyes whilst he was taking aim.

Once inside the porch Mervyn Harper paused, waiting until the congregation had been told to kneel. Then he opened the door while the coughing and scraping of feet muffled the click of the catch. He needed only seconds to confirm the location of the man he wanted. Only one person looked up at him, a big, rough sleepy looking countryman: he smiled but the man looked blank. As he left the church so he shut the door behind him quietly and stepped out, walking quickly yet quite openly around to the far side.

It was when he turned the corner and was making for his firing position, that the church door opened again. But he was too far away and never heard it. Harry Tucker, home on leave for the weekend, did not like the look of the man who had just smiled at him. Moments before, the newcomer had been scowling as he looked around and the smile he gave had been a mite too quick. What was more the fellow had backed away almost as soon as he came in as though he did not wish to be seen. Something wasn't right, indeed something looked very wrong and he got up to follow whoever it was, just in case.

Harper saw his target immediately, as soon as he had climbed onto the pile of logs, and it was while he was easing the long barrel of his pistol through the open windowpane that Harry Tucker turned the corner and saw him. The assassin licked his lips. He took hold of the stock in both hands then held his breath and half closed his eyes. As he took up pressure on the trigger, Harry shouted and ran forward. Harper flinched. It was a mere fraction before he fired but it was enough and his foot slipped causing him to stumble. Even as he ducked away he could see the figure closing in on him. He jumped, slipped and almost fell but picked himself up and began to run.

Initially Tod felt no pain but something kicked him hard in his right thigh causing him to stagger and half fall against the lectern where he had been standing waiting for the singing to finish. Later they found the spot on one of the heavy tiles where the musket ball had ricocheted before hitting him. It had struck the floor only a couple of feet from where Sir Wilmot Tucker had been standing.

The chase would never have been successful had not Harper's horse stepped into a rabbit burrow. The bay gelding stumbled heavily and its rider was thrown. Harry was way behind but he had taken the spare horse from the ostler and had started to give chase when he saw the fall. The man had been hurt but was making his way across the field so Harry rode at him. The horse knocked him to the ground but he got up again whereupon Harry rode him down once more, this time trampling over the body. By the time he had dismounted, the man had reached the hedge, but he was limping badly and turned as Harry closed on him. The soldier saw the knife but he was a mite too late. As his arms crossed to block the stroke, so the blade sliced through his heavy tweed sleeve and into his arm.

The first blow from the bare-knuckle fighter sent Harper flailing against the bank, the second drove him to the ground. Before he could move, Harry's knee was against his throat. Harper felt himself lifted and thrown half into the air before he was caught and pinned against the wooden railings in front of the beech hedge. He could not move and as his back was being bent further and further over the rails so he cried out. He tried to wrestle the man away to use his legs but they were pinned.

"Now, my beauty, us'll see." The words came quietly for the great brute was breathing steadily. "Talk or die, my little sunshine. Talk or die, simple as that." Harper was picked up again. This time he was hurled against a fencing post, then again for a second time. The wind went from him, then a rib broke and he felt the searing pain. Then a second bone snapped and it was his scream that brought the giant to a halt. The two were looking at one another. Harper, his face twisted in pain and forced back by the hand at his throat, was sneering, not in rage but in fear. Harry Tucker, red-bearded and foul-breathed was glaring down at his victim. "Now then. Us'll try again. Talk to Harry Tucker, my little friend, or it'll be your back first, and then your neck."

The terrible thumping began again but there were voices. Men were shouting, several of them. Harper was aware of two of them wrestling with the man on him but still he was picked up and thrown like a rag doll. The world became hazy. First he saw the branches of a tree spinning above him then the grass where his feet should have been. Then branches once more, then blackness. Harry dropped his victim to the ground and turned. "Cuh, the very devil," he cursed. "Damned fellow cut me new coat right up." He held up his arm. " 'Ere, look. Cut me right up so he did."

"Got you, too," a voice shouted.

"There's blood, Harry. Your arm's been cut...looks nasty."

"Damned fella." Harry turned his arm up and pulled at his blood-soaked shirt. "Bain't got no respect. Cuh...no damned respect fer nothing at all."

4

"*No* idea? That's a likely tale." Luncheon in The Reform Club would be in twenty minutes and the three men were sitting on one of the red leather sofas behind the bar in the hall. "You honestly mean to say that a fella comes up and tries to murder you in broad daylight...picks you out, and in church at that...and you've got no idea what it's all about? Oh...come *on* now."

"That was Sir Wilmot Tucker's line. Sir James Masterson's a damn good Defence

Counsel but he couldn't budge the man. Tucker swore blind that he'd never seen the fella, never heard of him and never heard of the character that was s'posed to have set it all up. No idea at all." The second diner, tall and urbane, drained his glass and summoned a waiter. "But it's not as though they're trying to get *Tucker* for God's sake…he was the poor chap this lot were after."

"Agreed." The third of the trio, both the shortest and most shabbily dressed, put his glass on the waiter's tray. "But they've got to start from somewhere and apart from being a prime witness, as well as the most likely target, Masterson was convinced that our good Sir Wilmot Tucker must have known what was behind it all…for that would have helped his case."

"But he didn't," the second man added. "Didn't know a damned thing."

"Well, there you are…David Prime and his prosecuting team are about the best in the business and they fairly pinned it on the guilty so and so."

The tallest of the three leant forward and raised a finger. "But I'll bet you that Sir Wilmot Tucker, chairman of one of the country's biggest shipping lines, knows a damned sight more than *that*." One of the others shrugged and their companion reached for a silk handkerchief.

"Well, apparently not and that was the end of it…attempted murder and the wretch…that Harper fellow'll hang for his troubles."

"And the motive?"

"Oh…a grudge. It came out in court that the man used to work for Tucker at Bideford…until he was sacked."

"Didn't Harper claim he knew the family…Wilmot Tucker's brother? A farmer or something?"

"Pretended to but Sir Wilmot would have none of it." The three of them turned as the waiter returned with their glasses.

Chapter Eighteen

William Gladstone was tired and it showed; Wilmot could see that yet even as he watched, the fire began to return. It had been a hard winter since Benjamin Disraeli and his Conservatives swept back to power in February. At first many believed that the years in office had drained the sixty-five year old but here he was joking again with his friends, his deep-set eyes twinkling behind the usually lugubrious façade. Business in the House that morning had been a noisy affair and the ex-Prime Minister had enjoyed himself.

"If Freddie Knight goes on like that they'll have to gag him." Sir James Caird, wiry, shrew-like and alert as ever, looked from one to the other. Only last week his Cambridgeshire constituency had been hit by the agricultural workers' strike, an event that sent ripples of alarm coursing through rural England. More than that, stories about the new union were filtering through to Westminster, setting fire to the debate on the importation of foreign food. Frederic had spoken out passionately against the proposed raising of quotas of foreign imports, claiming that rural life was withering away and that thousands dependant upon agriculture were being forced out of a livelihood.

"What d'you reckon, Wilmot? Our man from Exmoor let fly right enough. Eh?" Gladstone hitched his trousers and reached for the tall silver coffee pot. "Both barrels and spot on," he chuckled. The Reform Club was packed out, many having come into town hoping to witness the beginning of the Liberal fight back. There had to be two sittings for lunch and the whole place, in William Gladstone's opinion, resembled some hysterical school reunion. The four had decided to escape the throng and were taking coffee in the quiet, book-lined Committee Room off the mezzanine floor landing. Not only was it quieter than anywhere else but they could talk freely - as good friends should be allowed to do.

Wilmot stretched his leg. "That's our man, all right. Get Young Knight on to the lot of the farming community and he's away. Mind you, he's always been like that...remember his arguments last month about the Poor Law and its various rates...or whatever they were. Our good friend, the Prime Minister, was damned glad of some support from his own back benches and Freddie did him well there, too."

"Support for what?" Sir Thomas Gibson, still with his blond mane at sixty-one but now heavier and redder in the face, cocked an eye. "Suez and what have you?"

"Well, that and the whole business of British shipping being reined in over food imports." Wilmot grimaced at the memory of his own industry being used as the whipping boy. "It's a very fine line and there's no way that people in the business're going to stand back while the home market's screaming out for cheaper and better food...and it's all out there waiting to be shipped in. If we don't do it ourselves then the damned French will…or the Americans. And what are we going to do? Mmm?" He looked from one to the other. "Blockade ourselves in with the navy, I suppose, while the rest of the world gets on with moving commerce about all over the place?" He scowled at the idea. "Huh, what madness is that? No, I'm sorry but we're going to have to find a balance. I'm a farmer myself and we're all feeling the pinch, certainly down in Devon."

"What about this strike of yours, Jim…Newmarket, isn't it?"

For over a week news had been of markets being picketed and labour withdrawn from farms. In Newmarket itself a crowd of more than two hundred had marched on the town hall. Pickets had been checking produce on market stalls and anything that looked remotely foreign had been destroyed on the spot. The result was ugly: fighting between farmers and wholesalers, suspicion and distrust everywhere. Similar incidents had broken out in Saffron Waldon and Bury St Edmunds.

"Oxford and Wantage…Swindon, too." Sir Thomas Gibson, High Sheriff of Oxfordshire caught Gladstone's eye. "Your old parish, William, and there's news of rumblings further north as well. What about the West Country, Wil?"

"Not that we've heard of yet.…"

"Freddie'll let us know, all right." Gladstone threw his head back and laughed silently. "Oh dear, yes. One squeak from down there and he'll be on his feet, blasting away with order papers windmilling about. But no, I agree with Wilmot, we've got to tread carefully." Gladstone eased himself up in his chair. "They're far too many…far too many members who just don't understand what life out there's like. Either that or they don't *want* to know. But it's difficult to blame them, and there's a point, y'know." Gladstone raised a warning finger. "If you're member for South Oldham or Wigan then you've got several thousand redundant cotton workers on your hands. Well, they've no money and they've all been bellyaching like mad about the price of food…so you're not going to get much sympathy by telling them that the poor old farmers deserve every penny of it. They expect something to be done."

"Trouble is that the farmers don't get every penny…in truth they're getting precious few pennies. It's the men in the middle, just as Freddie said in yesterday's debate. The farmer, the man who rears the beast ends up getting less for his cow than the price of leather on a half-decent pair of shoes." Wilmot stood and thought for a moment. "And that's the whole point of the argument. The wretched fellow who's out there in all weathers, flogging away rearing the cattle or growing the corn…they're the ones who're suffering. They get a fraction of what's paid for the stuff so it's no wonder they're terrified of all these cheap imports. Undercut them any more and they'll be starving…*lit*-erally starving while this great industrial nation of ours gets fat on cheap imports."

"Well…young Knight certainly got them thinking." For one so small, Sir James

Caird had remarkably angry eyebrows and luxurious, black sideburns. He sat forward eagerly, clasping his hands together. "Trouble is that as soon as most of 'em get into the dining rooms around the place they forget where it all comes from and just pick at the best of it."

"Well, let me tell you this, we ignore the situation at our peril." It was Gladstone's turn to rise and he levered himself laboriously out of his deep armchair. He pulled at his collar and walked to the window where he glanced down at Pall Mall, searching for nothing in particular. He sighed heavily, then turned and leant against the sill. "Just think about what's been happening on our doorstep these last few years. *Think.* Seems only yesterday that we were standing by and gawping while the Austrians and Prussians were at each other's throats. Then the French...took those awful drubbings at Woerth and Sedan, and then there was Paris. And the Turks're fighting anyone they can lay their hands on. It's a very unstable world out there and come the day we can't feed ourselves and have to rely on what we can bring in...well, *poof*," he lifted his arms. "We haven't got a Nelson in the wings waiting to see it all safely home, have we now?"

"Or a fleet."

"Exactly...exactly." Gladstone stabbed a finger at his three luncheon companions. "When we can no longer look after ourselves, when we're quite helpless then we deserve everything we get. Civilisation's two fundamental requirements...since the caves...have been food and defence. Everything else, gentlemen, everything else is subordinate to that and we've got to find a way through this mess or there'll be trouble."

2

Brad Stone was a big man, as big as his name suggested. He had worked the mills on the River Yeo since leaving school at twelve. Arthur Grant, the miller, liked big men. The sacks of corn coming in from the new threshing machines were heavier than the old ones they used to fill by hand, while the new hemp sacks he had been told to use for his flour were heavier still. The gantry needed big men, as did the filling room. However, sales had fallen and the Bridgewater Canal company was now running only two barges each week. London, so word went, had found better and cheaper corn from across the Atlantic. Bigger ships were bringing it in more economically and the new mills in the capital's docklands were producing it more cheaply than Arthur Grant could ever do.

He had been forced to cut back just as had the millers at Anstey, Morebath and Milverton. All the way along the Barnstaple to Taunton railway line, men had been laid off. And it had been the same at the woollen mills at South Molton and Dulverton. The new line had been in place for little more than two years yet it was already part redundant.

Brad looked at the four sitting around the storm lantern in the waiting room. None of them were now working, yet between them they had three wives and more than a dozen children and they looked hungry. They *were* hungry just as their families were. He could see it in their eyes and the way their clothes seemed to hang from their limbs. None had money so they poached. Everybody did, and it was that which had brought them together.

"Five hundred yards back down the line. Stop the train there, Harvey, where the track to Yeo Farm crosses the line. Driver knows to look out for the light. Just stand up when I blows the whistle an' swing the lantern too an' fro, gentle like. Not go swinging hard, mind, and he'll bring 'er to a stop right by 'e." Harvey Trant nodded. All three of his grandchildren were living with him and his wife in their two rooms while their father went looking for work. Poaching it had to be, but at the age of fifty-eight it was no longer easy and they all knew the penalties if they were caught.

"Then you, Len. You an'me'll take the two long racks o'rabbits. Nigh on fifty on each pole, mind, and there's two lots so they'm'll weigh a bit and us'll have to look sharp." Len Bowden, nineteen and still at home in South Molton, had been laid off for over a year. His job as a cattle drover at the market had gone. The numbers of animals coming through were no longer enough to give him work so he, one of the youngest and unmarried, had been the first to go. His last pay packet had been a sorry affair…seven of the ten shillings going straight to his mother.

"And the venison's back in the wood? Yeah?" Brad Stone looked at Smales. "Where it comes right down to the line, right in close, both sides, like?"

"Aye," Tom Smales nodded. The three deer carcasses had been cleaned and prepared. They were lighter like that and the guards on the trains preferred them that way. Two had been easy enough to find but they had had to fight for the third, an old hind. Somebody else, a man from Molland, had been after the same beast. He had shot first but only wounded the animal and Wes Smales, Tom's brother, had finished her off. The other man, bald and sunken-eyed, had fought hard for the carcass but had been no match for the two brothers. "Aye, clean an' ready. Us've got them in the culvert under the line…one on the higher side." He pointed from where he was sitting, half turning and gesturing back down the line.

"We'll need them up wi' the rabbits then. Get everything ready in the same spot, hundred paces back from where Harvey stops the engine. Be a little whiles yet." As he slipped his father's old steel-cased watch back, Brad Stone was thoughtful. Should the guard pay well, and he would have to pay handsomely, they would be all right. But, only if he did. Far more likely would be the same old story that the guards were having to watch out for themselves and the butchers from Smithfield gave no more than a frown for what they were offered. There was always an excuse from somewhere up the line.

✳

"One hundred an' eighty five." Brad stood by the open door and looked up at the boots of the guard. Tall though he was, he barely came to the level of the floor of the guards' van. The guard seemed less than interested and was already muttering about signalling the driver to move on. The figures standing on the track beneath him were still gasping for air having had to run more than a hundred yards along the track weighed down by their fare. "Thrupence each," Jed panted. "That's two pounds, twelve shillings an' three pennies."

"One pound, ten shillings." The guard held out the lantern to see the faces more clearly. "One, ten. That's yer lot."

"Damn and blast, man." Brad looked up but could see nothing beyond the boots in front of his face. Further up the track, the engine hissed impatiently; somewhere a coupling squeaked and groaned as a truck settled. "That's tuppence a skin...us can't never break even at that. Say two, two pound...give us two pounds. Us've got mouths to feed, y'know."

"One pound twelve then, an' that's my last...what's of yer venison then?"

"Three...all clean and near on twenty seven stone between 'em. Seven pounds's a fair price. That's what us agreed last time."

"Let's be seein' them." The lantern lowered. "Hmm. Four pound an' that's it."

"For mercy's sake. 'Tis first class meat, man, an' taken yesterday. 'Tis the best there is."

"Four pounds, ten shillings. That's it or we're on our way." Another lantern with a green filter appeared above their heads. Jed heard them talking. "Four, ten an' one pound twelve that's...that's six pounds an' two shillings in all for the lot. Right?"

"Goddamned robber."

"Hush, Tom." Brad Stone cricked his neck looking up into the dark. "Make it six pounds and ten shillings, man. Us've got wives and chillern, y'know...an' bain't got no work nor nuthin."

"Six pounds and two, 'tis. Here." A hand was held out. Jed tried to see the face while reaching out for the money. Above him a green lantern was already waving and a whistle blew. "Here, take it...that's all there is." One by one the couplings clanked as each truck took up the strain. Silence came quickly as the train moved off, the three rear lights of the guard's van showing clearly until the next bend snuffed them out. The five left on the track trudged wearily back to the waiting room.

3

June that year blazed as hot as Jack could remember. They waited in vain for rain to sweeten the grass that had been left for hay but in vain. The crop was thin with the stalks only half grown and they were forced to cut early, almost on top of shearing. By then the sheep were suffering from the heat. Jack lost several while the flock lay panting, packed together wherever they found shade. They opened the gates above the river, letting them roam freely and to drink whenever they wanted but, by the end of the month, Sherdon Water had dried to little more than a trickle running between stagnant pools.

Every window and door at the farm was open in an effort to catch whatever breeze there might be. In the hall, the dogs lay lethargically on the flagstones just out of the sun's reach, unwilling to move even when somebody going to work stepped over them. The level of the well had dropped and Jack decreed that only water for the house would be drawn. And the garden, or rather what had not died already, was kept alive by Frank and Anna bringing pails of water tapped from the spring in the field beneath the house. Even in the usually chill grey hour before dawn, those who could sleep lay naked and restless on top of their beds.

The last of the shearing clothes had been boiled and Kitty had shaken them out before spreading them along the top of the low wall by the shippon. They seemed heavier than ever and Frank had got through three pairs of thick cotton trousers, each pair greasy with lanolin from the wool. She had to boil them twice, adding more soda than usual until at last she was satisfied. She walked slowly towards the shade of the shearing barn, now quiet at last, and dropped her wicker basket and bag of pegs. Then she turned slowly, threw down her straw hat and sat, resting her back and head against the wall, easing herself until she found a spot free of sharp edges.

She had not dared mention it but the coughing and pains were returning. Twice, when bringing tea and scones to the shearers, she had had to stop. She reached round her chest, took a deep breath and lifted her other arm. It was still there. Jack would have to know but only when they had finished the hay.

For a moment she rested, her eyes closed and body relaxed, listening to the silence. She felt for her hat, picked it up and fanned herself, lifting her chin to catch the slight zephyrs of warm air. A few matted strands of red-grey hair on her forehead wafted from side to side but that was all and she wiped the back of her hand across her brow before letting both arms fall listlessly. She savoured these few precious minutes but knew she had to get on. The eggs had to be collected and there was more bread in the oven to check. Half rolling onto her knees, she clambered to her feet but, no matter how she tried, the sharp stab of pain returned as if it had been hiding and waiting for that moment. She caught her breath and bent forward to ease the discomfort, steadying herself against the wall before moving on.

*

It was Frank who found her. Luckily and for no apparent reason he glanced into the hen house on his way back to the hay meadow. She was half sitting, crouched against the wall with her body curled up. Anna had come up from the field to collect another hayfork and the two of them helped her into the kitchen. "You're *not* all right, Kitty." Anna squatted by her chair holding a glass of water. "Honestly, it's no good pretending any more. You're not at all well…we all know it and there's no need to worry about father. He knows, or at least he suspects you're poorly 'cos he was talking about it to Arthur Fisher and Gaile at lunch."

Kitty nodded and put a hand to her brow. "'Tis a real useless business, and now at this time an' all. Feels's though I'm burdenin' myself…just another problem fer you all to worry about."

"Nonsense. Heavens, Kitty, don't even think like that. Here look, I'll cool you down." She rinsed one of the sink cloths in cold water then mopped her face while Kitty, her eyes closed, raised her head to meet the refreshing coolness. "I'm going to get you upstairs and onto your bed until Dr Bailey comes."

"*Him?*" she started. "Oh, fer mercy's sake who's gone about the doctor when there's a deal enough to be done outside."

"Shush, stop it. Now come on, let me give you a hand." Even as she helped her, Anna could feel and hear the breath rasping. She seemed so light and frail, barely able to help herself but at last they were there and she lifted Kitty's legs onto the bed.

"Thank'e, love." Kitty took her hand and Anna sat beside her. "What a to do but us'll manage. Gaile said her would come over when you's up in Lunnon next month."

"We'll see, Kitty."

"See about what?" Kitty lifted her head then grimaced in pain before lowering it once more. "See about what, eh? I don't want no talk about you putting it off just because of this y'ere."

"I said we'll see. There's heaps of time to be doing all that…all the time in the world and Sebright'll be happy enough to wait."

"Don't, dear. Don't go stoppin' an' startin' no more…you'll lose the man else. Honest." She struggled to sit up. "You go, my love. 'Tis a chance of a lifetime an' I've told you before he's a loverly young man…a real gentleman like his dad, so don't go testin' 'im. Anyways he loves you dearly, us can all see that."

"Then he can wait a bit." Anna adjusted herself on the bed and squeezed Kitty's hand. "I'm very fond of him too but nothing on earth's going to take me from you all when there's so much to be done. I'm part of the place, you know. I was born here and I love it, so that's that." She saw Kitty looking at her, then reached out and felt her forehead. "Kitty, you're hot…I'll go and get the cloth." At the door she turned and smiled reassuringly.

Kitty lifted a hand but it was to somebody else. Years ago another person used to turn at the door and smile like that, somebody else who gave up everything for Sherdon. It was the girl's mother all over again and she could see her so clearly. Time and time again she used to watch Katherine and wonder how it was that such a beautiful person, one who had everything, could forsake it all for a life where sheep and cattle, and hens and turnips came first. Where there was no escape from the washing tubs or stew pots, or the lashing gales, the driving rain and the deep clinging mud, or the harsh winter frosts when everything was frozen hard.

Kitty closed her eyes and turned her head. The girl was not going to leave; she could sense it. Perhaps it really was because of her love for the place. But perhaps the child was desperate to get away yet could not bring herself to go while something was wrong. She must be torn. Kitty sighed. It was so hard on young Anna and so unfair on them all that she, Kitty, should be lying here like this when she should be up and about, laughing and scolding and hurrying to and fro. Yet she was none of it, just a dead, useless weight. A tear fell, running straight to the corner of her mouth, then another. By the time Anna returned she was lying curled on her side, both hands to her face.

The girl stopped in the doorway. Sebright, she knew, would never understand, not now and no matter how much he tried. She could see his look of anguish. He would stretch out his arms and pull her to him but it would be to no avail. She knew he loved her but her own feelings remained mixed. He made her happy, she longed for his company and was always saddened when he had to leave. If that was love then love it was but how could she tell? Maybe the next man, if there was to be another, would make her feel the same. Would that also be love? How could it be, how could she love first one and then another? Or was there something deeper and more binding that she was supposed to feel? So perhaps her desire for Sebright was nothing more than how one good friend might long for the company of another. Quite simply she did not know. She put a hand to her face frowned unconsciously, shaking her head in uncertainty. But one thing was for sure; she would stay and see this through. And after that? She shrugged.

4

Damon Hartley thought about leading the dark bay out of the stable to finish the grooming outside but decided against it; it was too hot and the flies were bad. The mare was Sir Wilmot's largest horse, one of his favourites and he had insisted on riding her again today. The young second groom would be escorting his master, riding Barnwell the chestnut with the two white socks and thin blaze, and they were due to leave in half an hour. The mare pushed at him with her brow, blew and shook her head.

He knew Whitechapel Manor well. If they went along the Twitchen road and down Folly Lane the journey would take little over the hour. Sir Wilmot had been asked for lunch and he knew that he, Damon, would be looked after also. Malcolm Locke would be sure to ask him in for a bite when he would be able to catch up on the gossip. Damon Hartley, slim and with his brown beard neatly trimmed, whistled cheerily.

*

Wilmot was in a reflective mood; the face that scowled back at him from the hall mirror told him that. Rebecca had left for Barnstaple earlier, leaving him to clear his mind over what had to be done. He had decided to work in the library where Steer had brought his coffee. It was lighter there, even so they had moved the oval writing table closer to the window. His sight was getting no better and he now needed the light. As he picked through the books, he kept changing position to see better. His hair, longer and grey-flecked, fell untidily over his winged collar, due partly to him scratching in frustration and partly because he had forgotten to have it cut.

The two days spent at Sherdon last week had been their usual wonderful escape, although he had been saddened at the news of Kitty and shocked at how frail she appeared. She was better now but the pleurisy had taken its wicked toll. Anna, he thought, was the very image of her mother in those surroundings and Frank, though shorter and broader, and with a more prominent nose, was exactly as he remembered his father at that age. And as for the man himself, Jack had looked well enough. The drought had been a worry and the cause of yet more work but he looked fit. Age was taking its toll and, even in the last couple of months, he seemed to have lost a bit of weight around his face.

Their ride down Sherdon Water to where it ran into the Barle had been a moment to savour. They had been alone and talked freely about the family, first about Lottie then their neice. The young woman had been causing a stir, of that there was no doubt. However the bad news had managed to reach as far as Jack. It had caused him to become hurt and angry, unable to comprehend how any member of the family could behave in such a manner. Never one to go quietly through life, Sarah was bursting through one door with a crash while the last slammed shut behind her.

"Beg pardon, sir." The butler rose on his toes and pulled at his lapels. "Hartley'll be round the front in a minute or so."

"Ah, fine…thank you Mr Steer." Wilmot sat up and began to collect his papers together. "I'll be along shortly."

"Very good, sir."

*

Lunch had not been easy but less strained than earlier when he found her very prickly and edgy. Sarah was defensive so he decided, and suspicious of his visit, her replies coming abruptly as though she were a child blurting out some silly excuse for this or that. She had indeed taken wine with the meal so perhaps the rumours about drink had some foundation yet she seemed easy enough when he declined her offer, preferring spring water instead. And there were signs of age, of course there were, but of age rather than drink. After all she was the mother of two lively youngsters, the younger of whom, Amelia, had shyly brought him a posy of half crushed wild flowers and with whom he was now helplessly in love. The gardens were enchanting and he was happy enough that she had decided to take coffee on the metal coalbrookdale under the willow beyond the summerhouse. From there the manor looked exquisite as it lay basking dreamily in the August heat. It was as though the place was making a special effort on her behalf, perhaps compensating for the awful Northboroughs who had caused such mayhem with his niece.

She left him briefly, walking briskly and purposefully back to the house, her endless nervous energy still pouring from her. Exhausting he thought; exhausting but intriguing. On her return, he rose and held her chair. "But I don't see why I should make the rounds of the family, uncle. If Jack's so worried about what he's hearing then he should come and see me. Why should I be the one to present myself here and there in order to satisfy people's curiosity…and anyway I really cannot be bothered."

" I suppose I could answer by saying that he is your uncle after all and now, at the age he is, he's custodian of the family. And he's worried…."

"Hmm."

"Oh yes, my dear." Wilmot stroked back a lock of hair, turned his head slowly and smiled. "He is the man of the family, you know. All of us acknowledge that, but it's a family he loves dearly and there's nothing more important than to be loved."

"Then how do you explain all this conflict with Sharland's family? The disasters…Lottie and Harry. I'm sorry but it was a dreadful business when that great buffoon came barging in here like he did…dreadful."

"I cannot answer that." As soon as he had mentioned Sherdon earlier, she had bridled sharply. He thought she was bound to bring up the mystery of the jewels, how her husband had come across the necklace, and her father-in-law's assumption about how it came to be there in the first place. But she had not. Perhaps she had forgotten about them or perhaps these other family matters were uppermost in her mind. "All I can say is that I have known my brother all my life and that these sad events hurt him deeply."

"And then there's this woman in his life. I've not met her but from all I've heard she seems to have pushed herself in and taken over…forced poor Lottie out of the place." She paused and raised a hand meekly before suddenly stiffening as if a thought had suddenly occurred to her. "And look." Sarah leant forward and rapped the table. "There's still all this ill feeling between Sherdon and my father-in-law. It's beastly…they've nothing in common, nothing whatsoever. In fact Bertie, that's Herbert, cannot but think darkly of him ever since he killed Kenton Knight in front of his eyes. What on earth do you expect…and there's never been the slightest hint of remorse." Wilmot inclined his head, acknowledging to himself that this would be brought up sooner or later. "And then…and then there's all the business about the shipping…about the loss of orders and the men and that sort of thing. It's been very, very difficult for me, you know uncle." Wilmot glanced sharply at the sound of her raised voice. "The devil himself knows what was going on but the Duke has been forced out of business and after all those ridiculous allegations in court he's left…gone for good. Gone back to Blagdon, and he really did love it down here."

"We were all dragged through the court, my dear. It was most unpleasant. Hard business is one thing but murderous intent is another."

"Well, I can't help that but you must surely see what a position I'm in, and I'm hardly inclined to go about begging forgiveness for goodness knows what." She paused flushed, her chest rising and falling sharply. "No, I'm sorry but until this visit of yours today nobody, *nobody* at all has had the decency to come and see me. I'm here…a woman on her own…what in God's name are they all trying to do to me?"

Wilmot looked down, his fingers toying with the metal leaf on the tabletop. He started to talk then stopped, considering further what to say. "Listen, my dear." His head was bent back towards her, making him look up with his eyebrows raised as if surprised. "I cannot persuade you otherwise, that I can see. All I can do is to come as one of the family…and, I had hoped, as a trusted friend of your sweet self. I came with nothing more than love and affection in my heart to pass on the worry that we have for you."

"You've told me that already, uncle. Twice now."

"And I'll tell you again." He sat up straight and turned towards her. "Do you honestly believe that I would come here and submit myself to this exchange were I not convinced…and were I not determined that some good may come of it. I've not come here to hurt you, my dear. I've come because I wish to promote a reconciliation…between all of you. That is why I am here." His eyes remained on hers even when he lifted his head and pulled slowly at his untidy apple-green cravat. "That's why, m'dear."

She was confused, he could see the doubt but there was also this stubborn pride. "Well, I'm simply not interested…and I'm certainly not going to do anything right now. I'm off to Hartland next week until the end of the month. It's not going to be easy after that, you know, living here with this atmosphere. Do they think that *I* have no feelings about it all? You're asking a lot of me to go up to Sherdon as though it's *me* that's the guilty party. What am I supposed to do, walk in wearing sackcloth and with head bowed? For Heaven's sake…what next? And I've never set eyes on this Kitty woman…I'd be walking into her home when her mind'd be full of all these charges against me. No…I'm simply not prepared to do it. Why should I?"

"Because I think you need to for your own good, my dear. There is a part of you that lies tucked away and about which, for some reason best known to yourself, you are afraid, ashamed of perhaps. No, wait…" he raised a hand. "Think about it. Think hard, that your uncle, Jack, who holds you so dear and who has faced life with such courage represents that other part of you. It is my contention that if you saw him for what he is and in his true light then you would see your other self…the real you, and that you would no longer be afraid. Really, I do. I honestly believe it to be so."

She shook her head. They were looking at each other, neither feeling the urge to drop their eyes. "I cannot say any more, uncle. Right now I want none of it. My mind is made up."

"But do not say no…neither to me nor to yourself. Ponder these things with care. I came here to seek nothing more and I shall leave well satisfied that you did not show me the door."

She was so strong and so resolute yet he could see the nervous insecurity underneath. They talked no more about it but when he came to take his leave he begged her, once again, to consider what he had suggested. It was sad and his heart was heavy for she was alone and, as he rode down the drive he rose three times to wave, the last just before he turned out on to the road. She was still standing in her doorway, but now her children were with her and all three waved in reply.

5

"Amelia…*seven*? My goodness me, where has that little girl gone?" Jocelyn Orchard was not the only one who could scarcely believe how time had passed and how the children had grown. "And Isaac *ten*…that shy, curly-headed little boy. Just look at him now." But it was Jocasta who shook Sarah. She was still the same fun loving, bubbly girl that her governess remembered but now she was nineteen. She was slimmer and taller and had just returned from Florence. In a few weeks time she would be away to London to stay with her uncle and aunt but, for the moment, they would be together at Hartland.

Sarah tried to persuade the Duke to join them but he had declined. He had not lost his appetite for shipping at all, rather he was more determined than ever and was looking at another business in Portsmouth. It was a huge, busy and well established port, far more congenial and he would be sure to find something there, he avowed. It was also closer to home from whence he could get back to Blagdon or strike out for London with considerably more ease than from far off Ilfracombe.

He had reminded her that, in just over a month, the London season would be underway and he would look forward to her company. So she had come to Hartland alone bringing Daisy, her maid, and the children's new governess. Eileen O'Shea came from Dublin. She was a generous, happy girl, bright and well read and one to whom the two children warmed immediately.

✳

Amelia and Eileen were singing. Daisy Price opened Lady Preston's bedroom door to hear better and smiled as the little girl kept faltering when the words escaped her then hurried along to catch up with the soft Irish voice. It was a beautiful lullaby, something about Galway and the River Shannon, one that Eileen sometimes sang to the child when the curtains were drawn and the lamp turned low. She glanced at the clock on the walnut chest-on-stand for they would be coming in a few minutes.

Amelia loved nothing more than to play with Sarah's jewellery and a routine had developed whereby, after a long day and if she had been good, she could spend a few minutes in her mother's bedroom when Daisy and Eileen would bring out the boxes and unlock them. Sometimes she would try them on and stand in front of the mirror turning herself to catch the light. At Blagdon and Whitechapel, Daisy held the keys in her room which was always kept locked but here at Hartland, where her mistress brought mostly her travelling jewels, Daisy kept the three little keys in an empty face cream jar on the dressing table.

"Come on, Miss Daisy." Amelia was by her side even as she was opening the lid of the ornamental porcelain jar. "It's the turn of the big ones tonight. You promised...come on, quickly," she whispered excitedly. Eileen joined them, still humming, and the three sat on the quilted bed covers, Amelia with her bare feet dangling over the edge and her toes rubbing against one another in anticipation.

The first brown leather case contained bracelets, trinkets and rings, most in their own presentation boxes but several simply wrapped in tissue. Eileen watched while Amelia, her blond hair still wet from her bath and now falling over her face, peered into the box as her fingers searched eagerly. "Whoa, whoa, steady there, Miss Amelia. You'll have them all on the floor. Here, look...look at this bracelet, it's all real gold. Give me you arm." Daisy bent down to fasten the clasp but the chain was too large. "You'll have to keep your hand up in the air....up like that. Now we'll find those two rings you like...the blue one, sapphires they're called and the one with the three white diamonds."

"Now the big ones." Amelia had returned from the mirror and watched carefully as the jewels were put away. "The ones in the black box. The one with two locks on it." She stared intently, following Daisy's every movement as she opened the black, badly scuffed leather case. "Can I see the necklace with the pearls and the red stones."

"Rubies."

"Yes, the one father bought for mama."

"Mmm hmm." Daisy nodded and lifted out the dark green oval case. Eileen and Amelia bent forward to watch her lift out the necklace, still wrapped in felt. "There we are...fit for a queen." Even as she held it up, the rubies, caught in the last rays of the September sun, twinkled and flashed. "Now then, off the bed and we'll make Her Majesty look beautiful. There now...turn around and keep quite still. *Right*...now go and look at yourself." The two women watched as Amelia stared at herself then, holding out the necklace, turned this way and that. They knew her mother had told her that the jewels were hers already but that she was far too young just now. She would wear them properly when she was presented at Court after her eighteenth birthday, twelve long years away.

"That'll be all fer tonight." Eileen rose from the bed. "Come along my little queen of fashion, 'tis to bed with ye now or you'll never be up in the mornin'. The little people'll be keeping hold of ye onder the sheets and I'll be in trouble with yer ma'am, so I will."

"One more song, Miss O'Shea." Amelia's head was one side. "Please, just one. Can we?"

"Just the one...but after your prayers. Away with yer now and get yerself ready and oi'll be there in a trice."

✽

The next day was hotter still and the gardeners at Hartland despaired of ever seeing a cloud again. August had been the driest they could remember and, the first two days apart, this month had been just as bad. Harold, the pipe-smoking boatman with the old fashioned greased pigtail that fascinated the children, had taken them out to check the lobster pots. Sarah and Jocasta had joined them for a picnic on the beach but, such was the heat, that they had come back early to rest before tea.

Much later, when all the fuss had died down, Sarah was told that it was Isaac who first had the idea. He had crept to Amelia's room and after a whispered consultation where she sat with her knees tucked under her chin and her eyes wide open with excitement, she nodded eagerly. She knew exactly what to do and would join him. He tiptoed to the door, checked the landing and nodded. In a moment he'd gone. Amelia followed him but turned down the corridor and pushed open the door of her mother's room.

The curtains were drawn to keep out the sun but she found the jar on the dressing table easily enough. A chair was all she needed to reach the black leather box but it was too heavy and she half fell to the floor when she lifted it. The keys took ages to fit the locks but the oval case was on top of everything else so she simply pushed open the catch and took out the necklace. She had watched to see how Daisy fastened the clips and now she copied her, frowning in concentration, before pulling the jewels clumsily over her head. Once on she ran to find her brother.

Isaac had found the two low walls behind the rhododendrons. He had been watching the gardeners cutting back the scrub and when he learned that the rocks were all that was left of an old strong house, he had waited until they had finished for the day before exploring further. Now, he suggested, he and Amelia should hide themselves away in their castle. It was to be a secret place, where no grown ups would be allowed to go. He would be king and, if she wanted, Amelia could be a princess but she would have to get properly dressed and wear her jewels.

"Come on, hurry up or they'll see us." Even as she was running across the lawn, the princess did as she was bidden. "Up there look," he directed. "Through the bracken behind those big green bushes. There's a path." So hot had been the summer that most wildlife hid themselves away during the day. But not the adders. Perhaps the burning midday heat was too much for their scales, but late afternoon, just as the sun was dipping behind Stoke church, was their favourite time to venture out.

"Come on 'Melia…up the path, there by the bush." Isaac watched her disappear behind the tall rhododendron and had turned away when he heard the scream. It was a piercing scream of terror and he ran. He found her staring at the ground with her arms held up in horror. Then she screamed again.

"The snake, Isaac. It…it bit me. Bit me hard and it hurts." She screamed hysterically, crying out in pain. "Oh, it hurts, Isaac, it really does…and it feels all funny." Her brother watched in horror as the bracken moved while the lithe brown and black body slid from sight.

"What happened?"

"I trod on it. I didn't mean to…it was a mistake," she sobbed. "It wrapped itself around my leg and then bit me…just here." She lifted her skirt to her knee. "There." she pointed to her calf. "Oooh, look. There, there's blood and two holes. Help me, Isaac. I feel funny…I want mama and Eileen." She turned and started to walk then fell to one knee. "Help me, Isaac, I feel all strange and it hurts…I want mama." Isaac ran as he had never run before, shouting as he went.

＊

The doctor had gone. He came as soon as the groom reached his house with the news. He was not unduly surprised, for adders had been a common sight throughout the long dry summer when several people had been bitten and one of them, a lad of twelve, had died. He just prayed that what had bitten the girl was a young reptile rather than one fully grown.

But no, one look told him that it had been an adult. He could tell by the teeth marks and the height of the bite. The opium took a little while to bring on her drowsiness but he had to cut quickly and the child had screamed out in pain. It was difficult to tell if all the venom had worked its way into the bloodstream but he sucked at the wound as hard as he could, spitting out the blood into his white enamel bowl. When he took it to the window he could see traces of the milky venom. They might be lucky because she had hardly moved from where she had been bitten. Some of the poison, anyway, had not begun its grim journey. The poultice he put on to draw the wound was almost too hot to touch and she had cried out again.

Dr Stoddart returned two hours later. The child was asleep but her breathing was too shallow and too fast. Her brow was paper dry and the wound, when he undid the dressing, was swollen and red. The crisis was yet to come but there was little he or anyone else could do. The child had to be kept still and cool.

It was Sarah who told him he should go. He had done everything he could, she told him, and she would sit by her daughter to see her through, no matter how long it took. The doctor departed, urging them to call him at once should anything worry them…anything at all. An hour later night had fallen.

"Mama, I'm so hot…I feel all funny."

"Does it hurt, my darling?"

"No…" she murmured. "All faint…and…and funny." Even as her mother bathed her brow, her head lolled to one side.

"Dear God," Sarah whispered as she bent forward. "Please…please, no. Please don't take her." She stroked back her hair but the child lay motionless. "Oh, dear God…no. Amelia, darling, don't leave us…stay with us, my little one…please don't go." For an hour the crisis raged as the dark evil of the venom battled with the child's very lifeblood. The conflict ebbed and flowed. All her mother knew of what was happening was when her child tossed and turned, sometimes awake and calling out to be cooled, at other times lying inert and still as the death that stalked her. There was nothing to be done; nothing except to wait and pray.

Some time before dawn the moment passed. As the light grew Sarah saw that her breathing was stronger and her head and body had cooled. But it was Daisy Price who tiptoed into the room. By then Sarah had fallen forward in her chair with her head resting on the bed and she started at the hand on her shoulder. Daisy had seen for herself that the child was sleeping peacefully.

"Come on, m'lady," she whispered. "You're all in. And now, see here. For mercy's sake the child's calmer and sleepin' more easily. The Lord himself has seen her…praise be." She settled Sarah in the chair and walked to the window. "'Tis another wonderful day ma'am…and now it's surely a day for us all to give thanks." She reached up and drew back the curtains allowing the morning sun to brighten the room.

"No." Sarah half turned as if to say something but stopped. Daisy saw her half in the chair and half out. Slowly her mistress raised a hand. "Oh...my...God. Daisy, *look*," she hissed. She remained as she was, one hand pointing at her dressing table. "Daisy," she whispered. "The necklace...*look* at it...look." Daisy followed her hand to where the first rays of sunlight were playing on the jewels. Somebody had taken it from Amelia last night and in the rush had left it there. It had half slipped over the edge and was now hanging full in the bright sunlight. As the sun poured in through the window, it was as if every ruby was alive and dancing with fire. The whole magnificent set of jewels seemed to be a mass of tiny scarlet flames each one burnished by the morning sunlight.

"Amelia was wearing it, wasn't she." Sarah had got up but was still pointing, her eyes transfixed by the necklace. "Wasn't she, Daisy? She had it on when we found her. My God, it's them...it's the jewels. *They* did it. They're cursed. There's a curse of the devil on them." She turned to her maid. "First there was Katherine...then Lottie...and then Sharland. Madam Tissini was right, you know. She warned me about a fire from the deep. It's them, the rubies. And those pearls from, from that troubled water of hers. *Look at them.*" Her voice was raised. "There's something ghastly and evil lurking there, Daisy. I can see it...I know it's so. My heart's telling me. Here...gimme." She leapt at her dressing table, snatching up the necklace and held it to the light. "Damned and blast you, you evil, accursed monster. But I have you now. Time after time you have struck us down, one by one, and last night your wretched, evil spirit tore at the very heart of my child. But now I have you...now I have you."

Daisy stepped back, her hands feeling for the wall behind her. She had it in mind to say something but was watching fearfully. Her mistress was shouting and staring wildly as if she had seen a ghost. "So, back to the deep from whence you came." Sarah was turning, this way and that as though she was looking for something. "My shoes, Daisy, and quick. Shoes and cloak, I'll go as I am. Quick, girl, hurry."

✳

Even before she was through the gate at the end of the park she was gasping for breath yet still she ran on. She never knew how long it took her to reach the cove where the shepherd had his cottage and where Sharland was killed. Twice, or perhaps three times, on the way she stopped to lean against a tree or the bank beside the lane to catch her breath. But still she ran on, sometimes stumbling and sometimes running freely as the track wended its way down to the shore.

Before she reached the cove she turned up the shepherd's path and began to climb. She remembered the spot, high on the cliffs from where she had often looked down on to the rocks where the dying wreck had taken her husband. The path went close to the edge, but not too close for the cliff was undercut and they had been waiting years for it to tumble into the sea. No matter, she would go there today. The last part of the climb was hard and she bent forward, her hands driving down on her knees to help her legs force her body on, while the necklace dangled and swung.

Then she was there. Her whole body shook as she gulped and gasped. Sweat ran down her face. Her eyes were shut tight with the pain of the climb. Her hair was a mess and her mouth agape as she drew in deep lungfuls of cool sea air. She turned off the path and half stumbled towards the cliff edge, right to the very edge itself from where she could look down. Beneath her, the calm azure-blue sea was lapping gently against the rocks. Further out there seemed to be a stillness and a silence as if everything had mysteriously stopped and was watching her. There was barely a movement across the water save for a smooth wide sweep here and there where a current was drawn over whatever lay beneath.

She never glanced at what was in her hand; simply drew back her arm high over her head and hurled the necklace as hard as she could, watching intently while it spun and curled on its way down as if it was waving in desperation. Motionless she stared until all sign of it had long gone. Then she turned and began to walk back but faltered before slumping heavily to the ground where she sat with one arm supporting her and her head bowed low. At last, at last she was rid of the terrible thing.

Chapter Nineteen

"Now then, I daresay your patience is running thin." As he spoke, the visitor put down his glass, picked up his linen napkin and dabbed at his mouth, delicately and discretely. "It is high time for me to declare my hand."

Mr Benjamin Disraeli reminded Florence Knight of a dapper little bird, precise in his movements and dressed, as always, in a brightly patterned waistcoat. Today it was scarlet and gold with dark green and blue leaves winding their way outwards from the pearl buttons. Somehow the musky fragrance of the lotion he used seemed exactly right. She nodded in reply. Ever since his card arrived two days ago, both she and Frederic had been intrigued.

"And so I shall," he continued. "But first of all permit me to apologise once more for this unwarranted intrusion of mine. It was an outrageous assault upon your forbearance, I must confess. Such hospitality as this in your beautiful home, dear lady, has been a privilege indeed." He gestured theatrically. Frederic, at the other end of the dining table sat back. "And to invite myself as I have done…well, I am indebted…to you both of course." He smiled disarmingly, flirtatiously almost at Florence, then at Frederic. "So…I wonder, if perhaps we might be able to speak alone?"

Frederic nodded and turned to the butler. "Thank you Maynard. Coffee in the drawing room when we're ready, if you will…and please be sure that we are not disturbed."

"Very good, sir." The three remained silent until the double doors had been closed.

Mr Disraeli pushed back his chair. "The reason for wishing to speak like this is that I had it in mind to talk last week but you have not been in the House, of course…West Worcestershire detained you, I know. However, in addition, I would have to say that the office of the Lord Chamberlain does not always move with the due sense of urgency we might sometimes expect." He raised one eyebrow. Benjamin Disraeli, Conservative Prime Minister once more, liked nothing more than to have his audience waiting upon his next word.

"And so to my point…let us dally no more." Unnecessary though it was he bent forward conspiratorily, as though eager to retain their attention. "I have recently submitted my recommendations for a number of members, of both sides of the House, to have their long and devoted service to our country recognised." Frederic moved in his chair. "Among those I suggested, in fact high on the list, my Honourable friend for West Worcestershire, is your name…Colonel The Honourable Frederic Winn Knight." He paused and glanced at Florence who caught his mischievous twinkle.

"Well, sir," Frederic stared at him. "I don't know what to say. I'm quite over-whelmed that you...."

Disraeli raised a finger. "You have done us well, my friend. You have served the House and your country faithfully and with devotion...and I am not alone in recognising the fact. Time and again you have raised points without fear or favour concerning the well being of the yeomanry, and they are deeply indebted to you...I have that on the highest authority from the War Office. *But*...more than that you have, with what can only be described as the most dogged persistence, brought the situation regarding those less fortunate...the poor and the needy, to our attention. Twice you have undertaken the mundane and onerous duty of secretary to the board and, still, now, you do not permit even the most indifferent of members to overlook their obligations."

"Nothing more than *my* duty, sir. Of that I can assure you." Frederic lifted a hand as if to demonstrate there had not been any alternative. "What else could I have done...or indeed wished to have done for that matter?"

"Oh, a very great deal less." Disraeli frowned and waved dismissively. "You need not have done a thing. It came from the heart, that we have all seen, and such virtues deserve their reward. *Now*." He looked darkly from one to the other. "I have proposed that such signal service should be recognised by the award of the Order of the Bath...Knight Commander of the Bath no less." He sat back. "And I am here today on behalf of Her Majesty to ascertain if you would be happy to accept...no objection, I presume, Young Knight?"

Frederic was still staring, first at his wife then at his visitor. "*Well*," he blew. "No, sir. Not at all," he muttered. "Really, I simply...words quite fail me."

"Uh, silenced for once," Disraeli laughed, throwing his head back. "I never would have believed it."

"Freddie, that's marvellous, dear." Florence left her seat and moved quickly to stand behind her husband. "That's wonderful, Mr Disraeli...wonderful news indeed."

"I know, dear lady...I know, I know. Indeed we all know and are mightily grate-ful...and here I speak for both sides of the House. William Gladstone agreed most heartily with my sentiments. This award is nothing less than a just and fitting tribute." Disraeli paused then rose to take Frederic's hand. His host rose immedi-ately. "My congratulations, dear boy...just and deserving. And you, dear lady." He took Florence's hand gently and lifted it to his lips, bowing solemnly. "You may be forgiven for being *sing*-ularly proud of your man." He stepped back, stretched his short frame and drew out a slim gold watch. "But now then..."

"No, no...coffee. Coffee this instant." Frederic pushed back his chair. The man was pure theatre; whether to a packed and silent House or in private company,

Benjamin Disraeli's ability to hold court never failed and it was the same now. "Come, sir, I insist. A quick cup before you depart."

"Perfect…and what could be better after such an enjoyable exercise…and in such delightful company." He was shorter than Florence, even before his further deep bow. His wavy, grey-black hair was combed neatly back and his cream silk cravat had been secured by a large pin whose head was a golden claw clutching a single pearl. The cut of his dark morning coat, his finely checked trousers and white spats completed the image. Benjamin Disraeli looked and behaved exactly as she expected, even now.

✳

"Now come on, Freddie. Tell us what she said." Wilmot, having heard word about the investiture from Florence and Sebright, was intrigued as to what the Queen might have said to him after the Lord Chamberlain and an equerry had stepped forward with the insignia. Sir Frederic Knight had risen from the kneeler and bowed as he had been instructed, then waited while the Queen placed the decoration around his neck. It was then, and to the surprise of many, she had momentarily held up proceedings to talk to him while those present looked on. The Ballroom had watched in silence as Frederic had twice nodded, at which point one of them said something which made both the monarch and her subject laugh. "Durnford and I are mighty jealous for we got nothing at all like that…simply a nod to inform us that we should be on our way."

"The colour of my eyes…that's what did it. She might have been our Queen for nigh on forty years but she still knows a fine looking fella when she sees one." Frederic grinned. The dinner at Simonsbath was the one celebration he had permitted and they had come together less than a week after his summons to Buckingham Palace. He had been concerned about the frailty of his mother, for she would be eighty-one this year, but Elizabeth-Jane and Durnford had been determined to join them and with Sebright there were seven. "No, seriously…d'you really want to know?" He looked at Florence and smiled.

"Exmoor ponies, would you believe? Yes…and that's the truth." She loves the countryside and asked me what I thought of the Exmoors in comparison with her own Highland ponies. I said we should judge them side by side. She agreed and suggested we should try it both here and at Balmoral. I replied that the animals would find that most diplomatic and she laughed…simple as that."

"Incorrigible, Young Knight." Durnford reached out for the port. "Quite the Court jester. But keep them smiling, my boy, or they'll be having your head."

"Well, I think it's marvellous that she shares our love of the countryside." Elizabeth-Jane looked around the table. "You see we are not alone." Then she paused. "Well, Florence, dear, it's been an evening to remember, it really has and it's all taken me back…oh, goodness." She frowned and lowered her head in thought. "Forty years? No, must be more. The old house doesn't change one bit. It's the same as ever and I can just see John chasing you all about."

"I would have loved to have met him." Rebecca looked at Elizabeth-Jane.

"Terrifying," Durnford interjected. "You never knew him, Wil. A wonderful man indeed but, by jingo, once he was away on something then the whole earth shook. Oh, my word, yes. And you should've seen Lombard Street when he was in town...sheer panic."

"Only one person could really handle him...one man that is." Frederic glanced round.

"My brother?" Wilmot glanced up and pushed back a lock of hair. The table fell silent.

"Indeed." Frederic cleared his throat and nodded slowly.

"Ah...dear, Jack." Elizabeth-Jane glanced down at her glass as if some small memory from the distant past was whispering to her. "John adored him, you know. Even when...well, even when things turned upside down as he put it. There was always a big soft spot there...and it was the same for me."

"Should be here tonight." Frederic looked around the table. "I tried to get him but it's April now and that means lambing at Sherdon, would you believe. Lambing with Jack and that's that."

"Typical."

"Wouldn't have been himself though. Not here, not even with us."

"It would have been lovely, though." Elizabeth-Jane smiled to herself. "He's just so much a part of it all. He's part of our history, from right the way back when the gallant Sir Frederic, here, was the little boy dressed in his velvet knickerbockers who kept running off down to the stables."

"Yes," Frederic mused. "Yes indeed...and that's a fact."

2

Winter for Sarah had been darker and longer than usual; even spring seemed to have come slowly. Try as she might, she could not throw off all that had been on her mind. Visits to London and Paris, including the persistent and amorous attentions of young Harold, the elder son of the Marquis of Bridport, had provided interesting if temporary relief, but the clouds had gathered once more. In the main, life at Blagdon and Whitechapel had been dreary and lonely.

The melancholy and glowering eyes of one uncle, Wilmot, and his words of advice kept returning. Family matters, the distrust and suspicion and the difficult relationships, remained a muddle. She could not gather them into any semblance of order while, behind it all, lay the sinister memories of the necklace. She knew she would have to find out the truth about its origin and why her other uncle had sold the jewels, the idea of which still hurt deeply. It was as if the necklace, like the adder at Hartland, had worked its way into the family in order to strike out. But exactly how she was going to solve the mystery she could not imagine.

Every idea that came to her seemed fraught with difficulties. Facing her uncle at Sherdon, with such anger still simmering, would be impossible. The whole family would be ranged against her. She could see them clearly. There would be Wilmot, clever, rich and powerful who had come to see her but whose ruthlessness had brought down the Duke. There would be Kitty, the new wife about whom she had heard so much obsequious and honeyed flattery; her cousins Tod, the curate, Frank and Anna, and the brutish oaf, Harry, together with the others she had never met would be there also. Even her own parents would side with them: they would all be there in spirit and she would be on her own. Yet she knew she must determine the truth.

However she chose to phrase it, her letter to Rebecca read more like a cry of help. She tried to disguise the fact but then that was exactly what it was. At first she had thought little of the woman but, of all those she knew, there was something comfortable and steady about her uncle's wife. She scarcely knew her but she had watched and listened when they had been together. Rebecca remained herself; there was no façade, no pretence and, most certainly, no show. There was no threat or hostility. Her lack of concern about how she looked or dressed was, in an odd way, refreshing and one could not but warm to her. When she spoke, she did so directly, eye to eye, engaging whoever it was with no concern or furtive looks as to who might be over the shoulder or who had just entered the room. She rarely, if ever, spoke about others except with benevolence and affection. She was discreet and, if there was anyone who might give her the strength she needed, Sarah decided, it was her. She sent the letter by courier.

✳

"Of course. Of course." Rebecca nodded. Her dark brown silk afternoon dress seemed strangely out of keeping with her untidy mass of hair yet, in spite of the distorted bustle, it looked comfortable. Sometimes, when she was listening, she appeared older than she was, perhaps nearer fifty than forty, Sarah judged. In part this was due to her lack of makeup and her natural, ruddy complexion accentuating the creases around her eyes.

But she would listen keenly, her earnest frown shutting out any distractions around her. When she smiled, her face would light up and her laugh, loud and unrestrained, was that of someone much younger, someone who appeared to have not a care in the world. "You *have* been through a wretched time, you poor thing. To be honest, I have been worried about you ever since dear Sharland was killed, and then just last autumn you had that dreadful business with Amelia. I think you've done quite remarkably well…you've been marvellous."

"I try, I really do but there're other things as well." Sarah took a deep breath. "There seems to be so much going on, so many things I don't understand about my life and which I find so painful."

"Wilmot?" The question came softly but with no side to it, as though Rebecca knew her feelings. Sarah looked up sharply as if there was more to follow; some point to be made which would break the friendly spell. But there was not. "Don't worry, I know how you feel and have done so for some time."

"No…it's not just him. But, yes. I know he came to see me. I have to say it's hard to believe what took place. It seemed…well, it seemed so cruel and Bertie was trying so hard to make a success of it. I just don't see why it had to be done."

"I hate it…loathe and detest all business. It's dirty and mean and, in London, it's quite dreadful." Her cheeks blotched in sudden anger. "*Ooh*…all the intrigue, the double dealings and back stabbing…*ugh*. And then the loss of trust and friendships. I want nothing to do with it and that's why I'm down here so much." She laughed suddenly at what she had said but then frowned compassionately.

Sarah looked down. "It's still painful."

"Business always is. It's beastly and I'm just so sorry that it came between Wilmot and your father-in-law." She could see Sarah was hurt and had it in mind to continue but for a moment her visitor sat silently, considering what had been said. Rebecca knew instinctively that she had come to pour out her heart. "There's more, isn't there?" she murmured. "You're here because you want to talk…about things. I knew from your letter, my dear, so don't be afraid. Whatever you tell me will go no further. I keep my own counsel."

Sarah sighed and put down her cup and saucer. "It's the family." When she looked up there were tears in her eyes. "It's all such a horrible mess…and I just don't know where to begin."

"Well try. Come on…we'll sit by the window." At first they talked about Sherdon. Rebecca said little and it was when Sarah had finished, and there had been the short silence there is at the end of every tale, that she began to speak of her failings, of her insecurity and how she had striven so hard to hold her place in society.

She knew, she went on, that she had alienated herself from so many and that, even though nothing was said, how those she thought might be her friends had backed away and rejected her. She had tried to find happiness in the company of others but had been used by them. She spoke freely about her relationships and went on to talk about Wilmot's visit and what he had advised. He had been right, she admitted, but she found it so difficult to do what he suggested yet, the longer she delayed facing her family, the more awkward it became. She was confused.

"And he was right." As Sarah was speaking, Rebecca had taken her hand. "You *have* been fighting yourself, you know. Wilmot and I've seen it but you mustn't worry," she added hurriedly. "I'm just as concerned as he is." Sarah nodded. All the strength she had mustered before the visit had disappeared. Her defences, such as they were, and any fight she may have brought with her had diminished and she sat meekly, awaiting whatever Rebecca had it in mind to say. "It's that inner self about which Wilmot was speaking and he was right. We all have a different personality hidden far away and deep inside, you know. It's our very soul and so often it's not very pleasant…it's the dark side to us, a whole swirling mass of uncharitable ideals that we keep suppressed. I have them, you have them…we all do, it's just that you have been battling away with perhaps less success than others."

"You mean it's so obvious?"

"No…no, I wouldn't say that. But you allow your perceived weaknesses to get on top of you. Now look here." She adjusted her dress and sat back. "I can talk freely as I married into your family but I have been blessed with a man who's at peace with himself over what is really important in life. Wilmot, your mother, Emma, and Jack all came from a humble background but each of them, in their own different way, has relished it, drawn strength from it, if you will. Wilmot loves nothing more than going back to Molland or out to Sherdon. He loves it there, far, far more than the beastly, pushy, insecure world of London and business. He feels in harmony with his roots…he becomes his real self." She squeezed Sarah's hand.

"*But*, and here's the point, not everyone in the family seems able to live with this fact. Jessica, for one. She drives us mad with her silly little airs and graces as though it's all some sort of veil she's drawing over her background. Harry's another one in quite a different way. He's better now but for years he battered his way about the place desperate to get away from something and I suspect…no, I'm sure, that you, too, have this needless worry about your lineage. It eats away at you and you have become determined to hide it rather than living comfortably with it…and being proud of it. And it's then that all these silly things get done and said which you regret later."

The room was very quiet. Sarah's head was bowed for now Rebecca had dug deep and prized open Sarah's soul. She felt exposed and helpless with nothing to cover herself. Suddenly her whole life seemed so shallow; all the titles and trappings and great wealth were so much insignificant veneer. In that instant, she saw herself for what she was and a hand went to her face. Rebecca put an arm around her shoulder.

"Everybody, but everybody, loves your family, you know. Your dear, dear mother is a sweet soul and your uncle, Jack…he's a fine man. What took place all those years ago on Brendon Common was seen by the world as honourable and just. Honestly, my dear, if nothing more comes from this visit today, let it be that you understand what I've been telling you and that, once understood…and accepted, you can be at peace with yourself. There is nothing, nothing but pride and honour in your blood. Anyone who thinks otherwise either does not know you or else they are making up for their own sad inadequacies." Rebecca nudged her. "We'll go together…you and I."

"*What?*" Sarah lifted her head. "What d'you mean – go? Go where?"

"Out to Sherdon, of course. Come now, you're fighting yourself again, I know you are." She laughed sympathetically and removed her arm.

"But I don't think I could."

"Oh yes. With me you can. Anyway, I want to go and see Kitty. We'll send the horses on ahead and take the chaise as far as Sandyway, then ride on from there." She looked at her. "Don't worry…you'll find your uncle just as I said, and he…all of them, will think much of you."

"D'you really think so?"

"Yes, I'll arrange it. There's so much here that's tangled and muddled…so much that has been exaggerated or misconstrued. It needs to be undone…has to be and it's best that we see to it together."

✳

The short ride to Sherdon was more difficult than Sarah could have imagined. Most difficult of all was coming to terms with the fact that Rebecca, who, in her mind she had so foolishly slighted, was the strength she needed. She warmed to her, her happiness marred only by the worry about what might lie ahead and her anger at her own initial feelings about the woman riding beside her.

Twice she wanted to stop and turn round. Once was on the bridge over Sherdon Water when she seemed trapped and helpless in the bottom of the deep valley. It was the moment when she felt herself finally committed to whatever was in store. But it was after they had ridden on and crested the rise and saw the farm in front of them, so close that they could hear the dogs, that she pulled up. Rebecca stopped with her and watched but said nothing, leaving her to muster her own courage.

Frank, fair-haired and dark tanned, smiled and took her hand as she slipped from the side-saddle. Anna, so different to the young woman she remembered in the officers' marquee the year before, and now dressed in her drab farm clothes and with her hair tucked into a serving girl's mob cap, helped her up the steps to the front door. Sarah nodded her approval but noticed the tautness in the girl's face and the sidelong glance she gave her brother. They were wary of her and, suddenly, she was wary of them, too, and ill at ease. Jack, who looked taller and older than she imagined, stood quietly in the doorway.

For a moment she paused, letting go of her habit she was holding up and looked at him. There was a tension; everybody pretended to be doing something but all were acutely aware of the moment. Behind her, Rebecca and Frank said something to each other and she could hear the grooms watering the horses. Somewhere a cockerel crowed. It was a different world and she felt her heart racing. Her mouth was dry and, for a moment, she felt unsteady. But there was warmth, also. She could feel it in their very presence around her. The family had set out to make her welcome; her own family whom she had shunned and about whom she had harboured such cruel thoughts.

"Sarah, m'dear." Jack stepped forward. "'Tis a wonder to see you here...a real wonder." She stood on tiptoe, inclining her peaked riding hat with the dark green ostrich plumes so her uncle could embrace her. His hands, supporting her under her elbows, felt strong and held her just long enough to give her confidence. She smiled, more in relief at the deep calm in his voice than what he said. "And Rebecca, welcome, my dear." Even as he reached out for Rebecca, one hand remained on his niece's arm, giving her more strength.

Inside it was cool and, momentarily, dark. The sharp smell was of cooked food, of sweat and dogs. It was the breath of a working farm but to Sarah it was new. She moved cautiously into the gloom of the room, her eyes taking in the sparse furniture, the bare walls and the sights and smells of a kitchen where ash had spilled from the hearth, where flies busied themselves on cups and glasses that remained unwashed on the long oak table; where a folded sack lay under boots put close to the fire and where a black and white cat dropped silently from a chair and slunk away.

"'Ello, Sarah, m'dear...I'm Kitty." She looked so small but there was the same warmth in her eyes as she saw in the others. Her hand was cool and boney but the grasp was firm and her other hand came on top of her own. "Welcome, m'dear...us've bin longing to see you here, reelly, us have." Suddenly she felt foolishly overdressed. Her clothes and make up seemed out of place, unnecessary in this farmhouse. All around her, her own family stood calm and assured. No doubt they had their own thoughts, yet she could sense their curiosity about her and what she might do next. She had no idea what to say; instead she took off her hat and made a gesture at freeing her hair of the pins and nets that now felt ridiculous. She swung round a bit too quickly and smiled self-consciously but it was Jack who put her at her ease once more.

"Us'll take tea presently, dear." He smiled at his wife. "You an' Rebecca stop here. Our Sarah bain't seen nothing of the farm an' I've a mind for her to see what us've got." He led the way back into the hall and, as she followed him, her riding boots rang out on the flagstones. When he reached the porch from where they could see the farm he stopped and turned to her. They were on their own, the others having gone off and the kitchen door behind them was closed.

"I'm glad you've come, m'dear. Your mother's told me you've things on yer mind.

I would have come down to see you but didn't want to interfere and anyways," he shrugged. "Always summat here or hereabouts to keep a man at home. But you're here and it's grand to see you…really it is." His face was peaceful, even the grey-blue eyes that might have so easily been cold and hard were kindly. "Why don't we sit together awhile, just you an' me." There was a strength about him just as Rebecca had said and as they sat together, opposite one another in the stone porch, she found his company easier than she dared hope.

"Tell me, dear," he continued. "I've a mind as to why you've come, but I'd like to know. Summat's been in your thoughts. Summat, I daresay, that's been a worry. Mmm?" They looked at one another and he smiled. "I'll take a guess," he continued. "'Tis about the jewellery, I'll be bound. Eh? Katherine's jewellery. 'Tis that what's been plaguing your mind."

"So you do know?" Sarah could feel the surprise on her face. "And how, might I ask? I made Rebecca promise not to say anything."

" 'Twasn't anything to do with her, m'dear…nort at all." He leant back against the wall. "News, bad news like that comes back every which way. Staff mainly…down at Whitechapel, young Locke and that…then Wilmot picked it up. And that's just about your littl'un out at Hartland. Us've known all about the necklace since it was bought down in Exeter, way back…why, you showed it to your mother, for one. Remember? 'Bin common knowledge with the family."

"But why did you sell it, uncle? It was a terrible thing to do…awful. It put such dreadful thoughts into my mind." She raised her eyebrows. "Even now I feel angry…it's awful."

"*Sold* it, m'dear? *Sold* it? Never, ever would I have done that. No…never." He leant forward, resting his elbows on his knees. "No matter what you've heard, and I'll mind it's a lot. But, no matter…I'll tell you." He paused and pulled on his nose. "'Twas your poor dear aunt, Lottie. She had taken them from Kitty, from up here at the house and had hold of them down at the cottage when they found her. Some dastardly villains came upon her and beat her to the ground, half beat her to death for them, so they did.

"It were stolen, my dear, stolen not sold…torn from out of her hand as she lay helpless back down the road. Anna an' Victoria found her. Half dead she was. Ask Anna." He saw the look on her face. "Oh, aye," he said. "Never think for a moment we sold it. Times were hard, real hard, but there's some things in life you never do. But wait…there's summat you should know, and I daresay it's summat for all of us to know for certain. Bide here a minute."

She was alone. Her heart was beating wildly and she swallowed then wiped her mouth with her hand. How could this be so and why had she not been told? What had happened to make her think otherwise? What had gone so horribly, horribly wrong? Then he was back. He took her arm and helped her from her seat. Sarah said nothing, just looked at him."'Tis all right, my dear. Must have bin a shock to hear that but us'll find out now…find out once and for all." He led her back into the kitchen where Rebecca and Kitty were sitting together at the table.

"Right dear," he nodded at Kitty. "Here, then, take a seat." He pulled out a chair for Sarah, brushed it with his hand and waited for her to sit, then sat himself. "Us've wondered fer sometime if they were the same or not. Kitty'll tell."

"Well," Kitty smiled. "This is how I remember Katherine's necklace. Now then, there were forty one stones rangin' from about three carats up to, let me see," she screwed up her eyes. "About six, or p'raps six and a half, but the drop was around nine, circular cut an' with back spray. An' the pearls were pink…Bombay. Beautiful they were. Yes?"

"My God…yes." Sarah's face fell. "How on earth…how on earth…."

"I'll tell'e in a minute." Kitty leant forward. "They were Flemish. I could tell by the flaws on the first two, the settin' stones as they're known. Th'inclusions or the flaws're what are called rutile or silky needles…cat's eye as we used to call 'em. Round cut they were, the end two an' all the others're step cut, sort of oblong, like. Remember them as clear as day." She sat back.

"Go on, dear." Jack simply nodded.

"Y'see, years ago when I were a child, I were a stone polisher down in Plymouth. Worked for a man in Devonport who brought in raw cut stones and polished them before selling them on. Shady business mind and us never knew how'e came upon them but 'twas work nonetheless. Worked there until I were twelve or thereabouts when father left home. Worked with Hammond for nigh on four years, I did…learned all I know there. Should have bin able to say who the jeweller were that made it 'cos that's how he marked his own…with they two stones. Forget now but I knew 'twas foreign, Flemish or Dutch."

"But what happened…why did you leave?"

"Oh, makes no odds." She waved a hand. "That's another tale and a long one at that but Gillan found me an'…well, here we are." She shrugged and smiled. "But that were the same necklace, weren't it?"

"Yes…exactly. Every detail as you've described. Exactly." Sarah looked from one to the other. "It's such a shock, all this. All these things I'm hearing here and all that I'm finding out…it's all so, so different. But it makes so much sense…about so many things."

"And where's it now?" Jack looked from Rebecca to Sarah. "Where's it to?"

They all felt the long silence.

"I have to confess that I got rid of it." Sarah looked down. "It sounds awful, I know, for it should be here, back safely with you from whence it came. It's yours, uncle, yours and it was taken from you." A hand flew to her face. "Oh my God, what have I done...I can't believe it," she whispered. "I rid myself of it. It's gone, gone for good."

"Rid for ever, I hope." Kitty looked at Jack.

"*What*?" Sarah's voiced was raised in disbelief. "Why d'you say that? It belongs here."

"Aye." Jack looked at her. "Sounds daft, I know but after Katherine were killed by her fall like she was and then when Lottie were taken bad, and then when she was beaten an' robbed. Well," he glanced at Kitty. "Sounds daft but we reckoned that the thing had a curse on it." He gave a little laugh. "Sounds dreadful, I know, but we never really wanted to see the damned thing again...and never came to see you about it, that's for certain." He looked at Sarah again. "But 'tis gone now...eh? That right?" He frowned and looked at her.

"Oh, Heavens, I simply cannot believe it." Sarah rose, one hand still to her face. "What I've heard this afternoon...all this...I, it's too much."

"Steady, dear. Bain't nothing to worry about. If 'tis gone, 'tis gone. Here." He stood beside her. "All right, are you? 'Tis all right, y'know...there's nothing to be done. Not now."

"No," she whispered. "No it's not just the jewels, it's so much more." She covered her face. "It's everything...oh, dear God, what *has* happened." For a moment her uncle watched, then gently took her into his arms.

3

There was a definite touch of autumn in the air. Although still only late august he could feel a crisp freshness and rubbed his hands vigorously. The heather on Withypool Common had been in flower for a week and already the bracken had begun to die back. Jack took another deep breath before walking down the front steps and into the yard. A flock of swallows that had gathered on the roof swooped away. Not long now before they would be off. Any minute now, Victoria would be back from her ride. She and Little Jack had risen even earlier and she had taken him up the Barle valley where her father thought they might catch a glimpse of some deer. Soon the boy would be six. He could ride well enough but she had put on the leading rein nevertheless.

It was lovely having them up at the farm. His grandson's piping voice and the constant bustle of a high-spirited child about the place brought memories. Were he to know it, the boy had brought new life to the place. At that, he stopped. Victoria had come almost two weeks ago just after Kitty had fallen ill once more. The doctor had come out and ordered her to bed: it had helped and she was up again but still delicate. He remembered watching her moving about the kitchen and wondering how much weaker she could become. Before he left, Dr Baillie took him aside and broke the news Jack guessed might be coming.

"That bad, is it?" Jack pursed his lips.

"I'm afraid so, Jack." The doctor took off his glasses and huffed on the lenses as he considered the situation. "The heart's very weak, just about keeping pace with what it's s'posed to do but it's that cough that's the worry. You know it's back again and, if it gets to her lungs then, well, I fear for her."

Jack nodded. Baillie knew he understood and waited for the questions to come. "Anything to be done?"

Baillie blew, raised his eyebrows and pulled a face. "No, Jack. It has to be said that there's not much apart from keeping her rested as much as possible. She's not very old, I know. Not yet sixty she said but then everybody's heart's different, so we've to keep her quiet."

"Some hope there."

"I know," he laughed reflectively. "She's not the sort, is she? Then best let her lead her own life. If we can keep her health going then that'll be one thing. But the heart, well...they've a mind of their own, you know, and it's impossible to say when they've had enough. Could be a week, could be five years...could be next year."

It was then that Victoria came to stay bringing her son with her and the much needed joy when she told them that another child was due early in the new year. Little Jack took to Kitty and she to him. He was, she told the others, her fingers and toes and between them they made a busy person. There were stories by the fire after supper and again when he was in his cot but only when Kitty was strong enough to climb the stairs. But Little Jack would have none of it and would get out of his cot to sit on the landing and call endlessly until she came; which most nights she did. There would then be another story before the curtains were drawn.

Victoria stayed on. Jack explained what the doctor had said and she wanted to be with them a while longer. Kitty's spirit, the doctor had told him, was as strong as ever but the little body and the heart that drove it was tired. And tired they proved to be.

*

Later, when he was able to talk about it, Jack began to realise how grateful he was that she went the way she did, but it was the suddenness of it at the time which shook him. Anna and Victoria had gone to Withypool in the dogcart. Little Jack was due to stay and help Kitty with the carrots and dried peas but, at the last minute, decided he wanted to go as well. Frank had been in the shippon but came back into the house where Jack and Kitty were together in the kitchen.

"I'll be up at Sixty Acres, father. Coupl'a gaps in the top hedge where the deer've bin breaking through."

"Be back for dinner, dear." Kitty looked round from the sink. "Others'll be home by then and us can have it all together."

"Aye, an' I'll take the littl'un up with me after…need another pair of hands up top."

Kitty turned again, smiling warmly. "Ah, bless him…don't go getting him too tired, mind." Then she stopped, started suddenly with her eyes wide and clutched at her chest. "Jack…'tis…'tis."

"*Kitty…*" Father and son rose up and cried out together. She tried to reach a chair but half fell and it was Frank who caught her. At first he thought she had stumbled but the body collapsed loosely in his arms and he struggled to get her to the seat.

"*Kitty.*" It was Jack who called, louder, but he stood frozen, unable to move and quite helpless. Frank lifted her again, struggled with her in his arms then lowered her gently to the floor and knelt beside her. His father knelt also. "Kitty, 'tis me, dear…Jack. 'Tis Jack. Speak, dear…oh, Kitty, talk to us. Say summat." He half pushed his son aside then reached down before rising with her head cradled in his arms. Frank moved, then sat back on his heels and shook his head.

"There must be summat, Frank." His father's voice sounded frail, almost childlike. "Must be summat us can do…help her, Frank.." He still had not moved but remained kneeling with his body hunched as though he was exhausted. Frank rose quietly, bent down and put his hands on his father's shoulders. Eventually he, too, rose unsteadily. "She's gone, Frank. Gone dear," Jack muttered. "Gone hasn't she?"

All of a sudden, the strong leader of the family who had held sway for so long looked old and spent. His son reached out for him. It was something he had never done before and, for a moment, it felt strange to be comforting his own father. But now, in his moment of despair, it seemed the most natural thing to do. It gave him the strength he knew his father needed. "Come on," he whispered. "I'll see to her, father…bain't nothing more to be done."

✳

Anna was quite clear in her mind. She and Frank had discussed it time and again. At first he tried to persuade her otherwise but she was adamant in that she would remain at Sherdon with her brother and father. Jack begged her to think again but she would have none of it. "It's no good, father. I'm staying. You and Frank need me here but it's not only that…I love it and my mind's made up."

Even as early as Kitty's funeral at Simonsbath there was talk about what was to be done. Wilmot suggested a manager but Frank persuaded him that the farm must remain in family hands. They would go on just as they were, he explained. They would manage as they always had done and, if help were needed, then it would be brought in. Their father could do as he wished. If he found the memories too strong then he could leave. Already Victoria said that she and Edwin would welcome him at Molland. It was warmer down there and he had many friends. If he wanted to stay, then they would be more than happy.

Frederic saw it first. He had ridden down from Simonsbath with Sebright and the two had stayed on for the meal. It was afterwards, when Jack wanted to show him the new bullocks, that they found themselves alone. Sir Frederic Knight had been watching his friend anxiously and noticed the change. "You're tired, Jack...done in."

"Ah, well." Jack shrugged. "Bain't getting no younger are we now, sir?"

"No, not that. Here." Frederic put a hand on his shoulder. "It's not your body, my friend, it's your spirit I'm talking about. There's a heaviness about you I haven't seen before...it's getting to you, isn't it. All this sadness here. You're worn out."

Jack leant over the gate, his hands clasped in front of him. He sighed, glanced down then up at Frederic. "Aye, you're right," he muttered eventually. "Gets hard from time to time...sometimes nigh on too hard to bear." He half turned to look back at the house. "There's a lot here, y'know, Master Frederic, a lot to live with. But would be a lot to leave behind as well. Not sure it'd be easy."

"It won't. Not for a bit anyway but the place'll be in good hands. Frank's a fine young man and Anna...well, she's determined to stay with him no matter what we say. She's a strong personality...a resolute character there." Frederic glanced up at the house then back at his friend.

Jack saw his face and smiled ruefully. "More like her mother every day, so she is. Hmmph, stubborn as well. Stubborn as her mother an' won't hear nothing about leaving, that's fer sure." He paused. "Daresay your boy's a mite saddened."

Frederic looked at him again. "She *is* her mother, y'know, Jack. Every *inch* of her and my lad loves her dearly...as dearly as we all loved Katherine. Y'know, when I saw her preparing lunch, there at the fire, with her hair cut short like she's got it now...and when she walked over to the table with the plates, with that straight back of hers and her shoulders back. She was the very image...almost frightening."

"And your lad's the image of his father as well, Master Frederic." Jack smiled and nodded. "Cuh, don't know what's to do about it all, but time'll tell...one way or another. Us can't be telling the young how to live their lives, y'know." For a moment both men were silent then Jack sighed heavily. "Aye...and I reckon you're right, sir. Perhaps it's time to be moving on after all...time for a change up here as well, an' the young'll have to sort themselves out."

"They'll do that…they'll manage."

"Aye…we managed all right."

"They'll be fine." The two men pushed themselves off the gate. Frederic put an arm on Jack's shoulder and pulled at him gently. "They'll be fine, just like their father."

4

Hounds had just drawn up Sherdon Water when the covered wagon pulled out of the yard. It had been raining most of the night and a stiff November breeze blew up the valley. The wagon was covered to protect his few belongings but Jack rolled up the back canopy and stood looking out, one hand holding on to the metal hoop above his head. Edwin was driving and, as the cart rolled and jerked on its way down the lane, his passenger was alone.

Anna raised her hand first, then Frank, the two of them standing side by side in the porch. For a second their father did nothing. Behind him in the cart, something fell and he glanced down and then round, twisting himself to see what it was. When he looked up again they were still there and he raised one hand in reply.

For a moment, just a fleeting moment, he saw himself there with Katherine. It was just as she used to stand, upright and with her head held high like that. Lottie and Declan, the Irish boy were there, too, and he leant further out to see if he could see anything behind the shearing barn. He thought he could hear the tin whistle but perhaps it was the squeaks and groans of the cart. Billy and Davey would be there as well, all of them in fact, unless the children were still at school. He raised his hand higher and waved back, smiling to himself as he did so.

Just after the road crossed over the rise and dropped down to the bridge he saw the cottage. It had been empty for sometime but it looked just as he first remembered it. The clothes line was still there but the forked stick he had made for Kitty had long gone. The front door really did need a new coat of paint and somebody ought to come down and cut back the creepers on the front wall. The wooden hut where he first saw her was there, too. The door was hanging open and he peered closely to see if there was anything inside. Then he turned to look at the front of the cottage again and it was there, just inside the left hand window that she had stood with her hands on her hips and laughed in the quiet, alluring way she used to. And it was there, just by the porch, that she had wept on his shoulder after he helped her move Gillan downstairs.

Once more he steadied himself as the cart rocked, then he backed clumsily onto a seat as they began the long climb up from the bridge. They were all memories now, some happy, some sad but then it had been a long, long journey. Now they were bringing him home. In a funny way he was glad: glad to have lived as he had done and there were few regrets, very few.

✳

Christmas was less than a month off. The leaves from the tall beeches around Great Champson had long gone and Victoria bent down to fasten her son's coat against the chill wind. "Make sure you take care of grandpa, now," she instructed. "Oh, *Jack*, come on. Stop fidgeting…let me do the top button. Wait…there…now take hold of Naomi's hand." She stood and grinned at her father. "You all right, dear?" she queried, standing up to pick a spot of fluff from his cap. "Not too cold, are you."

"Us'll manage, maid. Won't be long." Jack smiled warmly. His daughter was heavy with child and, this time, he would be there for the occasion. For once he would be the first to know and the idea thrilled him. "Right then," he cried looking around. "On yer way now, Littl'un, but none of this running on ahead an' leavin' me and your little sister way back, like that." He squeezed his granddaughter's hand. "Right, my dear? If the little legs get tired, we'll give'e a lift."

✳

"What d'you doing that for, grandfer? Why're you putting holly and things on her grave like that for? Mmm?"

Jack rose unsteadily then stepped back to check the wreath on his mother's grave. The walk up to the church had been far enough and he reached down for the little girl. Naomi lifted her arms and he picked her up, adjusting her collar and bonnet when she was comfortable in the crook of his arm. She smiled at him. He smiled back and cradled her face against his cheek before looking down at her brother. For a moment he was silent and pushed back a wisp of grey hair. Then a sudden gust of wind snatched at their coats.

"'Cos she's there, dear. Your great-grandma's still there." He cleared his throat noisily and took the boy's hand in his. It was warm and soft and he felt the little fingers curling around in his palm. "'Tis our roots here, y'know." He looked at the child in his arms and bounced her gently.

"Aye…yours and mine, m'dear," he told her. " 'Tis where us all belong, y'know. Back here at Molland. All of us…you an' me."

THE END OF THE STORY

275